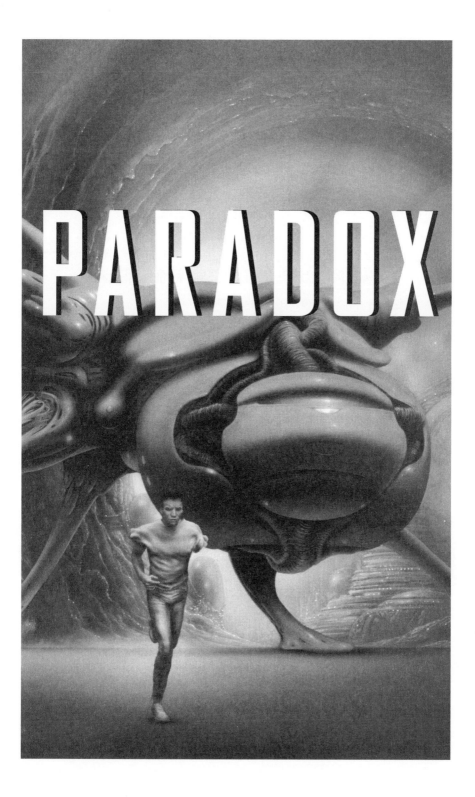

THE CROWN ROSE
Fiona Avery

THE HEALER
Michael Blumlein, MD

GALILEO'S CHILDREN: TALES OF SCIENCE VS. SUPERSTITION
edited by Gardner Dozois

THE PRODIGAL TROLL
Charles Coleman Finlay

PARADOX: BOOK ONE OF THE NULAPEIRON SEQUENCE
John Meaney

HERE, THERE & EVERYWHERE
Chris Roberson

STAR OF GYPSIES
Robert Silverberg

THE RESURRECTED MAN
Sean Williams

PARADOX

BOOK ONE
OF THE NULAPEIRON SEQUENCE

JOHN MEANEY

an imprint of **Prometheus Books**
Amherst, NY

Published 2005 by PYR, an imprint of Prometheus Books

Inquiries should be addressed to
PYR
59 John Glenn Drive
Amherst, New York 14228–2197
VOICE: 716–691–0133, ext. 207
FAX: 716–564–2711
WWW.PROMETHEUSBOOKS.COM

09 08 07 06 05   5 4 3 2 1

Library of Congress Cataloging-in-Publication Data

Meaney, John.
    Paradox / John Meaney.
        p. cm. — (The Nulapeiron sequence ; bk. 1)
    Originally published: London : Bantam Press, a division of Transworld Publishers, 2000.
    ISBN 1–59102–308–4 (hardcover : alk. paper)
    1. Civilization, Subterranean—Fiction. I. Title.

PS3613.E17P37 2005
813'.6—dc22

2004027137

Printed in Canada on acid-free paper

To *Anne McCaffrey*—
who weaves bright dreams
and changes destinies.

1

NULAPEIRON AD 3404

Like scarlet/amber fireflies hanging in the tunnel's darkness, the floating tricons read:

His desperate hooves are flying, flying—
Hunt the moon which now lies dying
Where all about, and all around
Falls barren, grey and broken ground.

Tom froze.

Patchy fluorofungus, clumped upon the tunnel ceiling, palely pushed back the shadows. No visible motion. Had there been the faintest whisper of a sound?

Nothing.

Heart beating faster—he did not want to be caught by the other market boys, not when he was writing poetry—he returned his attention to the battered blue infotablet on his lap. He was sitting in a cold stone alcove, and when he shifted position the holodisplay jerked in mid-air.

Something . . .

No. Shaking his head, Tom unwrapped a sweet-ginger jantrasta strip and bit off a piece. He chewed, thinking, then swallowed. He gestured for dictation mode.

"Hard-striking sparks are pounding, trying—
With bursting heart is crying, crying:
Pursue the love his . . . no, er, damn it . . ."

Left hand arcing horizontally, right index and forefinger scissoring together, he killed dictation and wiped the final stanza.

With another glance into the shadows, Tom leaned back, reached inside his coarse-weave tunic, and drew out his talisman on its black throat cord. It was a silver stallion: wild-maned, its hooves frozen for ever as they cut through the air.

He remembered the day of its creation: Father, sweating, bent over the white-hot graser beam; the metal block spitting, bubbling; the air redolent with the close, heavy scents of oil and scorched metal. The joy which leaped through Tom when Father gave the stallion to him instead of selling it.

It was his good-luck piece, his inspiration when the words would not come. Stroking the smooth metal mane, he closed his eyes.

And heard: "Don't stand up on my account."

Paralysed, Tom could not have risen. The woman before him was cloaked in burgundy, her hood drawn, but he could see the elegant, pointed chin, the clear olive complexion. Her silver voice was a flautist's dream.

"May I?" she asked, and somehow she had slipped the cord and the small stallion was in her slender hand.

Throat constricted, Tom could only nod.

"Quite beautiful."

"It—" Tom swallowed. "It's a stallion. A mythical beast."

"Hmm."

"My father made it." He started to point in the market's direction, then stopped. The woman was bent over, examining the hanging tricons.

"And this poetry?"

"Mine." An odd emptiness in Tom's stomach. "I write—"

"Competently." She gestured to rotate the display. "A nice sense of space, for someone who has never seen the sky."

How did she do that? The infotablet was keyed to Tom's gestures alone.

"Good harmonics, too." Enlarging the tricons, she pointed to the subtlest colourplay: grey to silver, suggesting shivering cold, agoraphobic chill. "Do you ken mathematics?"

Wordlessly, Tom brought up the triconic lattice of *My Market*: crowd-flow as fluid dynamics. Poetry and maths combined.

"Ah," the woman breathed. "Nice. Perhaps"—she pointed into a floating hamiltonian matrix—"you could be more rigorous here with the third differential. But it works."

Tom inclined his head.

"What's your name, young poet?"

"Uh, Tom Corcorigan, ma'am."

"I—" She stopped, listening. "Time, I think, to go." A small hesitation, then she seemed to come to some decision. Holding the stallion talisman, she held out her other hand. "Take this."

It was a small, black, ovoid capsule. *Strange*, Tom thought, picking it up. *Looks slippery, but isn't.* Almost as though it was not there at all.

A small needle adhered lengthwise to the capsule.

"Trust me now, for a moment." The woman wore a dark copper thumb ring. Briefly, it sparked with a ruby light. "I won't damage your father's work."

Suddenly the stallion lay in two silver halves on her palm, its once solid core hollowed out like an empty womb. Tom was speechless.

"Hold the stallion, and give me back the nul-gel cap."

Taking the black ovoid, the woman gave Tom his sundered talisman, which he accepted automatically. He flinched as though burned, but the metal felt cold.

"Quickly, watch me." She unfastened the needle and stabbed it into the capsule. "Push this, and the processor's accessible." Swiftly removing the needle, she laid it lengthwise once more against the capsule. It held in place. "Download just one module at a time, then disengage, otherwise they'll detect emissions."

With deft fingertips, she placed the capsule inside one half of the stallion, closed the other half over it, and gestured. The stallion was whole once more.

"Did you see the control gesture?"

"Yes," said Tom. "Like this—"

"No, don't show me. Left hand opens, right hand closes."

Tom nodded to show his understanding: one control gesture to undo the two halves, its mirror image to meld them together.

"Damn it." The woman's fine mouth grimaced. "If only I had more—Well, I don't." Another glance along the corridor. "Life is a mortal pilgrimage, my friend."

She closed Tom's fist over the talisman, enclosing his grip with her own. Her hand was smooth.

"When the dark fire falls, seek salvation where you—" Her head turned swiftly to one side.

And then she was standing.

"I won't tell anyone." The words came straight out of Tom's mouth, surprising him.

Gentle fingertips brushed his cheek. Her touch was electric.

"Good luck."

Her farewell seemed to hang in the air as she slipped into the shadows, broke into a silent run, and was lost among the darkened turns.

On his way home, infotablet tagged to his belt, Tom halted suddenly. From a side tunnel, a militia squad appeared. They were running in time, a distance-eating jog, graser rifles held at port-arms, boot soles slapping softly on the worn stone. As the squad disappeared around a bend, two militiamen dropped out of formation and came back towards Tom.

He felt caught, a blindmoth trapped in a hanging web.

"Hello, lad." The bigger militiaman smiled, then continued in thick-accented Nov'glin: "Seen a stranger, have ye? A woman?"

Tom could only shake his head.

"Where, then?"

Tom stared at him, confused, but the other trooper laughed harshly. "We're in Darinia Demesne," he said. "Part of Gelmethri Syektor."

"Yeah. So what?"

"So"—the trooper brushed Tom's head with a rough hand—"round here, a shake of the head means no."

"Bleedin' Fate." The big militiaman scowled at Tom. "Ya wouldn't lie to me, would ya, mate?"

Tom started to shake his head again, then stopped.

"Wastin' time. Come on."

Suppertime. Silent tension seemed to knot the air. Mother bustled about the small family chamber, her startling red hair tied back, her pale, beautiful face lined with strain. Father, looking blocky and resigned, followed her with his gaze. Tom said nothing, unable to tell them what had happened.

Throughout supper, he was conscious of the talisman beneath his tunic, warm against his skin.

Meal over, Tom ran the dishes under the clean-beam, then retired to his sleeping-alcove and pulled the hanging across—failing to shut out his parents' icy tension. Placing his moccasins on the floor, he sat on his cot, infotablet in his hands, thinking about the mysterious woman. Eventually, with a sense of distant surprise, he realized he was exhausted, and lay back, clutching the infotablet.

Grey sleep seemed elusive, and his mind drifted—

And then he was *clinging by his right hand, void beneath him, desperate, and a flake of stone broke off and tumbled into space . . .*

"*Fate," he murmured, feeling the danger. Strong winds rocked him, turbulence tugged.*

Turbulence. Chaos. Terms of ancient days, before fate became hardwired in humanity's souls.

He clung to his precarious hold, aware of the weapon sheathed at his back, fuelled by the inner core of rage, murder in his heart as he was jerking awake, and Father's broad hand was on his shoulder.

"Nightmare again?"

Father's square, fleshy face, beneath his heavy thatch of grey hair, was creased with concern.

"Sorry." Tom struggled up into a sitting position. "I don't remember."

But his body was drenched with sweat.

Cold breakfast, bitter daistral. Tom and Father left early, but there were already people moving in the quiet corridors. The old trinket-seller, carpet roll across his shoulders, nodded wearily.

At the market's entrance, Trude Mulgrave waved her thin, bony hand.

"Hi, Davraig." She brushed back a long, grey lock of hair which had escaped from her red-and-white headscarf, and her large earrings jangled. "And Tom. How are you both?"

"Good," said Father. "And you?"

"'Twixt great and middling." A typical Trude reply. "Good business today, I think."

"Let's hope so."

Grey shadows, pale rose-hued glowglobes: early morning in the market chamber. The unpacking—the head trader's surly sons unloading their lev-platform—and the setting-up. The dragging-in of carts; the untying of stalls' fastenings, for those who relied on the nightwatchman to guard their goods. The fish-vat woman's gaggle of children. The unsnapping of membrane tents and the tying of knots; the scents of heavy hemp and dusty fabric.

The hong-owner's daughters, caped and beribboned, on their way to school, flanked by patient housecarl bodyguards: "Darling! Isn't this wild?" Holding up a shawl or jewellery which they would not buy. "Perfect for Darkday."

The girls grew quickly bored, as always, and continued to the market chamber's centre. Waiting until their earstuds flashed, confirming IDs, they stood aside as the silver ceiling disc rotated and the flanges spiralled downwards and snapped into place.

Slender ankles flashed beneath their capes as they ascended the helical stairway to the stratum above, a place Tom had seen only in his imagination.

"Tom?"

"Sir?" Tom flushed guiltily.

"Put these on the front display, would you?" Heavy medallions.

"OK, Father."

Tom laid them out on the velvet tray and checked the rest of the cluttered booth: perfumed candles, bronze dragon lamps, pewter amulets and cape clasps. Twisted-knot brooches and amber tag-holders.

The stairway had folded back up into the chamber's ceiling, solid and impenetrable.

Gradually, the market-going crowd built up. Within two hours, the chamber was filled with the sound of haggling, the digging for bargains. Among the multitude of matt ochres and dull blues, among the brown and grey tunics, bright silk flashed here and there. Trude's stall, with its bolts of exotic fabrics, was as popular as always, though many were merely looking.

An eerie hush descended.

Soft movement brushed through the crowd: a shuffling, a drawing-apart, forming clear passage from one entrance all the way to the chamber's centre. Tom's skin prickled as a squad of militiamen marched in. Up close, their goose-step was not silly, but an expression of controlled power: wide shoulders, muscular gait, heavy weapons held one-handed as though they weighed nothing.

Their prisoner was in the centre, surrounded.

The woman! Tom's heart pounded. *No—*

Hood drawn forwards, burgundy cape torn, her slender wrists manacled to a heavy silver bar: her bent posture spoke of defeat. A sympathetic ripple passed through the marketgoers, a tiny forward motion as though to assist, then a retreat.

Please . . . The words cut through Tom's mind. *Help her, somebody!*

What was her alleged crime? Somehow it made no difference. The crowd held its collective breath as the militiamen halted. At their centre, the woman slumped: a figure of broken grace. Ahead of them, an officer strode forwards and raised his baton. It blinked scarlet, and the ceiling disc span as silver slats spiralled downwards.

It must have been what she was waiting for.

Tossing her head back, she freed her mass of black, curly hair from the hood's confines. Her olive-skinned face was triangular, almost feline. She reached up, despite the manacle bar's weight, dabbed at her eyes and flicked something aside.

Her eyes were obsidian black, without surrounding whites. Glittering jet.

"Sweet Fate!" Father's voice was a shocked whisper. "A Pilot!"

Pilot? Weren't they just a legend?

In each eye, a tiny spark grew. Remembering the stories, Tom glanced away just in time, as golden fire coruscated across her eyes and lightning flashed, a blinding light, and people screamed, clutching at their eyes.

When Tom looked up, the Pilot's chains and manacle bar had fallen to the flagstones. She tossed her cape at a trooper. Lean, clad in tight burgundy, she whirled into motion, and ashen-faced militiamen staggered back.

A big, grizzled trooper lunged forwards, arms wide, but the Pilot's shin scythed into his ribs and the blade-edge of her foot whipped into his knee with a sickening crunch. He dropped.

And she ran.

She faked to one side, then sprinted *into* the main squad. Tangled among themselves, unable to bring their heavy graser rifles to bear, they fell as she span, almost dancing, through their midst: ducking low to elbow-strike a groin, leaping high to arc her knee into an exposed throat, palm-striking the troopers into each other's line of fire.

Then she broke from the mêlée and leaped for the spiral stairs.

Run! Tom clenched his fists. *Hurry!*

She landed on the fifth rung, ducked beneath a graser beam's sizzling crack, then launched herself upwards so fast that she looked weightless. For a moment Tom thought she was going to make it but more beams lanced through the air, impaling her. Arm flung out, she began to topple back, turning her face towards Tom. Half of it was blackened, roasted meat, her one good jet-black eye focusing on him for a moment . . . Then more beams split the air, and her lifeless body dropped.

It lay there, twisted and ripped on the cold, hard flagstones: a shattered thing, a broken shell.

2

NULAPEIRON AD 3404

After tragedy, a strange, disjointed day.

Tourists, on wander-leave from their Lord's demesne, passed through: oblivious to the stained floor and lingering stench; to the eyes-squeezed-shut desperate prayers of the Largin faithful; to the silent looks exchanged among the stallholders. To the food vendors packing up early, departing almost furtively.

When the glowglobes finally flickered to rosy dimness, Father and Tom trudged home empty-handed. Tom could not recall the last time they had left their goods overnight.

"Ranvera," said Father, as they sat down to table, "there was a prisoner today—"

"None of that talk"—Mother let a ceramic pot down with a thud—"in my home."

Father and Tom exchanged glances, used to her responses.

"What's for supper?" Father's voice held a hint of strain.

"Stew." Mother brushed back a damp lock of red hair. "Nothing special."

"Smells great."

A clap sounded from the corridor outside just as Father was reaching for the pot.

"Only me!" Trude's voice.

"Come in," said Father, as her liver-spotted hand drew the hanging back. "Join us."

"I won't stay. What did you think of—?" Trude stopped as Father shook his head, almost imperceptibly. "Well, I wanted to ask a favour. Can you spare Tom for an hour or two, later tonight?"

"Of course." Mother smiled brightly. "Tom would love to help out."

"Just to Garveron Place—"

But Father was lifting the stewpot's lid, revealing the dark meat-and-dumpling stew, and the aroma of roasting meat ascended, filled Tom's nostrils, mixed with his breath as he remembered the Pilot's face crisping, cooked beneath the questing graser beam . . .

He staggered, gorge rising, as he pushed back from the table and lurched past Trude out into the corridor, barely making it to the communal washroom in time.

After rinsing his mouth with warm water, Tom waited before returning to the family chamber. Thoughts whirling, he walked slowly back; at the hanging, he clapped absent-mindedly to announce his arrival, and went inside. Trude was no longer there.

He reassured Mother about his health. At her insistence, he put on a heavy overtunic, and headed for Trude's place.

She let him leave the overtunic there—"The temperature at Garveron Place is the same as here, Tom. Don't worry"—and handed him her smoothcart's handle.

He tugged the flat plate along the tunnels, its near-frictionless lower surface bucking and sliding across the uneven granite floor. Already his knees were aching, and it was an hour-long walk to their destination.

It pulsed.

As they entered Farlgrin District, zeitgeist-deco salsa pounded in the tunnel's walls, as though music were the heart of the world, of Nulapeiron itself. Mutated fluorofungus and hand-tinted glowclusters shone electric blue.

Other tunnels lay in black shadow, low-ceilinged and dripping with moisture.

They passed worn steps which wound into a darkened bar. The beat thumped loudly here, and the air was heavy with the sweetness of ganja masks. A pale woman, triple silver bars inlaid along each cheekbone and across her fingers—flesh entwined with metal, screwed into place during childhood—stared at them with feverish orange eyes. Baring her teeth, she snapped her clawlike fingers: a muted clash.

Trude laid her hand on Tom's shoulder and they walked away, taking a left turn, spiralling gently downwards.

"So, Tom." They came out onto a worn balcony above Garveron Cavern. "What have you been reading this decaday?"

The term sounded old-fashioned, overly polite. Anyone else would have said "tenday."

"Xiao Wang's *Skein Wars*."

Their path became a footbridge, bordered with floating holoflames, spanning a pit whose sides were stores and taverns. Bronze globes circled in the air: a lev-orrery.

"What's it about?"

Lone women loitered at curved niches, each with a small velvet cap lying beside her on the balustrade.

"Er, self-organized criticality." The phrase was awkward on Tom's tongue.

A nervous-looking man made his selection, picking up one of the caps and walking away, shoulders hunched. The cap's owner followed him docilely, too tired to sway her hips.

"Emergent properties," added Tom, "in their virtual environment. The sudden appearance of the Fulgor Anomaly."

"I'm surprised," Trude muttered, "that it got past the censors."

They took a spiralling ramp downwards. Unloaded, the smoothcart's very lightness made it awkward to handle, and Tom was sweating by the time they reached flat stone. In the cavern's pit, dark storefronts were like eye-pits in skulls. The taverns were open and late-night crowds sat outside, beneath stained orange glowglobes.

Above, the cavern roof was lost in darkness.

"It's a very old crystal." Tom was puffing now. "Centuries old. Text only. Found it on Darin's stall."

"Even so."

Passing through the crowds, among the clink of glasses and clack of go stones, the hiss of baby narls in tabletop serpent fights and the gamblers' encouragements and curses, Tom and Trude threaded their way to Tenebra Shaft, where love poets sweetly recorded whispered seductions for their clients.

"And it explains"—Tom tugged the cart out of a small black man's path—"why they do things differently now."

"Ah." A knowing look crossed Trude's lined face. "Shoring up the status quo." There it was again, in Trude's speech: a touch of educated precision, as though she belonged two or even three strata above. "Here we are." She clapped, and tugged a heavy hanging aside. "Hi, Filram."

"Trude!" A hook-nosed, sallow man, dressed in a voluminous smock, looked up from a counter piled high with fabric. "Long time."

Their business took a while, conducted in low voices while Tom, outside, sat on the small, flat smoothcart, heels on the ground, rocking frictionlessly. Then he helped load bolts of fabric—heavy burgundy and silver, light mandelbroten in a hundred shades of green—and tied them in place with cord.

"Full rate." Trude was handing over cred-flakes.

"I usually give a discount to fellow—" The man, Filram, gave a phlegmy cough, eyes flickering in Tom's direction. "Fellow traders."

"Wouldn't dream of it. My love to your family."

Trude held out a small, grey-wrapped parcel. Filram accepted it with a nod; it vanished within his stained, baggy smock.

"Go in freedom, Trude."

Lash!

Heading upwards on the spiralling ramp, climbing towards the footbridge, Tom was bathed in sweat.

Crack!

"What—?" He stopped, panting.

Trude frowned.

Unable to control the cart's frictionless wandering, Tom had no choice but to continue upwards, hauling the cart up onto the level footbridge. Then he leaned over the balustrade, looking down.

Another wet lash of sound.

"Fate!" Trude, coming up beside him, muttered: "Could it be?"

Down below, crowds edged back as a snub-nosed bronze lev-car slid into view. It was an open vehicle, its curved, curlicued bench-seat occupied by a vast, white-skinned man: bare-chested, hugely round, like stacked tubes of fat. Bald head gleaming with a sickly sweat. Behind him, on a footplate, a narrow-bodied slave rode, shaven-headed like his master, raising a sinewy arm—

Trude's bony fingers clamped around Tom's upper arm.

The slave swung forwards.

His chain-whip whistled through the air, towards his master's bare, wide back. *Lash!* Cherry drops on white: blood sprang out on smooth, glistening skin.

Trude: "What's he doing here?"

She almost spat the words, like a curse. But Tom was watching the women: they had filed down from the footbridge and laid their velvet caps on the flagstones. Even from up here, he could see the tension drawn across their faces.

In the now halted lev-car, the gross man's head lolled to one side, tongue protruding. The slave, ignoring him, pointed to two of the women.

They glanced behind them, but a big, grim-faced man with triple braids knotted into loops—pit-fighter style—gestured them onwards. No-one in the crowd tried to help the women. Fearfully, they stepped up onto the footplate beside the slave.

"Destiny." Bitterness swirled through Trude's low-toned words. "All tools, all trapped: even him."

They watched as the lev-car moved, heading for a low, dark tunnel, and slowly slid from sight.

"Who—?" Tom's voice was hoarse.

"We're honoured." Indecipherable emotion webbed Trude's lined face. "That was an Oracle, young Tom."

It was as though the stone bridge had dropped away beneath him.

An Oracle?

"It—No, it couldn't be."

Down here?

"Creator of truecasts. Destiny's voice." A bitter laugh, cut off. "Hard to believe, isn't it?"

Oracle.

A twisted intersection. Almost home.

"You were there, weren't you, Tom?" Trude's voice cut into the swirling images inside Tom's head. "When the, ah, prisoner was killed?"

Pilot. Stench of roasting meat—

"I can't . . ."

Beyond the intersection, a group of tall youths loitered. One of them called out, "Hey, Corcorigan." He made the forefinger-and-looped-thumb gesture. "Heard your momma's quite a dancer."

Trude glared, and they turned away, grinning.

"Getting worse round here," she muttered, then looked at Tom. "Are you OK?"

He shook his head, unable to talk.

"Don't worry. It got to me, too."

The Pilot's death. But there was more, and the stallion talisman felt hard as guilt beneath his tunic, yet he could not explain. Not to Trude, not to anyone.

Beside him, a wall hanging shifted and he jumped, heart pounding, and dropped the smoothcart's handle.

It was a storage alcove filled with cleaning equipment. A young couple stepped out—he thin and acne-scarred, she plump and smooth-skinned—and looked at Trude sheepishly. Holding hands, they simultaneously blushed.

Chuckling, Trude helped Tom to pick up the handle and get the smoothcart moving again.

Later, alone in his cot, Tom drew the stallion out from beneath his tunic and curled his left hand into the control gesture. Halved, the talisman fell neatly apart.

He looked at its contents for a long time: black, ovoid capsule, needle fastened alongside. Then, pressing the two sections together, he twisted his right hand.

Whole again: forever frozen, galloping for freedom.

He tucked the talisman away.

3
NULAPEIRON AD 3404

Astymonia patrol: a large, blank-faced man and a fit-looking woman. Black helmets. Behind them, night shadows etched the tunnel.

"Are your parents in?"

Tom had been nearest to the hanging when they clapped.

"Er, sure. Dad?" He turned, and the male officer walked in past him. Tom's gaze was drawn to the long knife at his hip, its hilt worn smooth with practice.

"Come in, come in." Father was standing by the table, smiling hospitably. "Please sit down."

The woman followed Tom inside, removed her helmet and placed it on the table, but remained standing. "Thanks all the same." She ran a hand through her close-cropped hair. "May we ask you some questions, ah—"

Father's ID stud flashed in his ear.

"Davraig Corcorigan." The male officer looked up from his thumb-ring display. "A trader?"

"That's right." Father's broad face looked cheery.

The officers were astymonia, not militia: locals, not foreigners. Armed, but no energy weapons.

"Were you in the market," the woman asked, "yesterday morning?"

"I saw the prisoner escape. The troopers"—Father spoke carefully—"had no choice, that I could see."

The woman nodded.

"A Romaner." The male officer looked intent. "A thief, separated from her people."

A Pilot, Tom wanted to say, but could not.

"Seems reasonable to me," said Father easily. "Thank Fate we've got you and the militia, officers—Say, there's supper in the pot. Would you like to join us?" He patted his ample belly and smiled.

The male officer snorted, but the woman declined politely. "No thanks. We'll be getting along."

"The boy?" The man nodded in Tom's direction.

"My son, Tom. He's fourteen Standard."

Only a hectoday, Tom thought, *until I'm fifteen.*

"One moment." Checking his display, the man narrowed his eyes. "Is there anyone else here?"

"Only my—"

At the chamber's rear, the sleeping-alcove's curtain moved, then Mother looked out: radiantly beautiful, her hair a copper nimbus, picking up highlights from the small floating glowcluster.

"Because it's cold in Farlgrin District," she said to Tom.

He closed his eyes in embarrassment.

That was last night's conversation, Mother. Opening his eyes again, he saw her ID stud's ruby spark. *Please concentrate.*

"Ranvera Corcorigan, officers." She smiled brilliantly. "Nice to meet you."

A sharp intake of breath: the male officer.

"Ma'am?" It was the woman who spoke. "Were you in the market chamber yesterday?"

"I don't allow that kind of talk in my home."

The officers looked at each other.

"Dreamtropes," murmured Father. "Disturbances . . . upset her."

"I see." The female officer frowned, then retrieved her helmet from the table. "I don't think we'll trouble you further."

"Oh, a moment." Father held up his work-roughened hand. "The injured militiamen. There must be medical costs—"

"Taken care of." Snapping her helmet into place, the woman nodded. "Sir. Madam. Thank you for your co-operation."

After they had gone, Father sat at the table, shaking his head.

"Never known it." Puzzled. "Young troopers, refusing payment."

Mother, retreating to the rear alcove, pulled the faded red hanging across.

When Tom returned home, halfway through the afternoon, the chamber was still untidy from the morning, and the sleeping-alcove was still curtained off. Tom shook his head, but went into his own alcove and sat cross-legged on his cot.

"*Kwere ost?*"

Stallion. Not too dissimilar from his talisman.

Tom gestured for lower audio volume before answering in Eldraic: "*Est ekwos.*"

As he had left the market chamber, Padraig and Levro had cast him sour glances, for none of the other traders' sons or daughters could shirk their duties. But Mother wanted Tom to "better himself."

"*Karoshe.*" The holo image shifted, morphing into a twisted spiral organism with hexagonal flukes. "*Eh kwees?*" A lava-dweller of some sort. "*Kwere ost?*"

A stirring outside. Mother, getting up at last?

"*Ne savro.*" Tom could not identify the species in any language.

"Ah, Tom!" Mother tugged the hanging aside, smiling brightly. "How lovely!"

"*Ost thermidron.*"

Spirit sinking, Tom saw that Mother was wearing a one-piece baggy black sweatsuit: her old rehearsal outfit.

"*Kwere ost?*"

"Never mind." Tom gestured the display away, closing down the language tutorial.

"The Borehole Lilt?"

Tom forced a smile. "Great." Tricons filled the air above the infotablet, and he pointed.

"Dancers—"

"—are special people." Tom sighed as the familiar strains of music began. "Yes, Mother."

She took a towel from a shelf, and Tom knew that the Shawl Dance was next. It would finish with a spectacular sequence of pliés, but that was not reason enough to stay. She might drag Tom out onto the floor and force him to try some steps.

But her eyes, a distant blue, were filled with dreams, and it was easy to slip past her, out into the tunnel, and head back towards the market chamber and sanity.

Hands jammed into his tunic pockets, Tom took the long way round, not wanting to face Father.

"You should have stayed with her, Tom," he would say. Then, "It's a sickness, that's all."

Two figures up ahead in the gloom, where the fluorofungus was patchy.

Tom shook his head. In a mood like this, Mother might be lost to them for days, dancing her dreams while he and Father tidied the chamber, bought and cooked the food, on top of their normal work.

Something about them—But the two figures were still, heads bent together, talking in low voices.

No matter. Perhaps he should go back.

He had never dared to ask Father why he stayed with her, but Father had told him nonetheless: "I love her, son."

And there was nothing Tom could say to that.

"—origan. Check them—" A freak whisper echoed down the tunnel, was lost.

Coming this way.

He recognized them now: the two patrol officers. Heart thumping, Tom looked around, saw a familiar wall hanging, and remembered the young courting couple who had given him a fright. Before he could think, he had slipped inside, into darkness.

"Come on, Elva." The voice was right outside the alcove. "She was pretty odd, don't you think?"

"Of all the people we've seen today"—the woman officer, exasperated—"she must be the least dangerous."

Tom swallowed, trying not to breathe. They were standing outside, at a junction: a natural place to stop.

"Besides," the woman continued, "she showed all the symptoms. Dreamtrope addict, for sure."

"Yeah, but . . . She's a babe, isn't she?"

Something in here with him.

"Keep it in your trews, Pyotr."

A sense of dark presence. A . . . *drip*. Wet, on his cheek. Tom thought he was going to be sick.

"I'm calling it in, anyway."

"You sure we're in range?"

Idiot. Just old cleaning gear.

"Just about. Who are we?"

"What?" The woman sounded puzzled. "Oh, Tango-Aleph."

Tom shifted uncomfortably, and touched the old mop: it scraped, and he froze.

"Did you—?"

But the woman's voice was lost beneath her companion's officious words: identifying himself by their call-sign and requesting access. "Citizens' Details. Current district, deepest detail."

In the darkness, Tom moved by millimetres, fingertips questing, and found it. Ceramic carapace. An old scrub drone, standing on end.

"What have you got?" The woman.

"Corcorigan, Davraig." Reading from a display. "Zero records. No criminal future."

"What about history?"

"Or history. He's clean."

Lowering himself—slowly, slowly—into a crouch, body aching

with tension, Tom bit into his bottom lip, stifling his desire to call out and be done with it.

"And as for the babe—" The man fell silent.

"What is it, Pyotr?"

"Corcorigan, Ranvera." Quietly. "Silver star."

"You're kidding. Show me."

After a moment, Tom could hear her chuckle. He was halfway down now, behind the disused drone.

"Well . . . Bad luck, mate. Watch, don't touch. Trust you to fall for a silver star."

"Very funny." Scorn in his voice. "Hey, young Elva. Wanna know what they call you in the men's chamber?"

"No." Her tone grew hard. "Shut up!"

Light cascaded into Tom's hiding place. The woman, dragging back the hanging.

"What are you—?"

"Nothing." She scanned the storage alcove's darkness. "Thought I heard something, that's all."

For a moment Tom could have sworn her grey eyes locked with his, but then she was turning away and the hanging fell back into place, and shadows hid him once more.

"Come on, big-brain," he heard her say. "We've got work to do."

It made a great lightball court.

Zing!

A hollowed-out spindle formed the round chamber's centre, its elliptical window-holes revealing the cracked triangular altar inside.

Pow! Green streak flying through a hole, rebounding from the outer circle's wall.

Once-red tiles were cracked, and many were missing, revealing blackened stone. Some said the old Zharkrastrian temple was haunted.

"My point."

Wham! The lightball sang as Padraig's palm slammed it across the chamber. It bounced, flew past Tom's face, and had already dropped to the floor with a dying whine by the time he made a grab for it.

"Play or stay away, Corcorigan."

"Sorry." He picked up the ball and threw it awkwardly, underhand.

"Friggin' Chaos!" The voice was behind Tom, but his heart sank: only one person used language that bad. "What you doin' here?"

"Just heading home."

Stavrel scowled. "You like lightball?" His wide face, splashed with a purple birthmark, was a frightening mask. "Anyone who don't, must be queer. Am I right?"

"Er, yeah," Tom lied. "I love it."

But that was not good enough. He backed away as Stavrel came close, pushing Tom hard against the spindle wall.

"Listen, pretty boy." Big hand, pressing against Tom's sternum. "Know what I'm gonna do?"

Tom's diaphragm was paralysed. He could not speak. No talking his way out of this.

Stavrel spat. "First I'm—"

Running footsteps. Coming into the chamber.

"Come quick!" Almost skidding to a halt: small Levro, Padraig's younger brother. "There's hundreds of 'em!"

The pressure of Stavrel's hand increased. Tom thought his heart might burst.

"What's going on?" Padraig grabbed Levro's shoulder.

"Militiamen! Ain't never seen so many—"

"Where?"

"Heading down Skalt Bahreen. Straight for the market."

"Better get home." Their father, the head trader, was rumoured to have shady dealings. "Come on!"

Stavrel looked from one brother to the other. Padraig glanced back at Tom, shook his head, but spoke only to Levro: "Come on." They exited together, moving quickly.

What now?

Stavrel thumped Tom once in the chest. Then, wordlessly—as Tom braced himself for more—he turned and hurried out, bearing left instead of right: away from the market.

Out of danger.

Pain and shame kept Tom pinned to the wall. Then, blinking back tears, he slowly sank to his haunches. His arms were trembling, and he leaned back against the solid stone, feeling the dull vibration. A marching army's rhythmic beat: two hundred troopers' bootsteps pounding in counterpoint to Tom Corcorigan's thumping heart.

4
NULAPEIRON AD 3404

The noise was greater here.

Sick with tension, Tom scrambled along Split Alley—an almost disused tunnel—over broken, tilted flagstones, not knowing what he would find in the market chamber.

"Destiny help us." An old woman's voice floated down the narrow, jumbled route.

The repetitive stamp of marching feet from the larger Skalt Bahreen, off to the left, accompanied him. This tunnel ran almost parallel: a short-cut. Would he reach the market ahead of them?

He hurried, not knowing why. Perhaps he should be looking for somewhere to hide.

Flames. The acrid stink of smoke.

Father . . .

Tom tripped over a broken block, and pain shot through his shin. But the market was just around the corner.

There was no panic.

Rapt, the crowd's attention was focused on something to Tom's left. Slowing down, he limped into the market chamber and leaned against the terracotta wall. What was happening?

Grey banner: faded narl, fangs agape.

There was a group of blue-robed, masked Largin wives in front of Tom. Huge cycle-eunuch guards—on-phase: muscles massively pumped with testosterone—formed a protective ring around the women.

The serpent banner was in flames. As Tom watched, the burning remnants dropped. Marketgoers and stalls blocked Tom's view, but it seemed that the fire sputtered out.

There was an old bale of rough sackcloth beside Tom, and nobody was paying attention, so he awkwardly clambered onto it. His shin, where he had banged it against the stone, was sticky with blood.

The pain faded instantly.

Someone had burned away the banner to clear the entranceway from Skalt Bahreen. Fully revealed, it was greater than Tom expected: a black semicircle wide enough to hold six men marching abreast.

And they did.

At the crowd's rear, near Tom, a small white-haired woman, bent beneath the weight of years, made the double-claw ward-sign with arthritic fingers. Tom shook his head and raised himself on tiptoe atop the unsteady bale, one hand against the wall for balance.

Hundreds of them.

Flanked by ranks of local astymonia in ceremonial headbands and gauntlets, a wave of scarlet-uniformed militia marched into the market chamber. They wheeled in formation, bootsteps reverberating, forming a red arrow into the chamber's centre as the market-going crowd fell back.

The ranks split apart, forming a wide, straight avenue and a hollow circle below the ceiling hatch. For a moment, Tom thought that the hatch might open and *she looked at him with one good eye from the blackened ruin of her face* but he shook the vision away.

"Present . . . arms!"

Heavy graser rifles spun through effortless curves. Onlookers flinched at the simultaneous clash of bootheels and the discharge flash of guide beams.

Then: nothing.

They stood still as statues, waiting, while Tom—riveted—held his breath.

Then, swallowing, he lowered himself from the bale and crept around the perimeter. Quietly. As he neared Trude's stall, she turned, sensing him, and nodded once.

"Up here." She was standing on a storage case, and helped Tom to clamber up. "We should be able to—"

Movement.

Cobalt blue and gleaming silver: a lev-car, moving slowly, slid from Skalt Bahreen into the market. The troopers' rigidity increased as the vehicle glided past them. Shivering, Tom watched the lev-car settling to the flagstones at the market's centre. Its cockpit grew transparent.

The man who stepped through the membrane was wide-shouldered and narrow-waisted, deep-blue cloak thrown back, tunic impeccable. He dismounted easily, light of step, and a grin briefly lit up his square, handsome face, neatly framed with a dark beard.

Trude's body was tight, angular with tension.

"Is that—?" Tom stopped.

Dark-liveried servants took up position around their master.

"I know this one." Trude's voice was a bitter whisper. "Oracle Gérard d'Ovraison."

But not much like the other one. A very different Oracle.

"And he's staying for a while." There was no pleasure in Trude's voice.

A black dodecahedron rose from the lev-car's rear on extruded, narrow legs. Spiderlike, it walked to the chamber's exact centre. It sank to the floor. Its legs momentarily retracted, then arced out in long inverted-catenary curves and touched the flagstones. Its feet were points on a circle some fifteen metres wide.

"Tom, I think you should go home now."

"But . . ." He looked over at Father's stall. Nothing. Father was watching the Oracle just like everybody else.

At the market's centre, the dodecahedron rose on its legs until it touched the ceiling. Then a black, translucent film flowed down between the legs, filling the interstices.

"It's a tent," murmured somebody in the crowd.

That's right, thought Tom. As the film reached floor-level all around, it hardened into opacity, forming a matt black hemisphere. *Neat trick*.

"Please, Tom." Trude's voice jerked him back to reality. "I wish you would leave."

Tom opened his mouth to ask why—and then he saw: copper-red tresses beneath a blue silk scarf, a slender figure in the crowd, passing through the cordon of militiamen into the cleared space.

"They're expecting her," said Trude.

Sway-backed dancer's walk.

"Sweet Destiny!" Above the heads of clustered traders, from behind his stall, Father's anguished voice clearly carried. "No . . ."

Mother?

At the black tent, she stopped by the smiling, broad-shouldered Oracle, who waved a courteous hand. The membrane puckered open.

Mother.

She and the Oracle walked through the opening, and the tent sealed up behind them.

5

NULAPEIRON AD 3404

Hating himself, Tom gestured the thing into motion:

"She was wringing her hands." Father swallowed. *"Did it for hours, in her sleep."*

"Oh, Davraig—" Trude, sitting across the table from Father, placed her hand briefly on his. *"But she did come home last night."* It was not quite a question.

Cut. The image froze.

Tom leaned back, heart thumping. He was sitting on his cot, stone at his back, and it felt icy cold.

"Fate, Mother." He kept his voice low, though the chamber was empty. "Why?"

He pointed, and the holo resumed.

"Yeah." Father looked to one side, to where the infotablet had been lying on Tom's bed, with the alcove-hanging open (and seemed for a moment to stare straight into Tom's eyes). *"She came back excited. Talked about the marvellous conversation, amazing food."*

"She danced for him last night."

"Oh, yes. The Shalko Troupe was quite famous, up there." He pointed at the ceiling, meaning: famous in the stratum above. *"Still is, probably."*

The troupe Mother had danced with. Had run away from, when she was scarcely older than Tom was now . . . And that was all Tom knew of Mother's early life.

"So he was impressed with her credentials." Trude. *"Doesn't explain why he was expecting—But then, he's an Oracle, isn't he?"*

Father looked down. "I'm not good enough for her, Trude. I never have been."

"She loves you." Trude's tone was not convincing.

"Dancers aren't stupid, you know." Father leaned back in his chair—

Tom glanced up at the empty table in the chamber, then back at the image floating beside him.

—and ran his blunt fingers through his untidy grey hair. "She was trained in physiology, voice control, drama . . . And it must have been glamorous, performing."

Trude shook her head. "Glamour's always on the outside," she said. "Other people's perceptions."

"Maybe. But it must have been better than here." He waved a hand around, indicating his surroundings.

Once more, Tom looked around the real chamber. What was wrong with it?

Trude: "Remember how you found her."

"She was down on her luck." Father was defensive. "That was all."

A strange, sick feeling took hold of Tom's stomach.

There was a long silence, then Trude said: "The hand-wringing you described . . . It's a bad sign, Davraig. If you can get her away from here for a few days—"

"I've no travel permit."

"Just a klick or two away. I know people in Farlgrin District . . ."

Father shook his head.

"What about the hand-wringing?" he asked, after a moment. "I've seen her do it sometimes, when she's very stressed."

"Just something we talked about once." Trude tapped her bony fingers on the tabletop. "When she was—Never mind. Girl talk." She stopped tapping and stared straight at Father. "Just follow my advice. I don't often give it."

"No?" Father forced a laugh. "I remember that time—"

The edge of Tom's hand cut the air and the holo image vanished. He was ashamed of himself: leaving the infotablet recording without telling anyone. But no-one would explain what was happening.

Forcing himself, he scissored his fingers together, wiping the log from existence. He got up from the cot, then sat down again, not knowing what to do. Stared up at the ceiling, seeing imagined episodes of Mother, dancing.

What the Fate was going on?

"Hey, little Tom." A youth—knotted-chrome headband woven into his forehead, amber ovoids like pustules beneath each cheekbone—was sitting on a ledge halfway up the wall at Pentangle Interchange, swigging from a flagon. "Hear your ma's out of retirement . . ."

He leaned over, handing the flagon down to a group of young toughs. One of them turned, and the purple birthmark made Tom's heart sink: Stavrel.

Tom clutched the new charge-bead for Father's cutting-tools. What if Stavrel tried to take it?

Last straw. Overload.

For three days now, Mother had paid visits to the Oracle in his tent, while his militiamen roamed the local tunnels and astymonia intelligence questioned everybody. No-one quite knew why. One word—*Pilot*—was in everyone's mind, but never spoken.

This morning Mother had tied her hair back with silver cord, used precious cred-flakes to buy a basket of jantrasta-filled gripplefruits, and taken them into the black tent.

I know more about the Pilot than anyone, Tom realized. *But all I care about is—*

Stavrel had jerked the flagon away from one of his companions just as the youth had been about to drink, but stopped now, and stared at Tom.

Up on the ledge, the chrome-headbanded one laughed shortly.

"Dancers learn lots of positions, don't they?" He spat to one side. "First there's—"

Overload. Tom opened his mouth to—

"Shut up." Stavrel. Looking up at the ledge.

Metal-headband stopped, blood draining from his face.

Stavrel glanced at Tom, then turned away.

Unsettled, Tom took the long route back to the market.

He had been halfway to Garveron Place, getting Father's charge-bead; the astymonia-regulated power booth served both Farlgrin District and Salis Core. Standing in line, Tom had caught sight of a grey-headed figure in a mandelbrot shawl. Trude? He had not been able to—

A Jack.

For the first time, icy fear swept away the constant background images of Mother and the whining question about Father: why didn't he *do* something? Suddenly, Tom was afraid for his own sake.

They will detect emissions—

Holodrama heroes were golden-skinned and muscular. In real life, this Jack was slender, almost emaciated. His spindly arms and legs were bare, exposing the motile dermaweb.

Across bone-white skin, fine blue tracery *crawled*.

Just for a moment, he—it—glanced in Tom's direction. A diffractive rainbow shimmered across microfaceted eyes.

My fear is natural. Tom was aware of his own sweat, his soaring pulse. *He won't stop me, will he?*

Behind the Jack, keeping their distance—not to overwhelm the Jack's hyper-reactive senses—were four militiamen in dark combat fatigues.

If I'm subvocalizing—

There was a small, unnamed side tunnel and Tom took it, quickening his pace, hoping no-one would follow.

He hurried through a low, dank inn where hooded men and women were sitting cross-legged around bubbling communal beakers, sipping leth'aqua through narlskin tubes. More hooded robes hung from sticky-tags on the bare rockface wall: clients used them, for anonymity.

Should he borrow a robe?

No, he needed to keep moving. And you couldn't hide from a Jack. Unconsciously he touched his chest, feeling the silver stallion against his skin.

Detect emissions—

Tom halted where the chamber narrowed to winding tunnel once more. Something about one of the hooded figures . . . He turned back.

"Trude?" he asked uncertainly.

There were three of them huddled by the wall, ignoring him. He must be wrong. Not Trude: not in a place like this.

"There's a Jack coming this way," he added, feeling foolish.

That got a reaction.

"Are you sure?" Pulling back her hood.

"Fate, Trude. It is you."

"Time to leave, gentlemen." She addressed the two still-hooded figures beside her. "Come on, Tom. We'll go first."

Dropping the robe to the ground, she took Tom's arm and hurried him out along the tunnel.

Though she gave him one or two strange, appraising looks, they spoke not a word, all the way back to the market chamber.

Laughter.

"Come on in, Tom." Father, waving a bronze cup. "You ought to have a drink, but—"

Mother grabbed Father's shoulder, pulling him to her, whispered something into his ear and giggled.

Father sputtered, spraying wine, then choked it down and shook his head, laughing. He was red-faced with drink, happier than Tom had seen him for a long time.

Mother winked at Tom.

"Er . . ." Tom stood at the family chamber's entrance. "Padraig and Levro asked if I could stay at their place tonight. Can I?"

"Huh?" Father looked blearily puzzled. "Are you—?"

"Anything you want, Tom."

"Thank you, Mother." Not letting the doubt sound in his voice.

"Aw . . . A family should stick together."

"It's OK, Father. I want to go."

He let the hanging drop back into place as Mother spoke again in a low voice, and Father laughed once more.

Everything's going to be all right. He sighed, leaning back against the wall.

After a while he started walking, wondering where he might sleep that night.

"—why the Uncertainty we're bothering."

Tom jerked awake.

"You what?"

Cold. Just one of those anomalies, perhaps to do with hidden running water: it happened sometimes, in Split Alley. The temperature must have dropped while Tom was sleeping. He shivered.

"I heard His Wisdom say it. The Jacks won't find the witch's transmitter."

"Some kinda joke."

Tom retreated farther into the rough nook, trying to make himself small. The troopers were near the market chamber, just a couple of metres inside the tunnel.

"Nah, he meant it. Said the trip would be worth the effort, though."

"What's that supposed to . . . ?"

Their voices faded: moving away, or submerged beneath the rushing of blood in Tom's ears. The Jacks' search would fail.

I'm safe.

"Father! Morning."

Father, picking desultorily at cold rice and shredded gripple, merely pointed with his tine-spoon. "Have some breakfast."

"Er, thanks." Tom, bursting to tell someone his good news, was struck by Father's downcast expression. "I'll get a bowl."

As he sat down, though, Father stood.

"I'm going to set up." He shrugged a jerkin over his plain tunic. "Early start."

It was not like Father to leave food uneaten. Puzzled but ravenous, Tom tucked in to his own breakfast.

Afterwards, he cleaned and stacked the two bowls, grabbed the infotablet and sticky-tagged it to his belt.

"Tom?"

He stopped. "Yes, Mother?"

"Come here." Leaning past the hanging, she kissed him on the cheek. "I love you, Tom."

"Oh, Mother . . ."

"You have your grandfather's eyes, you know." Her own blue eyes were unreadable: Tom could not tell if the resemblance was a good thing or bad. "I guess I've never—Anyway." Unfocused dreaminess entered her voice. "Your father needs you. Go now."

The hanging swung back into place.

Unsettled, disoriented, Tom almost bumped into a dark-clothed trooper.

"Sorry, I didn't—"

A stiff-expressioned officer was standing in front of Father's stall, his scarlet uniform immaculate, throat clasp and bracelets gleaming.

"Father . . ."

Nobody paid attention to Tom.

The officer was holding out a small bag. "Please, sir." He spoke through clenched teeth. In a lower tone: "He can afford it."

Father's expression was wooden. "No."

"Please reconsider." The officer waited. Then: "My respects, sir."

He bowed to Father, low and precise, as though to a senior officer. Then he wheeled on his bootheel, and for a moment self-disgust washed across his features.

"Escort: atten-*tion*!"

Six troopers snapped their heels together. In time with the officer, they marched away towards the chamber's centre.

And then he saw her.

It was too early for marketgoers, and the scattered stallholders moved to the market's perimeter as the militia ranks formed with the same precision they had shown before. At their centre, the black tent had already lowered itself into the lev-car's rear luggage hold. It pulled its narrow legs inside.

From the same entrance Tom had used, she came. Cupric tresses. Elegant, controlled walk.

There were militiamen standing to attention, but he could have slipped through the gaps between them—were he not paralysed. This was not, could not be happening.

The Oracle, big and impossibly handsome, was waiting by the lev-car.

No . . .

Courteously, he helped her aboard, then climbed in after her.

Mother!

And it moved off slowly, the lev-car, its cockpit membrane still transparent, the couple inside clearly visible. Her hand was upon his gauntleted forearm.

Two hundred militiamen stamped and turned in unison. Then they marched out, squadron after squadron, as the lev-car edged out of view, and they followed into Skalt Bahreen's darkness while Tom could only watch, pinned, until only the echoing bootsteps remained, lingering in the market's still air like the waking fragments of a bad, lost dream.

6

NULAPEIRON AD 3404

Where was she now?

"Tom?" Trude called after him, but he pretended not to hear: head down, holding the empty containers by their loop-handles.

He passed people he knew, but their gazes slid guiltily from his face, never meeting his eyes.

Ten whole days.

It burned at Tom. His own fault for eavesdropping, for using the infotablet again, but Trude's words would not leave his mind.

"Stop belittling yourself, Davraig." Impatience in her tone. *"You ought to ask: what would the Oracle see in her? Beyond the obvious, I mean."*

Father had been despondent, but anger rose in Tom at the memory.

"She'll return, you'll see." A pause, and then she added: *"I could get a call session booked. I've got some, ah, associates who owe me a favour."*

"I could talk to her?"

"We can try. Should take about a tenday."

And it had been ten days, of despair.

In the Aqua Hall, there were too many people—he should have come earlier—but he accepted a token anyway, set down his containers, and sat on a red ceramic bench, awaiting his turn.

So, where? Some other stratum? Another demesne? Where would the Oracle have taken her?

"Are you all right, son?" A white-haired man with a concerned expression.

Tom shook himself, unclenching his fists. "Just a headache. It's nothing."

"If you're sure . . ."

"Thank you. I'm fine."

Tom watched the old man make his way out, bent beneath the canister slung across his shoulders, water sloshing inside. The old man looked back from the tunnel outside—nodding as Tom waved—and then he was gone.

Tom leaned back, watching triple braids of water arc through the air above the pool. Inset wall aquaria were filled with fish: purple, red, yellow-and-black with impossibly long, trailing fins. Normally he liked to watch them—

"Gamma nine? Last call."

Tom checked the ceramic token: his turn.

He waited while the attendants filled his containers, spiked Father's ration flake and helped him sling the handles over his shoulders.

Awkwardly, trying not to slip, Tom made his long way home.

"Ranvera Corcorigan, if you would."

Trude—as he had never heard her. Not with such refinement and precision.

"A moment . . ." Above the table, the impossibly smooth-featured head was replaced by a human figure: a white-bearded man, with parallel purple scars cut into one cheek. "Chef-Steward Valneer, at your service."

Tom, who had been standing frozen in the doorway—this was only the third realtime call he'd seen—slowly lowered his water containers. Neither Trude nor Father even glanced in his direction.

"I am calling on behalf of Master Trader Corcorigan"—Trude nodded towards Father, who remained stone-faced, unimpressed by his apparent social promotion—"whose wife is a guest of His Wisdom, I believe."

A grim pause. "This call is not unexpected. I have been asked to assure you that Madam Corcorigan is well."

Father, like a statue, merely watched.

"She, ah . . ." The old man, Valneer, cleared his throat. "She is where she wants to be."

"My wife." Father.

"I'm sorry." The pain in Valneer's eyes looked genuine.

"Not good enough!" Trude, flaying him with her voice.

"Ma'am, I—" The old man stopped, then wavered: his image split into a thousand revolving fragments which coalesced once more.

Oracle Gérard d'Ovraison.

"Sorry, old friend." Spoken to one side. "This is my burden." Then he turned his handsome regard upon Trude, and bowed slightly to Father. "My regards, sir."

Father's skin looked suddenly grey.

"Ran"—a smile tugged at the Oracle's lips—"is truly fine. But I promised her . . . harmony. She cannot be disturbed."

"She is my wife."

"Not—ah, damn it." The Oracle shrugged his massive shoulders. "There is a thing—I don't want to tell you." An odd smile flickered, was gone. "But I already know I will."

"Ranvera is my *wife*."

"Not for much longer, I fear." A sudden resonance in the Oracle's words, like nothing Tom had ever heard. "But I haven't told Ran . . . of your impending death."

Trude's hands caught Tom's attention: gripping the table edge, bloodless white with tension.

"No!" Tom, filled with sudden rage.

"The son." Grey eyes, impossibly deep, meeting the force of Tom's anger, absorbing it. "Our first meeting, chronologically speaking."

Trude: "Ranvera's nothing to you."

"I can pull into timeflow more than . . . Well. Let's say she has qualities only I can appreciate." His gaze grew darker. "My regrets, all of you." He swept a courteous bow to everyone in the room.

"Davraig—if I may call you that—it would be wise to get your affairs in order."

A strangled sound escaped Trude's lips.

"Five tendays." The Oracle looked at her. "That's how long your friend Davraig has to live."

His image winked out of existence.

Minus thirty. Three tendays remaining.

Aleph to Zeus: tricons instantiated with a cycle time of 0.11-recurring nanoseconds. The names of God flowed past.

Background: the nasal prayer-hum, the whistling spin-chain.

Hb:7.3g dl⁻¹ Glowing amid the incense vapours. *Parietal-delta amp: 112.3 μV.*

A touch on Tom's sleeve: the assistant priestess, scarcely older than Tom, motioning him aside, as the Antistita, the elder priestess, swept past Father's bed once more, with a rustle of heavy purple silks.

"I don't . . . believe . . . in this." Father's voice was soft.

The shaven-headed priestess paused in her chants. "You used to."

Beside Tom, the younger assistant checked both displays: mediscanner's holo to the left, prayer processor to the right. Then she swung her thurible again, and a puff of violet incense fumes made Tom cough.

Blinking away tears, he watched the Antistita perform mudras above Father's chakra points, chanting softly, while pastel phase-space manifolds billowed and blossomed in the holodisplays.

Then she bowed to Father, who nodded weakly, slack-faced, from his bed.

"Be infinitely blessed."

The young assistant gestured, wiping the holos, and gathered up the processors. When she was finished, both purple-robed priestesses left quickly, surprising Tom. Then he realized, and went outside to the tunnel, where they were waiting.

"I'm sorry." The Antistita's eyes glistened in the half-light.

"You can't find anything, either." Tom had already tried a cheap diagnostrip, taped across Father's forehead: status red, prognosis/treatment a noncommittal white.

"There's a great deal wrong with Davraig." She reached out and touched his forehead with her ancient, palsied finger. "You must prepare yourself."

Tom looked away, still blinking from the incense.

"I can't."

Minus nine:

Spitting light blackened cheek and one eye stared at him—

A clapping . . .

—toppling, for ever.

"Huh!" He jerked awake, dragged himself bodily from the microsleep dream.

"Tom?" Outside.

He stood up. Padding barefoot across cold stone, he checked on Father, then went to the hanging and pulled it back. He had not seen Trude for several days, but she was here, with a yellow-tattooed, brown-skinned man behind her.

"You'd better brace yourself, Trude," said Tom, "for a change in Father's appearance."

He felt more than heard her sharp intake of breath as she came inside. The glowcluster was at low intensity, but she could see the grey, emaciated husk hunched foetally in the bed.

"This is Dr Sukhram." She gestured at her companion, who was already placing tiny discs across Father's skin.

Torn attractors pulsed in a hundred displays.

"Not battle-wounded," Sukhram muttered, as though to himself.

"He's a friend."

"The access codes—" Sukhram looked up, then turned back to his diagnostics. "Never mind."

Shifting hues, blurring—

"Sweet Fate, lad!" Strong hands catching him. "When did you last sleep?"

A cool sensation against his neck, then blackness.

"Past and future."

His tunic was rich, Tom noticed. Upstratum, for sure.

"This is the past event." Dr Sukhram pointed, and a golden node lit up. "And here the future event." Another glow.

"Each event sends out two waves: one directed to the future, one to the past."

Drifting. Trude asking something. Tom focused in again, on Dr Sukhram's answer.

"Between the events they reinforce. Before the past event and after the future event, the waves cancel out because of phase shift . . ."

Waves, hanging in time.

"Quantum predestination, Trude. Don't you ever attend technical briefings?"

"I . . ."

Grey haze, then sleep.

And, when he awoke properly:

"There's nothing wrong with my father?"

Dr Sukhram slowly shook his head. "That's not what I meant. Nothing organic, in one sense. The mediscanner and diagnostrip weren't wrong."

"So you can—" Tom stopped.

The doctor's eyes were dark and liquid: full of sorrow, quite devoid of hope.

Minus five.

Incredibly, the fragile thing tottered on its bent legs.

"Oh, Pa . . . Back to bed." Trying to be gentle.

"Stall . . ." A dry whisper, scarcely a sound.

"We've closed the stall. Sold lots. Time to rest now."

"Stall . . . Rest."

The ivory disc—the only one Dr Sukhram had left behind—hummed softly, plunging illegal narcocytes into Father's bloodstream.

A soft clap, and Trude came in.

"Ran-vera." Attempting to wet his lips. "Knew . . . you'd . . . come."

Silently, Trude sat down on a stool beside Father's bed, and took his hand. Tears, tracking down her lined cheeks, glittered in the glow-cluster's light.

Zero.

"Go away."

The hour before dawnlight.

<<status:>> The ivory disc's display lit up.

"Go away go away go away."

What devils did Father see, to terrify him so? Shaking, Tom moved out of Father's line of sight.

<<agonal phase transition>>

Breathing change.

Trude held one frail hand, Tom held the other.

Panting now: a long-distance runner, fighting for breath, fighting for life—

Not long.

<<phase ends>>

"We love you!" Tom shouted.

Coming faster. Sprinting for the finish—

Soon.

<<morbidity . . . >>

"We—"

Breath, rattling. Unmistakable.

<< . . . is 100 per cent>>

Now.

<<patient deceased>>

Finish line.

And silence.

Clap.

Automatically, Tom walked across and pulled the hanging back.

"The Antistita sent me." The young priestess. "She said—" She stopped, eyes wide with fright. "She said it's Davraig's time."

7

NULAPEIRON AD 3404

Don't look away.

It swirled beneath the acrid stench: Vortex Mortis, twisting with colour, while the young shaven-headed priestess swung her thurible, trying to overcome acidic fumes with herb-scented purple smoke.

Look.

Tom gripped the observation balcony's rail as the thing slid forwards.

And remember.

The Antistita's prayer-hum; Trude's black-headbanded form; the mourners' small shoulder banners. Clear, yet distant: a dislocated place and time.

Always remember.

Whirlpool, gathering pace.

"*. . . among infinity's shimmering lights . . .*"

Tom's lips moved with the prayer's words, but his thoughts were numbed.

"*. . . commit Davraig Corcorigan . . .*"

Slowly, slowly, an elongating membrane lowered the thing—that husk which had once held Father's spirit, his life—into the swirling pool.

"Davraig!" Trude, almost whimpering.

Remember.

Released, it floated for a moment, the twisting corpse—and then it sank, spinning, beneath the surface: already burning apart, decomposing into minerals.

Clasped hands over the lifeless chest.

"Time to go." One of the mourners, hand on Tom's shoulder.

But Tom kept watching as turbulence caused the body to bob upwards once more. Clasped hands, forefingers pointed stiffly in blessing. White bones showing, already scoured by acid.

A fingertip broke loose and plopped back into foaming solvent.

"This way."

The body disappeared beneath bubbling waves—

Father!

—and was gone.

Dirge.

"My sympathies."

A skirl of strange pipes.

"Thank you." An automatic politeness: Tom's consciousness seemed disembodied, suspended from the reality of the mourners, maybe thirty of them, taking their places at the spiral table.

The man who spoke was strong-looking and dressed in green; square-jawed and with hair as red as Mother's.

"This," said Trude, "is Dervlin. An old friend."

Twinkle in his eyes: he wanted to make a joke—not so much of the *old*—but he repressed it for Tom's sake. It showed manners, and Tom appreciated that.

"Pleased to meet you, sir."

"Ah, no need to call me sir, lad." Running blunt fingers through his cupric hair.

Mother—Tom forced the thought down.

The man, Dervlin, turned away. Across his back—wide shoulders tapering to a narrow waist—was a diagonal sheath holding two slender, black rods.

Musician.

One of the women, Heleka, carefully taking her place at table, had a black hip-sling. Inside, her tiny red-faced baby slept, miniature fist closed, thumb in mouth.

Had Father been like that once? So small, with all of life ahead of him?

In one corner of the heptagonal chamber, Dervlin was setting up floating drum-discs, while a young woman sang:

"To the caverns of my youth
Where shouts were glad
And children laughed:
I return now, seeking truth . . ."

The Antistita stood at the spiral table's focus, murmuring a blessing in Old Eldraic while the wake-aria continued. *"Beneh y blagos neh repas . . ."*

"The singer's wonderful," Tom said to Trude, in between bowing to mourners as, one by one, they touched fingertips to forehead in benediction.

Minrastic cakes and fragrant rice balls. Other dishes, which Tom could not have named. All arranged by Trude.

"In the shadowed world of death,
Our works are dead:
Sad, hollow boasts . . ."

Dervlin, unslinging the slender black drumsticks from his back, stood before his floating discs, waiting for his cue. A soft murmur of conversation, as people began to eat, formed a backdrop.

"Yet hear the newborn drawing breath.
Standing, around the bed:
Rejoicing shades, our dearest ghosts."

For the meal's duration, Tom remained calm. Polite to well-wishers; charming, even to those few who had borne a grudge against Father, but were shocked now that he was gone: an intimation of their own mortality.

Then it was over, and the mourners were filing silently out. Once more Tom bowed to them, completely composed, as though all were well with the world.

Remember.

Low tavern chamber. Glowclusters of turquoise and jade. Discreet tang of ganja masks from the rear alcoves.

"Dance?"

Tom shook his head, and the girl moved on. Her white dress was slashed through with violet, patchily redyed to suit the fashion.

Dervlin played, his sticks a blur, while the woman sang and metallic sparklets danced in a glittering cloud around her.

Remember.

Not just Father's death, but that Mother did not come—

"Are you all right, lad?"

Break. The music had stopped, and Dervlin was standing over him, a stick held lightly in each strong hand.

"Sorry, s—Dervlin."

"Aye, maybe"—a stick lightly touched the end of Tom's nose—"I'm the one who should apologize. But this gig's been arranged for a while."

"I understand." Tom looked aside.

There's something else: something wrong. But he doesn't want to tell me.

As the wake-fest had ended, Tom had seen Trude talking to a fit-looking woman dressed in grey tunic and red trews, and it had taken him a moment to recognize her *sans* uniform: the woman trooper. What had the male officer called her? He remembered: Elva.

They had been discussing him, and he had read one phrase from the woman's lips: *fourteen SY old.*

Too young for a dwelling-permit.

"Time I took you back, lad."

Almost gone.

"Ah, Fate." Dervlin's voice was a lilting murmur. "I'm sorry, Tom."

Nowhere to live.

"Don't worry," Tom said steadily. "I was expecting it."

They were waiting in the corridor: fifteen or sixteen men and women, dressed in shabby tunics and shawls.

". . . all you're owed," Trude was saying to the hunched man at the head of the queue.

Father's creditors.

The hangings were down, in a heap upon the stone floor. Young Alycha and Old Alycha, from the chamber on the left, were damp-eyed as they extended their own hangings into the space which had been the Corcorigans' family chamber. On the other side, the new young couple—who had lived there for only a hectoday, if that—were fastening drapes, ignoring Tom.

"Not that one." Trude, sharply.

A bent old woman, about to take a small ceramic box, paused.

"It's mine." Trude held out a carving: a triplet of entwined narl-serpents. "Take this."

I remember Father making that.

The woman took it, polished it on her dirty shawl, and clucked to herself. She turned and shuffled away.

"I'm sorry, Tom." Trude let out a long, shaky breath. "I thought we'd be finished by now."

"I have to get back." Dervlin tapped Tom's shoulder. "Take care."

Soon they were down to the last creditor: a hunched, plain-robed man. Accepting cred-flakes, he stopped, looked at Tom, and handed some copper mil-creds back to Trude. "For the boy."

Then he, too, was gone.

Where the family chamber had been, strange colours now hung: faded ochre, unfamiliar green.

Snick.

It rotated: coated in a patina of rust, but gleaming silver at the disc's circumference, polished by friction against the rim.

Snack.

The sounds came from below: facets snapping into place, forming a spiral staircase down to another stratum.

"Don't be afraid, Tom." But it was Trude's voice that shook as her permit tag sparked with ruby light.

Some two metres in diameter, the floor hatch. A segment swung aside, revealing the helical stair.

I didn't think it would be like this.

"Can you take this?"

Tom took the small, fabric-wrapped bundle from Trude. All his belongings.

Trude was a little unsteady, leading the way downwards. Tom held back, swallowing nervously, then followed. When he had dreamed of visiting another stratum, it had always involved climbing *upwards*.

Stained walls. Trickle of dirty water. A dark echo of distant people, talking.

Above their heads, a grinding noise. The slatted steps pulled upwards, folding into the hatch, as it rotated shut.

Another stratum.

Down again. Two strata below home.

Grey mesociliates scurried away as Trude and Tom clambered through a natural-rock junction, then down a sloping, dank corridor which ended in a small cavern.

"The thing is, it's—"

There was a double image, blurred, with odd parallax effects as they walked past: a big floating Yarandian tricon, script code common to thirty languages.

*** RAGGED SCHOOL ***

"—better than it looks."
Trude led the way inside.

8
NULAPEIRON AD 3404

*** PniO, WENHS something.

"Are you awake, boy?"

*** PniO, LLENHSAN . . .

"Uh, yes." Tom squinted. "Yes, sir."

Obermagister's study. Shelves piled high with crystals. Tom swung himself upright on the couch.

"Hmm." Long white hair, tied back with white cord. "I've let you sleep in, since you arrived so late. It will be the last time."

"Yes, sir."

*** PnrD, LLENHSAH NEDLOV .isM *** Ancient holo flat-script, not triconic, floating near the black-curtained portal. Hard to decipher, even when seen the right way round.

Steam rose from a bowl of herb tea. Not for Tom: it was on the Obermagister's black desk.

*** Mzr. WOLDEN HAZHNELL, DrNP ***

Reversed, it made sense.

"Your benefactrix, Madam Mulgrave, is gone." Obermagister Hazhnell turned, making some sort of control gesture. Tom's view was obscured by the desk, overflowing with crystal-racks. "You're free for the remainder of the morning. Attend class after lunch."

A clap from outside.

"In." The Obermagister looked up as a tall youth came inside. "Praefectus Bruan. This is Corcorigan. Put him in dorm Seven-Beth."

"Sir."

"Think old Wally's a nice chap?" Bruan asked.

The dorm was low-ceilinged: four rows, eight beds in each. Very clean. Cubbyholes lined one wall.

"Seems OK."

"Really?" The lightness left Bruan's voice. "Watch your step and you may be all right. The opportunities are here, if you appreciate them. Know what I mean?"

"Uh, sure," Tom lied.

"Good." Bruan paused at the short flight of steps which led out of the dorm. "One thing more . . ."

"Yes?"

"Try to lose that accent."

Silence.

The dorm was empty. Tom sat on the bed which was to be his own, and pulled out his infotablet from the small bundle.

Reaching inside his tunic—He stopped, looked around. Nothing. No-one looking. Heart beating fast, he drew out his stallion talisman.

Father . . .

The Pilot, the strange witchlike woman—*jet-black eye staring as she died*—had marked it somehow, making it more than a symbol of lost childhood. But it was Father's hands that had wielded the graser tool, creating beauty from a metal block.

The stallion fell apart into two halves: Tom had correctly memorized the control gesture.

Without any command, his infotablet's holodisplay blossomed into life: *a metre-wide representation of an Aqua Hall, blank-faced people queuing up with empty containers in their hands. Beside one figure, a descriptive tricon, hanging*:

THIS IS TOM.

"What the—?" Tom was confused.

The figures moving, shuffling forwards.

TOM FETCHES WATER FOR ALL IN THE MARKET WHO DO NOT FETCH THEIR OWN.

He swallowed. This fragment was not downloaded from the crystal: that was still wrapped in its black nul-gel coating. Either it had transferred itself just now, by induction from the needle which lay alongside the gel-coated crystal, or the Pilot had directly transferred it into the infotablet just before she—

"You're the new boy?" A strange voice, from the dorm's narrow entrance arch.

Tom just had time to see the final tricon, shaded an interrogative pink—QUESTION: WHO FETCHES WATER FOR TOM?—before he shut down the display.

"That's me." He powered off the infotablet completely. "I'm Tom. Tom Corcorigan."

The oriental boy grinned. His black hair was a spiky brush. "Not your fault, I suppose."

"Er . . . Who are you?"

"Zhao-ji. Pleased to meet ya." Another impudent grin. "Really."

Massive vibration. Blast of air, screech of noise.

The cargo engine was huge, greenish bronze and grime-streaked, and its roar filled the tunnel. Even from up here, the pulse of its brake jets was enormous.

"What are we doing here?" Tom raised his voice above the din.

"Following them." Zhao-ji pointed downwards. "Algrin and his gang."

Tom and Zhao-ji were high up near the cavern's ceiling, hiding behind an embrasure. Down below, on a cargo platform, six boys from the school were dodging behind dumb-crates, keeping out of the stevedore crew's sight.

Black studded spheres rolled down an unloading-ramp from an opened cargo car. As a crewleader waved her control baton, the spheres stopped, shuffled into position on their short, stubby protrusions, and split open to disgorge their goods.

"Don't we have to get back?" What would happen if Tom missed his first lesson? "Come on, Zhao-ji."

"Wait a minute."

Down below, a group of brown-garbed men had disembarked, and Zhao-ji laughed shortly. "Professionals. Brown Panthers. No-one would steal from them, except maybe—Well, not Algrin."

Tom shook his head. He had allowed this boy to lead him outside the school during the midday break—when leaving the school bounds was allowed—and he realized that he was going to miss lunch, if nothing else.

"Aw, no!"

"What's wrong?" Tom was concerned.

"Follow me."

Dead.

"Those bastards," Zhao-ji said, meaning Algrin and his cronies.

"An accident?" Tom looked at the poor thing. "Or the cargo men?"

Zhao-ji glanced back—they were in an alcove just off the main unloading-chamber—and shook his head. "I saw them."

The pool of blood was thick maroon. The feline's head lay in the pool, amber eyes focused on infinity, its long body arched in one last leap for freedom which would never end.

"Just because they couldn't steal anything. Damn it," said Zhao-ji, as a soft mew sounded. "Fate—"

A tiny white neko-kitten, up on a ledge. Thin enough for ribs to be outlined through fur.

"We can't keep pets." As though Zhao-ji had read Tom's mind.

Tom held out a finger. The kitten swiped at it, purring loudly. "We can't let him starve, either."

Zhao-ji sighed.

"Evening break. We'll come back with food."

"Good."

Tom smiled; it had been a while since anything had amused him.

"What the little fella needs," said Zhao-ji, "is a name."

"How about"—Tom thought for a moment—"Paradox?"

"Paradox. That's perfect."

After lessons and the evening meal, they sneaked out, bearing proto-block. They left Paradox hungrily lapping at the food, and hurried back, barely making curfew.

It was the middle of the night when Tom jerked awake and stared into darkness, the puzzle looping over and over in his mind. Then, moving quietly, he took his infotablet to the corridor outside the dorm—he could not leave the school's confines at night, when alarm fields were enabled—and powered it on.

QUESTION: WHO FETCHES TOM'S WATER?

"No-one," whispered Tom. "He only drinks daistral."

BREAKING CONTEXT, read the answering tricon, RESOLVES ANTINOMY. LATER, MORE SOPHISTICATED SOLUTIONS WILL BE REQUIRED.

"I don't—"

NOW, USE THE NEEDLE TO DOWNLOAD MODULE ONE

"Module one?" But he remembered the Pilot's words: *Download just one module at a time.*

He took out his talisman, split it, and dug the needle through the nul-gel coating, making contact with the embedded crystal.

COMPLETE.

Hurrying, he resealed the thing, remembering her warning about emissions.

ACTIVATE MODULE?

"Go," said Tom.

9

TERRA AD 2122

<<Karyn's Tale>>

[1]

Fear and elation gripped her simultaneously.

UTech from the air: verdant parkland, copper-bright Virginia forest. Octagonal central plaza, tiled in orange and green, among golden walkways and silver domes, gleaming beneath a clear sapphire sky.

Face pressed against the plexiglass, Karyn watched the campus rushing up to meet her—

{{*Tom swallowed, sick with vertigo, pressing back against solid stone, grateful for reality's anchor.*}}

—as the air-taxi swooped down.

Hovering at the plaza's edge, it raised its gull-door as Karyn thumbed her bracelet's cred-transfer. Grabbing her holdall, she slid out. Within seconds, the taxi was airborne; she stepped back to watch its soaring ascent.

"Watch out!" The shout coincided with a bark behind her, and Karyn jumped.

Wolf.

Huge and glowering, the timber wolf growled, silver highlights playing across its ceramic cowl. Behind the beast, a visored man roundly cursed Karyn.

"Stupid cow!"

Karyn stepped to one side, holding her bag in front of her. Two heads, human and lupine, turned in perfect synchrony, following her motion.

"Sorry," she said. "I didn't see you there."

"No kidding."

The wolf's growl deepened, threatening.

"An accident." Karyn swallowed. "Really. My first time here."

The man removed his visor.

"I can see that." A smile twisted across his face and was gone. "In a manner of speaking." Ripples of frozen scar tissue filled his eye sockets. Temple-mounted i/o ports clicked as he refastened the visor. "Spacer's outfit?"

"Er, yes." Karyn had removed her jumpsuit's UNSA insignia. "I'm Pilot Candidate Karyn McNamara. Very pleased to—"

"Bitch!" Real venom in the blind man's voice. "Damn you to hell!"

She could only watch as the symbiotic pair stalked away across the plaza, muscles bunched with fury.

"Jesus Christ!" Her own shoulders were knotted with tension. "This'll be even harder than I thought."

<<MODULE ENDS>>

10

NULAPEIRON AD 3404

It was five tendays—half a hectoday—before Tom received any contact with the world he had left behind. Fifty days in which he learned the Ragged School's immediate lessons: which of the bigger boys to avoid, how to insinuate himself into the crush for meals, when it was safe to bathe in the gel-bloc.

During breaktimes, the cavern fronting the school became a light-ball court and tagfight pit all in one, while Tom would sit quietly to one side, infotablet hidden, working on poetry or strategy algorithms in his head. He had replayed the first module many times (though never without a sickening sense of vertigo at the sight of Terra's open sky); yet he could not download the next module without solving its initial problem.

A ring of men, seated at a circular table. An empty bowl before each. In every gap between the grey-robed diners, a single chopstick lay.

One morning, when Zhao-ji was playing solo smartball nearby, a large praefectus snagged the ball from the air. Tom was only half paying attention, still thinking about the problem which would lead him to the second module.

At the table's centre, a full bowl of noodles. Each man would need two chopsticks to retrieve food. QUESTION: HOW DO THEY EQUALLY SHARE THE MEAL?

"Hey, little slit-eyes."

Two more praefecti came up. Each of them was twice Zhao-ji's size.

"On your knees." They laughed as Zhao-ji sank, obeying their command. "And beg, you little yellow—"

Tom thought his first answer had been efficient: THE LEADER COMMANDS THEM TO EAT IN TURN. But the algorithm had been rejected because . . .

Zhao-ji sprang up, arms flailing at the three youths, and pummelled away—

Tom, frozen, could only stare at them.

—until the biggest of them stepped back—"Destiny!"—and squarely kicked Zhao-ji in the groin.

Zhao-ji dropped.

They let the ball fall to the ground and walked away, shaking their heads. Tom, shaking, walked over to Zhao-ji.

"Leave me alone." Hunched foetally, hands between his legs. "Just go."

Tom went inside, ignored by the on-duty praefectus who should have stopped him: he had earned respect by proxy, from Zhao-ji's mad bravery.

But I was too scared to help.

Always the same. Always the bigger ones, the strong ones, abused their strength.

But in the puzzle world of his downloaded code, such concepts did not apply. THERE IS NO LEADER, it had told him, rejecting his first solution. THE DINERS ARE EXACTLY EQUAL.

Scared.

TRY ANOTHER STRATEGY.

That evening, Tom went alone to feed Paradox, while Zhao-ji lay alone in the dorm, silent in his pain.

TRY ANOTHER STRATEGY.

Magister Kolgash Alverom—known as "Captain Kolgash" or merely "the Captain" to the boys—was hook-nosed and possibly one-eyed: a black inverted-triangle patch was permanently fastened where his left eye should have been.

"Again, boy."

"*Balakrane,*" Tom recited. "*Balkerina, baelkrenitsa . . .*" He rattled through a hundred Laksheesh terms for cargo: nuances bespeaking dumb containers or smartbugs, small bundles or large sacks, their mode of transport and stacking-algorithms.

Tom was in the alpha group, and that meant logotropic enhancements, administered in the Captain's study. Always, it was the Captain's clawlike right hand, from which three fingers were missing, that held out the femtocyte injector for the boys to take.

"Good."

White fingerbone, toppling into the swirling liquid—

"And the rest?"

An ancient equation: $(-\hbar^2/2m)\nabla^2\psi + V(\mathbf{r})\psi = i\hbar\delta\psi/\delta t$

"Concentrate, boy."

The sound of waves, breaking against a shore.

"Talk to me, Tom."

Sapphire sky, and a lone bird flying.

"Tom?"

A screech as it descends, falling upon its prey . . .

Burst of light, pungent fumes inside his nostrils. He snapped back into reality.

"Are you all right?" The Captain's hawklike features showed concern.

"Yes, sir."

Synaesthesia flash: he knew what it was. Caused by his sessions with the downloaded code?

"Keep visualizing, or the routines lose plasticity."

"Sir."

"—a disgrace." The woman's voice, coming from the doorway, was familiar. "What are you doing to that boy?"

Tom whirled.

"Trude!"

"Tom . . . I can only stay for a while."

They chatted, in fact, for hours, while the Captain served daistral but otherwise remained unobtrusive. Finally, at Trude's invitation—her expression becoming grim—he drew an old graphite chair forward and sat down to join Tom and Trude.

"You're dispensing logotropes." She brushed back a long, white-grey lock which had escaped her mandelbrot scarf. "Do you know what you're doing?"

Tom held his breath. No-one talked to the magisters like that.

"Belageron Class-4 protocols." The Captain's voice was matter-of-fact. "With quick-dispersal tetani matrices and bipolar potentiators."

"What?" Trude's tone was scathing. "You'd put the fear of death into—?"

"Oh, no." The Captain shook his head. "Not military grade: I've reduced the apoptotic inhibitors. Weakened the time gradient."

"You tailor them yourself?"

"Quite." A grim smile. "I learned how, under pressure . . . some time ago."

Trude looked at him, expressionless, then turned away. "These boys aren't fighting for their lives."

"No," said the Captain. "But for their futures, even this far down. For the lucky ones."

When her time was up, Tom escorted Trude as far as the outer court, where she embraced him.

"For this stratum—" she began. Then, "The school's better than I thought."

"It's OK." Tom smiled, deliberately. Trude had done her best.

"Now I've two reasons to come and visit," she said, surprising him, then turned and walked away without a backward glance.

"How many times d"you pull the weasel, Kreevil?"

Rainbow dragon, writhing in the air above the lanky boy's bed.

"In one night, I mean."

Tom started. For a moment, he thought he had seen his old nemesis Stavrel, standing in the arched doorway. But it was Algrin, whose reputation was known throughout the Ragged School.

Kreevil's dreamy voice—"Up to seven times"—was almost lost among the sniggers.

Only Zhao-ji was impassive, sitting cross-legged on his own bed. He had warned Kreevil not to try the psychflash—femtofeed and holostrobe—knowing that the others would take advantage of its truth-serum side-effect, but it was white-haired Petyo whose will had won the day.

From the doorway, Algrin laughed: muscular, and with just the same cruel expression Tom remembered from his market days when the disfigured Stavrel had taunted him.

More laughter. Only Petyo—the only one of Algrin's gang in the alpha group, and therefore resident in this dorm—did not join in.

I should have stood up for Kreevil.

Always the strong forcing their will upon the rest.

TRY ANOTHER STRATEGY.

The glowclusters dimmed, and Algrin left before the night praefecti strolled past. Everyone went to their own beds. Kreevil moaned, but slid from flashtrance into sleep.

ANOTHER STRATEGY.

Beneath the bedcovers, Tom brought up the infotablet's display, minimizing its size and disabling audio. *Round table, grey-robed diners. Single chopsticks in the gaps between them: thirteen men, thirteen chopsticks.*

Opening a code volume, Tom entered design algorithms by gesture alone, working furiously. Then it was done.

The simulation executed.

Each diner modelled as a separate entity, an autonomous control process, choosing right or left at *random*—a matter of context: can randomness exist in a predetermined universe?—then waiting for the chopstick on the other side to become free.

The tiny figures moved. One helped himself to food . . .

People acting in parallel. No slave, no master.

EVALUATING . . .

Tom tweaked the design, avoiding deadlock whenever two reached for a chopstick at the same time.

OPTIMIZED.

It was a very *democratic* paradox.

USE THE NEEDLE TO DOWNLOAD MODULE TWO.

Solved it.

11

TERRA AD 2122

<<Karyn's Tale>>

[2]

Utter darkness. Soft matting, slippery beneath her bare, damp feet. Sweat gathered under her neck pendant and trickled between her breasts.

The pendant beeped, giving away her location.

There was massive movement in the darkness: no time to react. *Impact.* A brief moment airborne. Then the mats smashed into Karyn, knocking the breath from her body.

An iron grip pinioned her arm.

"I know." The mat, pressing against her mouth, distorted Karyn's voice. "I screwed up."

"Lights," said a gravelly voice, as the armlock was released.

"Ongoing scan, requested parameters." The pendant's unwelcome voice was tinny. *"A third mu-space vessel, found floating in realspace near its insertion—"*

Karyn thumbed the thing off.

In front of her, a large, bearish man was already kneeling in *seiza* position, sitting back on his heels. He was wearing a loose white jacket and black *hakama*, the traditional split skirt of aikido masters. His wrists and forearms were massive.

"Sensei." Karyn knelt, blinking against the light. The walls of the sparse gymnasium were stark white and the padded floor was bright blue.

High up on one wall, discreetly, a small blue and gold UNSA logo slowly rotated.

"Centre—"

"—and balance." Karyn nodded. "Yes, Sensei."

"More important to you," said her sensei—Father Michael Mulligan, SJ, Ph.D., D.Sc.—"than being able to fight."

Karyn let out a long, slow breath, calming herself.

"I haven't changed my mind."

{{*Tom checked the timestamp. This was* before *Karyn's arrival at UTech: a prologue, of sorts.*}}

The grizzled priest's flat, grey stare revealed nothing. Then he sighed and rubbed a massive spadelike hand across his buzz-cut, receding hair.

"When you get to Virginia, look up my son."

"Your . . ." Karyn let her voice trail off.

Sensei—Mike—had been ordained late in life. The rumour was, his wife and son had been killed in a shuttle crash; Karyn had never thought there might be another son.

"It's the second time"—there was old pain in Mike's voice—"someone I care about has chosen the darkness."

The next day, she left for the civilian shuttle flight to Richmond. UNSA guards saluted as her autoskimmer slid through the main gate's scanfield; otherwise, there was no-one to say goodbye.

Outside, a grey rain was falling. Behind her, the glistening domes of Saarbrücken Fliegerhorst slowly receded, while high winds whipped the surrounding oaks. A chilly draught seeped through a gap in the skimmer's cabin; its sound was a low, moaning complaint.

<<MODULE ENDS>>

12
NULAPEIRON AD 3405

In the changing-stalls, by the shoulder-high block of translucent bathing-gel, they came for him.

"Hey, it's a girly!" Algrin's voice, eerily echoing in the damp chamber.

Complacency dropped away from Tom.

A Standard Year without incident had made him overconfident. There had been the field trip with the Captain, when Zhao-ji wandered off alone into a dead zone—not noticing the absence of the air's normal woody smell, nor the too yellow autotrophic fluorofungus: a sure sign that it lacked oxygen-producing cyanobacterial symbionts—and the Captain had carried the unconscious Zhao-ji to safety.

But in the school itself, Tom had grown to feel safe.

Mistake.

"I got a real problem with girlies."

Tom shrank back towards the wall, tying the small, torn towel around his waist. He stopped, with cold rock against his back.

Behind Algrin shadows moved, and for a moment Tom's heart thumped with hope, but it was only Algrin's gang members. Their faces were pulled into smiles but their eyes were dead.

"And she's got a necklace."

Tom clasped his hand tightly around his talisman.

A white-haired figure stepped forward. Petyo.

"One chance, Tom. We need a runner, maybe a spotter."

Tom's knees felt weak.

"I can't run," he said, feeling awful. "Not like Kreevil—"

A whisper from outside—"Captain's coming"—and they turned

and began to move out. Petyo remained for a moment, looking at Tom, then shook his head and followed Algrin and the others out.

I've betrayed Kreevil.

Tom leaned back against the chill wall, chest pounding, feeling sick.

The Captain took the whole of his alpha group along: fifteen boys, including Tom and Zhao-ji. From a natural ledge near the top of Laridonia Cavern, they watched.

*** RED DRAGON EMPORIUM ***

The tricon was huge, enwrapped by a holo dragon: scarlet, with bulbous white eyes and a long tongue. Its wings unfurled slightly, shook, and were laid back upon its long, narrow body.

"Wow," said one of the boys.

For a moment, the dragon's eyes seemed to glance upwards at the ledge, and Tom felt a shiver of fear and delight. He glanced over at Zhao-ji, but Zhao-ji's face was pinched with tension. Tom wondered what was wrong.

Forcing aside thoughts of Algrin, Tom determined to enjoy himself. It was not often that a magister would take boys out on any kind of trip.

"They're caravanserai." One of the brighter lads, Hekron, trying to impress the Captain. "Wouldn't you say so, sir?"

The Captain's eye gleamed. "Could be. What do you think, Corcorigan?"

"I'd say"—Tom paused, as a giant blue horizontal disc flowed on a thousand tendril-like legs into the cavern below—"that's a travelling yurt, sir."

There was a ripple of laughter among the boys, which stopped as

the great disc halted and blossomed into a wide tent, extruding corri-
dorlike extensions, until a star-shaped temporary edifice covered the
cavern floor.

From small tunnel entranceways, more groups of local people came
in to see the visitors.

*** wholesale *** retail *** bonded ***
suppliers to gentry
since ad 3197

Local oriental storekeepers—Zhongguo Ren—had set up small
displays of produce on ledges two metres above the cavern floor. From
the large tent, an artificial dragon came—holo projected around a flexible frame, beneath which men's legs were visible.

"Dragon dance," said the Captain, as cymbal players accompanied
the dragon below—*clash-clash, clash-clash, clash-clash*—and the storekeepers held out good-luck offerings of green vat vegetables which the
dragon "ate."

"What do they sell there, sir?" asked Hekron, but it was Zhao-ji
who answered:

"Anything you can afford."

The Captain looked at him sharply.

Below, dance ended, the dragon retired inside the great tent, and
the growing crowd began to mill around. Then tiny holo tigers—
more mythical creatures: Tom's hand strayed unconsciously to the talisman at his chest—sprang into being and raced across the cavern
floor, clearing a space, and the spectators drew back with a sense of
anticipation.

And then they came.

Clad in orange, performing spectacular feats: butterfly kicks and
spinning punches (and Tom, throat dry, remembered the Pilot); heavy
halberds flying, one passing so close to a girl's head (as she dropped

into splits, avoiding the cut) that some of her long, black hair was shorn away.

They broke blocks of ice with hammer-fist strikes and even head-butts; whirled flails and chain-whips which left white fluorescent trails in the air, marking complex nonlinear trajectories as the warriors leaped and spun and fought.

"It's called *wu shu*," murmured Zhao-ji, as though naming it could take away the magic.

A small boy, maybe six SY old, performed an intricate form along-side a shaven-headed master. The old man's face was lined with age, seventy SY at least, but he lowered himself into a splits position while the crowd watched, struck into silence, then burst into thunderous applause.

"I wish I could do that," said Tom, surprising himself.

Afterwards—after the old man had defeated six opponents in a spectacularly choreographed fight—the warriors returned to the star-shaped tent, and small holo flames danced above the cavern floor, inviting customers into the emporium.

The crowd began to break up: some to go inside the tent, others to go back about their normal business.

"Sir . . ."

On the high ledge, the boys turned to the Captain, wondering if their trip was over, but Hekron was pointing downwards, to the winding path which led to their position. A small boy, Durfredo, was running up towards them.

"The old man," said Tom, ignoring Durfredo's arrival, "was incredible."

"Sigung Pin." Zhao-ji grinned at Tom. "If we get permission, I'll introduce you."

"Permission?"

"Oh, yes." Some of the humour left Zhao-ji's eyes. "Uncle Pin will be glad to see me."

Dark. Membranous corridor, leading towards the hub.

"*Nǐmen hǎo.*"

Old woman, almost invisible in the shadows.

"*Nǐ hǎo.*" Zhao-ji bowed; Tom clumsily followed suit.

Low-intensity holos. She led them past mythological scenes—"Monkey King," said Zhao-ji, pointing at a small figure spinning a staff—and stopped before a black velvet drape which furled up at her approach.

Like a graven statue, the old man sat cross-legged on a folded mat.

"*Nǐmen hǎo.*"

"*Lǎo shīfu,*" Zhao-ji bowed low. "*Nín hǎo.*"

"Master Pin," said Tom, attempting to bow gracefully.

There was a sense of *presence* in the room: not physical, but formed from the strength of the old man's spirit.

Chuckling, the old man turned to a small table beside him, took a small porcelain cup and drank from it. Strong liquor: Tom was surprised. Nevertheless, the old man's presence was strong.

"This is Tom Corcorigan, Uncle."

A nod of acknowledgement.

Speaking softly but rapidly, Master Pin and Zhao-ji conversed without glancing at Tom. How long would this take? The Captain had told them to be back soon.

It was not like the Captain to be imprecise. But young Durfredo's whispered news, whatever it was, seemed to have unsettled him.

The Captain knows this is Zhao-ji's family. Tom was suddenly certain.

Master Pin clapped his hands.

"Ah, Feng-ying." He smiled as a slender girl, about Tom's and Zhao-ji's age, entered the tent chamber bearing a black cushion. "One for each of our visitors."

Half a dozen narrow silver bracelets. Tom took one from the cushion, then watched as Zhao-ji took another and bowed to the girl, Feng-ying. Her skin was unblemished, her black hair long and lustrous.

The look which passed between her and Zhao-ji was intense but momentary.

"Young Corcorigan."

Fear swept across Tom's skin as the old man addressed him directly.

"Your travel permit will expire in two tendays. Visit us, before then. Zhao-ji will instruct you."

Travel permit?

Swallowing, Tom fastened the bracelet around his wrist.

"Thank you, Uncle." Zhao-ji.

"*Zàijiàn.*"

Tom knew they had been dismissed.

As they left, awareness of the old man's presence trailed like spider-webs across Tom's back. He shivered with relief as they stepped back out into the main cavern, and the tent's wall sealed up behind them.

"*Stokhastikos*, Zhao-ji." It was a curse Tom had recently heard for the first time.

Zhao-ji said merely, "There's Durfredo. Looks like he was left behind, to wait for us."

"Why—?" Tom stopped, as young Durfredo hurried towards them.

Travel permit. Travel to where?

But Durfredo's words swept away his thoughts: "Guess what? You'll never guess. Old Kreevil's been arrested. Would you believe that?"

"Kreevil?" asked Zhao-ji. "Arrested? Why?"

Tom's spirit sank.

"Robbing, with Algrin. Only Kreevil got caught."

Sweet Destiny! Tom closed his eyes. *What have I done?*

13

NULAPEIRON AD 3405

It glowed electric blue.

"Where's Kreevil?" Tom's voice was a shaky whisper. "I can't see him."

Half-shadows drifted in the sapphire liquid.

"There." Zhao-ji leaned forwards, and the warmth of his breath caused faint orange ripples to spread across the membrane, attenuating to nothingness.

"I can't—Fate! Is that him?"

There was a dark, fibrous core at the chamber's centre: a shadowed mass of deeper blue. Around it, the slowly changing parabolic curves of tendrils, and the suspended figures of the boys. Perhaps twenty of them: engaged in tasks—Tom could not make out details—like so many attendant fish.

From behind them, the bulky overseer spoke. "You've seen him now, lads." There was an odd, strained note in the man's voice. "Let that be enough."

Zhao-ji did not turn away from the membranous wall.

"We have the right to talk to him." Orange pulses accompanied his words. "Your boss said so."

Tom shrugged, about to apologize for Zhao-ji's rudeness, but the overseer's expression stopped him. It was hard to tell in the eerie blue light, but the man's eyes looked damp with tears.

He waved Tom and Zhao-ji aside, formed a control gesture with one stubby-fingered hand, and the membrane pulsed visibly as orange waves accompanied his words: "Kreevil Dilwinney. Egress now."

The man turned back to Tom. "Go easy on him."

Tom swallowed.

Swimming with painfully slow strokes, one of the shadowy figures moved through the viscous phosphorescent medium and drew close to the membrane, hanging there, corpselike in the blue light. Kreevil's bare hands and feet paddled gently. Behind him, a tendril—some sort of safety line, perhaps—stretched back into the fluid.

A brusque gesture from the overseer, and Kreevil slowly jack-knifed forwards, thrust one hand through the membrane—"Don't touch him, lads," the overseer warned—then wriggled and pushed forwards until he was through, and he knelt down, coughing up blue liquid onto the bare flagstones.

"Fate, Kree—Ah!" Zhao-ji jerked back his hand as though stung.

"Bleedin' Chaos!" There was a small pouch sticky-tagged to the overseer's broad belt, and he tugged it off. "I told ya not to touch him."

Sparkling silver motes sprinkled from the pouch, covering Zhao-ji's finger—but not before Tom saw that the flesh itself had blackened.

"Cold," whispered Zhao-ji.

"You'll be all right, lad."

From the floor, Kreevil looked up, mouth working like a fish out of water. Then he coughed up more liquid and said: "Tom. Why? Made me . . . get out?"

Confused, Tom glanced at the overseer, who shook his head.

"Let me in." Kreevil turned back towards the fluid-filled chamber. "Back in . . ."

There was a hiss from Zhao-ji, and at first Tom thought it was from pain; but then he saw it, too.

From beneath Kreevil's torn, dripping tunic, the thick tendril was *growing* from Kreevil's back, part of his flesh, stretching back into the sapphire fluid and connecting him to Fate-knew-what. And below Kreevil's ribs, a series of suction holes pulsed open and shut, as though gasping.

"Go back inside, Dilwinney," said the overseer.

Tom and Zhao-ji could only watch as, trembling, Kreevil crawled back along the floor and rolled through the membrane, back into the supercooled fluid's embrace.

Joy flared briefly in his eyes. Then, pushing with his hands like flippers, he swam slowly backwards, until he was lost among the half-seen shadows, suspended in the blue.

It was a Shyed'mday, their first free day since the arrival of Zhao-ji's family. The first day they had been allowed to visit Kreevil.

"He was lucky," said Zhao-ji.

Tom halted. Around them, the narrow tunnel's fluorofungus, somehow overstimulated, glowed intensely.

"How can you say that?"

"They could have executed him. That's the maximum penalty for theft."

"Oh." Tom began to walk on. "I hadn't thought of that."

And it's my fault.

"Still . . ." Zhao-ji held his injured finger against his chest. The silver motes sparkled as they moved, repairing the flesh. "Four SY."

My fault, Tom wanted to say. *I mentioned Kreevil's name to Petyo.*

"By the time he gets out," Zhao-ji added, "he'll be nearly twenty."

Coward.

"I—" Tom swallowed. "Did you see that overseer? The look in his eyes?"

"Ex-prisoner." Zhao-ji coughed. "Leaving that blue stuff must be worse than being put inside."

They walked on in silence. Only their footsteps in the winding corridor made any sound: damp echoes bouncing listlessly back from the fault-cracked walls.

"Maybe we can come back next Shyed'mday," said Tom, dreading the thought.

Zhao-ji stopped.

"Not possible." Still cradling his injured hand, he looked away from Tom, along the empty tunnel. "I won't be here then."

"What do you mean?"

Zhao-ji, not speaking, started walking again.

"It's your family—" Tom should have realized before, but it just had not occurred to him: most of the boys' families were dead, or forever missing. "You're leaving with them."

Mother. Where are you now?

"I—" Zhao-ji stopped again, and held up his wrist. He was wearing his permit bracelet. "You don't have to come visit, afterwards."

Master Pin's invitation. Tom's own bracelet was tucked inside his belt.

"But the Master, the Sigung—he invited me."

"Half a dozen strata up, in Gerberov Santuario. In fifteen days. That's where we'll be."

Six strata?

"But—"

"The bracelet permit will let you ascend." A strange, impenetrable look in his dark eyes. "You don't have to do it, Tom."

Six strata up.

The image took him aback.

TWO BOYS HAVE BEEN CAUGHT, SUSPECTED OF STEALING. The images might almost have been of Tom and Zhao-ji, sitting outside the Obermagister's study after some misdemeanour. THEY WILL BE INTERVIEWED IN TURN.

A blank-faced figure, beckoning one boy inside for interview.

IF BOTH BOYS REMAIN SILENT, THEY WILL RECEIVE JUST EXTRA ASSIGNMENTS. IF ONE "DEFECTS" BY ADMITTING THE OFFENCE, HE WILL BE LET OFF, WHILE HIS PARTNER WILL BE BEATEN.

"I know this one," said Tom. "Too easy."

But he was impressed: the 'ware must be tailoring the problem to his own experience.

IF BOTH BOYS REMAIN SILENT, THEY WILL RECEIVE THE LESSER PUNISH-MENT. BUT NEITHER BOY KNOWS WHETHER HIS PARTNER WILL CONFESS.

With his fingertips, Tom sketched a grid, entered the possible out-comes, and highlighted the equilibrium point: where both boys con-fess, so they both get punished, but relatively lightly.

"Not defecting is dangerous: if one boy stays silent, he risks betrayal by the other." Tom added his verbal comment, knowing that the downloaded code wanted more than the mathematically correct answer: it wanted an explanation.

"Defection," he continued, "is the only way to avoid expulsion for sure, even though they both get punished."

Tom sat back. This was one of the classic two-person scenarios from ancient game philosophy, but he had not thought through the implications before. The equilibrium point, where you assumed the other person would act in the worst possible way, and you acted accordingly . . . was bad for everyone.

NEXT TENDAY, THE TWO BOYS ARE CAUGHT AGAIN.

"Oh, really."

That changed the scenario, Tom realized. If one of the boys had ratted on his partner last time, it would be remembered now—

"Come quick, Tom!"

"Damn it." Tom quickly killed the display. "What's going on, Durfredo?"

"It's a rakkie!"

Sighing, Tom sticky-tagged the infotablet to his belt. For some reason, young Durfredo had latched on to him and Zhao-ji over the last few days.

"What are you talking about, Durfredo?"

"In Laridonia Cavern. A bloody big rakkie!" Durfredo was almost breathless with excitement. "It's come for Zhao-ji!"

Shiny grey-brown and dappled with black: a huge bulbous body, suspended some ten metres above the cavern floor. Pale underbelly. Thorax segueing to dark purple where its tendrils extruded.

"What is it?" Tom stared up at the thing, shivering.

Cablelike, the tendrils stretched from the rounded body to the cavern's walls, ceiling and floors. Flattened pads, adhering to solid stone, formed each tendril's end.

"It's an arachnargos." The Captain looked grim. "You rarely see them this far down."

At least fifty boys trailed behind them, maybe more, and a couple of the other magisters. No-one was going to keep the boys concentrating on work with a spectacle like this in progress.

There was no sign of the Red Dragon Emporium: the black tent and all its inhabitants had departed upstratum a tenday before. Instead, there was just this strange . . . thing . . . hanging at the cavern's geometric centre, while the Ragged School's wide-eyed pupils looked up in awe.

"Where's Zhao-ji?" Tom looked around, searching the boys' faces.

"Here I am." Face unexpectedly solemn beneath his brush-cut black hair. Satchel slung over one shoulder. "Goodbye, Tom."

"Goodbye." There was nothing more that Tom could say.

The Captain shook Zhao-ji's hand. "Good luck."

"Thank you, sir."

Then Zhao-ji was walking, a diminishing figure, across the cavern's shadowed floor, while the boys' applause, starting softly, rose to a crescendo—"Way to go, Zhao-ji!"—and sustained it as the arachnargos's lower belly puckered open, swiftly dropping a cord-thin tendril at Zhao-ji's approach. It looped itself, figure-of-eight-wise, around his body—"Fly, Zhao-ji!" "Good luck, mate!"—and drew him swiftly upwards.

Tom raised a hand in farewell.

Be nice to people—

Spinning as he rose, Zhao-ji's small figure might have looked in Tom's direction once before being pulled inside. Then the bulbous body rippled shut, became smooth-bellied once more.

—unless they're not nice to you. Petyo's white hair was visible among the crowd of boys. *Then you take revenge. That's the strategy.*

The arachnargos moved.

Thwap!

One tendril unfastened itself, whipped back into the body, then spat out again at a forward angle and adhered farther along the cavern roof. Then another tendril unhooked, retracted, whipped forwards. Another . . .

"There he goes."

The tendrils moved ever faster, and the central body's motion was a smooth trajectory high above the broken floor as the tendrils became a blur and the arachnargos accelerated, arced down towards a wide tunnel's entranceway, turned sharply and sped away.

And was gone.

14

TERRA AD 2122

<<Karyn's Tale>>

[3]

Steam rose from the cup, rising in the shaft of sunlight which poured through the tall, crystalline window. The assistant registrar—"Call me Anne-Marie"—sat behind her hexagonal desk and sipped her tea.

"You won't get much sympathy from the VL Institute, Karyn." Another sip. "But to the UTech students, you'll be some kind of hero."

The steam rose close to her randomly shifting eyes.

"Wonderful." Karyn looked out across the campus. "That's all I need."

"I don't think," said Anne-Marie, "that the intention is for you to be comfortable here."

"I know. If this doesn't make me change my mind, then nothing will."

"Exactly." Anne-Marie's blind eyes continued to shift as she placed her cup down.

It would be tough. For three months, Karyn would be expected to continue her training—including her physical awareness drills—all by herself. No lecturers, no instructors. No sensei.

That was part of the ordeal. They knew she could take discipline: they were testing her *self*-discipline.

"Are there any other Pilot Candidates on campus?"

Anne-Marie smiled. "One left, from the previous intake."

"I see." Karyn did not want to ask how many there had been initially. The drop-out rate, here at the final hurdle, was very high.

"His name's Dart. He'll be going through with it."

"And what about me?" Karyn could not help asking. "Do you think I'll see it through?"

"Bad choice of words," said Anne-Marie, then smiled ironically at Karyn's discomfort. "I don't know. But I'm rather hoping you don't, because I think I like you."

Great. Part of the act? Or genuine concern?

"So"—Karyn let out a long breath—"what do you think of us, Anne-Marie? Crazy, or plain stupid?"

"Oh, no."

Anne-Marie was silent for a moment, then added seriously: "Most of the time, I think you're all as brave as hell."

And the rest of the time?

<<MODULE SUSPENDED>>

"What?" Tom looked up from his infotablet. He was sitting cross-legged by the school's main entrance.

"Feelin' lonely, now your little friend's gone?"

Tom minimized the display. "What do you want, Algrin?"

It had been eleven days since Zhao-ji's departure.

"Hear you might be payin' him a visit." Algrin's foot nudged Tom's knee. "Got a permit."

Closing his eyes, Tom said: "All right, Algrin. The permit will work for a group. Up to six additional people, and we have to go tomorrow." He heard Algrin suck in a breath, surprised. "After that, it expires."

The Captain had explained how it worked, when Tom had asked permission to go upstratum on his rest day.

"Hey, not bad, girly."

Behind Algrin, more boys came up. At their head was Petyo, even paler-faced than usual. His tunic was open to the waist, and *something moved across his stomach*. Fear gripped Tom as it shifted: a red dragon outline, wings beating, travelling across Petyo's skin.

"And that's for your little friend." Algrin grinned as Petyo fastened his tunic up.

"What—?"

"You explain." Algrin reached into the group of boys and dragged out young Durfredo, pulling him by one ear. "We got better things to do. Come on, lads."

Tom waited until Algrin and the others had disappeared behind a milling crowd of lightball players. Then he asked Durfredo: "You all right?"

"Bastards!" Moist-eyed, Durfredo rubbed at his ear. "Yeah, I'm all right."

"What was all that about?" Red dragon across Petyo's flat stomach. "The motile tattoo, I mean."

"Supposed to be yours." Durfredo sniffed. "An old Zhongguo Ren woman. She came to the gate, asking for you. Petyo said his name was Tom Corcorigan, and she injected the thing into him."

"Chaos!"

He was half glad that Petyo had done it. Who would want femtautomata crawling inside their skin?

"It's a message or something, for Zhao-ji." Durfredo sniffed again. "That's all I know."

Zhao-ji had not seemed enthusiastic about Tom's visit: maybe because he knew there was a price involved.

"Listen, Durfredo. Just stay out of Algrin's sight for a few days, OK?"

"Don't need to tell me that."

Tom watched as Durfredo slipped away. *Be nice*. Strategy, or cowardice? *Be nice, until you're pushed too far.*

<<MODULE CONTINUES>>

Music wound through the corridor, past Medical Physics. A pus-yellow holo sign proclaimed the bar's name: THE FIZZY CYST. Karyn shook her head, but went inside.

"*Genki*, pretty lady?" An ivory-skinned young man, hair falling across his eyes. "You FourSpeak?"

"Uh—" Karyn looked where he was pointing.

Silver holotext strung in text-planes over a black glass table. There were half a dozen students in the booth, all young-looking.

"My name's Chojun."

"Karyn."

As they slid into the booth, the others made room for them.

"Your turn, Akazawa." One of them handed a set of finger cursors to Chojun.

"Right." He winked at Karyn. "Time to see the master in action."

Ignoring derisive catcalls from the other players, he reached into the display.

Karyn examined the sheets of text. References to Ragnarok made some sort of sense, but the overlaid puns, the geometric planes formed between node words, were indecipherable. Watching Chojun—only a few years younger than Karyn—rearranging words and dictating text, she felt suddenly old, out of step.

Chojun's gestures became almost manic in their intensity, and he muttered voice instructions while his friends cheered or made sarcastic comments, as he built up a disembodied text structure. A story—Twilight of the Gods as comedy—was part of it. But it was also a game, and something more.

Beyond me.

Murmuring, "Excuse me," she slipped quietly from the booth. Neither Chojun—his sweat-damp face lined with concentration—nor the others paid any attention.

The bar. Despite the little ten-legged robot on the zinc top, there was a real barman behind it, and rows of bottles.

"I think," muttered Karyn, hiking herself up onto a tall stool, "that I know how this works, at least."

A tall, black-jumpsuited man was sitting on the next stool.

"Tesseractions," he said.

"Beg your pardon?" The little robot clanked along the bar, and Karyn tapped its sensor plate. "Cocktail. Anything. The strongest you've got."

The big man beside her let out a low whistle.

"Serious drinker."

"I don't drink."

The barman, who looked young enough to be a student, was carefully monitoring the robot's progress. Probably his engineering project.

"Tesseractions." The big man nodded in the direction of the booth she had left. "Pointless game."

"I don't know." The drink which arrived was a shade of burnt orange, and the glass was warm. There was a small eye-dropper beside it. She looked up at the big man. "Maybe it's just beyond us."

His face was ugly, as though carved from wood: not good-looking, but a solid presence. A black lightning-flash decal decorated his left cheekbone. "Maybe. That's no reason to—"

Karyn took her glass from the robot's back, and tossed back a slug. It clawed at her throat like acid, and she half choked, almost dropping the glass.

"—burn your brains."

"Jesus." Through tear-blurred eyes, she could see the room sway from side to side. "Shoulda warned me."

"I tried." His grin was broad. Very . . . physical. Intense. "You're supposed to use the dropper on your tongue. A drop at a time. The effect's instantaneous."

She sniggered. "Nah."

Another swig. This time she coughed only a little.

"You . . ." She reached out to touch the lightning-flash decal, but his face was suddenly swaying, as though on a pendulum. "Know you. You're—thingy. Him."

A chuckle. "That's me, all right."

"Dar'."

"Give or take a consonant. Pleased to meet you."

"Tryin'"—Karyn squinted at him—"to be funny?"

"I was hoping for hilarity."

"Huh." More liquid fire. "Preacher's son. Thank God for agnos—nossicism. Iss what I say."

"You're wondering, how can you navigate in a fractal continuum if you can't even play a kids' game. Right?"

"Uh . . ."

"But you're making a—never mind."

Bright lights swirled around her. Holos twisted apart and flowed.

"*Mu-space*," she said, or thought she said, as she toppled from the stool.

<<MODULE ENDS>>

15

NULAPEIRON AD 3405

Kaleidoscope: cream panels, mother-of-pearl inlays rimmed with gold. Sparkling fountains; clouds of silver motes dancing. Soft melodies came from crystal birds, soaring and gliding through the rose-scented air which filled the high, spacious halls.

Things had brightened progressively as the seven boys ascended; the last of the six ceiling hatches had melted away and great brass ramps had slid into position. Like nobility, they had been carried upwards, into this place of light and music.

"Beautiful," breathed Petyo.

To one side, dodecapears stirred softly on a table, and a uniformed attendant asked if they would like to try free gripplefruit or purple sprima.

"Not likely," said Algrin, face twisting in disdain.

If only I could stay up here, thought Tom, staring at a freewheeling copper construct that might have been lev-sculpture or a functional device. *But who would look after Paradox?*

Paradox was a lean young feline now—a pure white near-adult neko, and a solitary denizen of lonely tunnels—yet he regained his kittenish ways whenever Tom (or Zhao-ji, until a tenday ago) brought a small lightball with the food.

"Look." One of Algrin's other cronies pointed at a game of airpetanque, played by laughing youths in velvet tunics and soft caps, while gracefully gowned girls looked on.

Tom knew nothing of Zhao-ji's parents, or how Zhao-ji had come to the Ragged School in the first place. Left behind by Master Pin's caravan, perhaps, on some earlier journey through this demesne.

Gold pavilion floating above a limpid pool into which impossible waterfalls arced. Purple fish flitting through the water.

If only I could join Zhao-ji's people. Able to travel anywhere . . .

On a confectionery stand, a ribbon-wrapped jantrasta dragon was on sale for thirty coronae. Where Tom came from, that much credit would feed a family for half a Standard Year.

Past strange fluted columns among which eerie music drifted, by more floating pavilions beneath soaring panelled ceilings, the seven boys walked on, through a series of colonnades, into a market area. But it was nothing like the market of Tom's childhood.

Here, lev-bikes, for sale, hung from gleaming racks. A crystal case held rows of shining foils and epées. One could buy jewel-encrusted chess sets, psychflash globe-holders of twisted platinum, or heavy velvet capes which fluttered and billowed to unseen breezes.

A slender young woman of heart-stopping beauty, golden hair tied back with a sparkling net, her ivory gown trailing filmy scarves, walked past racks of clothing—gaudy tunics and fanciful hats—trailed by a retinue of servitors in black and ivory livery.

She stopped by a stall, pointed to something, then walked on, moving like a floating dream.

"Sweet Fate!"

Behind the girl, one of her servitors carried the item she had just bought: a thin marble sheet, like a tabletop, upon which tiny figurines danced and cavorted and sang with voices like flowing silver.

Tom stood stock-still, watching as girl and servitors passed by.

When they had gone, Tom looked around. Only Petyo was standing beside him; Algrin and the others were gone.

Petyo flicked his white hair back from his eyes.

"You don't want to know, Tom." A knowing smile twisted across his smooth face. "But we'll see them again soon enough."

"It's always nice"—the thin woman smiled beneath her high coiffure, which looked on the point of toppling—"when young people take an interest in local government." She waved them inside.

I hate this. Tom closed his eyes momentarily, then snapped them open for balance. *The drop—*

Vertigo clawed at his guts as he and Petyo took the transparent walkway alongside the District Council chamber. Below, representatives and their aides sat in curved tiers. Personal holodisplays blossomed and twisted while, in a central pit, a huge tesseract of evolving tricons mapped out issues, context fields, realtime voting-scores.

"And now," said one of the speakers, his voice amplified around the amphitheatre, "my private bill on behalf of Madam Karlkinto and other animal traders, allowing free flight of avian species within designated—"

"The Parrot Lady!" came from the floor. Then a chorus: "Caw!" "Free parrots!" "Caw-caw!" "Caw-caw!"

Petyo, shaking his head, pointed up at an observation balcony, where an old woman, parakeet on shoulder, was peering down at the speaker.

"Serious business, this politics."

Sniggering, the two boys took the first exit, and Tom's knees almost gave way with relief on their return to a solid, polished floor. Then Petyo added a surprising comment: "They haven't a clue, you know. It's all show."

"What?"

"Their council. Playing at politics, when they haven't any real power at all."

Narrow silver blades, cutting through the air.

The unseen drums' rhythm accelerated; pipes and strings strained towards crescendo.

Beat and clash of simultaneous parries, then all the attackers leaped backwards together, suddenly on the retreat, as their opponents pressed forwards, blade sliding along blade, then thrusting out in sudden riposte.

"Destiny," breathed Petyo. "They're deadlier than Zhao-ji's crowd."

Different. Tom shook his head. *Not better*.

Down below, on a velvet-carpeted stage, the pairs of fencers disengaged, stepped back, raising their blades, then swept them downwards in intricate salute, just as the music ended. Around the dais, the crowd applauded.

"What's happening, ma'am?" Petyo asked a matronly woman beside them on the balcony.

"Just part of the celebrations," the woman said, and beamed. "Haven't you heard? Rumour is, there's a Lady all the way down from the Primum Stratum, visiting."

Primum Stratum! Blood roared in Tom's ears. The mystical, mythical highest level . . .

"Come shopping, most likely," the woman continued. "Getting Darkday presents early."

On the other hand, I thought the Pilots were legend, too.

A crystal bird glided past the balcony as, on the stage below, the blue-garbed fencers removed their masks. In front of them, an older, purple-suited man—their instructor, perhaps—bowed to the assembled crowd.

"Is the Lady watching?" Petyo, leaned over the balustrade.

"Not yet." The matronly woman beamed, the colour high in her cheeks. "But I think I saw her, er, vehicle, earlier . . . Levanquin, isn't that what they call it?"

Petyo shrugged, and Tom answered: "Yes, ma'am. I think that's the right term."

"Good boys." The woman smiled again, then her face grew serious. Like Petyo, she leaned forward to get a better view.

A murmur passed through the crowd below.

"Call that a fencing display?" The voice drifted up from beneath the balcony. "Dancing, more like!"

Then a wide-shouldered, green-capped figure leaped up onto the stage, and a collective gasp arose from the onlookers.

"It's one of the musicians," muttered the woman beside Tom. "Thieving gypsies. They ought to be flogged."

A live band? Tom had not heard live music since the day of Father's—

Dervlin.

Had he spoken aloud? Beside him, the woman drew back. But down below, the intruder whipped off his soft green cap, revealing a shock of bright copper hair, then slapped it across the fencing-master's face.

Dervlin, for sure.

"Since you insist, sir." The fencing-master, his voice carrying upwards in the suddenly still air, took a blade from one of his students. *"En garde!"* He stepped back into a fighting stance.

"Ah, see . . ." Dervlin, shaking his head, stepped back, circling away to make some distance. "Yer fancy words won't help ya now."

Reaching over his shoulder, Dervlin drew the two black drumsticks from their sheath across his back. One stick in each hand, he began manoeuvring across the stage, taking odd arcing steps, spinning the sticks.

The fencing-master lunged and retreated, measuring distance, while Dervlin's sticks whirled in a blur, like propeller blades cutting the air.

From beneath the balcony, music grew.

The other fencers sat down cross-legged around the stage's edges, defining a fighting-area, while their teacher and Dervlin leaped and turned, engaging with a clash, then breaking off. As the music quickened, the watching fencers began to clap in time.

From the crowd, a burst of relieved laughter.

Spellbound, Tom watched as Dervlin and the fencing-master fought, disengaged, renewed their blistering attack, while the spectators, realizing the truth, clapped along. Faster and faster, building to a climax as Dervlin leaped high, dropped low, elbow-striking as a stick went flying—

I've seen that movement before.

—then he fell as the fencing-master swept his legs out from under him—to a clash of cymbals—and lay there, panting, with the master's blade at his throat.

No. It couldn't be.

"Do you yield, sir?"

"Aye." Dervlin grinned. "Grant me mercy, an' ye will."

"I do."

The crowd roared its approval as they stood and took a bow.

I've never done sports. What do I know about physical movement?

But he couldn't force the notion aside. Dervlin's technique, his flowing tactics, struck a strong resonance inside Tom's memory: of the market where the Pilot whirled, striking troopers, moving and fighting against the odds until they cut her down.

After the demonstration, as the crowd began to break up, Tom made his way down the staircase, sighting on the red hair.

"Tom Corcorigan! How are you?"

"Hello, Derv—" Tom began, then: "You're injured!"

Dervlin was leaning back on a deep-green slab against curlicued abstract sculpture. A small, dark stain showed below his ribs.

"Not from the demo, lad." He blanked his features, then smiled. "Yesterday, some fellers got playful. Their enthusiasm outmatched their ability."

"But why?" Tom shook his head, not understanding. "What about an autodoc?"

"No time. I'd made the commitment to help out here."

Blinking, Tom glanced back among the gold-trimmed ivory colonnades, looking for Petyo, but he had slipped away while Tom was descending the twisting staircase from the balcony.

"Anyway, lad. How's the school?"

"All right." Tom remembered Trude's words. "Better than you'd think, given where it is."

Dervlin's blue eyes sparkled.

"So," he said finally. "You hate it that much, do you?"

Tom tried to argue, but could not.

"The other boys—?" Dervlin began, then stopped. "I see. That bad, is it?"

Deep, shaky breath. *Don't cry.* That was one lesson he had learned.

"About this little scratch . . ." Dervlin pointed to his ribs. "It would have made medical sense to get treatment, but I gave my word that I'd do the demo."

"I don't understand."

"You have to live with your own self. When you can't change the circumstances, you can still control your own reactions, don't you see?"

But Algrin's bigger than I am . . .

"Kneel down, lad. Let me help you."

Tom knelt, then sat back on his heels, like Karyn and her sensei in Karyn's Tale. He sensed surprise from Dervlin, then a quiet chuckle.

"Interesting. Now, think of . . . Let's see. Think of *freedom.*"

Tom shivered at the word. Reaching inside his tunic, he clenched his fist around the stallion talisman's hard, curved form.

Stallion . . .

"This"—Dervlin's voice, oddly lilting; a light touch on Tom's fist (and Tom realized his eyes were closed)—"is stronger than you think. It can hit solid stone without injury, if you focus your intention."

Drifting.

". . . intention, and intensity . . ."

There were other words, but Tom no longer truly heard Dervlin's voice. Instead, he was *adrift in a sea of sharp-tinged moving air, washed by cold air beneath a yellow/purple open sky. Silver grasses whipped back and forth by weather. And, on a curving beach by a steel-grey sea, a stallion raced, hooves plunging, mane wildly flying—*

"Hold the picture, lad. It's *your* image."

Fist . . . and stallion.

Running for ever. Chasing liberty, scorning fear.

Fist and stallion.

"Remember . . ."

I will, Father.

". . . and wake up as I count . . . three, two, one."

Tom rocked back on his heels, pain throbbing in his knees.

"What—?" Wincing, he pushed himself into a sitting position on the hard flagstones. "What did you do?"

"Call it voodoo, lad, or call it Zen Neuronic Coding." Dervlin laughed. "Either way, it works. Just—"

"Don't worry," said Tom quietly, surprising himself. "I'll remember."

Fist and stallion.

16

NULAPEIRON AD 3405

Low, grey ceiling covered in something that might have been soft fur, embossed with metre-wide silver hemispheres. In a wide sunken area, the restaurant; each table, a floating crystal disc. A hushed sense of relaxation: a place to take one's ease.

Maybe I'll see Mother.

Who knew where she was living? Or where Oracles lived, for that matter. Was she this high up, or in some stratum below his feet?

"Hey, it's the girly."

But Mother could be anywhere in Nulapeiron; anywhere in the world.

"Aw, we've finished all our daistral. Sorry, girly."

Tom wished that Dervlin were here, but the other band members had fetched him for some function they had to attend.

I never asked him about his fighting style . . . But then, Tom had never mentioned the Pilot to anybody, ever.

"You boys. Time you left." A waitress, hands upon her hips, unimpressed by Algrin's sneer or his cronies' contemptuous slouching across the U-shaped seat.

The crystal table tipped in the lev-field as Algrin levered himself upright. Bobbing, it adjusted itself.

"Watch your language, you old hag." Algrin nodded in Tom's direction. "Our girly's here."

"Out!" The waitress looked at him, then walked away, stiff with purpose.

"Better leave," one of the others began, then shut up. Nevertheless, all four of them slid out from behind the table and clustered around Algrin.

"Where's Petyo, then?"

Tom shrugged. "I don't know."

"Chaos!"

That was how Tom felt, too. He was to meet Zhao-ji at Gerberov Santuario, but he could not go without Petyo and his subcutaneous femtautomata.

"Wait. Is that a great tunic, or what?"

Tom looked. In a fluted maze of arching crystalline threads, a small group of handsomely surcoated youths stood among racks of clothing. Beside them, a hovering mirror field and a servitor anxiously watching.

"That's mine."

Moving skull. In one eye-socket, a lick of crimson flame.

"Come on."

The black tunic was certainly Algrin's style. Why any of these rich lads would want it was another question.

"Out of my way!"

Oh, Fate!

Then everything happened quickly.

Algrin was running, laughing, with the tunic clutched in one hand. On the floor, two of the rich youths lay in shock, too stunned to cry out, while even Algrin's cronies were wrong-footed.

They hesitated, while on the ceiling *shining things moved* and a silver light flashed and Algrin reacted instantaneously, changing his run, sprinting towards Tom while *they moved again* and there was a thud as Algrin crashed into Tom and was gone.

Silver hemispheres.

It took less than a second for Tom to realize that he was clutching the stolen garment, but that was a lifetime too late as the ceiling's silver hemispheres flowed downwards to the floor, forming elongated quasi-humanoid shapes. *Mannequins.* Before Tom could move he was caught in the cool, hard/soft embrace of an extended liquid-metal limb, moulded into place around his wrists.

No!

Twisted, distorted face. Pale with shock. His own reflection in the security mannequin's curved mirror-face.

"Well, now." The waitress's brassy voice. "You got—"

Caught.

"—one of the little bastards, anyway."

Freedom's end.

"The prosecution"—feminine, cut-glass accent—"argues for death?"

The void is purple and grey.

"Er, yes." Male voice, coarse and nasal. "Indeed so, my Lady."

It spins, whirling, filled with motes of sparkling black like a million hungry eyes.

"And the defence?"

"Waives commutation rights, my Lady, in view of the evidence."

A tiny round shape amid the flowing strangeness—

"You'll pardon our presence, gentlemen, and conduct the case as normal. My daughter has an interest in judicial matters."

"Of course, my Lady! It's our honour."

—growing larger. A flat ellipsoidal stage, on which Tom can see himself.

"You have your own executioner?"

"Indeed, my Lady. He's, ah, away right now. But back in three days."

"If that's the sentence."

"Indeed—"

"Then let us proceed."

He is standing, stolen garment in hand, while the others flee. Two of the victims lie, stunned and hurt, upon the ground.

"—incontrovertible, as you can see. The defendant condemns himself."

Then from above—from nowhere, in the swirling grey/purple void—silver shapes elongate, take humanoid form, and one of them traps Tom's wrists.

"Awaken the accused."

Ice-fire, jolting through brain and arteries—

No!

—slamming Tom into wakefulness.

"Thomas Corcorigan. You plead guilty."

He hung his head, unable to argue against the fading holos which ringed his chair.

"Is there anything you can say in your favour, as regards sentencing?"

His wrists were embedded in the chair-arms; the chair itself was on a crystal floor, and the sense of vertigo was sickening. Below him, beneath the crystal, lay the District Council chamber's empty tiers.

Tom shook his head.

"Remove the squid claws."

Unseen hands pulled away a thousand hard points, tugging Tom's hair, scraping at his scalp.

"Look at me, Thomas Corcorigan."

Something beyond fear dragged Tom's head upright.

She was resplendently gowned, and a platinum-inlaid wimple, from which several silver-grey locks of hair artfully escaped, surrounded her heart-shaped face. Her pale eyes shone with a startling strength.

But it was the maiden beside her who caught Tom's attention. Golden hair, tied back with a glittering net. The girl he had seen earlier buying the tiny moving figurines.

So beautiful . . .

"You have nothing to say?"

"My Lady—" Tom cleared his throat, then stopped.

What can I say?

His mind raced, but fear and confusion blocked his throat. Blurred vision, a kind of darkness pressing in; a strange insulation making their voices fade. It was inconceivable that they were talking about ending his life—his *life*, for Fate's sake—yet he had to do something, say something.

But what?

There were four ruddy, stern-faced men—two on each side of the Lady and her daughter—sitting behind a curved obsidian table.

What did he know of the nobility? What would move this Lady's heart?

Wordplay and paradox.

All he knew of their class, besides the fact that they ruled everyone, was that they were master logosophers, wielding massive intellects, hunting abstruse problems for amusement.

"Sylvana?" The Lady addressed her daughter. "Your opinion?"

"That it should be quick." Piercing glance, with her mother's strength. "The boy should not undergo cruel or unusual punishment."

Tom swallowed, strangled by fear, unable to speak.

The briefest compression of the Lady's mouth, the ephemeral appearance of lines across her cheeks, and then she nodded. "Very well. Take him to a holding—"

"But that's cruel." The words burst out of Tom's mouth before he could consider them.

"You *dare?*"

One of the men half rose, hand reaching for something at his belt.

"It's all right." A languid wave of the Lady's hand; but her eyes were intent. "Explain yourself, boy."

Reluctantly, the red-faced man took his seat once more.

"You would have me . . ." Tom stopped, swallowing again.

But it's the only chance.

". . . You'd have me taken to a cell, expecting leniency. But I heard one of the councillors say"—Tom reached into his memory of the squid trance—"that the executioner returns in three days' time."

All four men were frowning.

"So . . ." Tom expelled a long, trembling breath. "I expect to be held there, having been told that I will live, *thus saving me mental torture*, until the time arrives for the executioner to kill me."

The men were puzzled; but the Lady raised one eyebrow.

Only chance.

"But the wait itself is, er, cruel and unusual punishment, since, reasoning thus, I expect to die. So—"

Go on. All the way.

"—by your own logic, you have to pardon me."

Stunned silence.

Then outrage erupted. "Damn you, boy!" "How dare you!" "Kill him now—"

One raised finger halted the commotion.

"My Lady." The men bowed hastily.

Tom's eyes stung.

And the Lady's daughter laughed.

"He argues prettily, Mother." Her voice was both warm and cool, like a gentle fountain's plashing upon a pool. "And we need more Palace servitors."

The men were discomfited, but fearful of the Lady, their faces blotched with conflicting emotions.

"Gentlemen."

They grew still as the Lady spoke.

"I shall buy the boy for a thousand coronae."

A palpable hush. The amount was staggering.

"Lady Darinia," murmured one of the men, head bowed. "Enlightened ruler of our demesne." His words sounded like a traditional formula.

The Lady—Lady Darinia—inclined her head towards her daughter. "The Lady Sylvana will decide the boy's punishment."

Frank blue eyes, appraising him.

"An arm, perhaps?"

Paralysis encircled Tom's throat.

"Very well." Lady Darinia stood, and chairs scraped back as the four men hastily followed suit. "Before you deliver him, remove an arm."

Her grey gaze swept over Tom.

"Either arm will do."

17

NULAPEIRON AD 3405

"Catch!"

It arced through the air and Tom reacted late, knocking the light-ball aside. It dropped to the ground with a dying whine.

"Just checking." The big man, his upper arms swollen with muscle, shook his head. "Don't seem like either hand's much use."

No—

But the mannequin was already hauling Tom across the brick-red chamber's floor. Its unbreakable grip around his left wrist drew him across a round, flat-topped slab; its other hand pushed implacably down upon Tom's shoulder-blade, anchoring his arm in place.

Face pressed against hardness, Tom forced out the words: "Executioner's . . . not here."

"But I ain't the executioner." The man hefted a big, two-handled vibroslash. "I carve stone for a living."

The shear-field crackled into life.

"Please!"

"Orders, son."

Ozone stink as the buzzing field burned the very air.

"No!"

Touched his skin.

Burning . . .

Beyond pain, shock hammered into him as the cutting shear-field bit into his upper arm, just below the left shoulder, and it burned as Tom kicked out uselessly at the mannequin's immobile form but it was too late and fat bubbled and spat while it burned past all imagining and the rising stench of burning meat hauled back memory flashes of the Pilot's death burning surpassing agony but this pain was his.

He screamed again and again as the field descended through grinding bone burning until bloody blackness fell and dropped him to oblivion.

And it burned.

For days, it burned.

Over and over, while lightning spat and comets of his imagining fell through blackened space, his pain was an endless fire submerged beneath the deadening blanket of femtocytic invaders in his blood. Sometimes he saw her ethereal face and dared to say her name—Sylvana—but always it became Father, shaking his once fleshy face with a new darkness hidden in his eyes, before licking flames carried Tom back to agony.

And then he awoke.

It was three days later, and the room in which he lay was all of jade, pale and elegant, and his mind felt cold and lucid.

Pain dreams fell away as he sat up in the too comfortable bed. He was naked—though his talisman still hung from its throat cord—and the opalescent sheets were cool and smooth against his skin.

"Fate . . ." A hideous nightmare.

A bubbling laugh rose in his throat, suddenly cut off.

How could I have imagined . . . ?

So he looked, and saw the short stump protruding from his left shoulder.

Nothing at all, where his left arm should have been.

When he came to for the second time, fresh clothes had been laid out at the foot of the bed.

His outfit was all of ivory and black, his new owner's livery. Black boots and trews edged with gold; black sleeveless jerkin, loose ivory shirt.

With awful thoughtfulness, the shirt's left sleeve had been removed, and the abbreviated remnant closed up, trimmed with expensive brocade.

18

NULAPEIRON AD 3405

A tenday had elapsed.

"You're being assigned permanent quarters."

Ten days, passing in a lucid dream.

"Yes, Major-Steward."

They stood at the briefing-chamber's exit.

"Stop," Major-Steward Malkoril murmured. "Gentry coming."

The corridor which crossed in front of them glowed with an opalescent, pearly light. Rich burgundy carpet ran along the floor.

Ten days. Why do I feel no pain?

Puzzled, Tom tugged at his right ear. The feel of the earstud was still strange, but not unwelcome. Malkoril's earstud was identical: a ruby droplet. Similar to the IDs worn by adults—Mother and Father included—in Tom's home stratum.

Two small children drew near, laughing. A boy and a girl, hair in golden ringlets, their lace-ruffled smartsatin suits shimmering with deep richness.

The girl, stuffing some confection in her mouth, tossed aside a gold-embossed wrapper.

Neither one showed a flicker of interest in Tom or Malkoril.

"There's a protocol," said Malkoril in a low tone, after they had passed, "which lets us pass in front of young nobility—"

The discarded wrapper lay like an accusation on the perfect burgundy floor.

"—if our task is urgent, that is."

Tom started to pick the wrapper up, but Malkoril was already walking. Tom hurried to catch up.

"Will I learn—?" Tom stopped.

Motion at the edge of his vision: a distortion on the wall.

"The protocol?"

The opalescent wall gathered itself, elongated, *reached out an arm* for the discarded wrapper and, retracting, took the wrapper inside itself.

"Yes, you'll learn." Malkoril glanced back at Tom. "Hurry along."

A downward-spiralling ramp took them past two levels. Some parts of the Palace were twenty levels deep, Malkoril had said, though it was all within the Primum Stratum. Then they hurried along, turning at half a dozen intersections while Tom tried to memorize the sequence.

Then they stopped dead.

"Very funny." Malkoril glared.

They were faced with a blank, pearly wall.

"Kitchen complex." The colour was rising in Malkoril's face. "Usual way. Now."

An opening melted away. Beyond, a gold-lined corridor twisted to the right.

"Damned Palace," muttered Malkoril, "would reconfigure every night, if we let it."

"I'm Shalkrovistorin Kelduranom." The bald man's pate glistened. "But you can call me Chef Keldur."

Around them, processor towers shone with silver, glowed with lustrous mother-of-pearl.

"Chef." Tom bowed.

"Corcorigan. Sub-delta servitor." Malkoril introduced him. "He's all yours, Shalkie."

"Right, boy. We'll start you with—" Chef Keldur stopped, frowning.

"I don't know my lines!" A distraught man, long-faced and pale, came from behind a processor. "It didn't take!"

"Hold it." The Chef was a short man, but when he held up his hand the new arrival stopped dead.

A golden microdrone passed by overhead, then hovered over a row of dessert dishes.

"You." Chef Keldur pointed to the rust-uniformed servant who stood by the desserts. "Personatropes for Eldriv."

"Sir." The servant waited for a moment, checking the microdrone as it began to pour sauce over the desserts, then hurried off along an aisle.

"One refresher dose only," Keldur called after him. "No more."

Malkoril asked the pale man: "How goes it, Eldriv?"

"The play will be magnificent." A haughty sniff. "You'll excuse my frustration: the creative urge."

Malkoril kept a straight face as Eldriv withdrew.

Chef Keldur and Major-Steward Malkoril walked along a wide aisle, trailed by Tom. Silver drones floated and golden microdrones flitted among the square, ornate columns.

On one steel table lay a slab of meatblock, carved into an elaborate double helix. Keldur and Malkoril halted.

"Ah, Chef." A long-mustachioed man was replacing a lattice blade, from a matched set of six, in its velvet-lined brass case.

"Bertil."

Behind the mustachioed man, eight anxious-faced young servants were huddled.

"My trainees"—with a disdainful glance—"have ruined this food sculpture. We'll need another block."

"Your section's already over budget, Bertil."

"But perfection—"

"—is a balanced ledger." Keldur stared the man down. "Don't ask again."

Then he and Malkoril walked on.

Tom stayed three paces behind, but he could hear Chef Keldur's muttered complaint—"Am I a pharmacoder, a circus manager, or what?"—and Malkoril's answering chuckle.

The trainees are going to pay for Bertil's loss of face. Tom glanced back at their worried expressions. *But why doesn't that bother me?*

"Tray duty, boy."

They had stopped by a shining copper workbench, and were looking at Tom.

"You'll start here."

"And call it."

For repetition after repetition, under Keldur's supervision, Tom summoned the tray.

"Again."

Each time, it floated slowly across the workbench, hovered, then Tom placed his right hand—his *only* hand—underneath, and swung the tray to his shoulder.

"One thousand. Stop now."

A thousand repetitions.

"Sir." Tom's shoulder and forearm burned.

"Go to store number three. Ask for Jak."

Trembling with fatigue, Tom bowed.

Outside in the corridor, he looked right and left. Opalescent walls, but an unfamiliar teal-green, furlike carpet. The wrong corridor? Or had it changed?

Confused, Tom tried to construct a mental map.

"Left," he decided, but a strange ripple passed through the soft, green floor.

He stopped.

"Wrong way?"

One wall's shining material shifted, extruding a stubby arm, and a thick finger pointed back along the corridor.

Tom knelt down to pat the soft floor. "Thank you very much," he said and smiled, bemused.

"You're Jak?"

"Right." The tall youth had lank, dark hair and was dressed like Tom in ivory and black. "Like the holodramas."

"Sorry? Oh—like a Jack."

But real Jacks were not heroic: Tom remembered the blue, motile dermaweb, the microfaceted eyes, searching for the Pilot's hidden crystal.

"You're Corcorigan, then."

"Tom."

A smile flitted across Jak's face. "This way, Corcorigan."

"Alexon, Tat, Jyonner, Mazh—he's the ugly one—then Driuvik . . ." Jak pointed them out in turn. Twelve, including Tom, at the black table in the gleaming obsidian room.

"And the pervert opposite you is Jak," said Tat, a strong-featured oriental. "But he answers to 'cretin.'"

Rectangular membranes—black, like everything else in here— marked the dorm's walls: entrances to their individual rooms.

"Forceful answer, too." Jak hooked fishblock from his bowl with a tine-spoon. "If you push me."

"In your dreams."

When the meal was over, Tom retired to his room—not before seeing a blank-faced serving wench come in to clear the table: there were hierarchies even here—and sat down on the black bed.

Luxury.

"Hiya." Jak's head and shoulders protruded through the membrane. "You OK?"

"Yes. Too much OK."

"What do you mean?" But Jak's glance flickered across Tom's abbreviated left sleeve.

"You know what I mean."

A pause.

"That'll be the implant," said Jak.

He drew back through the membrane, leaving Tom alone.

19

NULAPEIRON AD 3405

Late night: a dim orange lustre to the Palace corridors. Tom was "shadowing" Jak, learning by observation.

The stolen brass cylinder was hard, tucked inside Tom's waistband. Lattice blade.

They bore left, into a plush, wide tunnel, eerie in the muted light. A slowly revolving impossible triangle, three or four metres to a side, hung in mid-air.

"Get in here." Jak, without dropping his tray, stepped smartly into an alcove.

"What—?"

Tom was staring at the triangle, bone-white and inlaid with platinum, trying to figure the perspective. Was it holo or solid? A composite?

Jak tugged Tom into the alcove just as three silver shapes whipped through the air.

"Mad buggers."

One of the lev-bikes hurtled *through* the turning triangle's hollow centre, catching the opportunity just right. Manic laughter echoed back as all three lev-bikes zipped along the tunnel's diminishing perspective, hooked into a dangerous turn, and were gone.

"Thanks, Jak." As they stepped back into the corridor, Tom checked the smooth brass cylinder: the lattice blade was still secure, hidden beneath his jerkin. "Thanks for mentioning the implant, too."

"No secret." Jak shrugged his narrow shoulders, then hoisted his tray back into position. "Coming?"

Earlier, totally submerged in the bubbling black aerogel of his bathing alcove, Tom had found the implant: a lump, buried between his chest and left shoulder-muscle. Too big for femtotech.

At their destination, Jak went first through the membrane. Gossamer-fine, it slid over Tom's skin as he followed, hand held against his waist to secure the secreted brass cylinder.

Inside, a polished red granite floor shone beneath the groined ceiling, the floating amber glowclusters.

"You can't go any further." A small, chubby-faced child, maybe five SY old, looked up at them.

Jak stopped dead.

Beyond, on soaring, twisted, stalklike columns, two grey marble platforms hung. Facing each other, each platform held two rows of seats, but currently held only four youngsters.

It was a junior debate, and the moderator—a small black-skinned boy—sat on a jade chair dangling in mid-air from a cable extruded from the high ceiling.

"Why's that?" asked Tom.

The little girl's eyes grew round. "Zeno's paradox." She spoke with a slight lisp. "Before you reach the table"—her small chubby hand pointed to a lev-table near the moderator's chair—"you have to get halfway there. Before that, you have to get a quarter-way there. Before that . . ."

She continued in a singsong voice, enumerating fractions.

Jak was standing stiffly, not moving, because of the girl's implicit command. He gave an almost imperceptible shake of his head.

I'm breaching protocol, Tom realized. *But if I don't, we could be here all night.*

From the suspended chair, the moderator announced: "The motion before the house is that this motion, its outcome being predestined, is not a motion."

"We can get there," Tom whispered, interrupting the girl's continuing recitation, "in no time at all."

She stopped, mouth open.

"If I take lots of small steps, really small," Tom began.

"Infinitesimal," the little girl said solemnly.

"Right." Tom was impressed. "And it takes no time to cross each infinitesimal distance, so . . ."

The girl's face lit up as she spotted the conclusion. "It's instantaneous."

"That's Tom's paradox."

"Tom's paradox," she repeated. Then she stuck her thumb in her mouth, turned, and scampered away.

"Salle d'armes," said the sous-chef. "Tertiary studio. You know the way?"

"Yes, sir."

It was the morning shift, and things were busy.

"It's for Maestro da Silva."

Not nobility, then. If Tom had not been available, they could have sent a smart-tray via a drone.

Once outside, tray over his right shoulder, he checked the direction in which the salle d'armes lay. "This way?"

A ripple of agreement along the wall.

"Thanks."

Clash of blades, stamp of feet. Exertion's heavy scent; aggression's tingling edge on the cool air.

A tremor passed through Tom as he reached the open archway.

Inside, the fencing-master's students stamped and lunged, span and cut. Blue-clad, masked, their blades a fast-moving blur.

"Watch your line, Master Adams!"

"Maestro." A blade salute, and the bout was rejoined.

"Better."

The fencing-master wore black, and his long hair and goatee beard were dark, tinged with grey. He was lean and his eyes were quick.

"Bind, disengage." He walked among his students, alert to every-thing. "Mistress Faledria: flèche with the hips low."

Maestro da Silva was not the fencing-master whose demo had fea-tured Dervlin, but he was of the same physical type: whipcord-thin and very fit.

To one side, three maskless fencers practised individually within holospheres. Colour-coded radii spiked through the air, arcs hung in brilliant curves, as their blades traced the intricate sequences.

Tom looked for a table, found one.

"Ow!"

A light foil bent almost double: stop-hit against a charging oppo-nent's exposed ribcage.

Tom set down his tray.

A buzzer sounded, and the fencing-master called out, "*Arrêtez!*" The fencers stepped back from their opponents, sketching formal salutes with their blades.

"Out of my way, oaf!" A burly youth pushed past.

"Sorry, sir." Tom made the requisite genuflection of apology, but the youth was already lost among the bustle of sweat-stained students, masks under their arms, leaving the chamber.

"Lord Avernon?" the fencing-master called to a pale-skinned lad who looked thin and exhausted. "Are you all right?"

The boy nodded. Unsteadily, he walked out.

As the others left, Tom watched. Some merely glanced at the fencing-master, a few gave short bows—the better fencers, Tom guessed—and smiles. But their teacher was not noble-born.

"Thank you, Maestro—" a young woman began.

A graceful nod from the fencing-master.

"—and I'll keep my hips low next time."

A smile tugged at Maestro da Silva's lean face, but then he glanced at the open archway and frowned.

Tom hurried from the chamber.

I hope Bertil's not sculpting food today. The lattice blade which Tom had slipped from the brass case was in his room. *But I should be more anxious than I am.*

As he walked on, the fencers were dispersing, taking different exits from the main corridor. No sign of the young Lord.

Not to worry.

Tom backtracked, taking his time. He checked three side corridors, going a little way along them before returning. In the fourth corridor, he spotted Lord Avernon: the boy was still walking, putting a hand out for balance.

Tom held back.

The boy's footsteps faltered and he coughed, rasping, then his knees gave way. Somehow, Tom caught him just before his head hit the floor.

What do I do?

Awkwardly, he pulled at the boy.

"Help me . . ."

Then the floor began to flow, carrying Tom and Lord Avernon along, though it seemed for ever before Tom finally dragged the wheezing, unconscious boy through the unadorned archway, calling out the maestro's name.

Blood spurted.

Fist and stallion. Tom fought to hold the image in his mind, but his naked body was drenched with sweat and the brass cylinder was slippery in his grip.

Again.

The lattice blade field crackled back into life.

Fist and stallion.

Logotropic flashback from the Captain's classes overlaid visual/proprioreceptive stimuli: between anterior deltoid and the pectoralis group, he sighted in on the target. Old nano, from its size, drexling nanocytes into the thoraco-acromial artery.

He whimpered as white light bit into his shoulder. Bloody rivulets ran down his chest.

Fist and—

The hilt twisted in his grip and he thumbed it off, put it down, then hooked his thumb into the open wound and pulled the thing out.

—stallion!

Tiny gobbets hung to the implant as it arced across the black bathing-alcove, bounced off the wall with a clang, and fell. It rolled to a stop.

20

NULAPEIRON AD 3405

The left arm burned.

Sliding in and out of sleep, among fitful dreams of *Mother dancing, callously laughing, while Paradox, no longer kittenish, was starving, ribs visible, and Father's corpse span endlessly in the Vortex Mortis*—the arm was there, but not in reality: instantiated in pain.

"—awake yet?"

Waves of grey exhaustion crashed upon Tom.

"I said, are you—?" Jak, leaning in through the black membrane.

"All right, all right."

"Visitor." He popped back out of sight.

Tom rolled to his left—and he could feel, exquisitely, every detail of his nonexistent left arm: had it been real, it would have been *inside* both sleeping-pad and floor—and sat up, just as Maestro da Silva came inside the all-black room.

"Morning. May I sit?"

"Er . . ."

Tom blinked as the fencing-master said: "Float-pad," and a lozenge of black wall slid out into mid-air and hovered.

"'Morning . . ." Tom cleared his throat. "Ah, good morning, Maestro." Tom pulled the sheet around his waist.

Maestro da Silva sat down on the pad and crossed his legs.

"With that accent . . . You're from Duke Khaznhov's realm?"

"No, here. This demesne, but—" Tom's gaze dropped to the floor.

"Ah. How many strata?"

"I'm not sure."

A pause. Then, "Sometimes, when an opponent has a sophisticated strategy of compound attacks, you can use intricacy and momentum to your advantage."

"Er, right."

"But you're not a sportsman." Not quite a question; the Maestro deliberately did not look at Tom's softly unathletic body. "What are your interests?"

"Poetry, sir." Tom swallowed. "And maths. Languages."

"Hmm." He pointed at Tom's stump. "Once you're here, the punishments for poor performance are quite mild. Demerits and the like. Had you noticed?"

Tat was currently working extra duties, to clear the twelve demerits he had earned for spilling soup on one of Lady Darinia's grand-nieces.

"Yes, sir."

The use of tranquillizer-implants was unmonitored: there had been no repercussions from cutting the thing out. The powers-that-be did not want their subjects to be mindless zombies.

Had he attempted to remove his ID earstud, that would have been different: a microwave alarm would have shrieked to the Palace systems, which would have tracked him until his apprehension by the Dragoons.

"A deliberately encouraging system, don't you think? Hence, too, the merits." Maestro da Silva stood. "Good day."

The float-pad drifted aside as he stepped through the membrane and was gone. Tom watched as the wall reabsorbed the pad.

"So?" Jak came inside. "What did he want?"

Tom shook his head.

"I've no idea."

"Rank: Lord-Meilleur-sans-Demesne." The steward-minor consulted the display blossoming above his wrist. "Name: Corduven d'Ovraison."

Tom nodded as a topographic tricon appeared in front of him, projected by his tunic's smartstrip.

"A problem," the steward-minor continued, "with the gentleman's wardrobe, I believe."

"I'll sort it out."

Once outside the kitchen complex, Tom stopped close to the softly glowing wall and whispered: "Is this correct? Level three, right spiral, twelfth chamber: guest name is d'Ovraison."

A ripple of agreement.

D'Ovraison?

"Er, thanks." Tom patted the wall, his thoughts a distracted jumble.

D'Ovraison.

His nonexistent left arm flared with pain as he walked. He could ask the Palace to speed up his journey, but refrained.

When the young Lord Avernon was in trouble, the floor had flowed. And late one night, when Tom had replaced the borrowed lattice blade in the kitchen, the Palace had caused him to sink *through* a corridor floor to the level below (though still in this stratum: the Palace was complex) to avoid a night patrol.

His footsteps slowed.

Psyching himself up to cut out the implant had involved classic double-think—he could do a better job if his mind lost its tranquillity: witness the length of time it had taken to come to Lord Avernon's aid—while the true reasons lay hidden in dark shadows.

But, as he stopped outside Lord d'Ovraison's chamber membrane, the force of hatred thrummed inside him like a deep, resonant chord.

"Tasteless, isn't it?"

Incense in the air. Walls decorated in a moving maze of soft maroon on ochre; regular-looking pattern, drawn with one continuously shifting line.

"I've seen better," said Tom, surprising himself.

The young man—maybe two SY older than Tom: blond hair; taut, elegant face; deep grey eyes—was standing by an intricate black and silver sculpture formed of intertwined Möbius ribbons and Klein surfaces. Thoughtfully, he tapped a fingernail against it.

"I expect a mercy killing would be in order."

"I'm sorry?" Tom exhaled softly, releasing tension.

"My suit. Buggy smartsatin." D'Ovraison crooked a finger. "Come this way."

Tom followed Lord d'Ovraison into the next chamber. A stack of opened penrose cases lay by the bed; on top lay a grey-black suit of clothes with impossibly elongated lace ruffs.

"Take this." D'Ovraison draped the suit over Tom's outstretched arm.

Tom started to bow, but *it moved* and the suit was slithering up his shoulder, lace ruffle embracing his throat, beginning to tighten just as d'Ovraison tugged the sleeve back and slapped it smartly. It fell limply, as though stunned.

"Disrupts the microwave op-codes."

"Er . . . Thank you, sir."

"Please don't call—Well, never mind. Just keep an eye on that thing."

Despite himself, Tom laughed. "Be a material witness, you mean?"

"With strong moral fibre." A raised eyebrow. "May I ask—?" But a low chime sounded, and he turned. "Go ahead."

Above the twisted metal, she appeared: pale and beautiful, blond tresses intricately tied up with white silk.

"Hello, Cord."

"Sylvana." D'Ovraison sketched a bow, graceful yet sardonic.

Lady Darinia's daughter.

"Old Drago's reciting the Elder Edda tonight, in Old Terran Norse. Did you know?"

"I've only just arrived." D'Ovraison gave a twisted smile. "Somehow that escaped my notice."

"You know how the rhyming works?"

D'Ovraison started to shake his head. From one side, Tom mouthed the answer: *Alliteration*. Not quite the correct term, but—

Taking the cue, d'Ovraison said: "Willingly would I/ Wend my way with thee/ Whither ever thou—"

"Yes, all right. But I was thinking of the lev-bike race tonight."

D'Ovraison folded his slender arms. "Sounds rather macho to me."

"But if you were to take me—"

"—then Lady Darinia's matchmaking proclivities would be satisfied." D'Ovraison glanced in Tom's direction. "And you could skip the Edda. Quite."

"Is there—? Oh, Thomas Corcorigan. How are you?"

Tom was rooted to the spot, and he felt his face flush.

She remembers my name. The constant fire of his left arm momentarily cooled.

"Er, well, thank you."

But she . . .

The fire of his missing limb returned; he felt hot, confused.

Her attention was once more on d'Ovraison. "Come on, Cord. Rescue me from boredom. Please?"

"Well . . ."

In the holodisplay, Sylvana held up a small violet crystal, shot through with milky inlays. "It's my only chance to give you Galdriv's latest paradoxicon."

"That's blackmail."

After Lady Sylvana's image had disappeared, Lord d'Ovraison turned to Tom.

"Where's this race meeting, do you know?"

"Veneluza Galleria." Since the terminal was still on, Tom sketched

out a control gesture—awkwardly, because of the smartsuit's weight—
and a topographic tricon grew into being.

"Got it." Cool, grey eyes. "Neatly done."

Tom bowed. "I'll take the suit to—"

"A moment, please." An ironic smile played across d'Ovraison's
delicate features. "Don't take this the wrong way—you're not my type,
old chap—but I'd like you to accompany us tonight, if you would."

"I . . . Of course."

"Chaperon duty. I'm sure you understand."

"Ah." Involuntarily, Tom smiled in return. "It's not only Lady
Darinia who has designs on your future."

D'Ovraison looked delighted that Tom had spoken so freely. "I
need a bodyguard. Deal?"

Tom shook his head, but only at the absurdity: a Lord could command him completely.

"Deal."

Tom began the ritual of bowing out, but d'Ovraison stopped him.
A penrose case unfolded at d'Ovraison's approach, and he pulled out a
small white object.

"Tom, wasn't it? This is a present for Lady Sylvana." He held it
out: a tricon, in metal. "What do you think?"

Solid, it lost the subtlety of a holo, but the meaning was clear: *This
statement is a falsehood.*

"I'm sure my Lady will appreciate it."

He wants me to identify it as Epimenides' paradox.

But Tom's reticence seemed only to amuse d'Ovraison. "Well,
then. Do you recognize the material?"

Tom shook his head.

"It's antimony."

Then something strange happened. Tom and d'Ovraison burst into
completely simultaneous laughter, shook their heads at the same time,
then chuckled in total unison as d'Ovraison replaced the tricon in its case.

"Subtle, my Lord." Tom bowed.

"Perhaps so." D'Ovraison gave the tiniest of bows in return. "Tom? In private, I'd prefer that you call me Corduven."

Back in the kitchen complex, Tom's sub-gamma-servitor status gave limited access to LineageNet, and he traced the arcs until one node was highlighted, its tricon slowly revolving.

Oracle Gérard d'Ovraison.

"Damn it," said Tom, then glanced around. No-one was listening.

A golden drone passed silently overhead as he shut down the display.

I like you, Corduven.

Tom closed his eyes, opened them.

Why did you have to be his brother?

21

NULAPEIRON AD 3405

There was no sound.

Early, seated in a balcony halfway up the high wall, Tom watched the riders practise. The groined ceilings were fifteen metres above polished marble floors, and silver lev-bikes hurtled along the halls, span into impossible turns, twisted upside down and came together in daredevil formations of four bikes, almost touching.

There was no audience, save some servitors on the flagstones below, and a cloud of microdrones which flitted out of sight as a lone lev-bike whipped past.

I could never do that.

Just leaning over the balcony's edge gave Tom vertigo. He sat back and adjusted the collar of his tunic: cream, slashed through with turquoise. Ugly, but expensive-looking.

"Selfish," Chef Keldur had said, while servitors bustled around him. "That's what Lord d'Ovraison is."

"Sir?" Tom raised an enquiring eyebrow, ignoring the warning look from Jak.

"It's his PenSextoMilDay tomorrow, and we don't even know his favourite dish." The Chef shook his head. "Visiting without his retinue. What's the world coming to?"

"I could, er, ask him tonight, if you like. At the races."

There was muted laughter from the other servitors. Driuvik murmured: "Awfully good of you, old chap." "Frightfully decent of you," someone else stage-whispered.

Chef Keldur glared.

"He asked me to accompany him." Tom swallowed.

"By name? You, in particular?"

Tom nodded.

"Well, why didn't you say so? Driuvik! Put that down, and order Corcorigan suitable clothing. Come on, boy! We don't have all day—"

There had been sidelong looks from the others, even Jak. Subtle adjustments of personal space, keeping their distance.

So? A lev-bike whipped past, perilously close. *Should isolation worry me?*

Down below, spectators were beginning to file into the spacious halls and galleries, while servitors and drones bore drinks and light pastries. Tom stood up, took the winding staircase down through the balcony floor, and slowly descended.

"Drink?"

Tom jerked back: a servitor had mistaken him for a freedman.

"No thanks."

Tom turned away before the servitor could say anything more, and searched the crowd for Lord d'Ovraison—for *Corduven*—or Lady Sylvana.

"We've brought in visiting specialists." Chef Keldur had waved an arm, indicating a group of young Zhongguo Ren, dressed identically in black satin suits. "A treat for his Lordship: they'll provide the luncheon."

Tom's association with Corduven had raised him in Chef Keldur's esteem. While they waited for Tom's clothing to arrive, Keldur talked to him.

"He's ordered Zhongguo Ren cuisine before?" Tom asked. But he had noticed Sous-Chef Bertil in the background, morosely observing, and guessed that intrahouse politics were also involved.

"Indeed, though—"

Wait.

"—he doesn't eat much." Keldur patted his own belly. "As for the dinner—Well, we'll wait till you've talked to him, shall we?"

I know her.

Porcelain-pale features, long hair reaching to her waist. One of the Zhongguo Ren.

"May I take a look?"

Keldur nodded, glad that Tom was taking an interest. "Go on."

The dishes were elaborate, the display as important as the taste. Most of the Zhongguo Ren were standing idle: these were just samples for Chef Keldur. Tomorrow, for a full-scale luncheon, everyone would be involved.

"Very nice," murmured Tom, moving closer to the young woman.

She gave a warning glance.

Lowering his voice: "Is Zhao-ji all right?"

A tiny nod.

"Do you see him much, Feng-ying?" Tom dredged her name up out of memory.

But she turned away then, an odd glint in her dark eyes, and Tom had no choice but to return to Chef Keldur's side.

"Congratulations, Tom." Corduven, dressed resplendently with a blue-gold cape thrown back over one shoulder, pointed for Tom to sit.

Side by side, on one of the balconies near the cathedral-high ceiling, they sat. Tom dared not look behind him: among the eight servants standing to attention were Jak and Driuvik.

"Yes, quite." From her seat on the other side of Corduven, Lady Sylvana leaned over and transfixed Tom with her smile. "Congratulations are certainly in order."

Tom swallowed. "I don't quite, er . . ."

"Consider this your official notification, then."

She sat back and nodded to Corduven.

"Ah, right," Corduven said. "You saved Lord Avernon's life, Tom."

"I—" Tom stopped.

He had merely raised the alarm. The Palace itself had dragged the young Lord to the salle d'armes, where Maestro da Silva had applied first aid until the drones arrived, followed by medic-servitors.

"—golden sash, old chap," Corduven was saying. "Just a symbol. But it's worth a thousand merit points."

One of Lady Sylvana's retinue, an auburn-haired young woman— something peculiar about her turquoise eyes, but Tom could not concentrate—handed something to her mistress.

A thousand merits?

Down below, the crowds were gathering. Was it their murmuring or the rush of Tom's blood in his ears that filled his hearing?

"Here you are." Corduven took the folded sash from Lady Sylvana and handed it to Tom. "Don't put it on now."

"Er, thank you."

Did he understand Corduven correctly? That he had been awarded a thousand merit points, along with this sash? He did not dare to ask.

Corduven presented Lady Sylvana with a small box, which unfolded to show the white metal paradox tricon Tom had seen earlier.

"What? Oh." She held it up. "An antinomy, cast in antimony." Her laughter was girlish, uninhibited. "That's very subtle, Cord."

Corduven turned towards Tom and winked.

Silver arrows whipping through the air.

"Sweet Fate," murmured Lady Sylvana. "I didn't know they could go that fast."

Earlier, she had joined in the applause as the bare-headed riders had bowed to dignitaries, who were seated on balconies. Then the young riders—some freedmen, some noble younger sons; one slender noblewoman—had pulled on their helmets and taken their mounts.

Twenty silver lev-bikes had risen as one into the air and hung there, quivering, until the start signal's golden beam had lanced through the air and they leaped forward.

Here, at the outer reaches of the Palace, the vast airy tunnels were natural stone, *sans* smart-tech. The lev-bikes whistled among gargoyle-spotted columns, twisted in and out of gallerias, soaring impossibly fast, and disappeared.

A tense silence overlaid the crowd: it would take about a minute to complete a circuit and reappear.

"Oh, for Fate's sake," said Sylvana.

Tom peered over Corduven's shoulder. The auburn-haired servitrix had given a crystal to her mistress; Sylvana's bracelet, reading by induction, was directly projecting a recipient-eyes-only display.

"We have to talk privately, Cord." She spoke in a very low voice. "In the corridor outside. Quickly."

Corduven stood, motioning Tom to remain.

"We'll be right back." A frown creased Corduven's taut-skinned forehead.

There was a back way from the balcony, and the two of them took it, oblivious to their servitors' hurried bows.

For a moment, Tom's eyes met Jak's, but Tom turned away, not wanting to get Jak in trouble.

Then Tom woke up.

He was in a medical ward: shattered ribs wreathing every breath with agony, his lower back a clenched mass of suffering. One eye was swollen shut, and swathes of skin had been torn from his pain-wired body.

22

NULAPEIRON AD 3405

"Retrograde amnesia," the voice was saying. "Not unusual in cases like this."

"Shouldn't have left him there, damn it." Corduven.

"You couldn't have known"—even now, with the ceiling a distant, swimming vision, he could recognize Sylvana's silver voice—"what the message was about."

"No, I—"

Everything went away.

Jak was sitting beside the bed the next time Tom awoke.

"How are you feeling?"

Tom's throat was dry. "OK . . . Better."

No!

Panic rushed through him and he raised his head, heart pounding, but the outline of both legs was there under the thin blue sheet, and he wiped sudden sweat from his forehead.

"You're all there." Jak smiled grimly. "As much as—Well, you know."

As much as before, yes.

"What about you?" Coming out of his own misery, Tom could see the translucent amber cast, filled with sparkling silver motes, which encased Jak's forearm.

"No problem." Jak brushed lank black hair from his eyes. "But Driuvik's dead."

"You've taken logotropic treatments before." Medic-servitor, white tunic. "That'll make this easier."

Holodisplays shifted and pulsed.

"I'm ready." Tom lay back.

Behind the medic, a junior officer of Lieutenant Milran's Palace Dragoons waited.

"Femtocytic infusion starting. And . . . go."

". . . Go, Erivan!" Hands waved in the air as the lead lev-bike flashed overhead. "Go!"

Tom leaned forwards in his balcony seat, everything else forgotten, as the next three riders flashed past in a tight group, the rest strung out behind.

Last lap.

A bald man down below called out: "Come on, Pitrov!" with hysteria in his voice. Tom wondered how much he had bet on the race's outcome.

Great circles of light leaped into being, and he saw her.

They were vertical rings, three of them hanging in space. Just for a moment, among the crowds, their white light illuminated Feng-ying's ivory-pale face, but then she was gone.

Tom stood up, searching.

But hundreds of people below were shouting encouragement and even noble spectators in other balconies were on their feet, clapping and cheering, as two lev-bikes whipped into sight, flying side by side.

They flashed through the rings—one strobing strontium-crimson, one copper-green—so close together that Tom could not tell the winner. Third: flashing orange.

The remaining lev-bikes were still hurtling to the finish as the first three slowed, dipped, and came back towards the rings. Teardrops of light streamed backwards from snub nose to rear: crimson on the winner, emerald for second place, orange for third.

Tom swallowed, and breathed. The riders must be insane, to fly at such speed, risking so much.

From the spectators below, a high jubilant cry: Pitrov had won.

As the presentation began, the three lead lev-bikes took up position.

At floor level, the crowds parted for a white-haired gentleman in ceremonial military uniform—mirrored breastplate, lev-bazookette hovering over each shoulder—who marched stiffly to a golden lev-disc, and stood to attention as it lifted him upwards.

"Field Marshal Belnikov," murmured someone.

Applause grew as three young women, with bejewelled torcs on velvet cushions, followed—robed in crimson, green and orange respectively—and each stood on a silver lev-disc.

He must have been mistaken.

But the discs revolved as they ascended, and just for a moment he saw her full-face: Feng-ying, clad in crimson and bearing the winner's torc.

Clapping and hooting echoed from the crowds below as the Field Marshal, from his golden disc, shook hands with the winning rider. Then he turned to the silver lev-disc behind him, held out a hand for the torc—

And stopped.

The Field Marshal crouched, raising an aged fist to activate his bazookettes, but too late. The young woman, Feng-ying, clasped her hands and bowed.

Tom tried to yell—

White light exploded.

"That's all?"

Cold tears tracked down Tom's cheeks. "I'm sorry."

"Are you—?" The medic stopped. The Dragoon officer's hand was on his shoulder.

"I think you've distressed your patient enough."

"If necessary I can—"

"No." The officer looked at Tom. "We won't trouble you again. Thank you."

"My Lady said I should check your needs have been taken care of."

"I'm . . . grateful for her concern."

Did I betray Feng-ying? I don't think so—

"The medic thinks you'll be out of here in a tenday."

—but I'm not sure what I said under trance.

"It was awful."

There was a kind of shiver in the servitrix's voice, and it dragged Tom out of his own concerns.

And Feng-ying's dead, anyway.

The servitrix was sitting by Tom's bed.

"Of course," he said. "You were there."

She had auburn hair, a pointed face and those turquoise eyes. This time, Tom could see what had half caught his attention at the race meeting: her left iris was a pupil-less turquoise disc, beautiful but nonfunctional.

"Yes." She swallowed; Tom noticed how slender her throat was. "My name's Arlanna, by the way. Arlanna U'Skarin."

"Tom Corcorigan."

He lay back for a moment, as the chamber seemed to keep shifting left, without ever moving: a kind of pulse effect.

"Shall I get a medic?"

"No, I'm—" He stopped at the cool feel of her palm on his forehead. "Just a dizzy spell, I think."

Arlanna took her hand away.

Silence, then:

"I—"

"There's—"

They started simultaneously, and stopped.

"There's no need to stay," said Tom, "if you don't want to."

"Well, all right." She began to rise.

"No, I didn't mean—" Tom bit his lip. "I'd appreciate the company."

Arlanna looked at him, then sat back down.

"It must have been worse for you," said Tom, after they had traded Palace gossip for a while. "I just saw a flash of light, and then I woke up in here."

Arlanna closed her eyes.

"It was awful"—her voice grew distant—"with the screaming, the blood. Clouds of choking dust." She shook her head, as though to wipe her memories away.

"Sorry. I shouldn't have—"

"That's all right." Arlanna sniffed. "Nobody's saying, but it was a suicide bomber. Must have been."

Tom looked away, not sure what his eyes might give away.

"Though I'd like to know," Arlanna continued, "how someone could get a microtak past the sensor web."

His right hand started to move, but he stopped himself. The talisman was still around his neck: he had already checked a dozen times.

You could coat a charge in nul-gel, he realized. *But that's offworld tech, isn't it?*

Offworld.

Not a concept Tom was used to: existence beyond Nulapeiron.

"Madness," he muttered.

"Bravery."

Startled, Tom looked at Arlanna, but her expression shut down, as though she had said too much.

Referring to the suicide bomber? To Feng-ying?

Tom cleared his throat, and returned the conversation to safer ground. "You know what I'd really like?"

"Anything." Arlanna forced a bright smile. "That's what her Ladyship said."

"Can I purchase an infotablet?"

"I . . . Yes, I should think so. You have a thousand merit points, after all."

Tom sat further upright in the bed. "That's nice," he said. "Though I don't really know what that implies."

She laughed.

"You've never had any merits, and now you've got a thousand. Good start, I'd say."

"What do you spend your merit points on?" He guessed that she earned some: there was something capable and determined about her.

"You can spend them on clothes, fragrances . . ."

"But you don't."

"I tend more towards holodramas, epics."

Tom looked at her carefully. "What about eduthreads or logotropes?"

"They're available. And you can earn more merit points from the house AIs," she said, "if you take exams at each module's end."

"Positive feedback."

"That's right."

But Tom detected the bitter undertone in her voice. "Where's the problem?"

"Amassing enough points to begin with. Initial momentum." She looked away. "With a thousand points . . ."

There was a stillness in the chamber.

"I don't know my way around the system," Tom said. "Can I sign points over to you, using them by proxy?"

"I . . . suppose so."

"We could start by buying two infotablets. One each."

She looked at him for a long moment. "Are you serious?"

"Definitely."

"Well then. Two infotablets. And register for aleph-track prepthreads?"

"Whatever you say."

A smile slowly grew across her pointed face. "That's a deal, then."

23

TERRA AD 2122

<<Karyn's Tale>>

[4]

In her dream, the other girls made her laugh—deliberately, of course—just as Sister Mary Joseph was walking past. Karyn flinched as the pale gaze was fastened on her.

She braced herself for the expected blow, but it never came: instead, the darkness.

No candles in the nightbound chapel.

Kneel and pray.

Burning pain in her knees.

Pray for forgiveness for all your wickedness, girl.

Shivering tension in her torso. Not daring to fall asleep.

Will the Good Lord send his angel for you tonight?

How could you die? How could you suddenly . . . not exist?

Better pray, girl . . .

Tears trickled coldly down her cheeks.

Creaking.

Soft, strange whispers.

Could it be only wooden benches settling in the dropping temperature? Faint wind among draughty stonework? If only that were all! If only she could close her eyes and sleep! But in the darkness, all around, unseen angels and waiting demons crouched.

"*No!*"

She pushed up, warding off the darkness.

"*Bastards!*" She twisted, struggling, with the dark weight upon her. "*Get off me!*"

She flung the cover back and rolled from the bed.

Combat stance: bolt upright, heart pounding, feeling dreadful.

Through the study-bedroom window, pale amber sunlight streamed into the clean, sparse room.

The floor was warm beneath her bare feet. Karyn raised an arm and sniffed: not good. Scratchy with old sweat, still wearing yesterday's jumpsuit.

She had no recollection of coming back here last night.

"Dart."

Her throat felt thick. She took herself to the bathroom, spat into the sink, stripped off and staggered into the shower.

Ten minutes later, blasted awake—clean but unsteady—she tapped a tabletop terminal into life.

"Sal."

An elegant, mustachioed, top-hatted man's head appeared. He doffed the hat with a disembodied white-gloved hand.

"Two things, Sal." Karyn addressed her NetAgent, Sal O'Mander, without looking at its image. "One: find the other Pilot Candidate on campus, contact his agent, arrange lunch. Two: ah, God—"

The NetAgent waited while Karyn rubbed her eyes.

"Ah . . ." The other thing: the mad concept at the back of her mind these last few weeks. Why not go for it? "Summarize missing-vessels info, scan for patterns, and . . . any mention of mu-space lifeforms."

The image winked out.

Official briefings were just that: brief. But the attrition rate on maiden voyages was rising, and her own first excursion into mu-space could be just six months away.

Lifeforms. No-one was considering the possibility. Not publicly.

"Sal?"

"Yes, ma'am?" A ghostly outline; Sal's image did not quite reappear.

"The Pilot Candidate—"

"Pilot Candidate David Mulligan, a.k.a. Dart Mulligan. Room twelve-seventeen, dome nine. Completing second phase of—"

"Enough."

"By the way, you're due to give your first lecture in quantum chaos at ten hundred hours, VL Institute, room—"

"I remember. Later, Sal."

The hint of a bow, and the image faded once more.

"Sensei's son." Taller than his father; but he had inherited Mike Mulligan's muscular strength and easy focus.

Karyn stared out across the campus, squinting at the brightness.

"Bloody hell."

<<MODULE ENDS>>

24

NULAPEIRON AD 3405

For freedom's cave, by open space,
Is strange attraction, pure love/hate:
That dreamt-of Chaos which our race
Subsumed within hardcoded Fate.

"And something-something-something," Tom murmured to himself. "Till Destiny is wild once more/And all the—"

There was a chime, and he froze the display.

"It's me." Arlanna's voice.

"Come in."

He closed down the verse. Not so much that he minded Arlanna's seeing it, but she might notice the way openness and freedom recurred in his poetry.

Sometimes, now that he had an infotablet once more, he would replay the opened modules of Karyn's Tale just so he could freeze an image, rotate and magnify, and—fighting down vertiginous nausea—stare at a landscape beneath a wide blue sky.

The talisman itself was almost impossible to open, being encoded for a left-handed control gesture; the requisite contortions gave Tom finger cramps.

"I can't do this." Arlanna almost threw her infoshard against the black tabletop.

They were in Tom's private quarters. The door membrane, for propriety's sake, grew transparent: outside, in the dorm's central chamber, Jak and the others were eating.

"What's up, Arlanna?"

"It's the very first problem in the module. Just look at it."

A sorites lattice: fifty-three triconic syllogisms linked by a network of colour-coded arcs.

"You've used concentric-context calculus before?" Tom rotated the display, pointed to a node; it unfurled into a rainbow-hued tesseract. "For functional in-drilling?"

"Not really." Arlanna's left eye was like a jewel, turquoise flecked with amber/orange; its lack of expression made her good eye harder to read.

"Let me show you what the Captain taught me . . ."

Funny that the Ragged School's methods should prove useful up here in the Primum Stratum.

"Do you want to postpone this? Your friends are still at supper."

"I know." Tom shook his head. "I'm not hungry."

"I noticed you've been losing weight."

An echoing chorus of warlike cries reverberated along the corridor. Surprised, Tom stopped, nearly tipping the heavy tray.

"*Heee!*"

The pearly walls glowed with evening rose, and the corridor was deserted, save for Tom.

"*Arrêtez!*"

Maestro da Silva's voice, for sure.

Still no clash of blades.

"Pair up!"

Heart beating faster, though he could not have said why, Tom hurried to the archway and looked inside the salle d'armes.

Fifty warriors launched themselves into the air, stabbed flying kicks in Tom's direction—"*Eee!*"—and landed lightly, throwing follow-up punches.

Destiny!

Tom, sitting on a low bench just inside the archway, was riveted by the spectacle.

White/black baggy jumpsuits, lean figures throwing elbow-strikes and punches, knee-strikes and kicks, against imaginary opponents.

"Pair up again." Maestro da Silva's voice cut through the chamber's charged atmosphere.

The tray, beside Tom on the bench, was quite forgotten.

"Faster."

In prearranged but earnest attacks, half of the students threw long, straight punches which their opponents intercepted, turned into and redirected: the attackers flipped over their opponents' hips and landed flat on their backs.

"Faster!"

Afterwards, Maestro da Silva watched the last of his sweat-soaked students leave, then came over to Tom.

"I'm sorry to have kept you."

"I shouldn't have stayed to watch, Maestro."

"But if anyone asks, tell them I kept you until this time."

Tom gave a short bow. Embarrassed and feeling shaky, he backed away to the exit.

"Mm, looks good." Maestro da Silva checked the tray's contents, then looked back up at Tom. "Yes?"

"May I ask . . . What was that you were teaching, Maestro? Not fencing."

"What's in a name?" The Maestro shrugged. "We call it phi2dao, or flow/focus."

"But the students—"

"—Aren't noble-born. Quite." The Maestro took a sip of juice. "It's a little rough for the gentry."

Tom looked back into the still-electric atmosphere of the empty salle d'armes, swallowed, then asked: "Can just anyone learn the art, Maestro?"

Thump. Mapping out his failures: he was awful, clumsy, the worst student by far.

"Tuck your head in, Corcorigan." Brunelow, an assistant instructor, was running the beginners through their drills.

Pain lanced through Tom's neck.

"Try again."

Slowly he rolled forwards through a breakfall and lay on the cushioned floor, breath sawing in his lungs.

"Once more."

Grappling: he desperately tried to hook his opponent's ankle, but again and again Tom found himself airborne, ceiling passing by in a dizzying blur, then he crunched into the mat.

"Slowly . . ."

Striking: blocking too late. Unable to raise his knee to the side, Tom's circling kick was slow, awkward, no higher than his partner's kneecap; in return, his partner's instep rapped neatly against Tom's temple.

Where did that come from?

The training session lasted for ever.

Abdominal exercises, finally. Here, his missing arm was not a handicap, but he could not keep up with the others.

Tom collapsed, knowing he could do no more.

"Stand up." Unable to see through stinging sweat and fluorescent vision flashes, he hauled himself to his feet. Everyone was coming to attention.

"And breathe . . ."

The class cooled down, and bowed in unison.

Staggering towards the exit, every step a nightmare.

"Ah, Tom."

Hardly able to stand, Tom nevertheless turned, breathing open-mouthed, and bobbed his head in an abbreviated bow.

"Did you enjoy your first lesson?"

Heart racing, stomach sickened, coated with slick sweat and beyond exhaustion, knowing he was truly useless at this art, Tom squinted through the haze.

"I loved it, Maestro."

25

NULAPEIRON AD 3406–3408

Flow/focus training: every D'vaday, Ped'day and Shyed'mday, Tom turned up at the salle d'armes. After thirty tendays, he could at least perform a breakfall.

Eduthreads and logotropic studies: the house AIs furnished the training shells; Tom sped through them, gaining merit points for each exam he passed.

But Tom could load no new modules of Karyn's Tale. Following the microtak explosion, Lieutenant Milran's Dragoons, advised by Jacks, upgraded the sensor webs throughout the Palace; Tom dared not risk detection of the characteristic emissions.

By the year's end, Arlanna's intellectual explorations had begun to diverge from Tom's, as she entered the administration and fine-arts threads more deeply. Lady Sylvana promoted her from gamma-plus to beta-class servitrix. (Older servitrices resented Arlanna's unexpected new responsibilities; she responded by working harder than any of them.)

Tom's duties remained much the same.

Second year. A dozen new servitors and servitrices—part of that year's reassignment—joined Maestro da Silva's class. They were already fit and strong: Tom (with a full SY head start) could just about keep up.

His studies led him to femtopology, fractal calculus, epic theory (strategic/historical, not literary), paradoxicology and some life sciences: symbiology, cognitive algebra and emergenics.

Third year.

He began to run. Allowed to wander as far as the Palace's outer core, he found a long, deserted gallery, quite disused, which became his running-route. The first time, he jogged, uneven-paced, until he had passed twenty shadowed archways—they occurred regularly enough to be used as distance markers—and ran faster on the way back. He stopped once, to throw up—apologizing to the Palace—then shuffled back home.

The next night, he completed the route without mishap.

By Darkday's Eve, when Corduven and Sylvana formally announced their engagement, Tom was running eight klicks every evening, in addition to his flow/focus sessions.

Returning to his quarters after that particular run, he noticed a peculiar expression on a freedman's face. Tom thought about it, stripping off his soaked tunic and running-tights in his room, then realized: it was *envy*.

Waving a control gesture, he caused a section of black wall to turn mirror-bright. The reflected Tom Corcorigan was lean and spare: all sinew and muscles. Hair a shade too long. His face had a distance-athlete's gauntness; his waist was narrow.

But . . . Envy? With a missing arm?

The reflection's smile was grim.

He was eighteen Standard Years old.

Jak, in a curiously gentle tone, said: "Have you heard? Lady Sylvana and Lord d'Ovraison are engaged."

"I . . . didn't know."

What? Did I expect her to be mine?

Next night, the Darkday Festival was in full swing: everywhere, wallshimmer was muted, fluorofungus covered with heavywrap, glow-clusters turned down low. After late duty, Tom had two free hours, and wander-access to the two strata below, though no farther than the Palace boundaries, projected downwards. His destination was the Caverna del'Amori, in Tertium.

"A nice massage, sir?"

Shaking his head, he wandered past the candlelit alcoves: a beguiling redhead (no!) in diaphanous green; a bulky woman sitting with her legs splayed (no other advertisement necessary); a dancing, slender blonde (motile tattoos rippling suggestively).

"Hi. I'm Lora."

And he let her take his hand and lead him into a shadowed nook. The curtain she pulled across was threadbare, spotted with unidentifiable stains.

"A hundred mils," she said, and accepted the cred-sliver.

He ran, feet pounding.

Only a dancer. The refrain hammered through his nerves as he forced the pace. *Mother! You were only a dancer, weren't you?*

The girl, Lora.

Tunnel-bat.

Fumbling, tugging at his clothes . . . He had almost gone through with it. But the simple stuffed-toy bat, lying on the cracked shelf, stopped him: a reminder of home, her home; and he had looked at her closely and seen the bruises beneath her heavy make-up.

"Take the money back, then," she said.

A ploy? He left without knowing whether she meant it.

Run.

The gallery's shadows grew deeper: he was farther from the Palace core than he had ever been before, but still he ran.

Faster.

He noticed it first as a chill draught; but as he ran, it increased until he was running into a wind which moaned among the darkened archways.

Faster!

The vertical shaft was huge.

He ran all the way to the low balustrade and stopped, then stretched lightly, catching his breath. It was a horizontal slit, man-high, opening onto a kilometre-wide chasm. Leaning over, he looked upwards—a strange, dizzying sensation: in the high shadows, a rainbow ripple of membrane—then down.

Movement.

It took him a couple of seconds to register what he was seeing. Half a dozen spots of bright primary colours. But they were a long way below, on the shaft's curved wall, moving slowly.

People, climbing.

Laughter drifted up. Climbing for pleasure? Vertigo clutched at him, and he pulled back from the balustrade.

Halfway back, running easily despite the distance, Tom stopped. To his left, a colonnade overlooked a sunken forum, no longer in use.

Could I . . . ?

He thought through the technique, then tried it out.

Foothold, foothold, then *let go* with his one hand and boost upwards, *catch it*, hooking his fingers into the next hold.

He fell off twenty times, but eventually he climbed perhaps four metres up the column, tried to rest by hugging the stone—arm shaking with fatigue—and painfully descended.

Slowly, he ran back to his quarters.

A woman was waiting for him: legs crossed elegantly, back rigid. Black-skinned, black-haired, with striking white streaks.

"Your chronodynamics exam showed a nicety of understanding," she said without preamble. "Bilking-antisymmetries are contextually extensible, wouldn't you say?"

"I, er, beg your pardon?"

Drenched with sweat, fatigue-sore.

"The basis of our culture, don't you think? Time trajectories reflected in political structures?"

"Um, yes." Tom swallowed drily. "I agree."

He needed fluid replenishment, electrolytes, some glucose in his blood before his brain could function at this level.

"Perhaps the AIs have overestimated you, Master Corcorigan." She stood easily. "I hope not. Report to my studio tomorrow at oh-seven-hundred."

"Yes, ma'am. Where—?"

"You'll address me as Mistress eh'Nalephi. Your tuition starts with kenning-matrices: be ready."

She left with a rustle of dark silks.

Tuition?

Slowly he pulled the sweat-soaked tunic from his body, then let it drop. "Sorry," he murmured, distracted, as the black floor flowed, dragging the discarded garment towards the clean-gel.

A personal tutor?

26

NULAPEIRON AD 3409

"So? What do they need?" asked Tom.

"I don't know." Jak fingered the wispy moustache he had been trying to grow for the last six tendays. "You're to go to the Sorites School, is all I know."

"All right."

"At least you'll probably know what they're talking about."

"If they speak slowly enough." Tom smiled, slyly.

"Don't give me that." Jak checked his display again. "Seminar-suite epsilon. Don't go showing them up, hear?"

Black glass pyramids. Twelve dodecahedral buildings, rippling with gold and emerald, slowly changing shape in unison: growing taller, extending towers, extruding annexes. Later, they would shrink in size, and begin a different growth pattern. What would it be like inside them?

I've never been so far from the Palace.

The cavern was enormous, so that the architecture looked like buildings beneath a dark open sky, and it made Tom queasy. The Sorites School, his destination, was a simple crimson cube, stellated with black, slowly revolving.

"—drunk again last night?"

Tom stood by a row of statues—famous Lords and Ladies wearing scholarly frowns—while a group of red-caped young men and women passed him, heading for the school.

"I certainly was . . ."

He waited until their voices faded with distance.

Hung-over. *Don't you know how lucky you are?*

Tom shook his head, then followed.

"Ah, there you are." Long, patrician nose, white hair pulled back into a queue.

"Sir?"

The room was bare: ivory walls, float-pad seats, a tiny infotablet hovering beside each one. Only the black-robed Lord was there, making adjustments to a master tablet floating at the front.

"The seminar's starting soon."

Seating for fifteen. Tom wondered what it would be like: for half a year now, he had been attending Mistress eh'Nalephi's exacting one-to-one tutorials.

"What can I do to help, sir?"

"None of that 'sir' stuff, laddie. We're all scholars here."

Tom looked around. By one wall, flagons of fruit juice and daistral were standing on a table.

"Shall I serve the . . . ?"

"Oh, no." The Lord raised one white eyebrow. "We need your brain, laddie: not your brawn."

"I—" Tom's back straightened. "That's interesting."

"I'm Velond. No, don't bow—That's better." Lord Velond: cousin to Lady Darinia, the High Lady of this demesne, and a Lord Minor in his own right. "My niece informed me, some time ago, of the puzzle known as Tom's paradox."

A flush rose in Tom's cheeks. "A veridical paradox, sir, as you know."

He meant, it was a puzzle only to a child who did not know how an infinite series might converge.

"She was five SY old. To her, it was a real antinomy."

Tom inclined his head. "That was why I chose that example."

"Mm." Lord Velond's stare was penetrating. "And an example of true antinomy?"

"This statement is a lie." Tom glanced at the nearest infotablet, then decided he could elaborate without its help. "Though that becomes veridical, if you allow meta-contextual recursion."

"Ah." An odd smile creased Lord Velond's long face. "And an example we can't dispose of so easily?"

"I don't know." Tom frowned. "But the nature of time would be involved, I'm sure . . . No, that's too difficult for now."

Turning to the infotablet, Tom opened up a display and wrote a tricon by gesture: *This statement is a paradox.* He made ten copies of the tricon, then linked each "this statement" identifier to the next tricon by two relations: one labelled "is true," the other labelled "is false."

Finally, he linked the identifier of the last tricon to the verb-attribute of the first, completing a strange loop.

"Not in our universe," murmured Lord Velond. "But an interesting way of looking at it."

What about a universe whose dimensions are fractal?

Tom's skin crawled. The thought had popped out of nowhere. Yet, to someone who knew that Pilots really existed, it was not ridiculous.

The possibilities . . .

If you could close off the infinite series, perhaps Gödel's theorem became invalid: allowing logic to be complete, so that every true statement was derivable from axioms—

But the others were arriving. Red capes were tossed over shoulders as they sat: scholars-designate, Lords and Ladies of Tom's age, making themselves comfortable, powering up the floating infotablets.

Lord Velond spoke quietly. "Tom, I'd like you to sit in on this."

I don't belong here.

A migraine pounded over Tom's left eye as he sat miserably in the front row. He wanted to make notes of everything Lord Velond was saying, but the other holodisplays around him remained still. Veridical qualification in self-referential representations was obviously child's play to scholars-designate.

"And how," asked Lord Velond, "may we contextually analyse paradox classes?"

Silence.

What does the question mean?

Sickened, Tom wished he could get up and leave without attracting attention. He looked around at the others—and saw puzzled frowns, carefully blank expressions.

But there were only three kinds of paradox: falsifiable, veridical and antinomy. Mistakes, misunderstandings and the real thing. Any other distinctions must be terminology.

"Er . . ."

"Yes, Corcorigan?"

"Well, if we start with the most difficult set . . ." Tom began to draw a branching logic-tree, as *This statement is a paradox* spread through successive versions of truth and falsehood. "The instantiations can be labelled with indices, i and j, alongside a loop formula . . ."

At some point Tom became aware of a latecomer joining the group, but he pressed on with his discourse until Lord Velond called a halt.

"Interesting exposition," he said. "Comments, anyone?"

No-one spoke.

Then a babble of voices broke as they questioned Tom's model, and he froze, throat paralysed, until a female voice spoke up: "But can't we equate Tom's indices to metarelations? Then it becomes analogous to the standard method, doesn't it?"

"No, of course not—"

But that lone supporting voice was all that Tom needed. Guessing what they meant by "standard method," he proceeded to show that his notation was shorthand for the same thing.

"What's more . . ." Inspired, he dreamed up examples whose

veridical status was immediately revealed in his model, while the other approach took a dozen calculations to produce the same result. There was a chorus of objections—

"Enough." The authority of Lord Velond's voice reduced the room to silence.

It was only then that Tom realized who had spoken up for him: Lady Sylvana, sitting at the rear of the group.

"That opens up some interesting possibilities," Lord Velond continued. "Let's explore them."

Using Tom's exposition as a starting-point, Lord Velond launched into dazzling realms of logical exploration—almost dancing on his toes, as holodisplays blossomed around him, often flaring with random bursts of colour as he gesticulated excitedly, forgetting to turn off gesture mode.

Tom watched in awe, oblivious to the scholars-designate except when Lord Velond said: "So it is intuitively obvious that—" and there were sniggers from the back row and an audible groan from one young Lord.

How can one man know so much? Tom wondered, as Lord Velond continued.

He felt a sudden lurch as Lord Velond brought his lecture to an end. Two hours had passed.

"Not bad, Tom." Lady Sylvana smiled. "See you tomorrow."

As Tom was leaving, Lord Velond said: "We'll be working you hard, Tom. Very hard."

Fate, thought Tom as he stepped through the membrane. *I hope so.*

Shyed'mday was the next rest day. Sleeve rolled up, Tom scrubbed out a processor-oven which refused to self-clean, wondering where his fellow students might be: partying at the Outer Courts, racing arachnargoi in Cavernae Brachialae.

After his duties, his private tutorial with Mistress eh'Nalephi, his training-session at the salle d'armes . . . he reviewed the tenday's studies, and prepared for the next.

It became a pattern—of hard self-discipline which no-one ever saw—with tangible results: soon only Lord Velond himself could withstand Tom's ferocious attacks on the consensual view of matters logosophic.

"For most of us," remarked Lady Sylvana after one gruelling seminar, "logodiscipline is a world-view, maybe even therapy."

"I hadn't thought of it that way."

"For you, though"—she stared at Tom intently—"logosophy is a weapon."

The next day, she was missing from the group.

Disturbed, for no reason he could think of, Tom was more blunt than usual in his presentation.

"I don't see—" began an intense, pale youth: Viscount Humphrey.

"By symmetry," said Tom, dispensing with an hour's worth of tedious calculations, "it's obvious that—"

He ignored the sniggers as he drew a dozen meta-related sorites together in one triconic knot.

"—as inevitable as an Oracle's predictions," he finished. "Any questions?"

Some of the scholars-designate looked stunned or angry. One or two were either bored—having given up trying to follow the argument—or quizzically amused.

"Could you—" Viscount Humphrey coughed politely. "No, that's all right. I'll read my download later."

Lord Velond was impassive.

"Do you have truecast access?" Tom addressed the room in general.

An angry murmur rippled through the group. Having a jumped-up servitor in the group was bad enough: but to discuss matters of noble interest—

"Truecasts are really artists' impressions—correct me if I'm wrong—of future events, based on Oracles' perceptions of their personal futures. OK so far?"

A vicious silence.

"So my argument is as inevitable as an Oracle's truecast . . . unless the Oracle lies."

Even Lord Velond's face hardened.

"I'm treating this as a logical exercise," Tom continued. "But there's an antinomy here . . . for another day, I think. Lord Velond?" He bowed in the Lord's direction. "My apologies, everyone. I got a little carried away today."

Then someone clapped.

Suddenly, the whole group was applauding, and Tom, stunned, let the sound wash over him.

Arlanna was waiting for him at his quarters.

"I need your help, Tom," she said. "Actually, Lady Sylvana suggested it."

"She wasn't at the Sorites School today."

"I know." Turquoise eyes unreadable. "She was trying on bridal gowns."

The ground seemed to fall away beneath Tom's feet; Arlanna's voice came from some distant place.

"You and I," she added, "are in charge of the wedding ceremony."

27

NULAPEIRON AD 3409

There was one good point: working on the wedding organization—
Sylvana's wedding, Fate damn it—meant that he gained access-control
codes for the sensor web. In his room, Tom twisted open his stallion
talisman and downloaded a new module for the first time in nearly
four Standard Years, and solved the opening paradox.

He had no chance to execute the storyline; details of the marriage
plans took up all his time.

"Shantzu Province, Byelasavyetski Commissariat, a dozen Lords-
Meilleurs-sans-Demesne . . ." Arlanna's fingertip traced the gantt-lat-
tice. "That's besides the contiguous surrounding demesnes."

"And a Commissario Proconsul is the equivalent rank?" Tom
looked up from his display.

"Fate knows. I hope so." She sighed and leaned back, massaging
her forehead above the good eye.

"How many settlers do you think there were?" Tom minimized his
displays to a string of shining beads suspended in mid-air. "Originally,
I mean: twelve centuries ago."

"Oh, I don't know." Arlanna rubbed her forehead again. "The current world population is ten billion."

"It is? I didn't know that."

"If you were alpha-class," she began, smiling.

"An urchin like me? I don't think so. But the colonization logistics . . . For that matter, isn't it strange how the multiculture's been so
stable?"

"Oracles, though there are only five thousand of them." Her

expression grew serious. "They're the real basis for—" She turned away, and bit her lip.

"What's wrong, Arlanna?" He could only see her jewel-like left eye: turquoise, amber-flecked, but expressionless.

"You don't—The day of the explosion, remember that? Remember how Lady Sylvana and Lord d'Ovraison hurried out, away from the balcony?"

"Uh, yeah. Yes, I remember. You'd just handed Syl—Lady Sylvana—a message."

"It was from an Oracle." She took in a deep breath, then slowly let it out. "It said: '*While you are reading this, a disaster has occurred. My apologies*—' There was more, but I didn't get to read the rest."

Tom stared at her.

Not a message from just any Oracle, I'll bet.

And he thought, as often before, that it had been worse for Arlanna: while he had been knocked unconscious by the explosion's percussive wave, she, at the balcony's rear and shielded by a buttress, had dealt with the aftermath.

But he was not going to discuss treason with Arlanna. Why would she broach this subject the day after he had mentioned truecasts in the Sorites School?

Instead, he said: "So what about this seating plan?" Dredging up a display, he drilled in with a fingertip. "A minimax co-ordinate in a sixty-dimensional phase-space. Just to determine where a bunch of people are going to sit . . ."

Arlanna remained silent for a moment. "You could request a transfer, Tom," she then said quietly, "to other duties. They'll probably allow it."

"There's nothing too onerous about this, really." Tom forced good cheer into his voice. "Do you fancy a walk around Aleph Hall?"

They were laughing by the time they reached the main doors. Behind them, the wide corridor glistened white, with rippling hints of pink and green.

"Can you believe those old guys?" Arlanna shook her head.

Shoulders hunched, two white-haired servitors had hurried past them, muttering: "There were none of these freeflow panels in eighty-nine," and, "I've walked this tunnel every year since Lord Rilker's accession, and we always used to . . ."

"Since Lady Darinia's predecessor took power." Tom looked back, but the two old men had gone. "Thirty years, walking up and down the same length of corridor, working with the same bureaucracy—"

"Wait a minute." Arlanna stopped. "Didn't we just spend ten hours devising a seating plan?"

"That's different."

"How?"

"Er . . ."

There were two dark-uniformed Dragoons at the main doors. "I know you're in charge of the seating," one of them said before Arlanna or Tom could speak, "but we can't let you in. Lieutenant Milran's orders."

Arlanna started to look annoyed, but Tom thought diplomacy might be in order: "Makes sense. We hadn't really thought about security."

"He'll be here himself in an hour."

"I'll wait." Arlanna had regained her normal composure.

"The kitchens are beckoning me," said Tom.

"Wait a minute." Arlanna drew him aside. "You're really OK about the . . . ceremony, and everything?"

"Of course." Tom spoke lightly. "Why shouldn't I be?"

"It's just that . . . Talefryn Tunnel, there, is where they're going to start from. Their honeymoon grand tour. I hear they need extra—"

Tom shook his head.

"Sorry." He turned away. "I must be getting back."

"Would you like company, sir?" The woman's face was creased with the pressures of a life Tom could not imagine. "We have nice girls waiting for you."

He shook his head and walked on, wondering what he was doing back in the Caverna del'Amori. Behind him, the woman was making coarsely worded invitations to a pair of off-duty labourers.

Should have dressed down, he thought, *if I wanted to blend in.*

"Hey, honey."

Tom held up his hand. "There used to be a woman called Lora—"

"Nothing wrong with me, is there?" But her eyes had shifted to the left. Tom nodded abruptly and headed for the alcove she had not quite looked at.

"Hello?"

The hanging was half-open, and he leaned inside.

White, glistening. It covered her face: wet, weeping fungus. The thing on the cot was skeletal, all flesh sunken in, cheekbones like razor-sharp protrusions.

A smile: an awful parody of invitation.

"Sorry," he muttered, and pulled back.

He walked away, shaking inside.

A rack of edged weapons: redmetal poignard, titanium chainflick, white ceramic darts and throwblades. Over the display a crude holo hung:

*** SeRiouS bRowserZ onLY ***

A stuffed narl-serpent, fangs agape, reared stiffly in a jar fitted to the rack.

This was Tertium, Fate-knew-how-many strata above the stratum of Tom's childhood, but this market was sleazier than any Tom had visited. The chamber was low-ceilinged, lit by randomly floating crimson glowclusters; the marketgoers moved heads-down, not talking, many of them with hoods drawn to hide their features.

Very pleasant.

Shaking his head, Tom started to move on, then stopped. The semiliterate holo was cast by an ancient laser, pulsing through translucent smoky ceramic on which arcs had been hand-carved: by knife-point, it seemed.

That's clever. Working out the interference pattern and drawing it directly.

Perhaps there was more to this than shabby first appearances. Behind the weapons display, a black velvet tent had been directed, closed to public view, and—apparently deep inside it—a virtual holo showed a tiny scarlet tricon:

*** KILWARE ASSOCIATES ***

He stepped inside the darkened tent.

"Worried about vendetta, my Lord?" The voice was high, genderless; the speaker was dark-robed, sitting in shadows.

"I'm not a Lord."

"But a gentleman. Still. What's the one factor that determines a weapon's suitability for a given occasion?"

Wary, Tom said nothing.

"Detectability."

"Er, OK."

"Some environments disallow energy weapons, or disable smart-tech with microwave bursts. But an edged blade may always be used to settle a gentleman's quarrel, provided it conforms to *Les Accords d'Honneur*."

Tom shook his head. "I'm not really—"

"But there's a level that deepscan can't go beyond. Implanted pseudatoms and other femtotech: no-one can nondestructively seek them out."

Scared of the direction this was taking, Tom said: "You're talking about mindware."

A clucking sound. "Perhaps, perhaps."

Tom turned away.

"We'll see you again, sir."

Tom had read Lord Pelishar's speculations on attotwist geodesics in the original Mardu, and enjoyed Arlanna's historic Laksheesh holodramas with translation disabled. He had smatterings of Zardais and Valraig. These were languages of regions passed through by the grand tour.

I would be an asset, to accompany them on their honeymoon.

"Loop, please," he said to his empty room.

A small loop appeared on the ceiling. On tiptoe, Tom hooked his little finger through the loop and pulled himself up—a one-finger chin-up—five times. He repeated the process for each finger, then did a last set with a full grip, then switched to one-hand press-ups—*the only kind I'll ever do*—for five sets of twenty.

Tomorrow night he would run to the big vertical shaft and clamber around on its walls for a while. But tonight—

"I'd like to run without going outside."

Laminar flow swept the black floor endlessly away beneath his feet as he began to run on the spot.

He gestured the infotablet into voice mode.

"Activate."

28

TERRA AD 2122

<<Karyn's Tale>>

[5]

//insert

{commentary.provenance = $\pi\sigma3\varsigma989$/Petra deVries/personal .journal/ KMcN}

   {   [[Critical event: turbulence-net intensifying]]
      [[P(phase-transition) = .979]]
      [[Recursion level = 10 exp 32]]

Rivulets of energy. The seed point: an insertion from another continuum, forced into a sea of golden light, studded with black spongiform stars. As the intruder's structure dissipates, the native event-pattern becomes detectable at higher and lower levels, spreading in both senses: expanding outwards, while growing inwardly more complex. Whorls and loops and spirals tighten as the pattern's growth accelerates.

Replication.

In its own universe, there is energy to prolong the pattern's growth. There is a correlation between shifting structures and the sources which might feed them. Selection acts within the pattern. Dendrimers branch endlessly, seeking sources and avoiding sinks.

Perception. Tropism.

It falters at first against antithetical labyrinths, against destructive interference from incompatible patterns. But slowly, slowly, it learns coping

strategies. One by one, defensive patterns fall before its questing tendrils and are
absorbed by the growing whole.

No self-awareness.

Not yet.}

end-insert//

The refectory was noisy, the clamour of hundreds of feeding students bouncing back from its crystalline domed ceiling, ribbed with soaring spars of pine and steel.

"I can hardly hear myself think!" Karyn raised her voice hoarsely above the din.

"Sorry?" Dart grinned. "Can't hear you, it's so noisy!"

"Funny, funny."

She looked at the black lightning-flash decal on his cheekbone. At school, some of her friends had been suspended for getting A-Life tattoos, and the deletion motes had inevitably left scarring. It had put Karyn off cutaneous decorations—but on Dart, it looked attractive.

Sensei's son.

"Listen," she began. "Do you—?"

Overhead, a bright macaw flew, screeching, then wheeled back and came to a fluttering landing on its owner's padded shoulder. The young man held up food for it, as sunlight glinted on his silver visor.

"For God's sake," Karyn muttered. "People have to eat in here."

Maybe a fifth of the students were from the VL Institute—the ones with visors and symbiont animal companions, or with experimental photoarrays where their eyes should have been—while the rest were students and a few faculty members from the main UTech campus.

"The Via Lucis Institute is right by the physics dome," said Dart.

"Yeah." Karyn stabbed at her salad with a fork. "And whose idea was it to meet in here?"

Dart shrugged his wide shoulders.

The macaw screeched loudly. At the same table sat a young-looking girl with a macaque monkey chattering on her shoulder, and an older man beside whom a black furry animal crouched—either a very large dog or, improbably, a small bear.

"Jesus Christ!" Karyn slowly lowered her fork. "That's why you brought me here, isn't it?"

Dart looked away, his ugly/sexy face momentarily hard.

"Another two weeks," he said, "and they take out my eyes."

Later, as they walked across the green campus, she slipped her hand into his. It seemed the most natural thing in the world; at the same time, she felt enervated, and warm all over.

"What's it like?" she asked, as they stopped beside a silver birch.

They sat down together on the grass.

"Almost normal." Dart tucked his knees up and clasped them. "Everything looks a little flat, a little grey, you know? But the viral insertion was only three days ago."

"Another few days," said Karyn, "and perspectives will start shifting."

"Yeah." Then he looked at her and grinned. His face was very close to hers. "But you'll still look beautiful, babe."

<<MODULE ENDS>>

29

NULAPEIRON AD 3410

It was a magical start to the new year. A noble wedding.

Aleph Hall was immense: a huge spherical interior, punctuated by a lucid crystalline floor low down, closer to the bottom than to the equator. The walls were lined with silver facets, transforming the hall from globe to high-order polyhedron.

On the flat crystalline floor, white tiers of ceramic seating were sufficient to hold two thousand guests, with much space to spare: wide aisles, and a large open area surrounding the monocrystal altar.

By the Lords' standards, it was a quiet affair.

"We do solemnly conjoin our lifepaths in parallel . . ." Corduven and Lady Sylvana recited their vow in clear, carrying voices, while Lord Velond, presiding, smiled benevolently.

There were exaggerated sniffles and quiet satisfaction among the congregated nobility, dressed in their finest satins, lev-silk confections bustling around hips and shoulders, holo-assisted to display impossible perspectives and paradoxical knots.

Tom, standing stiffly in brocaded tunic and heavy half-cape, watched as the couple exchanged platinum bracelets. Then the new Lord and Lady d'Ovraison, holding hands, bowed to peers and subjects.

Carillons rang—Aleph Hall itself acting as a vast musical instrument—and the floor became sapphire as floating holos tumbled through the air: pastel tricons for Lord Corduven and Lady Sylvana playfully interwoven into symbols for prosperity and budding, a three-dimensional colour-coded pun.

Conflicting emotions washed through Tom. He stood to attention, sweating beneath the heavy garb, part of the double row of servants lining the route to the exit as Corduven and Lady Sylvana walked past.

Corduven's grey eyes flickered once in Tom's direction, but then the couple were at the main doors, facing the cheering crowds in the cavernous chamber outside.

"Absolutely monstrous." The white-bearded Lord swigged purple wine. "Should have killed the scoundrel when they had the chance."

Tom, standing at the wall like all the other servitors who ringed the vast, round, cream-and-white dining-hall, stared at the stellated crystal sculpture at the ceiling's centre. His gaze appeared—he hoped—unfocused, but he was listening, riveted, to the nobles' conversation.

"But Rictos, my dear. Are they sure he was"—the Lady leaned over, featherlike hat flopping forwards as she lowered her voice—"a Pilot? Aren't they all dead?"

"The ones we knew about. This fellow was a trader; seemed legitimate. Only tried to arrest him because a truecast reported the warrant's being drawn up, just a tenday before the event."

Tom's skin prickled with the implication of paradox, as much as with mention of a Pilot.

"The premises"—the old Lord waited while Tom moved forwards, replenished the empty goblet, then retreated—"were destroyed. Microtak booby-trap. Damned insolence. Had my head of security whipped, I can tell you." Another swig. "He's damned lucky I let him live."

"But the escaped suspect—"

A discreet gesture from Jak.

Cursing inwardly, Tom kept his usual bland expression as he walked over. Around them, concentric rings of tables were occupied by increasingly raucous groups of nobles and a few successful freedmen. Dishes from the last course had been cleared away; drinks and sweets were all that remained.

"You're off duty." Jak wore a diagonal white overseer's sash. He was reporting directly to Chef Keldur who, directing the affair, had been moving between here and the kitchens all evening. "Off you go."

"The meal's not really over."

"Early tomorrow, by special request"—he glanced at the central disc-shaped lev-table, where Lord and Lady d'Ovraison sat, along with a majestic Lady Darinia, Lord Velond and the highest of visiting dignitaries—"you're to report to Talefryn Tunnel. The Aleph Hall end."

"But that's where—"

"Precisely. You need time to pack."

That's where Corduven and Sylvana are leaving from.

"Pack?"

"Funny," said Jak, though a smile was threatening to break through his studied irony, "I thought you were supposed to be the bright one."

There was a message on his room's holodisplay, directing him to Mistress eh'Nalephi's study.

"OK," Tom said to the empty room. "I'll get going."

He changed into integral-slipper running-tights and tunic, then pulled light, baggy trousers and surcoat over them. On his way back, he could shed the outer layer and go for a run.

Mistress eh'Nalephi was already sitting in a high-backed chair, waiting for him, when he arrived. Her ebony face was expressionless.

"You're going on a trip."

"Er, yes. Apparently."

"It's an honour, young man."

Tom blinked. "I know."

Accompanying Corduven and Sylvana on their honeymoon. Great!

"Do you keep a journal?"

"No . . ."

"Be precise, be positive." An old refrain.

"I . . . sometimes write poetry."

"Really?" A flicker of interest. "Make a copy. Have someone bring me the crystal tomorrow."

"Yes, Mistress eh'Nalephi."

"In the meantime"—she handed over a black and orange crystal of her own—"that contains modules sent over by Lord Velond, in addition to some I've drawn up. There'll be no slacking off."

"Of course."

"And keep a record of your travels"—a trace of a smile—"in any format. I'll want to see it on your return."

Tom bowed.

"In the meantime, Lord and Lady d'Ovraison have appointed you co-ordinator and chief translator."

Tom stiffened. This was news to him.

After reviewing this tenday's work: "It's not the done thing to transport AIs when travelling." Mistress eh'Nalephi's prejudice was implicit: that translator-AIs were hopeless at capturing nuance.

Tom nodded.

"Also, Tom"—with a hint of disapproval—"you've been granted limited delphic access. A prime duty will be continuously to review the itinerary for safety."

"I've never seen a truecast," said Tom.

"Perhaps it's time you did."

Her chair turned in place: a signal for a pale-blue holosphere to bloom, then coalesce into a panoramic scene.

Flat chequerboard flagstones: a wide boulevard beneath soaring buttresses, glowclusters floating near the marbled ceiling. Along the centre, a shallow toy canal: placid water, fish, decorative model boats.

"Interesting." Tom walked into the frozen image's centre, like a giant among the insect-sized people. "It's only a simulation. An Oracle attempting—with expert help—to recreate a forward memory from his or her own future."

"You think he was there?"

"Maybe . . . Or perhaps, he saw—will see—just a newscast. But this simulation's more detailed than I thought."

"So execute it."

Tom found the correct tricon, gestured, and the scene slid into motion.

A busy day. Thousands thronging the walkways. Lev-carts and skimmers in profusion.

"This must be Primum Stratum, maybe Secundum, of some far demesne—Ah, I see." Tom reached up to another revolving tricon: it unfolded into a tesseract of explanation.

In the miniature canal, a soliton wave slides along its length, disrupting the toy vessels, spilling them in all directions. The crowds change their motion, halting or stumbling: from above, the people are tiny specks caught up in turbulent flow.

Without bidding, another tesseract, pulsing gold in warning, blossomed into a phase-space of stresses and strains and breaking-points.

On the curved ceiling, high up, a crack appears . . .

"Fate," whispered Tom. "Duke Boltrivar's realm, Snapdragon 307."

. . . and sudden water spurts out, arcing down to the ground.

He cast an agonized look at Mistress eh'Nalephi. "That's only twenty-four days away."

The cavern roof explodes open. A white torrent smashes down upon the boulevard, a hail of rushing water and debris, as the subterranean river bursts into the inhabited stratum, and thousands perish.

"No!"

This can't be.

He span the display, magnified, opened secondary volumes depicting the flood's progress in the connected tunnels and corridors, while tesseracts scrolled through dynamic statistics of death and injury.

A wide hall, filled with diners, as a curling wave comes crashing through . . .

"We must—"

Children playing with dolls. A girl looks wide-eyed . . .

"—we *have* to stop it."

. . . and foaming water explodes into place, flinging a white-robed doll across the maelstrom's surface as the tiny, plump fingers disappear amid the spume.

"*No!*" Tom's hand cut downwards, striking the image from existence. Panting, as though finishing a run, he stared at Mistress eh'Nalephi's impassive ebony features.

"The expectation value noted here is ninety-seven per cent congruence," she said, "between truecast model and eventual reality. Usually, that means correlated impressions from two or more Oracles. Alternatively, it might be from one unusually eidetic Oracle: some are more talented than others."

I can't let this happen.

"If we start now"—Tom forced himself to speak softly, calmly—"we can mobilize emergency services, plan evacuations. Get Duke Boltrivar's subjects out of there before it happens."

She gestured. Beside Mistress eh'Nalephi, delineated in white, pink and gold, the Zimmer transforms hung: the core chrono-relative function-tesseracts.

"If you can point out the flaw in these equations"—her voice was like cold stone—"and save thousands of lives by changing the universe so that bilking" (she meant, acting now to change a predestined future) "is allowed, then please do so."

Tom stared at her. "But we can't do—nothing."

Thousands dying.

"Does it rankle that you've not been promoted, Tom?"

"I'm sorry?" Wrong-footed, he did not know how to answer.

"Chef Keldur was once a sub-gamma-class servitor, and has made it to alpha-plus. Maestro da Silva was born alpha-class, and received manumission when he won the Gelmethri Syektor championship. Of course, you're only delta."

Drowning.

"But the flood, the—"

"You will go far, Thomas Corcorigan. But not if you betray yourself and me with hysterical illogic."

Tom stiffened as though he had been struck.

"You can't save them." Her voice softened. "Neither can I. Nor can anyone."

30

NULAPEIRON AD 3410

I love you, Sylvana.

Grey shadows—*attackers!*—and he hurled the black sheet off his body, kicked out, stabbed with his fingertips—

No-one there.

Sylvana . . . Fate, had he spoken aloud?

In one corner, a glowing tricon slowly revolved. Shaded apologetic green, it nevertheless required his presence in kitchens-admin right now.

Groaning, he slid from the bed, fought down a curse as his toes knocked against one of his packed bags. The room's illumination grew bright.

Chaos! Three hours before dawn-light.

Gritty-eyed, he dressed and made his way to the office suite: fluted columns of dark blue glass, a basalt freeform sculpture; Chef-Steward Malkoril blearily sitting in his obsidian chair.

"Sorry, Tom. But the others were working very late."

"Sir."

"It's only a food order. But I want you to take a drone, and one of Milran's Dragoons as escort."

"OK." Tom was puzzled.

The red-tinged membrane slid across his skin as he stepped inside, followed by a small, gleaming drone. He stopped, drone hovering at shoulder height, and surveyed the guest suite. The young Dragoon trooper remained outside.

"Sir?"

Blue shadows lay across the chamber, and it took a moment for Tom's vision to adjust. Then he could see in the dark, sunken pit at the chamber's centre a bare, emaciated man—lev-bracelets around every joint in his body—floating in the lev-field, ringed by holovolumes cycling through newscasts, political analyses, financial reports.

"Your meal."

Spittle dripped from the man's slack mouth. The half-lidded eyes seemed to stir, blinking away some of the stupor as he turned in Tom's direction.

"N-nice." The man's tongue wetly licked his lips.

An Oracle.

"If that's all, sir—Thank you."

Tom turned and chopped his hand through the air in command to the drone: *remain here.* Then he strode quickly through the membrane.

"Everything all right?" The trooper's expression was open, unconcerned.

"Come on," said Tom. "Let's get out of here."

Two hours before dawn-light, but Tom had been out before at this time, in darkness. Every three or four tendays, when insomnia struck, he would rise quietly and do what he did now: get changed, stretch, and make his way to the deserted gallery for an extra run.

Dark grey shadows shrouded the diminishing perspective; the archways were black semicircles receding to infinity.

Tom crouched—

A cough.

—and froze.

"Who's there?"

A scrabbling sound, then: "Sorry, your honour. Meaning no harm."

"Who are you?"

Tom heard the fear in his own voice, but felt also the buried eagerness that wanted to prove his phi2dao training for real.

In the nearest archway, a dozen lumpen shadows moved, shuffling towards the dismal light. One drew back her hood, revealing a scarred, wizened face.

"Beg your pardon, yer honour. We was ordered to find a quiet place."

"Ordered?" Tom relaxed: these wretches were no danger to him.

"We're Oracle Palrazin's retinue." A measure of pride in her voice as she gestured back with a fingerless hand.

"We're not allowed"—it was a hunchbacked, heavily scarred man who spoke—"to stay in official quarters, like."

"We won't be no trouble," started another, but then someone at the rear spoke up: "He's one of us. Look."

There was a strained stillness until Tom understood and straightened up, turning so that the stump of his left arm was visible in the pale grey light.

"He tortures you," Tom said simply.

The woman looked at him. "Sometimes it takes . . . extra stimulation . . . to drag His Wisdom's consciousness into normal timeflow."

Sweet Destiny!

"Wait here." Tom forced his voice to remain calm. "I'll come back to you."

In the kitchen, Tom ordered a macrodrone to stock itself with leftovers from the wedding feast. Then it followed him to Tom's dorm and hovered in the corridor outside as Tom went in.

He quickly transferred all his essentials to one small holdall. There were formal outfits which he could not get rid of, but he packed the heaviest, warmest old capes and tunics, and took them out to the drone.

Then he led the drone back to the shadowed gallery.

"Thanks!" "Bless you, sir . . ."

As they gathered round the drone, unloading it, Tom gave the control gestures that would cause it to return to its docking-bay when empty.

I wish I could do more.

Eyes stinging from more than lack of sleep, he walked quietly back to his room to wait for the wake-up signal.

A huge arachnargos with shining thorax—blue/grey, shading to black underneath—bobbed in place, suspended by long tendrils fastened to ceiling, floor, walls.

"Amazing," murmured Tom.

Beyond, the clean-curved dark-nacre lev-car hovered: the new Lord and Lady d'Ovraison would travel in that.

"What I do to those lazy buggers will be amazing"—the stevedore captain gestured with his chin towards the loading-crews—"if they don't get everything on board before his Lordship gets here."

"Plenty of time yet."

Tom felt curiously displaced, exhausted. He had to crane his neck back to stare up at the arachnargos: its shiny underbelly seemed almost to glow with reflected eldritch light as it puckered open, extruded a slender thread down to the stevedores on the ground, and sucked up a bound cluster of penrose cases.

I'm going on a foreign trip.

The excitement mingled with his lack of sleep and his tangled feelings towards Corduven and Sylvana, so that, in a weird state of mind, he took every step carefully, watched everything minutely—

He stiffened.

"What are those?" In the main Talefryn Tunnel, and in some of the smaller cross-corridors, they hung: like arachnargoi, but totally black, with small, teardrop-shaped bodies and narrow, formidable-looking tendrils.

"Arachnabug escort." The stevedore captain picked his nose, examined his finger, then wiped it across his work tunic, oblivious to Tom's disgust. "One-man bugs. Military."

"There's a sick-bag, back of the seat."

The tunnel lurched and twisted, and the bottom dropped out of Tom's stomach as they left the ornate, marbled Talefryn Tunnel and plunged into raw cavern.

"Leaving Darinia Demesne." The driver's voice, muffled by his helmet, remained even, though the arachnargos control cabin tipped, then levelled. Their velocity increased. "Interdemesne territory for the next fifty klicks."

"You don't like travelling by arachnargos, do you?"

It was the co-driver who spoke, turning in the bench-seat towards Tom, who was webbed into the small jumpseat on the rear bulkhead. Taking off her helmet, she ran her fingers through her close-cropped hair.

Inside her discarded helmet, virtual holos pulsed with impossible depths: tracking vectors, monitoring the lev-car—with Corduven and Lady Sylvana on board—and the arachnabugs.

"It's my first time in one of these things."

Tom glanced through the wide horizontal slit of the forward screen. Amid the hurtling craggy buttresses and splotchy fluorofungal patches, the tiny black arachnabugs sped back and forth, criss-crossing the bigger arachnargos's trajectory.

"They're real mad buggers."

Tom swallowed, holding down bile. "Sounds as if you admire them."

"They're OK, for soldierboys." She flashed a grin. "I'm Limava. That's Lanctus."

"Tom."

"Nice to meet y—Oops! That was a good one."

They span to the right, tipped downwards forty-five degrees, pouring on the speed.

Bastard!

"Sure you don't need that sick-bag?"

Tom, teeth clamped together, shook his head.

They stopped overnight in the Burnished Caves: ornate and polished, complex-hued and elegant; gargoyles clustered along its baroque, intricate walls.

Relieved of duties, Tom went for a run.

After a late dinner, the lev-car crew camped out on the crystalline floor, leaving their vehicle discreetly to Lord and Lady d'Ovraison.

The arachnabugs were gone—"Patrolling," Limava said—and the arachnargos control cabin was quiet, peaceful at the day's end. Lanctus was asleep, softly snoring in his chair.

"Pretty, isn't it?" Limava spoke softly, pointing out at the cavern.

"Beautiful," Tom whispered.

They watched in companionable silence for a while, then Tom—with an involuntary glance out at the lev-car—excused himself, and left via the cabin's rear membrane.

His quarters were a catwalk overlooking the cargo hold. Wearily, he stripped off and slid inside his sleeping-bag: aching with exhaustion, but knowing he would not sleep.

"Hey, there."

It was Limava, barefoot and wearing a simple robe—with nothing beneath it.

"Uh, hi . . ."

She slid the robe down. Smooth, pale skin; strong shoulders; wide, flat breasts; a slight curve to her muscular stomach—

Tom gulped. "I thought, er, you and Lanctus . . ."

"Don't be disgusting." She crouched down and pulled back the sleeping-bag. "He's my brother."

"I didn't—"

"Budge over."

She slid in beside him.

Over the next fifteen days, Lord and Lady d'Ovraison swam in the swirling, multicoloured mineral pools of Lord Yelthiwar's demesne; saw the bat caverns of Upper Milthenos; watched Countess Relviko's Fire-lancers' combat display; flew lev-gliders along the Rivulet Borehole.

In Ralgakhtan, they listened to the sweetly complex baroque chants of the surgically altered Floating Singers of Kalgathoria; then joined in the MistDance at Ronivere Lake, among pale holowraiths and the Veritas Sprites.

Without wander-access to these foreign demesnes, Tom spent his time in meetings with the host servitors, or confined in the arach-nargos, working on the crystal's latest set of problems: he was on the point of solving them, allowing download of the next module.

During working-hours, Limava discouraged intimacy. But every night she came to Tom, though she would slip quietly out of the sleeping-bag later, leaving him to sleep alone.

His dreams were haunted by drowning children.

31
TERRA AD 2122

<<Karyn's Tale>>
[6]

She killed Sal unintentionally: by her choice of keywords; by her illegal upgrades to his heuristic query-probes, bought while on leave in SingaporeCube.

"Priority A: get all reports on life in mu-space," she muttered on her way to the shower. By the time she came out, drying herself with a rough white towel, it was over.

The image's voice was flat and uninflected; its expression held a generic polygon-transform blandness: *"I'm sorry."*

Sal O'Mander's features, but no doffing of the hat, no sardonic smile.

"I regret to say . . ."

"What did you—?"

". . . that this is a non-interactive recording. All instantiations of Sal O'Mander underwent omnithread deletion two point three minutes ago."

The use of the third person chilled Karyn: her NetAgent had a sense of self . . . but this was no longer Sal O'Mander.

"All template-classes and local snapshots were zapped from EveryWare within ten seconds."

Every copy of Sal O'Mander, even the basic template from which he had grown . . . Lost.

"Who could—?"

Sal's face was gone. In its place, the one/mu/zero prompt of the EveryWare logon display.

"Aw, shit!" Karyn threw her towel across the room.

Why the hell had she never dumped Sal to crystal? But then, who bothered with backups when EveryWare lived up to its name?

"I'm a total idiot."

It would take months to train up a template to even approximate Sal's versatility . . . but by then, she—and Dart—would be inhabitants of mu-space, leaving that strange, fractal continuum only to pick up or drop off their cargo: trade goods or passengers deep in delta-coma.

"Power off," she said, and the logon display winked out.

Poor Sal: killer-flamed by a firewall. That must be what happened.

Her own damned fault for using a highest-priority command with fuzzy wording. Sal had looked everywhere, following hints and links even to unauthorized black nodes.

She pulled on her UNSA-issue jumpsuit, kicked her chair viciously across the study-bedroom, and headed off to deliver yet another lecture to the too young students who were waiting for her.

Fractal sex.

Like a coastline whose length increased the more closely you examined it: her explorations of Dart's rugged, muscular body grew slower and more powerful, more fundamentally moving, as time drew on and the end of their affair drew near.

Then they took him away for the final stages, while Karyn, in grey despair, received her first nanocytic infusion.

And launch.

She walked out in the pre-dawn, footsteps receding into the endless desert air as she crossed the runway. Its huge shape brooded in shadow above her, and she shivered from more than the cold.

You're taking Dart away from me.

And in truth, vessel and Pilot would be wired in more intimately than lovers.

Look after him.

She waited until brilliant sun peeped across the distant purple mesa, dripping molten gold across the vessel's shining cupric hull, lacing fire across Phoenix LaunchCentral. From one of the crystal domes, a white TDV slid onto the tarmac.

Dart was somewhere inside its ceramic carapace.

The TDV, its thermoacoustic drive whispering into stillness, settled down beside the shining mu-space vessel. Mirror-masked ground crew stepped out.

Then the TDV's scorpion tail arced into its body, rose with Dart's white-shrouded cocoon, and deposited him through the dorsal opening, inside his new ship.

Ground crew swarmed over the vessel: they were on a countdown, and the bio-interface procedures were time-critical.

During the process, there was no way to talk to Dart, but they had already said—no, sang mutely with their bodies—their farewells.

She waited in the gathering heat, sickened by nerves or in reaction to the nanocytes, until the ground crew signalled, thumbs up, that the hookups were complete. They waved her on board the TDV and took her back to LaunchCentral.

"You can watch from there." One of them pointed out a spacious lounge with black leather couches beneath a soaring, aquamarine-tinted glass wall.

The window reconfigured, magnifying.

Karyn watched.

Flicker of blue jet-flame. Rocking on its lev-field.

Then the copper ship was racing above the runway, delta-wings spread, arcing up into the blue-green sky, sparking white/gold as it caught the sun, ascending faster, diminishing, bright dot, was gone.

A SatTrack holo opened beside her.

Soaring ship, darkness of stratosphere, into the orbital reaches and then a white-light crescendo. Transition radiation spilled out into real-space, the insertion four-axis angle optimized, twistors cohered, tunnelled, disappeared.

Subsidiary holovolumes settled down.

Mu-space projection achieved.

Gone, gone, gone.

"Sorry, Barney. I'm not much company today."

The dog gave a short bark as though in agreement.

"What he said"—Anne-Marie, the blind woman from the campus registry, patted Barney's powerful shoulder—"goes for me, too."

Karyn started to get up off the couch, but the room swayed.

Perspectives swung in and out of sensible geometric relationships: fractal-affine transformations crawling in her skull.

"I feel awful." She slumped back. "Everything I see is—Hell, you must hate me, for what I'm giving up."

"Maybe." Anne-Marie's voice was strained. "Perhaps you're trading in one reality for another. A better one."

"Ha."

"I've heard tell"—wistfully—"of golden seas of light, black spiky stars . . ."

"How do you imagine—? I mean, er . . ."

"I could see a little when I was young." Anne-Marie's sightless eyes shifted. "I can still tell the difference between a sunny day and pitch darkness, *mais c'est tout.*"

Is that better or worse than never having seen at all?

"The memory remains. And sometimes I dream . . ."

"Like love? Better to have loved and lost than . . ." Her voice trailed off.

"Oh, Karyn. It's been only three days. Some maiden voyages last a fortnight until reverse transition."

Before returning to realspace.

"You've got all the jargon, haven't you?"

"I've worked a lot with UNSA."

"Ah, hell—"

Anne-Marie leaned across and squeezed Karyn's knee. "It's all right. Really."

Bloody hell, Dart. If you don't come back to me, I'll—

She didn't know what she would do.

It had happened twice before.

She suspected it was pheromone-based, but it seemed supernatural: a skin-crawling certainty that someone was the other side of a wall, sensing their *ki* . . . and then they walked in through the door.

Am I kidding myself?

The first time, she had been kneeling in *seiza*, on her first visit to the Honbu Dojo in Kyoto; then the awesome sense of presence overwhelmed her, about twenty seconds *before* the legendary Harada Sensei had walked in.

Reality had seemed to centre around him, the light to grow brighter.

The second time was in a Manhattan dojo, a converted dance-loft, and she had sensed the half-Filipina, half-Anglo *rokudan* before she arrived.

Karyn herself held merely *nidan*, second-degree black belt . . . not advanced. But she was sensing it again—

There was a knock on the door.

"Enter."

A burly shape, half-shadowed from the bright corridor lighting.

"Sensei."

Mike looked at her for a long moment, then came inside. He had a straight-backed warrior's walk, big hands held loosely at his side.

"Oh, no," said Karyn. "Not Dart."

$$\Diamond \Diamond \Diamond$$

//insert

    {commentary.provenance = $\pi\sigma3\varsigma989$/Petra deVries/
personal.journal/
KMcN}

    {   [[Vortex.homeostasis = established]]
       [[P(phase-transition) = 1.0000]]
       [[Recursion level = 10 exp 37]]

It spreads there, a fractal web of recursive patterns, hovering on the verge of self-organized criticality: not aware, not unaware. Somehow, it has been trapped by its own potential . . . yet something new is happening.

The universe is a sea of golden light. In it hang black spongiform stars: stellated, fractally riddled with holes . . . and massive. Through the gold, streamers of scarlet and purple denote rivers of interstellar energy.

And the anomaly.

Its tiny copper form, born of unnaturally smooth geometry, is trapped. An event membrane surrounds it, shields it.

Tiny tendrils, offshoots of the main pattern, spread along the membrane. There are sparks, reconfigurations, as the pattern-levels evolve survival strategies in the new environment.

Slowly, slowly, the pattern's nucleus moves closer to the tiny trapped mote.

The vessel is like the tiniest of dust particles, a seed, about to give birth to the storm.

    }end-insert//

<<MODULE ENDS>>

32

NULAPEIRON AD 3410

Immense cavern systems, their ceilings swirling with pinks and oranges. Vast blood-red networks of slender tubes were threaded through the airy spaces: in them, half-shadowed shapes flitted.

Vehicles, Tom thought, craning forwards over Limava's shoulder. Cargo-bugs.

Arteries, suspended in mid-air.

Then the arachnargos whipped into a gold-white square-cross-sectioned corridor encrusted with intricate sculpture, and followed it to a pillared hall where the floor was of polished marble and granite: pink with swirling grey, black speckled with yellow-green.

"Lady V'Delikona's realm," Limava announced, taking off her helmet.

"Word is," said Lanctus from the driver's position, "that she's something of a dragon. Even Lord d'Ovraison's scared of her."

Tom, grateful that they had come to a halt, sighed. "I don't think that need worry us minions."

"That's where you're wrong, old mate." Lanctus pointed at a small holovolume. "Dinner tonight, and you'll be accompanying our Lord and Lady."

Tom glanced at Limava, then looked away.

"The thing I find oddest around here," Lanctus continued, changing the subject, "is that they have no dark-periods. Just continuous brightness. Or do I mean continual?"

"Continuous." Tom peered out through the front viewscreen. "But that's terrible. You need to sleep in darkness to avoid developing myopia, and to reach the deeper states."

"I don't mean they can't sleep OK in private. The public areas remain lit."

"Oh."

"Hey, servant-boy!" Limava grinned. "You're a well-travelled man, now. Exploring different cultures."

I ought to feel grateful.

But every time he closed his eyes he saw the same thing: a small girl's pudgy fingers disappearing beneath roiling waves, drowning in a maelstrom which had not yet occurred.

Quietly, Tom stood with goblet in hand, too diffident to ask for something different—this contained alcohol—and watched the nobles in conversation.

The setting was informal. They sat or stood in small groups, chatting, oblivious to the platinum-inlaid dendriforms, the antique statues of Kali in all her aspects.

The servitors were unobtrusive, attentive, blank-faced.

I should be with them. But those were not his orders.

He was dressed formally, half-cape across his left shoulder. Incredibly, he was a *guest*.

He observed:

Laughter, with a hint of strain. A young Lady leaning towards a Lord: her body-language unconsciously open, his arms defensively crossed.

There, an older Lord, arm around his younger companion, not noticing her discomfiture.

Beyond, a group of grey-haired men, each merely waiting his turn to speak, not listening to the others.

And me? I'm less than any of them.

"Depressing, isn't it?"

The Lady was slim, straight-backed, her white hair coiffed into a simple twist, bound with platinum.

"Ma'am?" Uncomfortably, he twitched his left shoulder.

"Never mind, young man. Do you know where Lady Sylvana is?"

"Ah . . . She went that way." Then something loosened Tom's normal restraint: "She went with a *personal* friend of our hostess, or so the gentleman took pains to mention. Several times."

"Really." A faint appraisal in the Lady's eyes. "And the gentleman's name?"

"Sorry, I don't know." He added: "I don't suppose Lady V'Delikona does, either."

"Perhaps she knows him as an *impersonal* friend."

Tom laughed.

Nearby, a servitor swayed slightly beneath the burden of a heavy tray.

"Something the matter?"

"Oh no, ma'am."

But she followed his gaze. "It must be hard, holding the food, unable to eat."

Putting herself in a servitor's position. Unusual.

"Actually"—he smiled—"I think you'll find he's already eaten. And very well, too."

"I trust you're joking."

"Oh, no." Tom shrugged. "How else can they make sure their stomachs don't rumble?"

The Lady looked at him, then turned away.

"I'm Tom Corcorigan."

The servitor, overseer's white sash over his burgundy livery, frowned at his holodisplay. Other guests, nobles, filed past Tom into the dining-hall.

"I beg your pardon, Master Corcorigan." The servitor minimized the triconic lattice. "There was a last-minute change to the arrangements. This way, please."

Some devilry made him do it.

Before sitting down, Tom slipped off the half-cape and draped it across the back of his chair. When he sat, the young Lady to his left visibly blanched.

The Lady to his right—the white-haired Lady with whom he had conversed earlier—was being treated with deference even by the nobility around her.

Lady V'Delikona.

At that moment, Lady Sylvana walked past the long table, almost gliding in her peach satin gown—and winked in Tom's direction, before continuing on.

Fate.

"What were you thinking, young man?"

Her voice cut through his thoughts.

"Er . . ." Tom gestured at their surroundings: octagonal chamber, pale orange and lapis lazuli; triple rows of tables parallel to each wall. Three hundred Lords and Ladies, attended by servitors. "I was just admiring this. Everything."

"Ah. So what do you think of the room's arrangement?"

"It's . . . all right."

Lady V'Delikona's wrinkles deepened as she frowned.

"What do you think?" She addressed the bearded Lord who was sitting opposite Tom.

"Well. Very fine." The man gestured with his half-filled goblet. "Tasteful, Lady V'Delikona, as always."

She looked around the table, and Lords and Ladies nodded agreement.

Tom turned away, suppressing a smile.

"What?"

"I was thinking, your Ladyship"—Tom hesitated: he was on dangerous ground—"that its leitmotif is rather subversive, in fact."

Frowns from the gentry. Even the young Lady at Tom's left glanced at him.

"And you appreciate—what?" Lady V'Delikona's gaze was piercing. "Explain yourself."

"The connection to . . . the past."

"And connectivity is important?"

Tom paused, then: "If you mean implicit connectivity in the universal sense"—excitement pushed his inhibitions aside—"of ancients like Bohm or Spinoza, then yes. We're temporary eddies in the flow. Far-from-equilibrium patterns which dissipate, soon enough."

"Flawed patterns, then." Again, the icy glitter in her eyes. "So tell me, young man, just how did you lose your arm?"

Shocked silence settled over the table.

"An accident." Tom smiled. "I got caught."

"A thief?"

Background clatter, but the Lords on this table were intent on Lady V'Delikona and Tom.

"More of an unwitting accomplice."

A studied pause, then: "Did it hurt?"

Bubbling fat. Stench of burning flesh.

"Always."

A frown.

"But you should have had an implant to—" Lady V'Delikona glanced in the direction of Lady Sylvana's table.

"I removed it."

This time, Tom felt the full weight of her attention upon him.

"How did you accomplish that?"

"I stole a lattice blade from the kitchens." A smile twitched at the corner of Tom's mouth. "But I returned it later."

"So. A reformed thief. But why did you choose the pain?"

"Because—it's mine."

Lady V'Delikona stared at him for a moment. "You didn't mention that some patterns are nearer to dissolution than others."

Tom blinked. "That would have been impolite."

The briefest of nods, then she turned to the man at her right. Touching his arm, she asked about his diplomatic envoys to Treston Province.

Tom understood that he had been dismissed.

"What did you mean"—the young Lady to his left, trying not to look at Tom's abbreviated left sleeve—"about subversion?"

"The trigrammatic table arrangement." Tom gestured around the octagonal chamber. "Following the *I-Ching*."

"I'm sorry?"

"From Terra, the world that colonized Nulapeiron. But we shouldn't talk about such things, should we?" Tom raised his goblet. "Not in front of the servitors."

Through the silver-tinted membrane, the huge caverns were visible: creamy apricot ceilings, crimson transport-threads.

"Did you enjoy the meal, Tom?"

Tom wheeled: he had not sensed Corduven's entrance.

"Yes, I—I may have overstepped the mark once or twice. Excitement."

"Maybe." Corduven tapped a floating rose-and-jet table with his fingernails. "Lady V'Delikona likes you, though."

"You're kidding."

"Not at all." But his voice was tense.

Tom looked carefully at Corduven. "What's wrong, Corduven?"

"You were discussing itinerary changes with your driver, Lanctus."

A chill settled across Tom's skin. "That's right. Hypothetically: otherwise I would have come to you, of course."

"It would have placed us in Duke Boltrivar's realm by 303, in five days' time."

Four days before the flood.

"I know it's a detour." Tom let out a long breath. "But I thought you'd like to—"

"There's something you don't know about me." A small smile tugged at Corduven's delicate features, then he glanced away, out into the caverns.

A silver mesodrone drifted past the window membrane.

He's nervous.

"I don't understand."

"The thing is, Tom. For one thing, my brother's an Oracle."

"I—"

He doesn't know.

"Gérard is one of the best. Never gets anything wrong."

"I thought . . . they can't. Make mistakes, I mean."

"Can't they?" Corduven shrugged. "They're relying on memories of future events. Their consciousness is twisted up and down their own timelines: most of them are scarcely human."

Tom looked at him.

"You know I saw the truecast, don't you?"

33

TERRA AD 2122

<<Karyn's Tale>>

[7]

Dart was missing.

No message. No contact. Nothing that anyone could do.

Comms technology could make the Earth—or that tiny skin of the living planet which people thought of as the world—appear small. But in the face of mu-space's vastness . . . In that literally endless cosmos, no-one could mount a search for one missing vessel.

In UNSA, nobody even pretended they were going to try.

Dart—

For three days she skipped her workouts, ate badly, slept little. Exhaustion frazzled her nerves: once, halfway through delivering a lecture, she suddenly came to her senses and realized that everyone was staring at her—a group of upturned young faces—and that her voice had just trailed off.

She resumed her routine, but listlessly.

A week passed.

Sometimes, when a novice Pilot miscalculated slightly, their vessel reappeared in realspace a few days late, with the Pilot's nerves jangled, but unharmed.

Another week. Then a third.

Karyn's life became an exercise in grey despair. She performed her duties automatically, without flair.

It was nearly a month after Dart's disappearance when Anne-Marie, accompanied by her dog Barney, tapped lightly on the lecture-theatre door.

"OK, guys," said Karyn. "Download the bifurcation diagram, and perform an order-of-magnitude . . . No, plot a Schrödinger"—Karyn nodded to Anne-Marie: a useless gesture—"and replace the del-squared with a Fordian, then compare."

That should keep them busy. She stepped outside.

There was someone with Anne-Marie: mid-twenties, oriental . . . Karyn ransacked her memory, then said: "What can I do for you, Chojun?"

Brief smile on Anne-Marie's face. Chojun Akazawa—the guy Karyn had met in the Fizzy Cyst bar: grad student, probably—shuffled his feet, embarrassed.

"I've, er, been running quester agents in EveryWare . . ."

"Yes?"

"I thought you should know—UNSA's been running a lattice search. Concentrating on the volume where Pilot Mulligan was supposed to, ah, reinsert."

Dart.

Chojun cleared his throat. "They've picked up signals—"

"They've found him!"

"—from a buoy. Not his vessel."

Karyn was dumbstruck.

"Give Karyn the crystal," Anne-Marie prompted.

Chojun handed over a small datacrystal. "It's the strangest phenomenon you've ever seen," he said. "Fractal lightning: that's the best description I can think of. But not transient—permanent. Actually, growing."

"What do you mean?"

"It's all over Pilot Mulligan's ship, trying to burrow through the event membrane. Almost"—he hesitated—"purposeful."

"I've got to—" Karyn stopped.

Got to reach him.

Anne-Marie reached down to pat Barney—the dog was watchful, tail frozen, sensitive to the emotional atmosphere—then she said: "It's six months before you get a ship, Karyn. Someone else will have to go."

"I know—" Karyn began, but Chojun interrupted: "I don't see what anyone can do. Sorry, but—You'd need to resonate with the event membrane, logarithmically increase its intensity . . . You'd do better to configure a new vessel that way, rather than refit one in service."

"What way?" demanded Karyn. "Reconfigure how?"

"More field generators, core transmitters . . . Your own UNSA guys should have a better idea."

"Right." Karyn glanced back into the lecture theatre: the students were heads-down, working on the quantum chaos solution. "As if"— she could not keep the bitterness from her voice—"they'd talk to me."

Anne-Marie spoke softly: "I have contacts."

What had she said before? *I've worked a lot with UNSA.*

"Anne-Marie, I've got to find him. Got to."

"Whatever I can do."

Chojun, stuffing his hands in his pockets, nodded abruptly.

"Thank you both." Karyn turned away, heart pounding.

Dart's alive!

<<MODULE ENDS>>

34

NULAPEIRON AD 3410

Specks of light in the darkness.

"Watch out." Limava started to gesture, but Lanctus had already reacted.

"I've got it. Spark and halt."

Tom grabbed the webbing, then forced himself to relax as the arachnargos stopped its forward motion, rebounded as Lanctus allowed the tendrils to behave elastically, then steadied.

"Spark" was the code which would tell the lev-car to stop. Tom winced as it grew larger in the rear-view IR display, but it span to a halt, just in time.

The smaller arachnabugs were no danger: skittering past, then sticking to strategic positions high up the natural-cavern walls.

"Fate," muttered Limava, opening up more real-holos for Tom to see.

Photo-multiplied images showed long queues of shambling people. Their lights were glowclusters tied in simple rope bags; the natural fluorofungus here was patchy, and the refugees were taking a risk, hoping that the air was breathable.

Tom was already moving.

We could have prevented this!

His nonexistent left arm flared with pain as he ran through the rear membrane and into the cargo hold.

"Command: release!" he shouted, and a dozen mag-clamps deactivated, dropping med-drones into a hovering position. Snatching a satchel from the catwalk, tagging it to his waist, he leaped into open space as he called "Rope! Now!" and caught the descending thread.

The floor puckered open at Tom's approach.

"Drones, follow!"

Damn them all!

The med-drones scattered flitterglows as they descended, lighting up the scene.

"Where are your wounded?" Tom called out the question in four different languages as he hit the ground running.

Drawn faces, dead eyes. One gaunt man pointed back along the straggling column.

"My thanks."

Behind him, the cavern flared with white light as leviathans, with lev-bike escorts, settled into place, popping their carapace doors. Hundreds of burgundy-uniformed men and women streamed out—Lady V'Delikona's most skilled servitors and freedmen-volunteers—followed by more med-drones.

It was endless: the grey shifting tableaux of walking wounded, the old folk bandaged with makeshift rags, the ancient stares of children who had seen their parents' deaths.

Tom stayed with the lead group, backtracking along the column of broken refugees—here, sliding down a scree slope; there, wriggling through gaps where rockfall had filled in the natural route—working his way closer to the demesne's flooded core.

Maintenance shafts led them down to a river: twisting whirlpools and turbulent eddies surrounding smashed columns, piled debris. The flowing water's surface was just two metres below the broken ceiling: it had once been a major thoroughfare.

With no swimming skills, Tom could only watch as smartmasked divers followed submerged med-drones, their white lights a rippling glow beneath the surface.

Images: Lady Sylvana laying her hand across an old man's forehead while medics worked on his broken torso. A child crying in her mother's lifeless arms. Torn limbs. Opaque eyes staring into Destiny.

"I can't save him." A medic, her face stained with grime, looked hopelessly up at Tom while holodisplays cycled above a boy's pain-ravaged body. "I need a euthanasia-dose, but I can't reach—"

Gently, Tom reached down and used finger and thumb against the carotid arteries, sending the boy to oblivion. Then he helped the medic to her feet, and took her to find a patient whom she could save.

More: long hours of organizing supplies, prioritizing evacuations, logging names and implanting tracers so that sundered families might later be reunited. Naming the dead, whenever they could; sampling DNA, tagging temporary burial mounds, encasing them in antibacterial gel.

"Oh, Tom! There are so many of them." During one of their few short breaks, Lady Sylvana came over to talk. She brushed her hair back from her sweaty face, heedless of the bloodstains across her torn garments.

"How's Corduven?"

Though Corduven was in charge of the overall effort, Tom had seen him earlier walking dazed, face unnaturally white with shock, among the laid-out bodies of dead children.

"You didn't hear?" She struggled to focus on Tom. "I had to sedate him. Your drivers, Lanctus and Limava, helped me do it where no-one could see. He's back in our lev-car."

"But—" Tom forced himself to shut up.

Why should I think I was the only one to feel the strain? Corduven knew what was coming, too.

"He beat his fists bloody against a bulkhead." She spoke softly, in counterpoint to swirling waters and the shouting of team co-ordinators.

"Destiny."

Then she was holding out her thumb ring, her official seal, to Tom. "There's a bounce-beam link to Lady V'Delikona's palace. You've Lord-Majeure status to commandeer resources. Take it."

Tom took it automatically. "But how can I—?"

"You're in charge, Tom." Transgressing etiquette, she touched his cheek, briefly. "Cord needs me."

Tom stared, then nodded. "Look after him."

Second day.

Though he usually steered clear of stimulants—distrusting any-thing that was not coded and tested to logotropic standards—Tom used them now. There had been time for a few brief snatches of sleep, but it felt worse than not sleeping at all. Gritty-eyed and greasy-skinned, he hacked agents to help the monitoring and scheduling—pushing the legal limits, enabling near-Turing capabilities—and sur-rounded himself with shifting holovolumes. It helped to watch the colourful schematics: but his eyes were drawn back, always, to the real-time images of grey despair.

The body count steadily rose.

More teams arrived from Lady V'Delikona's demesne. More vehi-cles joined the convoy transferring the wounded to safe havens. Still, thousands were threading their way on foot through broken tunnels.

When the nervous strain became too great, Tom would set the monitor nodes to auto, and help with the digging-out of collapsed cor-ridors.

The second night passed without sleep.

Twinges of chest pain warned Tom that he was pushing too hard: the heavier the fatigue grew, the higher the stimulant doses he had to use.

As the number of rescue personnel continued to grow, travel routes became more complex—while lower strata in this realm were being steadily evacuated, as a precaution—and Tom's state of mind grew increasingly inhuman, almost crazed.

"You ought to rest." Corduven, twitching from medication, vis-ited Tom in the arachnargos.

Tom raged at Corduven and threw him out.

◇◇◇

Third night.

Fourth.

At some point there was a ragged cheer—a survivor, dug out from a landslide of debris, way past the expected time limit—but it hardly affected Tom: only his left eyelid flickered.

He numbly checked displays, noted increasing throughput, pin-pointed bottlenecks, worked automaton-like to string everything together.

Fifth.

Next day, he was staring at a cycling display—had been staring at it for some unknown period of time, just letting the colours pulse—when Lady Sylvana shook his shoulder.

He felt sick, unable to speak.

"It's working smoothly now, Tom."

Slowly, he shook his head; even his neck seemed to creak.

"What's that?"

He followed her pointing finger.

A light touch on the back of his neck, and he reacted too slowly—*derm-patch*. Cascading blackness fell upon him and he drowned.

Entire universes collapsed.

It was literally true: a continuum requires consciousness to comprehend it; every death ends a universe.

When you die, it all disappears.

Semi-lucid waking periods; dreams in which all his limbs were missing; grey confusion of real sensations: strapped onto a hard bench, being thrown around in a comfortless military-grade arachnargos, stripped down for speed.

We were well prepared. The thought was comfortless: *Thanks to the truecast.*

Then—suddenly, it seemed—he was resting on clean, fresh sheets in a luxurious bed, in a bright chamber whose silver-tinted membrane window looked out upon startling caverns threaded with crimson transport tubes.

Tom closed his eyes, sighed, and slid down into sleep.

35

TERRA AD 2122

<<Karyn's Tale>>

[8]

Sensei punished her.

It was strange: a dark shadow seemed to blight his spirit, but Karyn could not use it against him. Over and over, he crunched her into the mat.

I needed that, she thought, kneeling to face him afterwards. *But I'll be bruised in the morning.*

"Sensei? Mike? What's the—?"

He shook his grizzled head. "Blackmail, Karyn. A dangerous strategy. They could throw you off the programme altogether."

Puzzled, Karyn said nothing: waiting for more detail.

"I had to OK your request," Mike continued, "since it counts as temporary leave. And since you bypassed three or four levels of bureaucracy."

"*Irimi*," murmured Karyn, referring to Mike's favourite strategy: entering directly to the centre of the whirlwind as the opponent attacks.

Again, she waited, but there was already a hint: a request of some sort had been placed using her ID. Since it was not her doing, it must have been Sal's, before he was deleted.

"I'll tell you straight." A hint of a smile on Mike's face. "You've some people worried. And that makes me interested, since I was on the ethics committee."

"Ethics committee?" Now Karyn was really puzzled.

"Not for the whole of Project Rewire. Just some of the experiments."

Project Rewire?

"I just want to reach Dart."

Mike stared at her, then: "I want him rescued more than anything, Karyn. I've been praying for guidance." His big hands were palm-down on his thighs: he looked like a kneeling bear. "Is it really best that you go, not someone else? You're not the next in line for a ship commission. And an experienced Pilot—"

"It will take longer to refit an existing vessel. It needs to be a new one."

"OK . . ." Doubtfully.

"And is anyone better motivated than I am?"

"The Zürich labs are shut down for a fortnight." Mike shook his head, but his voice was suddenly decisive. "I'll book flights to Jakarta for both of us. First thing tomorrow." His big hands closed into fists. "I won't let you do this alone."

Her terminal—controlled by her new packet-swarm of antlike agents: dumb but numerous—woke her at 4 a.m.

"Oh, God." She groaned, stretched, then blinked at the flat-text message hanging in the air above her bedside table.

"ITINERARY CHANGED. TRAVEL-PASS FOR PARIS IS APPENDED: DOWNLOAD TO C-FORMAT CRYSTAL. SEE YOU AT THE CAFÉ CATOPTRIQUE, SEINE LEFT BANK, 19:00 LOCAL, TOMORROW."

"Paris?" she said to the empty room. "*Merde alors.*"

<<MODULE ENDS>>

36

NULAPEIRON AD 3410-3413

Years flowed past, but changed his life. Relentlessly, Tom pursued his studies; ran every night, climbed often, sparred and instructed at Maestro da Silva's academy; performed his duties as servitor.

Arlanna was promoted to beta-plus, then alpha-minus servitrix: an almost unheard-of promotion rate.

Tom did not care. Cold and disciplined, he worked harder than ever. He replayed his downloaded modules of Karyn's Tale, exploring every hyperlink for clues to the science that was not on his curriculum.

New downloads, though, were out of the question. During Tom's convalescence in Lady V'Delikona's demesne, Lieutenant Milran had again upgraded the Palace sensor webs.

Lady V'Delikona. Though Tom had not talked to her during his tenday-long recovery, it had been by her orders that he had stayed in a lavish suite, attended by delta servitors. Afterwards, one of her Ladyship's own arachnargoi had taken him back to Darinia Demesne, where he was assigned light duties.

For a while, he was listless. Limava had remained in Duke Boltrivar's realm: she had transferred allegiance in return for command of her own arachnargoi squadron. Great career move. Bitterness and relief swirled through Tom in equal measures.

Then he knuckled down.

Attitudes towards him altered—some became friendlier; others more distant—but the real change was internal: certainty, knowing how far he could push himself.

He would have given that up, to have prevented all those deaths. Grey dreams of swirling waters and white-faced corpses visited every night.

Tom studied harder, relentlessly.

Occasionally, at the Sorites School, a slight, pale youth was seen conversing with Lord Velond and other logosophers. Tom heard the rumours: that the youth was a true genius, whose insight and intuition were like magic. He spent most of his time far away, at the famous Veritas Institute.

Corduven's marriage to Lady Sylvana was annulled.

He was gone: off to Lord Takegawa's military school—incredibly—or so it was said. Lady Sylvana resumed her studies at the Sorites School, withdrawn and intent: more and more, she appeared in her mother's place at official functions. Tom knew nothing of Lady Darinia's state of health.

One day, during a break at the Sorites School, Tom heard: "Genius, you wouldn't believe," from a huddled group of scholars, and sensed sidelong glances in his direction.

I don't think so. Did they not realize how hard he worked? Lord Velond knew the difference: otherwise Tom would have been transferred to the Veritas Institute, servitor though he was.

Jak left the Palace. He was relocated to a major bonded hong at the edge of Darinia Demesne, with pan-sector responsibilities.

No-one gave Tom extra responsibilities or promoted him.

His private tutorials with Mistress eh'Nalephi continued, and his respect for her increased: she was alpha-class, but had more ability, Tom suspected, than many Ladies. She pushed him to the limit, offering neither congratulations nor encouragement. But on his twenty-third birthday (a servitor's celebration: a noble would have celebrated his OctiMilDay), she presented him with a crystal shard.

It contained *Playing the Paradox—collected verses by Thomas Corcorigan*. His first official publication; payment received as academic merit points.

Nine Standard Years had passed since the mysterious Pilot had stumbled over Thomas Corcorigan, huddled in a lonely corridor, writing verse.

In the Sorites School, the atmosphere seemed changed: not just because of the respect Tom had earned, but because there was a sense of fruition, of training coming to an end.

Auntie Antinomy Dances the Fractal Fantastic was Tom's second publication, light-hearted but complex. The strangest moment occurred when he saw Lord Velond chuckling over a holodisplay, reading about Auntie's paradoxical exploits.

Then, early one morning, Tat, who was on the dawn-light kitchen shift, came into Tom's room and told him to report to the Sorites School immediately.

"I'm due there in an hour, anyway."

"I know. Thing is, Tom, while you're there, I'm supposed to pack your gear for a long trip."

A sinking feeling in Tom's stomach. "You don't know—?"

"Sorry, old mate." Tat shook his head. "I've asked the others. None of us has a clue."

Lord Velond's private study had a sweeping curved window overlooking the outer cavern, and plain eggshell walls. Crystals, as usual, were scattered everywhere: abstract mosaics of violets, blacks, oranges, reds—a schema Tom had never deciphered, but Lord Velond could unerringly pick up any required crystal. Dozens of abstruse holodisplays cycled through skeletal six-dimensional proof-dendrimers.

"Good morning, Tom."

There were three people waiting for him: Lord Velond, long, snowy hair brushed back, stern and regal; Mistress eh'Nalephi, aloof and self-composed; and a stranger.

It was the pale youth, the alleged genius from the Veritas Institute.

"Lord Avernon." Tom bowed, dragging the name up from memory. "Lord Velond, Mistress eh'Nalephi."

"Ahem." Lord Velond cleared his throat. "Very nice, but Avernon stands on ceremony even less than I do."

In Mistress eh'Nalephi's eyes Tom caught a flicker of disapproval of the Lords' informality. Her tone was businesslike: "You have a journey to make, Tom."

He smiled. "I promise to record everything. And to study hard."

A brusque nod. "This time, I have only one assignment for you." She held his gaze. "Plan your own logosophical research. And"—she held up a hand as Tom started to speak—"don't tell me. This is for you to do."

Solemnly, Lord Velond handed Tom a crystal. "Your itinerary. This year's Convocation is hosted by Count Shernafil's demesne. You'll both be attending." He nodded in Lord Avernon's direction.

"My Lord."

Then something surprising happened.

"I want to thank you." The pale Lord Avernon *held out his hand* as though Tom were his peer. "Though I don't know what to say."

Mistress eh'Nalephi gasped audibly.

"I—" Swallowing, Tom held out his hand.

They clasped wrists, in the noble fashion.

"I could have tracked you down at the time," Lord Avernon said, "but I didn't know what . . ."

Then Tom remembered: his first time in Maestro da Silva's salle d'armes, following the ill-looking boy out into the corridor.

"My Fate, it's you! The one who collapsed."

"I nearly died."

"Thank Destiny you didn't." Lord Velond smiled. "Or the Veritas Institute would have missed its brightest star for decades."

Lord Avernon looked embarrassed.

"Anyway"—Mistress eh'Nalephi cleared her throat—"I wish you luck, Tom. And you, Lord Avernon. May you both receive what you deserve."

[lemma 324.1]

$$Ai = \{\daleth_1(\mu), \daleth_2(\mu), \daleth_3(\mu) \ldots \}$$

$$(\nabla^2\psi = \Theta(\psi)) \Rightarrow \int \mu dr \in Ai$$

$$(\nabla^2\psi = \Theta(\psi)) \qquad\qquad q$$

$$(\nabla^2\psi = (\psi)) \quad \wedge \quad q$$

"Er, very nice." Tom peered at the display as Lord Avernon minimized it and waved it to one side. "What's that theta-function supposed to represent?"

"Total bidirectional temporal energy. Here." Lord Avernon tossed a crystal in Tom's direction, and Tom snagged it from the air. "Read up about it, and we'll talk."

They were in a modest passenger cabin; only occasional arcing acceleration reminded them that they were in a small arachnargos. There were no external views.

"So, what's a Convocation?"

"Ah, right. Annual gathering. Ours covers four sectors: that's about eighty demesnes."

"That many?"

"Hm? Oh, yes. Held in interstitial territory, at the boundary inter-section of all four sectors. Each year, one demesne provides the host services: the obligation rotates."

"And?"

"I'm sorry?"

"What do they do, my Lord?"

"Just Avernon, please." He looked distracted. "Policy reviews, dis-pute arbitration, that sort of thing. Ratify limited military action, if it comes to that. And then there are appointments to office."

"Oh, I see. You're hoping to become a full academician?"

Avernon shrugged. "I can't imagine anything else, really. Who'd want to run a demesne?"

"Mm."

Five days later, they arrived.

Congressio-Interstata Beth-Gamma was opulent: a shining red-and-cream palace nestling in a giant cavern, supported by silver but-tresses. The guest wing had black, shining floors, high ivory ceilings.

Servitors carried Avernon's baggage; Tom carried his own. But their guest suites were identical.

"Can we review some sorites before dinner, Tom? I wanted to look over cathartic transform strategies."

"In an hour and a half?" asked Tom. He wanted to go for a run.

"Perfect, old chap."

"Er—" Tom spoke up just as Avernon started to walk through his liquefied door membrane. "I would have thought there was nothing in drama theory you didn't know."

"There are always weak areas to be strengthened, don't you think?"

"Frankly?" Tom looked at him. "Not in your case, no."

"Damn it, Tom." Avernon stepped back from the membrane; it quivered, then vitrified. "Maybe it's your weaknesses I'm concerned with."

$$\Diamond \Diamond \Diamond$$

"Tom?"

"*Huh!*" Kicking the light sheets from him, Tom rolled to his feet beside the bed, crouched, his arm held in front of him, fingers extended, as though feeling the darkness.

"Can I come in?" Avernon.

"Uh, yeah." Tom pulled a cape around his shoulders as Avernon came inside. "Room: raise lights."

Diffuse illumination made the peach-coloured room warm. A brocaded chair slid up as Avernon dropped to a sitting position, raising a crystal.

"Display."

He was pale, eyes feverish.

"Authorized." Tom, the designated guest, gave the go-ahead. Then, "What's wrong?" he asked, as spectral manifolds unfurled.

"Look at this." Triconic lattices slid into place. "See here . . ."

And then he began to explain.

It took several hours for Tom just to learn Avernon's peculiar abbreviated metavector notation, but by then the excitement had taken him over, galvanizing his nerves so that sleep was forgotten. Layer by layer, drilling in through holotesseracts, Avernon laid out his theory's skeleton, fleshing in the details when Tom could not understand the principles.

"Destiny," Tom murmured at one point. "Just that corollary over there"—he pointed—"is what the ancients called a Theory of Everything, and never found."

Simplicity theory lasted a century; connectivity theory lasted a further three hundred years. Then, in the twenty-fifth century, the old paradigms had been overturned by the Amber Maze model: combining bidirectional time loops with contextual emergenics.

Sub-quantum twistors, vertebrate consciousness, stock-market dynamics and stellar evolution were linked by a web of step-functions which correctly predicted a plethora of phenomena, including the emergence of one-way timeflow at the thermodynamic level.

It was a view of the cosmos that had reigned four and a half times longer than Newton's once had, and now Avernon was challenging it.

And Tom Corcorigan was there to see it happen.

After Avernon closeted himself away—even he felt the need for some preparation before his summons—Tom continued to work through auxiliary problems by himself. Awe, like a subsonic chord, thrummed constantly inside him. How could these bright marvels have appeared in Avernon's mind?

He ploughed on, not noticing the time, distractedly eating snacks which other servitors brought in, then finally collapsed on the bed and slept.

And dreamed.

On black velvet, a string of white pearls lay glistening.

A necklace . . .

When he awoke again, it was fifteen hours after he had gone to bed.

Fading dream-tag: *ghostly pearls dissolved* as reality crowded in.

A waiting note from Avernon invited him to lunch. Tom said yes, and waved the tricon out of existence. Naked, he walked through the glimmering clean-film, dressed, and was in the dining-chamber within five minutes.

"They'll make you an Academician-Premier at least," said Tom, sitting down.

"I suppose. That would be all right, so long as I could do real work." Avernon looked morose, picking at his food with a tine-spoon. Suddenly he laughed. "Bet you a thousand coronae they never make me an administrator."

"Er . . ."

"Negative occurrence, right? Twenty SY, then. If I'm still doing research, you owe me a thousand."

Tom shook his head. "I hate to point this out—"

"No, no." Avernon interrupted. "You'll be able to afford it. But we'll make it one corona, if that makes you happier."

"OK. Done."

Just then, a rigid-looking servitor in the turquoise-with-violet-slashes livery of the host Lord, Count Shernafil, marched into the room and bowed to Avernon.

"The Review Committee, my Lord, requests your presence. At your convenience."

Avernon's smartchair extruded a tendril to wipe his mouth, napkin-like, as he rose. It startled Tom, whose own chair—reading his servitor ID from his ruby earstud—had remained in static form.

"Wish me luck."

"Good luck." Tom smiled at the mildly heretical form of words: Avernon's metavectors had not replaced the concept of manifest Destiny. "But you don't need it."

"Right. Um . . . You know they're not so much looking for one piece of work as for someone who can produce results consistently, over time."

"OK—"

"See you at the Grand Assembly."

But that's five days away, thought Tom. *What am I supposed to—?*

"In the meantime," added Avernon, "if I were you, I'd study hard."

He turned to the waiting servitor. "Lead the way, then."

On the fourth day, they sent for him.

Tom was exhausted, febrile, hardly able to speak: dosed to the limit with logotropes, their femtocytic networks extending his mental vision so that a thousand proof-dendrimers and phase-space manifolds coexisted in parallel.

Information-entropic logos-flow was embedded as kinaesthetic feel, proprioceptive stimulus, even emotional strength.

He was trembling from overstimulation. His training-runs—in his room, on his small running-pad—had been short, maybe fifteen minutes long, but he had run ten times a day, failing to burn off his adrenaline, while logosophical constructs whirled in his mind.

When the servitor came for him, Tom could not even acknowledge the summons; he let himself be led.

He scarcely noticed his surroundings until they reached the committee chamber's door. It was a wide copper oval containing a white membrane, growing transparent at Tom's approach.

He stepped inside.

Communication problem. He walked across the cold flagstones and stopped before the wide marble table. *How do I demonstrate everything I know?*

But the three Lords Academic themselves, beneath their canopied chairs, had the flickering eyelids and "infinity stare" of logotropic trance. They were prepared for his presentation.

"I, er." Tom cleared his throat. "I see you, my Lords . . ." A grey-cowled glowcluster floated overhead, and he pointed to it. ". . . by photons emitted from this, reflected from your skin, then travelling into my retinae, where the photons are destroyed.

"But, as a journey's speed increases, its duration decreases, changing by a factor of $(1 - v^2/c^2)^{-1/2}$. At light-speed duration becomes zero.

"So these photons, this multitude, have lives with beginnings and endings, but no duration in time."

Tom gestured holomanifolds into being. "In Old Terran philosophy, this phenomenon was known, but not yet appreciated . . ."

As he plodded through the classics, he sensed the Lords' increasing boredom, their slipping out of trance.

They—presumably—had seen Avernon's new approach, which showed how pure numbers and brane-tensegrity relations defined and were manifest through the universal subquantum matrix. The myriad contexts of emergence were tied together with well-behaved metavectors . . .

Tom was expounding ancient concepts, when Avernon had just changed everything.

By the time he came to demonstrate his own metalevel-recursion notation, he was becoming bored, and passed off the approach as caprice. His model, once instantiated in burning fire in his mind, now seemed a lacklustre trick; its time-saving proof solutions were chance results.

"And, er, that's it, really," he concluded.

There was a silence. One of the Lords coughed, then said: "And have you any notion of problems you might like to investigate?"

"One or two, in, um, visual-loop algorithms and paradoxicon representations. And . . . I write poetry."

"I see."

This time the silence lasted longer.

"Thank you for your time."

Another Lord, eyes bright beneath white, bushy eyebrows, spoke up: "I'm sure I speak for us all in saying that it was a privilege to hear your discourse."

The other two nodded.

"You have achieved well, given your, ah, provenance. Well done, Corcorigan."

It was a dismissal. Heart sinking, Tom bowed.

"Thank you, my Lords."

I've failed.

He turned, and walked across the cold, shining flagstones.

Necklace.

He remembered the pearls . . .

A string of them, glistening against velvet blackness.

Cosmic necklace.

Dream image.

Insight? Or delusion?

He stopped. Behind him, the Review Committee's presence felt like static electricity crawling across his back.

Fist and stallion.

A deep refrain, pounding: Dervlin's determined admonition, never to give up.

Heart thumping, Tom turned back.

"Sirs? My Lords?" Voice quavering: ignore. "A point of detail— something I missed. Can I go over it?"

An exchange of dour glances.

The central Lord nodded gravely. "Approach, young man. In your own time."

Breath control. As in Maestro da Silva's classes: mental state changes triggered by physiological transitions.

"You're familiar, my Lords, with Lord Avernon's work?"

A widening of eyes. Surprised that he should know of it.

Use your weakness.

The maestro's refrain to a small student facing a charging bigger opponent. Use agility, the surroundings, anything . . .

Unable to mix socially with nobility, Tom had worked on his Sorites School assignments alone. Lacking their access levels, he endlessly replayed Karyn's Tale, exploring the limited hyperlinks to Terran ecology, sociology, to mu-space physics.

I know stuff the others don't. Slow exhalation. *Use it.*

"Inspiring, isn't it?" He meant Avernon's theory. "Broad as well as deep."

Striding carefully across the polished floor, he gestured one holodisplay after another into existence.

"So revolutionary, no-one's had time to work through the implications." Animated now, he was surrounded by wafting, translucent phase-space manifolds: gossamer sheets manifested in light.

"If you think of it"—causing a burst of new volumes: blue, silver and a hundred pastel shades—"it resolves the ancient negentropy question, once and for all."

Stillness in the chamber.

Tom drew Avernon-style metavectors into position. The Lords, eyes flickering, descended into deep logosophical trance.

An easy picture.

His key display was a simple 3-D static image: glistening, roughly spheroidal, denoting a flat (2-D) universe. It started as a point, grew larger to a maximum diameter, then shrank again to another point.

The universe as a giant pearl; time as a horizontal axis.

Base everything around that.

It grew from the big bang—with entropic time flowing in the same direction: the big bang was in the past, the period of greater size was in the future—up to a maximum size.

Then the universe began to shrink towards the big crunch but *with time reversed*, so that, in the second half of the universe's life, the final big crunch was in the past, and, again, the time of maximum size was in the future.

From left and right, from two opposite points—like an east and west pole—golden arrows pointed across the surface to the vertical circle, like a 0-degree longitudinal circle.

Make the arrows glow.

There were, in effect, *two big bangs*. Two cosmic histories colliding in the middle, where time switched over from one direction to the other. The concept was called Gold-Sakharov negentropy, and it was so old that Tom was not sure of its origins.

Pause now.

Tom allowed the Lords to meditate on his display.

"Previous arguments," he continued after a few minutes, "have relied on symmetry. Avernon's—excuse me, Lord Avernon's—metavector actually requires it"—he pointed to a twisting manifold—"for consistency."

Beyond the simple pearl image, more sophisticated imagery showed the cosmos as a hypersphere (subtly different-hued, distorted spheroids nestling along a notional time-axis) and as a moving construct in 12-space.

"It would be interesting to see how that would map to mu-space—"

Destiny! The Lords, stony-faced in logotropic trance, said nothing. *What have I revealed?*

"—which I know nothing of, except that its mythical dimensions were supposed to be fractal. As a thought experiment, consider the possibility of an infinitely recursive, self-referencing statement, attempting to complete itself."

I'm doing it.

Excited now, almost forgetting the committee, Tom waved golden seas and spongiform black stars into being.

"The number of depths and the number of instances are both infinite. But is one infinity a bigger class of infinity than the other?"

He waited a moment, then plunged on.

"By applying the metavector"—almost dancing, he manoeuvred through his images—"we see that it negates Gödel's theorem as a direct analogue of negating unidirectional entropic time in realspace."

No questions.

There could not be, for the Lords were too deep in trance to verbalize, and Tom had full control of the holos.

"—which brings us back to the symmetry arguments. Our realspace cosmos begins from a tiny locus, expands with time until a maximum is reached, then contracts once more to a near-point."

Pearl. Simple image.

"The universe essentially has two origins in time, which grow forwards to meet each other. Two big bangs. *We can't know which half of the cosmic life cycle we're in.*"

Something strange about the Lords' regard . . .

"It means, of course, that while Destiny remains paramount as always, a physical interpretation is that the cosmos starts at maximum size and shrinks symmetrically in two directions, *against* the flow of time."

Unspoken communication between the Lords.

They're not surprised!

In his peripheral vision, Tom saw the near-subliminal gestures. *They know this already. And something more.*

He pressed on.

"Now the Avernon metavector"—Tom hid a smile, wondering if he had just coined a name for posterity—"requires the symmetry. But symmetry *cannot be broken* at the end points, at the big bang or crunch, any more than at the midpoint. So, in fact, the universal history must look like this."

The universe was no longer a single pearl.

It was a long string of pearls, one after the other.

Each pearl was one generation of the visible universe. But it replicated itself, over and over. Identically? Tom could not tell; he was not sure if even Avernon's metavectors would provide the answer.

It was the true cosmic cycle, revealed for the first time.

"The ancient questions were: (1) does the universe keep expanding for ever? When that was answered—definitely not—they asked: (2) does time reverse when the universe contracts? As we now know, it does."

With a grand gesture, Tom swept every one of his two hundred displays out of existence, save one.

Only the hanging string of pearls—*cosmic necklace*—remained.

"So now the question is (3) whether the string extends infinitely or is closed up to form a loop, as in a lady's necklace . . ."

He was bathed with sweat, pumped up with adrenaline, as though he had run for many kilometres.

"And that question, my Lords"—he bowed low—"you are much better equipped to answer than I."

The silence seemed to last for ever.

There were other things Tom could talk about, a dozen research topics suggesting themselves. Yet he held back, knowing he should keep something in reserve.

Blinking and, in one instance, yawning, the Lords pulled themselves out of trance. Their grave faces seemed blurred, tired.

I'm exhausted, Tom realized. *But I've done the best I can.*

Their eyes refocused on their surroundings.

Tom bowed again, low and courteous.

Let them judge me on this.

Then he left, chin held high.

37

NULAPEIRON AD 3413

Final day.

The Exedra Concordia was a huge hall: platonic solids revolving in mid-air, among lacy web-columns of fine white ceramic. Banked tiers of canopied smartseats. Tapestry banners bearing flat-projected paradoxi-cons; Tom whiled away the long wait by guessing the missing facets.

He was high up, near the rear. His crimson seat was at the end of a row, with neither canopy nor reshape-capability.

Down below, thirteen nobles—ten Lords Maximi, three Ladies Maximae—gave welcoming speeches. Each stood on a wide, floating crystal sculpture—sapphire, violet, crimson: spread-winged gryphons, eagles—which drifted into the foremost position when it was the rider's turn to speak.

Haunting music. Dreaming flutes; sweet strings; a distant roll of martial drums—*I wonder where Dervlin is now*—as Field Marshal Lord Takegawa, in full dress uniform, marched in with other senior military men and women to take seats in the first row.

A more splendid refrain of massed horns and a solitary pipe began to rise. Blue-robed Lords Academic filed in and took their places.

It was Lord A'Dekal who led the ceremony, his voice cast by the hall's systems across the thousands-strong audience.

"My Lords and Ladies, let us meditate."

His long, white beard lay in contrast against his azure robe; was complemented by the stiff, white cape, its ornately horned cowl framing his long, stern face.

Did you always look the part of Primus-among-Maximi? Tom wondered. *Or have you taken on the image that others expect?*

Down below, in the fourth tier from the front, the younger Lords and Ladies wore scarlet trimmed with yellow. They were awaiting the Nuntiatio Dominorum, in which promotions and fiefdoms would be announced, and secondments to heirless realms or elevation to the higher ranks of academia would be made public.

None of them knew their fate.

Tom had briefly talked yesterday with Avernon—"Surely you must know what position you've got?"—but Avernon merely shook his head, with an almost bemused smile.

He could see Avernon now, in the middle of the fourth row, his scarlet cap set at an odd angle. Carelessness rather than jauntiness. Two of Avernon's peers, the devil-may-care duo of Falvonn and Kirindahl, were stiffly formal today.

Your futures have been decided already. Tom almost pitied them. *You just don't know what it is yet.*

The ceremony's agenda had been printed in flat-text on crystalline laminae, and every attendee had a copy. Tom wondered how many of the audience could read the archaic format.

He checked the items still to come.

There were Lord A'Dekal's summary of the year's events in the sector; a chorale by the Floating Singers of Kalgathoria; talks on fiscal policy and interdemesne trade agreements; and the Lord Xalteron Anniversary Speech to be delivered by Duke Boltrivar, it being fifty SY since the distinguished logosopher Xalteron (now deceased) had codified his ethical calculus and overseen its widespread dissemination.

Ethics. After so many of Boltrivar's subjects had died three years ago.

And where were you when the riverflood broke, my Duke?

Tom knew the answer: far away on an "impromptu" diplomatic visit.

He closed his eyes.

His left arm itched. If only it existed, he could have scratched it.

Snapping his eyes open, he scanned the schedule again, estimating the ceremony's duration. Two hours, at least.

After Duke Boltrivar's item, there would be the announcements of ambassadorships and appointments to the Fora-Regnorum. They were for older nobles—the grander Lords and Ladies—and were temporary, often part-time assignments, though highly prestigious.

The futures of the more senior peers were not at stake today. They would have been party to the arrangements; the announcements were pro forma.

"*. . . like to review the events of a most propitious year . . .*"

There were few freedmen among the gathering's members. No proletarian promotions would be announced here.

Later, when the Convocation proper had ended, there would be three more days of meetings. Some commoners' assignments might be decided then, but it was still rare. A subject's future was normally decided by his or her own Lord.

But they brought me before the Review Committee.

Tom did not know what to expect. Maybe a teaching assistantship? In the Sorites School, perhaps. Or in some other realm.

"*. . . increased revenue by . . .*"

Today he was here only to watch Avernon's official recognition and assignment. But that was hours away.

I shouldn't have drunk all that daistral.

He slipped from his seat and headed up the aisle to the rear membrane. Outside, the corridor was a sweeping grey-black curve, almost deserted. He nodded to a servitor, who bowed awkwardly (discomfited by Tom's wearing a guest's scarlet sash but a servitor's earstud), and headed for the wash-chamber.

Afterwards, he returned to the corridor. It was cool and peaceful, and long black bench-seats arced along one wall.

I have no duties, Tom realized with a kind of eerie shock. *There's a grand ceremony going on in the hall, which most servitors would kill to see. But it's boring.*

Half amused at his own actions, he slipped off his half-cape and laid it on the seat. Carefully ignoring the servitors, Tom sat down, pulled his legs up into lotus, and closed his eyes.

He exhaled.

"Sir?"

Tom opened his eyes. From the hall, applause.

"They're announcing senior ambassadors, sir." The tall servitor, standing by Tom's bench-seat, spoke respectfully.

"Thank you."

Wisely, Tom had changed earlier from lotus to an easier cross-legged position. Now, as he slid off the bench and stood, there was only the tiniest twinge of stiffness. "I'd better get back to my proper place."

The other servitor bowed and backed away.

Don't treat me like that.

Tom slipped through the membrane and walked down the aisle to his waiting seat.

The audience applauded another appointment. Down below, Lord A'Dekal was handing a thumb ring of office to a distinguished Lady.

Nobody paid attention as Tom regained his place.

"*. . . to become Duke of Pelokrinitsa . . .*" The first of the younger Lords was now being awarded office. "*. . . by virtue of logos and thinatos, power in thought and deed . . .*"

Tom applauded, clapping his hand against his thigh. Then he sighed inwardly as Lord A'Dekal announced the next elevation in rank.

One by one the young nobles, Lords and Ladies, ascended on floating crystal stepping-discs to Lord A'Dekal's platform. Their scarlet-and-yellow robes were bright, almost glowing as they accepted their honours.

Finally, it was Avernon's turn.

"*. . . for a great leap forward in human understanding, in a sweeping but subtle reformation of deepest logos, soon to be known in every realm . . . I present* *the new Sapiens Primus of l'Academia Ultima, and visiting Isslyedavetel of Skola Na'wchnya, the most honourable Lord Avernon!"*

Tom joined in the thunderous applause.

You're winning our bet so far. The two positions were pure-research roles, the highest attainable. *Good for you, Avernon.*

There were three or four more appointments announced by Lord A'Dekal, and the clapping was prolonged. Partly, it was a continuation of the genuine warmth for Avernon.

But also, the long ceremony was drawing to a close.

". . . last of all, and most unexpected: an elevation from the common ranks. A rare event, my Lords and Ladies, and unknown in this sector for nearly a century."

Stunned silence.

"Thomas Corcorigan, would you stand, please?"

Blood-rush in his ears. The world slipped in and out of focus.

Shakily, he stood.

"Come down, if you would."

Scattered clapping.

He felt disembodied. Unsteadily, swallowing, Tom made his way along the downward-sloping aisle.

". . . with fewer advantages than the rest of us, and despite his background . . ."

There were attendants, alpha-class servitors, and their gentle hands helped him up to the first floating crystal step. Then he was on his own.

". . . and an outstanding presentation to the Review Committee . . ."

Above him, Lord A'Dekal beckoned.

Heart hammering, Tom climbed to the next crystal—glancing at Avernon's beaming face amid the crowd—then to the next, moving automatically.

Then he was standing, paralysed, before the tall Lord.

"Take this," Lord A'Dekal murmured. "Go on."

It was a silver thumb ring. Hand shaking, Tom reached for it.

"My Lords and Ladies . . ."

Lord A'Dekal turned around on the floating platform. His regal voice, projected by the hall systems, rang out across the great hall.

". . . may I present to you Lord Corcorigan. He will be ruler of Veldrin Provincia, a new realm bordering Lord Shinkenar's demesne."

Tom turned to face the rows of people. The applause was massive—

Destiny! It's really happening.

—a roll of thunder which stretched on and on, for ever.

Lord Corcorigan bowed, and descended to meet his peers.

38

NULAPEIRON AD 3413

Golden background powdered with black stars, slashed by a diagonal bend surmounted by a poignard gules . . .

"I don't think so."

He waved it out of existence.

Azure Möbius-strip inescutcheon, argent stallion rampant in the first quarter.

"Fate. How bloody pretentious can I possibly get?"

A soft chime sounded.

"Come in," called Tom, minimizing the holovolume.

"Were you busy, my Lord?" Avernon poked his head through the membrane.

Tom laughed. "Not really, my Lord."

"Designing a coat-of-arms, Lord Corcorigan?"

"*Noblesse oblige . . .* or *noblesse s'amuse.* Do come in, Lord Avernon. Make yourself comfortable."

Avernon came into the gold-appointed drawing-room.

"Stopped grinning yet?"

"No."

"You look as though you're floating off the ground."

Tom shook his head, but not in denial . . . just at the strangeness of the situation. The old market chamber seemed a lifetime away: somebody else's life.

"When are you seeing Lord Shinkenar?"

"Father?" Avernon shrugged. "On the way to l'Academia, I suppose."

"Don't forget—"

"—to thank him on your behalf. Right."

"Sorry." Not the first time Tom had mentioned it.

Though Avernon had spent many years fostered into Lady Darinia's extended family, his father was Lord Shinkenar: first proposer of Tom's elevation, and responsible for the creation of Tom's demesne.

He didn't come to see your triumph. Tom looked at Avernon. *But you haven't complained once.*

Yet nothing was that simple. Tom was now the ruler of Veldrin Provincia: a modest demesne, formed from some outer sections of Lord Shinkenar's own realm, plus reclaimed interdemesne caverns and halls which had lain unused for a century.

It was a very handsome gesture of gratitude.

"You saved my life." Avernon gestured to a couch, and it slid across the floor to him. "He wanted to repay you years ago, when it happened"—he lay down on the couch, crossed his hands beneath his head, and stared at the mother-of-pearl ceiling—"but someone had already bought you a thousand merit points—"

What?

Tom had always thought that merit points were an automatic award. A cost to the system, not to an individual.

"I didn't realize that merits could come from a donor."

"Over a certain limit, they have to." Avernon squinted at the slowly changing swirls in the panels above him. "I forget what the threshold is. A hundred points, maybe?"

In all Tom's time as a servitor, nobody had mentioned this. And he had never known anyone else to be awarded more than twenty points at a time—and even that was rare—so the issue had never arisen.

"But if it wasn't your father . . ." Tom's voice trailed off.

Who gave me my start? Lady Darinia?

The question burned in his mind.

Or Sylvana?

Intricate fairings swept back across a glistening carapace: it hung silently above the courtyard.

"Not bad," said Tom.

"Can't have a Lord without a lev-car, can we? That's what Father says."

"You won't have time to ride it." Tom clapped Avernon on the shoulder—an action which, a couple of days ago, would have carried heavy punishment. "Hobnobbing with the great minds of our age, unravelling the cosmic mysteries . . ."

". . . chasing women . . ."

". . . and chasing women, with no time for mundane activities like joyriding."

"You're exactly right." Avernon held out a small crystal shard. "That's why the lev-car is yours."

Tom was speechless. Not at the gift itself, so much as the implications: that he could go anywhere, ride it where he pleased.

He rubbed his earlobe where the ID stud had been.

"Want to try it out, Tom?"

The crystal shard, having transferred ownership codes to Tom's thumb ring, dissolved in his hand.

"I guess we'd better."

Tom gestured. The lev-car rose and floated across to the colonnade by which he and Avernon stood. Raising its retro-fashionable gull-doors, it sank to the flagstones.

"Beautiful."

Tom slid inside first.

They moved off, slipping beneath a trellis archway covered in cloying air-blossom. A group of Ladies, conversing on a high balcony on a silver buttress, stopped as Tom and Avernon passed.

Tom tuned the cockpit to transparency. He gave a cheery wave to the Ladies, then turned the lev-car and sailed towards a wide tunnel.

They came out in a vast, raw cavern. They were still in interstitial territory, belonging to no demesne, perhaps two klicks from the Convocation venue, the Congressio Interstata.

The natural stone was black, speckled with greenish yellow. Here and there, red-brown ferric insertions stained the walls like dried blood. Sparse fluorofungus glimmered.

Tom brought the lev-car's stately glide to a halt, and they hovered in place. In front of them five dark tunnel openings were like watching eyes.

"Is everything OK?" asked Avernon.

"I think so. Do you get motion sickness?"

"Er, no. Why do you—?"

"*Go!*" Tom slammed his fist down, whooping as the lev-car leaped forwards and status holovolumes went crazy. "Hang on, now!"

Banking to the left, plunging down, then arcing upwards, heading straight for the cavern ceiling—"Destiny!" muttered Avernon, clinging to his seat—then whipping aside at the last second, twisting, speeding into a tunnel entrance, pressed deep into their seats as velocity increased again and rock walls flew past like fluid slipstream while Tom manically laughed and red-planed the hurtling lev-car's acceleration.

"Not long till the Last Chance Dance."

It was the post-Convocation party.

Avernon, gripplewine in hand, nodded in the direction of a group of finely gowned young Ladies. One of them caught his regard and giggled.

"I beg your pardon?" The collar of Tom's formal half-cape was stiff with new platinum brocade, and he ran a finger inside to loosen it. "Last chance—?"

"Midnight Minuet, officially." Avernon raised an eyebrow. "But, y'know, for the guys who haven't managed to score during the Convocation—"

"It's Falvonn and Kirindahl, isn't it?" Tom indicated the pair who were heading towards them. "They're a bad influence on you."

"Hi, fellows." Avernon greeted the two devil-may-care Lords. "Tom thinks you're a bad influence. This is from a chap who breaks every flight regulation with a passenger who once had a cardiac infarction."

"Er . . ." Tom felt suddenly sick. "I didn't think—"

"Don't listen to him, Tom." Falvonn, swigging from a goblet. "They grew him a new heart when it happened. That's the one thing that definitely won't fail."

"I hope you're not insinuating . . ."

Tom tuned out their conversation.

He had learned that the party-going Falvonn and Kirindahl used to drag the naturally shy Avernon out to social occasions, helping him to meet Ladies, basically, in return for academic tuition. But sometimes their collective emotional development seemed to be stuck at the twelve-year-old stage.

Not sensible, like me. He remembered the mad lev-car flight, and inwardly smiled.

Come to think of it, Falvonn and Kirindahl always seemed to turn up in each other's company. A smart remark rose to Tom's tongue, but he held it back: latent homosexuality was not a topic for jokes in the Primum Stratum, at least in this sector.

He did not think it was true . . . but if it was, and if latency turned to actuality, then they would be disinherited, stripped of their new positions, and demoted to Lords-Minissimi-sans-Demesne. And shunned for ever.

"—do you think, Tom?"

"I'm sorry?"

"She's looking at me. Lady Arlath. What do you reckon?"

"I don't know, Avernon. Are you seriously interested in her?"

Avernon glanced at Falvonn and Kirindahl, and shrugged. "To tell you the truth—"

Tom snagged a glass from a passing tray, turning so that his half-cape fell open plainly to reveal his abbreviated left sleeve.

Lady Arlath blanched and turned back to her friends.

"Just a little social experiment," Tom murmured.

"Fate, Tom." Kirindahl, the quieter of the pair, finally spoke. "Underneath it all, you're an evil bastard. What do you think, chaps?"

Avernon raised his glass.

"We knew that," he said, "all along."

Tom beckoned a servitor—the gesture came too easily—and discarded his half-empty glass.

Laughter arose from the small group of Ladies near the marble archway. Avernon was in their midst, Falvonn and Kirindahl flanking him.

Tom looked around the gathering.

"Do you know anyone, Lord Corcorigan?" It was a young, plain-faced Lady who addressed him. "I'm Yeltina, by the way."

"Honoured." Tom, thinking carefully, gave the correct bow: half-radian angle (for peer-meeting-peer, first occasion), head inclined to the left (for male-meeting-female). "And I don't know anyone here, really."

Among the lacy columns, some three hundred of Gelmethri's elite mingled in small groups. Servitors moved around with trays, backed up by golden microdrones floating discreetly near the opalescent ceiling. Through various archways, neighbouring chambers were visible, filled with partying nobility. The celebrations extended far beyond this one grand chamber.

"That's Countess Nilkitran." Lady Yeltina pointed out a distinguished Lady with a fractal head-dress. "She devised contra-loop web-attractors."

"Good grief!" Tom was amazed. "I've read some of her work. She's brilliant."

"Come on. I'll introduce you."

She led him across to the half-dozen Lords and Ladies who formed Countess Nilkitran's audience. Drawing closer, he caught snatches of fine conversation, but found it hard to catch the words' meaning.

"Um . . . Your work is fantastic, ma'am," he said.

The Countess looked surprised, as Lady Yeltina introduced him: "This is Lord Corcorigan."

"Oh." Countess Nilkitran raised an eyebrow. "So you're the one."

But she smiled then, and everything was fine.

After a few minutes in conversation with the Countess and her admirers, Tom sensed another presence behind him.

"Ah, Lord Corcorigan." The Countess looked over Tom's shoulder. "Let me introduce—"

"Not to worry." An elegant, female voice. "Tom and I are old friends."

Tom noticed the surprised respect in some of the eyes upon him. He turned and said: "Lady V'Delikona. It's good to see you."

The white-haired Lady smiled as he kissed her hand. Then she tucked her arm in his.

"May I take Tom away for a moment?"

"Of course."

Her slender arm felt frail, but her spirit was still formidable. As they walked, she nodded to various Lords who bowed in her direction.

"You've attracted attention in some quarters."

"I guess so, my Lady. I'm having a lot of fun. And it really is good to see you."

"One grows so weary of sycophants." Her eyes were bright with energy in her lined, narrow face. "But when you say that, you mean it."

"I should hope so."

"Mmm. Come on." They moved into an adjoining chamber, a ballroom where slow music was gently playing. "Want to dance with a little old Lady?"

"My pleasure," Tom said truthfully.

As they moved slowly around the floor, she looked up at him. "You dance well."

"I learned mostly by watching . . ." Tom grinned slyly.

". . . standing by the wall," she finished for him, glancing at the servitors who even now ringed the ballroom. "Waiting on your *superiors*." Her irony matched his.

When the dance was over, she declined the offer of another.

"I was talking to A'Dekal earlier"—she was referring to Lord A'Dekal, ranked Primus Maximus—"and he mentioned an interest in meeting you."

"That's kind." Tom's voice was carefully neutral.

"Maybe, maybe not." Lady V'Delikona looked serious. She grabbed his forearm. "Promise me something, Tom."

"Anything."

"Remember that you deserve everything you've achieved." Her voice grew fierce. "What others have handed to them on a plate, you've earned by your own efforts. Believe in your strength."

"I . . . thank you."

"Don't forget. And keep your guard up. A'Dekal's a brilliant logosopher, but a rotten human being."

"Funny," said Tom, "how the two don't always go together."

"That's right." She tightened her arm in his again. "Except for you and me, babe."

Her sudden smile was heartbreaking, despite their difference in years, and Tom laughed. Inside, he was deeply moved.

Then she took him out to a small balcony, and left him alone with Lord A'Dekal.

$$\diamond \diamond \diamond$$

"I looked over the logs, Tom, of your Review presentation." Lord A'Dekal smiled frostily. "Most intriguing, though not in my area of expertise."

"Nor up to your standards, sir." Tom's reply was diplomatic more than truthful. "Your stochastic-certainty cytomatrices are required studies at Lady Darinia's Sorites School."

"Just so."

The balcony clung outside a marble-encrusted drawing-room. Below, in a low courtyard, an impromptu lightball game was in progress. Laughing white-shirted Lords, tunics and capes discarded, chased the whining, fluorescing ball.

"Builds backbone," added Lord A'Dekal. "The noble pursuit. I was in the first seventeen at l'Academia Ultima. Do you play?"

"Er, no." Tom realized belatedly that he was talking about lightball.

"Pity. Sound mind, sound body."

"I guess so." Tom thought of the thousands of hours he had spent running, stretching, practising phi2dao.

"You're welcome to visit my demesne." Lord A'Dekal's clipped tone made it sound like an order. "Come in two tendays. You can join in the bat hunt."

"Thank you."

"I don't suppose you've handled a graser rifle before."

"No, sir. But hunting doesn't sound like the kind of thing I'd be good at."

White eyebrows exaggerated A'Dekal's frown. "I suppose not. But you can stay for a while. You'll be welcome to use *all* the facilities."

Tom stared at the stony-faced old Lord, trying to understand his meaning.

"Any handicap in the sporting arena"—Lord A'Dekal's stern gaze was fixed determinedly on Tom's face—"can be overcome. My medical facilities are superlative; you know of my research."

He's trying not to look at my stump. Tom twisted slightly, moving his left shoulder forwards, and the tiniest of twitches plucked at Lord A'Dekal's right eye.

"My femtovats," Lord A'Dekal continued, "have clone and fast-grow facilities."

"Ah," said Tom. "I see. Thank you."

And he did see.

He can regrow my missing arm.

Cursing his lack of control, Tom glanced down at his abbreviated left sleeve. And when he looked up, there was the subtle, superior light of victory in Lord A'Dekal's eyes.

Of course. Bitterness flooded through Tom. *We can't have the newest Lord looking like a thief, can we?*

The regrowth could be achieved. There would be the long, painful physiotherapy afterwards . . . but in a few tendays, Tom could be whole once more.

White, glinting. A small teardrop-shape on Lord A'Dekal's palm: an offering.

Tom took the object.

"My Lord?" It pulsed with light: pure white rings, intricately revolving. Tom recognized the emblem now. "You're chairman of the Circulus Fidus, of course."

"An impartial think-tank," said Lord A'Dekal smoothly. "Though not without influence in matters politic."

Tom closed his fist around the holopin.

The Circulus's political philosophy was reactionary. Tom doubted that they favoured elevation of commoners to the noble ranks.

"I'm too new to this level, my Lord, to consider political alle-giances. I'd be a hindrance more than a help to anyone."

"You misunderstand me, Tom. There is no price attached to my friendship. Just visit me."

Tom regarded those glacial eyes.

You don't have friends, he thought. *You have allies.*

His skin crawled. Had he expected a life of gracious ease and no worries?

Allies. And enemies.

He made his choice.

"I . . . don't think so, my Lord."

The expression behind Lord A'Dekal's cold eyes shut down. "I see."

I could have my arm back.

But he remembered Lady V'Delikona's words: that he deserved what he had won, that he should believe in his own strength.

My arm.

Lord A'Dekal turned away.

"My Lord . . ." Tom let his voice trail off, knowing that A'Dekal would think he had weakened. "Thank you, sincerely, for your offer. You've been very gracious to this new Lord."

A curt nod, then A'Dekal headed back in towards the drawing-room, leaving Tom alone.

Believe in my strength, Lady V'Delikona?

Fist clenched, A'Dekal's holopin digging into his palm, Tom faced out across the courtyard. Raucous laughter from the lightball game below echoed back from the carved ceiling. But he was blind to the sport.

Hatred.

A hard lesson to learn. A bitter one. And he had never realized it, not before this moment.

It's hatred that feeds my strength. It always has been.

It was a moment of black enlightenment, thanks to Lord A'Dekal, which Tom would have preferred to live without. Cold hatred: of the Oracle, of the system that nurtured him.

Tom went in to rejoin the party. But everything was different now.

39
TERRA AD 2123
<<Karyn's Tale>>
[9]

//insert
{commentary.provenance = πσ3ç989/Petra deVries/
personal.journal/KMcN}
{   [[Vortex.homeostasis = established]]
     [[P(phase-transition) = 1.0000]]
     [[Recursion level = 10 exp 38]]

Inside the trapped vessel lies a paradox, an oddness. A form of life based on a twin-spiral molecule: a molecule which is simultaneously a chemical factory and a blueprint of itself.

The mu-space pattern . . . somehow, somehow, through some unsettling resonance . . . dimly perceives the intruder's form and function.

How can this be? How can a tool, a factory, be its own design? What could produce such a strange loop? What odd processing could manifest it thus?

The pattern is a maze of scarlet lightning tumbling and twisting through the omnipresent golden sea. Its core now firmly wraps around the strange intruder, but its tendrils spread outwards. Questing, questing . . .

It is self-organized criticality. Neither life nor not-life.

A new thing happens. An exploratory tendril meets another nascent pattern, another crackling turbulence. Before, they would have passed through each other without interference. But the intruding vessel has seeded a non-linearity, a growth algorithm . . .

The original pattern reconfigures, adapts, plunders the new pattern for its complex inner forms, and moves on. Fragmented whorls of dissipating energy spin off into the golden void, twist apart, and are gone.

It searches for new patterns to learn from: new configurations, new configuration-changing algorithms. Perhaps some algorithm will be subtle enough, shifting and strange enough, to burrow inwards, to pierce the unsettling intrusion now firmly embedded inside the pattern's core.

Searching . . .

The questing pattern is not quite alive.

end-insert//

New Year in Paris. Fireworks exploded in the dark night above the Seine, a cascade of brilliant hues, spelling out their message of good cheer:

BONNE ANNÉE!

Karyn sat, chilled, by a riverside table. The other diners sat indoors, inside the twisted labyrinth of mirrors which formed the Café Catoptrique. Carmine and silver liquid light trailed across its polished surface, reflecting the fireworks above.

No sign of Sensei. Hands wrapped around her glass of choco, grateful for its warmth, she looked up and down the embankment for the thirtieth time.

I should be badgering the project managers. But all her attempts at shifting UNSA bureaucracy had ignominiously failed.

Pointless.

At the centre of her sculpted-mirror table lay a holoterminal core, with a zigzag slot along its side. She stared at it, trying to figure out how one powered it up.

Dart . . .

Maybe Mike, Sensei, had just been delayed. If only she could check the arrivals at l'Éspace-Port Barbet—

"*Pardonnez-moi, mademoiselle.*" The young waiter who had brought her the choco reappeared. "*Il faut acheter un jeton*"—he gestured—"*pour le terminale, vous comprenez?*"

"*Ouais*," Karyn made her accent deliberately coarse. "I guess so."

A crimson starburst cracked open overhead as she pulled her Cred-Master ribbon from her bracelet. By the light of the dying firework, the waiter ran the ribbon through his handheld pad and handed it back.

"*Un moment . . .*"

There can't be a technological reason for this, thought Karyn, reeling the CredMaster back into her bracelet.

She watched the waiter walk inside, search behind a zinc-topped counter, then slowly return with the tiny bent token. He presented it to her with a flourish.

"*Merci*," she said.

"*De rien.*"

She fed the token into the holoterminal core. The one/zero/mu logon display blossomed just as golden explosions of light filled the night above the city.

"Bloody hell," she said. A trio of figures broke out of the slow-moving crowds and walked towards her. Sighing, she powered down the terminal.

"That's a fine greeting on a cold night like this." Sensei—Mike—looked bulky in his heavy coat, plain scarf tucked beneath his grey beard, dark hat pulled down low. "And a Happy New Year to you."

His two companions were a slender man and woman, elegantly dressed in sharp lightweight clothing, on which shimmering thermal elements formed curlicued decorative webs.

"Sorry." Karyn held out her hand.

"Jacques Lebrun." His handshake was dry and firm, lingering just a little too long. "Journalist, TechnoMonde Vingt-Deux."

"Pleased to meet you."

The woman remained watchfully in the background; neither Lebrun nor Sensei attempted to introduce her.

"It is my pleasure," said Lebrun.

He was an attractive man, Karyn realized. But that only intensified her longing for Dart, for the touch of his calloused hands across her skin . . .

She focused her attention on the moment.

"Your thumbprint," added Lebrun, holding out a transparent wafer.

Karyn looked at Mike; he nodded. "OK."

"I don't usually sign a contract," she said, pressing her thumb against the wafer, "without reading every clause."

"It has a . . . get-out option, is that right?" Lebrun turned to the woman, who nodded. "We will conduct the interview next week. OK?"

"*D'accord.*" Karyn smiled.

"I hope you decide to go ahead." He held out his hand, and they shook. Then he turned to Mike. "Be careful."

Then Lebrun and the anonymous woman left, footsteps clacking quickly on the stone embankment as a final flourish of rockets climaxed, then dwindled overhead.

Beethoven sounded among the Gare du Nord's high neoglassine-coated arches as Karyn and Mike descended from the high pedstrip.

"Our insurance policy," was all Mike had said in explanation. "If we get what we want, we cancel the interview. Jacques will understand."

"If you say so." Karyn had no idea what he was talking about.

There were a surprising number of people milling around the old platforms. But it was New Year, and the metropolitan services were free of charge, according to the flickering festive holos, until eight a.m.

The shinkansen-maglev was a grand old silver bullet-train emblazoned with the << *Beretta-Express* >> logo.

"Here we go." Mike grunted as he climbed aboard. "Don't worry. I've already bought the tickets."

"Jesus Christ." Karyn let out a long sigh as she collapsed onto her curved burgundy seat. "Oops. Sorry."

Mike—or Sensei: but it was always hard for Karyn to think of him as Father Mulligan, Jesuit priest—merely shook his head.

"Well . . ." Karyn cocked an eyebrow. "Weren't we supposed to be going to Jakarta?"

"I had a lesson in subtlety and indirection." Mike smiled. "My contact in Jakarta's BioCentre kept mentioning the two-week Zürich shutdown. Eventually it sank in: I could find what I needed *there*, not in the lab that was still open."

"So we're blending. Going with the flow."

"Exactly right. You have the data your friend prepared? What's his name?"

"Chojun." Karyn stared out of the window. The station was sliding smoothly past. Inside the train, the acceleration was imperceptible. "Chojun Akazawa. Yes, I've got the data."

"Between that and whatever we find in Zürich, we should achieve a strong bargaining position."

"Christ, I hope so."

Half mansion, half buckydome, outside the city: the UNSA facility was lavish, though not huge. They passed beside an arcing fountain and through a dozen security barriers of increasing thoroughness.

Two researchers were inside the lobby to meet them. Diffraction-grating strips, taped across their ID-tags, turned the two men's name-holos into anonymous sparks of random light.

A bright orange emblem, *RàFO*, was emblazoned beneath arrows of the same colour, on the walls of every corridor. There were other abbreviations, other direction indicators, but *RàFO* was the constant one. Their destination?

Underground, the facilities stretched farther than Karyn would have thought. In one corridor lay a small four-seater electric cart, but the two researchers walked past, ignoring it.

She was wrong about their destination. They passed a turning down which *RàFO* was indicated, but the four of them hurried on. Karyn barely had time to read the sign on the doors at the side-corridor's far end: <<*Réacteur à Fusion Optoélectronique*>>.

There were no labels on the heavy ceramic doors before which they finally stopped

Floating toroids. Glass rings through which a thread of blinding blue-white light arced. There were twenty rings, floating in mid-air, themselves arranged into a large circle.

"My God!" Karyn's whisper echoed back oddly from the big lab's shadowed walls.

"I fear," said Mike, "that it's not His work we're witnessing."

They were alone. In low tones, speaking guttural French, the two researchers had promised to come back in twenty minutes, when it would be safe to leave.

"It's a gateway, isn't it?"

One-dimensional, pulsing with secondary radiation, the light-thread opened onto another universe. To mu-space.

"No wonder," Karyn added, "they need their own reactor."

Mike was bent over a display. "I didn't know." He looked up at her. "Really."

"What is it?"

At first sight, it was meaningless to her. But Mike manipulated the holo, expanded and rotated it. He gestured. Text boxes and data lattices slatted into place.

"I had no idea."

Epigenetic history. Individual cytoskeletons analysed: micro-tubules, filaments, transmembrane receptors. Extracellular matrix, labelled and deconstructed. At the level of the whole: a history from the small hollow sphere of the blastula, through gastrulation, then the formation of the notochord, at which point external intervention began.

Secondary displays mapped histogenetic pathways. The full neu-ralation sequence, in a series of time-stamped snapshots, hung like multicoloured spiderwebs above Mike's head.

"We're looking at the contents of that toroid." He indicated the nearest glass ring, squinting against the light-thread. "It's just about visible."

A foetus, still growing.

Human.

The big discs of its eyes extended into tendrils. They branched, forming dendrimers: fractally dividing tributaries, ever narrower, which reached *into* the blinding one-dimensional interface between continua.

What have I uncovered? It was her use of Sal O'Mander—now deleted—that had begun this search.

"I think we have our leverage." Mike's voice was steady.

"But we have to—"

She stopped as *the foetus moved* and Karyn bit her fist, stifling the scream.

The intent was clear. Trying to force-adapt embryos: eventually to *grow* potential Pilots . . .

No excuse.

"The longest-lived foetus," said Mike, standing amid amber holosheets, "lasted ten days after interface." He pointed. "Autopsy results. Everything we need for blackmail, if we identify our target."

"But—" She stopped.

"I know. Dear Mother of God, I know."

Golden reflected light glittered on his silent tears.

<<MODULE ENDS>>

40

NULAPEIRON AD 3413

Dislocation; yet almost nostalgia.

My home.

Sitting in his study, in a wing of his palace—his own palace—able to do anything: access any crystal in his library, go for a run, order anything at all from the—from *his*—kitchens.

"Destiny."

Empty room. Sweeping shelves of narrow glass; a twisting baroque lev-sculpture; rows of crystal-racks. A huge bowl of candied gripple-cubes was set out on a side table.

No duties.

If he wanted, he could summon one of his servitors . . . Fate, he could summon *all* of them.

There was nostalgia, because it was like his childhood: neither owned by anyone nor weighed down by expectations. Yet it was also entirely new.

What do you do when your dreams are fulfilled?

Maestro da Silva had told him of this. When his ablest fencers were trying out for the sector squad, he would warn them. It was so hard to get into the squad, they would focus all their mental imagery —during an entire Standard Year—on passing the team selections.

Then, in the big inter-sector championships, the selected fencers would turn in a lacklustre performance: because their SY-long goal had been satisfied, and there had been no time to lay down a new objective in their deep, unconscious psyche.

So what do I do now, Maestro?

"Display schematic: Veldrin Provincia."

A long, tall, twisted shape, a multi-tiered cylinder bent out of true. Translucent layers. But the holo, slowly revolving above the glassine desk, was labelled not as Veldrin Provincia, but by its new designation.

Corcorigan Demesne.

Twenty-one strata (though bigger demesnes had more) were stacked beneath his Primum Stratum. Did the lower inhabitants know of their change of Liege Lord? How many would care?

Were there market chambers in the depths? Was a lonely stall-holder's son sitting now in some deserted corridor?

"Enough." He waved the holo away.

He looked at the gripplecandies, but did not take one.

Instead, unsealing his tunic pocket, he drew out the hard teardrop-shape. Immediately it pulsed with white revolving rings of light.

"Thank you, my Lord"—remembering the party—"for this reminder."

It was the emblem of A'Dekal's think-tank, the Circulus Fidus.

The rings flickered out as he laid the holopin aside.

I could remain here, in my palace, never seeing my demesne.

He gestured open an enquiry lattice; its intricate triconic webs pulsed, inviting exploration.

Rule unseen.

"Personnel enquiry." Indicating a multihued tricon.

Eat. Grow lazy. Collect my tithes.

The tricon's facets unfolded: a motile origami in light, a subtle semantic maze through which only a Lord might navigate.

Dispense justice by proxy.

Drilling in, plunging—with noble-house access—down strata of a different kind: the layers of information hidden away within the world.

Never see my subjects.

Rows of blossoming tricons, unfolding, blooming, as he picked their tiny seeds of light. Every symbol held at least six meanings:

1) its phoneme sequence;
2) its chromosequence;
3) its numerological facets (where phonemes rhymed with integer values);
4) its mythos resonances (where colour suggested mythical figures—hero or villain, warrior or dragon—and therefore psychological characteristics);
5) its socio-cultural import (denoted by speed of motion and topographic transformation as it revolved, twisted, turned itself continuously inside out); and,
6) subtlest of all, its logosophic gestalt, whereby the mode-of-combination of the other five elements could enhance a tricon's meaning, imbue it with personal or objective significance, even reverse (perhaps ironically) the surface message.

Talk only with my peers. Dissipate.
His equals.
Those trained in the labyrinthine thought processes which could appreciate a written language such as this. A communication modality of rich concepts and subtle, twisted connections.
Remain in my study, reading and researching.
By sheer good fortune, with Avernon's friendship, he could be an ambassador, of sorts, to the world of logosophy: one of the first to work on the new model. He could explore its ramifications, publicize its importance, link it to other modes of investigation. Bring his own skewed insight to bear on Avernon's magnificent work.
Write poetry, perhaps.
There was so much he could do here, reforming his demesne.
"But this is my time, isn't it?"
Whom did he address? Fate itself?
Father's knucklebones, falling into the acidic Vortex Mortis . . .
"And I have someone to thank, after all, for my Destiny."

Facets: petals of shimmering pinks, heartbreaking emeralds, unfolding over and over. An invitation to pluck forth meaning from its holo core.

Mother's cupric tresses. Her hips swaying as she stepped up onto the lev-cart.

"Show me where he lives, this one."

Intricate control gestures, matching the convolution of its parts.

"The one I have to thank."

Reaching inside, to its heart.

"Show me—"

Revealing . . .

"Gérard d'Ovraison."

. . . the Oracle.

Lady Sylvana was his first visitor.

"Sweet Fate, Tom! What is this?"

It was small, with a ceiling which sloped at forty-five degrees.

"Er . . . It used to be a Laksheesh-Heterodox chapel. Don't worry, it's been deconsecrated."

She stared up at the jumble of small protrusions across ceiling and walls. There were three or four hundred shapes fastened there: from small fingerholds to half-metre twisted ridges, with a few grinning gargoyles scattered around for variety.

"I won't ask." Highlights rippled across her golden tresses as she shook her head. "Why—? No. Let's go back outside."

Tom glanced back around the chamber—his training-room for climbing: already he had practised dozens of problems, tracing convoluted routes among the tricky holds—and his smile faded.

I used to climb only for fun.

"This, at least, is pleasant." Outside, Sylvana gestured along the gallery's length. "A cool walk before dinner."

It was Tom's running-gallery, his substitute for the outer reaches of Lady Darinia's Palace. Smaller, but his own.

"I've had one of the minor dining-chambers redecorated," said Tom. "And my study."

"Well, then." Lady Sylvana took his arm. "You'd better show me."

For a moment, Tom could scarcely breathe. Even through the heavy velvet of his black tunic, her touch electrified his skin. Then, regaining composure: "This way."

A phalanx of servitors, both hers and his, trailed them as they walked.

"I'm sorry I wasn't there," she said over dinner, "to see you invested. It must have been quite an occasion."

"Oh, yes." That same involuntary grin spread across Tom's face. "I'll say."

Amusement twinkled in her eyes. "Was that how you looked at the time? Smiling uncontrollably?"

"Oh, no." Tom laughed. "I've almost got used to the whole crazy notion by now."

"This is the subdued look? I really should have been there."

"I wish you and—" Tom stopped.

"Cord would have been there," she said quietly. "But the Field Marshal wouldn't grant him leave. I gather old Takegawa's something of a tyrant."

There was a silence, during which servitors unobtrusively came to the long table, took away the platinum dishes, wiped the marble down with white linen, and brought in the next course.

"I like this decor."

Sylvana's gaze travelled around the sweeping transparent shelves and columns, the slowly moving mother-of-pearl panels. Peacock blue predominated; other chambers were deep green or lustrous red.

"Smartnacre and quickglass." Tom gestured at a flowing translucent faux-buttress. "They'll form a leitmotif."

"Very nice."

Dessert was sorbet and wild dodecapears. Tom picked at his, then placed his tine-spoon down on the tabletop.

"I didn't know you and Corduven kept in touch."

Not since your marriage was annulled.

"Yes." Quietly. "Comms to that whole area are difficult. I think Takegawa keeps the academy deliberately isolated."

Time to change the subject.

"On Old Terra, you know, they had open non-fibre comms, worldwide, for a long time."

"Cooking their brains," said Sylvana, "with EM radiation. Didn't they also make themselves stupid with lead in their cooking-pots?"

"Don't you mean aluminium?" Tom frowned. "Or was that the Romans?"

"Before the Monolingual Stases, anyway."

"Probably." The global monopolies, first of NetAnglic, then of WebMand'rin, had caused education and research to ossify. "Before they figured out the need for diversity."

"Tell that to the Circulus Fidus. They'd like the whole of Nulapeiron to follow their stuffy ways."

Tom raised an eyebrow. "I haven't been following their polemic. Has—? Ah, there's the daistral. Well done, Felgrinar."

The grey-haired man who bowed in acknowledgement of Tom's praise was Tom's chef-steward. With the tiniest gesture of his white-gloved hand, he directed two junior servitors to set down the daistral pot and lay out the cups.

"Speaking of which," Tom continued after the daistral was poured, "Lord A'Dekal, after the ceremony, invited me to visit his demesne."

"I'm impressed." Sylvana raised her cup as though in toast. "Did you enjoy your stay?"

Tom kept his tone noncommittal. "I declined his offer."

Sylvana lowered her cup, untouched.

"You turned down Lord A'Dekal's invitation." A smile slowly spread across her clear-skinned face. "Oh, my word!"

✧✧✧

"The Lady Sylvana will decide the boy's punishment."

Frank blue eyes, appraising him.

"An arm, perhaps?"

"Very well." Lady Darinia stood. "Before you deliver him, remove an arm."

Her grey gaze swept over Tom.

"Either arm will do."

Tom jerked awake. He was bathed in sweat, dripping, and his nonexistent left fist was tightly clenched, every nerve on fire.

"Damn it."

It was the middle of the night, but he rolled from the bed, pulled on running-tights with integral shoes, stretched lightly and went out to run.

He passed the side corridor which led to the guest quarters, thinking of Sylvana in the ornate bed, swathed in white smartsatin—and jogged on.

Ghostly grey. No servitors in sight.

He ran up and down the long gallery for an hour. He was tireless: the more he ran, the stronger he became.

He finished with wind-sprints, then stretched out, performing variations on splits for fifteen minutes.

In his ex-chapel climbing-room, away from the main training configuration, a small looped cord hung from the ceiling.

Alternating, he performed sets of one-hand press-ups and one-finger chin-ups until his tendons were about to pop. Then he worked his abdominals, stretched lightly, and went back to his bedchamber.

He stripped, slapped a glob of smartgel against his chest and let it spread across him, cleansing and exfoliating. As the gel slipped off him and crawled back into its container, Tom climbed into bed.

Controlling his breathing, he began his relaxation: starting with his toes, working up his body, lightly clenching, then releasing, each muscle group in turn.

He slid into dreamless sleep.

"Who would have thought you'd come so far?" Sylvana's voice was musing. "You're hardly the same person . . ."

They were on a smooth ledge, by a wall encrusted with baroque carvings, overlooking a gentle slope. It was the edge of Tom's palace, where dwelling melded into natural cavern. In the depression below, the sapphire-and-gold jewel which was Sylvana's lev-car floated.

"A subversive notion." Tom hitched an eyebrow. "Personality formed by environment."

"Ah, Tom! Always looking for debate. Don't you ever just relax and enjoy yourself?"

Below, three servitors were setting out a silver picnic table by the lev-car. One was oriental in appearance, and Tom realized suddenly that it was Tat, one of his former dorm-mates.

"Truthfully, my Lady?" Tom turned his regard on Sylvana. "I've never had much time for that."

"No," she said thoughtfully. "I don't suppose you have."

She placed her hand on top of his, for balance, as they descended the slope together.

After they were finished, one of the servitors fetched a message crystal for Sylvana. She excused herself and went inside her lev-car, while Tom remained seated.

It was Tat who came over to clear the dishes. His face remained servitor-impassive as he worked.

"Thank you, Tat," Tom said quietly.

A chill worked its way along his spine. For the first time, Tom realized how wide the chasm was between his present circumstances and his former life.

Not once during the meal had Sylvana's glance so much as flickered at the servitors' hands as they laid platters, poured sauce, served drinks, took away dishes.

"A summons from Mother." Sylvana returned, looking thoughtful. "By courier to Lord Shinkenar, then femtopulse to your message centre."

Her complexion was flawless. Her pale-blue eyes were perfect. Soft, pink lips, wide mouth. Artfully arranged blond hair.

Tom forced himself to speak normally. "She wants you back home."

"Yes . . . But I don't think it's serious." Her smile was forced, but the worried frown which hid behind it caught Tom's heart. "I'm glad I got the chance to visit, Tom."

"So am I."

He stood as she prepared to go back inside her lev-car.

"Come and see us. Mother would like to see you, too."

"I will, my Lady."

Sylvana gracefully climbed aboard, while Tom could only watch, entranced.

Two servitors carried the dishes aboard. Tat, gesturing, caused table and chairs to collapse and fold themselves into a knotlike bundle.

"Thanks, old friend." Tom's voice was almost a whisper.

Tat stopped dead, eyes down, then gave the tiniest of nods before picking up the folded furniture and carrying it into the waiting vehicle.

From a colonnade, with a long cape wrapped around himself, Tom watched as Sylvana's sapphire-and-gold lev-car slid out of his realm and was gone.

Then he went back into the heart of his palace, shadowed by his own silent servitors.

41

NULAPEIRON AD 3413

"What's your ambition, Felgrinar?" Tom asked his chef-steward. "What's the one thing you'd really like to achieve?"

"Sir?" Felgrinar put down the infotablet he had fetched.

"Isn't there anything you really want to do?" Tom leaned back in his chair, put his feet up on the glass conference table, and crossed his ankles.

"Nothing, sir, beyond serving"—his face was a stone mask—"to the best of my ability."

Only a former servitor could have sensed the full depths of Felgrinar's disapproval. Did he and the other senior servitors resent their transfer from Shinkenar Palace?

"That will be all, Felgrinar."

The Chef-Steward bowed his way out of Tom's conference chamber.

"Damn." Tom stared, unfocused, at the smartnacre walls. "Damn it all!" He slid his feet from the tabletop. "Access the tablet," he directed the room's system. "Show me everyone in the palace. Start with alpha-class."

Tricons were arrayed above the glass table.

"Now that one looks familiar."

Chuckling, he pointed, and the tricon unfurled.

"My Lord?" A familiar voice from the archway: Tom had already dissolved the membrane.

"Jak!" Tom stood up, and restrained himself from rushing around the table to greet him. "Thank Fate you're here!"

"Anything I can do . . ."

"Sit." Tom pointed to a chair across from him, then seated himself, knowing that Jak could not sit down first. "You're here because of sloppy wording."

"I'm sorry?"

"I asked for a list of all alpha servitors within the palace bounds." Tom indicated the triconic lattice. "Not just those whose allegiance is to me."

"I've been negotiating with your warehouse steward," Jak said stiffly. "Importing procblocks is—"

"Don't worry." Tom held up his hand. "I'm sure that's all fine."

"Thank you."

Tom waited for Jak to say more, then realized he would not.

"I don't suppose you could call me Tom?" He stared at Jak's impassive face. "Ah, well. You've called me worse things—"

A smile twitched on Jak's face.

"—but perhaps you'd better not."

"What can I do for you"—Jak paused, just long enough—"my Lord?"

"Where do I start?" Tom sighed, and nodded at the tricons. "I've got thirty-four servitors and servitrices to interview, and that's just alpha-cl—"

"Begging your pardon, my Lord . . ."

"Any time, Jak. Say what's on your mind."

"You're going to interview them personally? The palace staff?"

"Well, yes." Tom frowned. "How else can I get to know them?"

Jak said nothing: but that was eloquence in itself.

"By Chaos, Jak!" Tom shook his head. "I really did need to talk to you, didn't I?"

"Looks like it, *my Lord.*" Emphasis on the title. The designation which meant Tom could never "get to know" his servitors.

"So what do I do? Tell me."

"Not fair. I don't know the details. But your chef-steward isn't too dynamic, is he?"

Tom sighed. "I didn't want to start by getting rid of people."

"No need to." Jak was reviewing the tricons' surface layers as he spoke. "Let him keep his title, just bring in a majordomo. Then you can—"

"Yes, that's right."

Tom stood up, motioning Jak to remain seated.

"Do you think you could do the job? And would you want to?"

"Chaos! Sorry, I meant—"

"That's OK. Do you want it?"

"I'm a lot younger than Felgrinar," Jak pointed out. "Could be awkward."

"So am I."

"You've other advantages, my Lord. But I'm up for the challenge."

"Good." Tom grinned. "Very good. I'll put in a request directly to Lady Darinia." He swept the triconic display into oblivion. "And I'll leave the interviews for my new majordomo to conduct."

"Sounds good."

"But first . . . Here's something I was going to ask everyone. What are your weaknesses?"

Jak frowned, but realized the question was sincere.

"Rough stuff," he said finally. "Peacekeeping. I can handle steve-dores—usually—but you need someone like Lieutenant Milran. I didn't notice any palace security on the complement."

"There are some watchmen and the like, at phi level," said Tom. "But you're saying I need a head of security?"

"Yes, sir."

"Maybe you're right." It was not a thought to bring him comfort. "Anything more?"

"I'm sure lots will spring to mind later."

Security. Servitor management. What else was he missing?

"I guess"—Tom looked at him—"there are things they don't teach in the Sorites School."

"I could have told you that . . . my Lord."

That night he fell asleep without the benefit of an extra training session.

Claustrophobia . . .

But there was a period during which he slipped in and out of grey wakefulness—

Things with him, in the shadows.

—never quite dropping out of the dream—

Dripping. A liquid dripping upon his cheek.

—then giving himself up to exhaustion, slipping back beneath sleep's veil, surrendering to the half-seen images.

It was huge: a big black cargo train, such as Tom had not seen since his days in the Ragged School. And it had been necessary to descend five strata to see it.

"My Lord." Jak looked concerned. "Seriously. You should not be down this far."

In truth, the twenty uniformed servitors surrounding Tom—some of them conscripted from kitchen duty just for the occasion—looked pale and nervous.

"Do they have any *particular* reason," asked Tom quietly, "to hate their Liege Lord here?"

"Nothing I've heard of." Jak peered into a shadowy side tunnel. "But I have a feeling—Hey!" He shouted to a gang of stevedores. "Watch those cargo-bugs!"

The near-sentient black spheroids, rolling on their stubby legs, had begun to veer off the ramps leading into the cargo cars. Quickly, the loading-crews brought them back under control with spit-wands and sheer manhandling.

"As I was saying, my Lord, you shouldn't be here."

"Damn it." Tom spoke out, knowing that he would be misinterpreted. "I ought to be able to walk safely in my own demesne, no matter the stratum."

"Even so."

"Yes, all right. I'm not going to hang around." Reaching inside his waist sash, Tom drew out a crystal sliver. "Take this, would you?"

"Of course. What's on it, my Lord?"

"Details of my new security chief, I hope."

Jak raised his eyebrows, but said nothing.

"When you get back to Lady Darinia's demesne, do some investigating, would you? See if the person would be interested in transferring allegiance. Check she's as suitable as I think she is. Let's confer before I offer her the position."

"OK." Jak spoke automatically, but his gaze was on the loading-crews, watching the cargo for which he held responsibility.

"And, Jak . . ."

"My Lord?"

"If you decide to transfer allegiance, and Lady Darinia agrees, I really will be your Lord. For the long term. You understand?"

Am I a hypocrite?

Jak bowed, very low. "I do, my Lord."

It was awful.

Hood up, hem of his tattered black cloak just skimming the foetid puddles, he walked along a twisted tunnel. Stepping aside to avoid two burly men hauling a battered smoothcart—its bottom plates worn, to judge by the scraping noise—Tom was careful not to lean against the damp, mossy walls.

My demesne.

Even the fluorofungus was mottled with black: the kind of infection that it was a public duty immediately to report, to avoid its spreading.

When Jak returned, perhaps Tom could get him to start some pro-grammes which would clean all this up.

But we'll need to get the Primum Stratum sorted first. Tom could almost hear the objection. Down here, ten strata below Tom's palace, noble intentions seemed far away and useless.

It had been two tendays since Jak's departure, and his return was imminent. But Tom had wanted to descend, to see the lower parts of his realm with his own eyes.

If it's this bad here, what's it like lower down?

Tom kept his long cloak drawn around him, not certain whether his subjects here would know of their new Lord's deformity.

"What d'you want?" Scowling, grime-blackened, warty face. Bleary eyes. A battered flask in a pocket of his tunic.

"I, er, was looking for the market," said Tom.

But he straightened his stance as he said so, relaxing his shoulders, and the other man unconsciously took a step back.

"That way," he said after a moment, gesturing with his wart-encrusted chin.

From the alcove behind him, two more men stumbled out and glared at Tom, oblivious to their comrade's drawing-back.

They stopped dead as Tom allowed his cloak to fall open: whether at the sight of his stump, or of the long redmetal poignard in a cross-draw position on his left hip, Tom could not tell.

"Thank you." He addressed the man who had given him directions.

Walking on across increasingly uneven flagstones, avoiding water dripping from ceiling cracks, Tom realized that he truly wanted to see the local market chamber. Would it be like the one he had grown up in within Lady Darinia's demesne?

He did not even know in which stratum his original home had lain. But it was not like this one. Surely, his home had been larger, not as grubby as this. The stallholders' tentlike awnings were stained and faded. The few marketgoers seemed bent by woe, malnourished and clad in near-rags.

It should not be like this.

Grimly, he walked around the chamber's pentagonal perimeter, noting the small barefoot children—one with the blank expression but sullen watchful eyes of a thief—and the spiritless haggling, the paucity of goods displayed on the old fabric-covered tables.

*** KILWARE ASSOCIATES ***

The scarlet tricon, just on the edge of his peripheral vision, caught Tom's attention.

Dark, and grimy enough to blend in with the surroundings, it might not even have been the same tent that Tom had seen in Lady Darinia's demesne. But it was the same tricon, projected virtually so that it appeared to hang deep inside the rock wall against which the tent was pitched.

Placing his hand lightly on his poignard's hilt, he stepped inside.

Dim lighting—low scarlet beams peeping out from gaps in a drape at the rear—and long shadowed tables, covered in translucent membrane. Inside were rows of weapons. Immediately, a poignard caught Tom's attention: silver rather than redmetal, but otherwise it could have been twin to the weapon at Tom's belt. He reached down—

"Stop! Don't touch the membrane!"

A slight, shaven-headed man in a dark tunic held out a hand in warning; Tom froze.

"Come here." The man crossed to a side opening in the tent, and beckoned Tom. "Take a look."

Adrenaline fading, Tom joined him. Unobtrusively, the shaven-headed man pulled the opening wider, and pointed out into the market. "See her?" It was an old grey-haired woman, autistically scrubbing her hands over and over—

"That's what the membrane does"—he let the hanging fall back into place—"unless I dissolve it. We don't encourage thieves at Kilware Associates. My name is Brino, by the way."

As Brino turned, a metallic glint in the small of his back denoted another discouragement to theft—as though his quiet, watchful bearing were not enough warning.

Scrubbing, over and over—

Tom shook his head. "I just wanted to look around."

"That's what the woman said. But don't worry"—Brino chuckled—"we'll get her the antidote when she breaks down and asks for it. That's more than most people would do."

"Antidote?"

"It's like a permanent skin condition until treated. Very unpleasant. And there's no generic treatment: the femtocytes have to be coded, exactly matching the toxin's receptors."

"Interesting," said Tom, wondering if it could be used for his palace's defences.

"Also expensive. That's why most people wouldn't treat miscreants for free."

Tom frowned.

"Let me just browse by myself. I promise"—with the tiniest of smiles—"that if I want to touch anything, I'll ask first."

"Very good." The man, Brino, bowed: as though to an official, not to his liege Lord.

Energy weapons were forbidden in all strata of Tom's realm; even his militia, when that was up to strength, would keep their hardware in armouries until needed. But some of these displayed items, among the blades and chains, skirted the intent of the law: brooches which used lev-fields to spit toxic needles, bracelets entwined with monofilament garotting-cord, belts which undid at a touch to form many-stranded blade-whips.

Tom looked at Brino. Small, but with a feline awareness. Much though he disliked the whole concept of this establishment, Tom realized: *This is probably the safest place in my realm.* No thieves in their right minds would try to rob this place.

A whimper sounded from the back of the tent.

"Don't worry." Brino spoke softly as Tom whirled. "One of our patients, that's all."

"Patients?"

Just then, black drapery rose, revealing a youth, face webbed with pain and glistening with sweat, limping out of a double chamber formed by the tent's inner partitions. A broad bandage had been fastened around his right thigh, outside his trews.

"Thank you." The youth's voice was faint. He nodded to a slender woman, clutched a small bag, limped past Tom without a glance, and went out into the marketplace.

The woman was dressed in a dark tunic, similar to Brino's. Beside her, on a bench, a hugely muscled man, running to fat—his face dangerously flushed—looked up fearfully.

"Your turn," the woman said, and the big man swallowed as the drapes fell back into place, hiding them.

Beside Tom, Brino was gently shaking his head.

"When it comes to weaponry, it pays to get the best."

"Weaponry?"

"Depending on your definition of the term." Brino smiled at Tom. "Implants, mindware—it's all part of the same thing."

Tom stared out of the tent's main opening. The bandaged youth was disappearing behind a stall, heading towards an exit tunnel.

"Cheap mindware was his problem." Brino spoke right beside Tom's ear, and Tom started: he had not heard the man approach. "Uploaded a close-quarter-combat logotrope. Shoddy workmanship."

"So what happened?" Tom, despite himself, was genuinely curious.

"Tried to throw a high roundhouse kick and tore his hamstring to shreds," said Brino, and laughed. "Loaded reflex-patterns his body couldn't cope with."

"Ouch." Tom winced.

"He wanted us to fix the problem with myolin-enhancers and monocarbon tendons." Brino shook his head. "Throwing good money after bad. We offered to deinstall the 'trope, or just treat the immediate injuries. Guess which he chose."

"I suppose . . . Not the long-term solution."

"Right."

Tom gestured towards the tent's rear. "And what about the big guy?"

"Muscle grafts. Silly bugger." Brino shook his head. "If he had the gym discipline to keep the grafts in working order, he wouldn't need them in the first place. Now they're just turning to fat."

Brino's body-fat percentage looked to be even less than Tom's own. Despite Tom's fitness and years of phi2dao training, he felt that he should walk softly around this man.

"So how many establishments," Tom asked, changing the subject, "do you have?"

He had already decided that this was not the same tent, nor these the same staff, which he had seen in the Tertium Stratum of Lady Darinia's demesne, near the Caverna del'Amori.

"A few." Brino's expression gave nothing away.

"Hmm."

"So what you need"—Brino talked as though Tom had been asking for advice—"is something subtle, don't you think?"

"If you say so."

"External smart-tech can be disabled, and at the very least is detectable." Brino ran his hand across his shaven head. "You should be looking for *sensitivity*."

Tom chuckled, though he knew Brino was being serious.

"Here." Brino took a fighting stance, slowly extending a punch and holding it so that his ribs were exposed. "Throw a side kick."

Tom did not ask how Brino knew he could fight. They both had the look: each could recognize something of himself in the other.

And the adrenaline was pumping. Two fighters, strangers, from different backgrounds: no matter how controlled and civilized the meeting, the possibility of sudden overkill lurked, waiting to explode.

Slowly, Tom chambered his right leg, extended, pressed the edge of his foot against Brino's lower ribs, then retracted.

"And if the opening hadn't been there?" asked Brino.

"I wouldn't have kicked. I'd have done something else." Tom extended a backfist which Brino blocked, exposing his own ribs. "Or created the opening."

Once more the path was clear for Tom's kick; he did not bother with the technique itself.

"Take your guard." Brino looked serious.

Right side forward, Tom's arm was bent at a right angle but fluid, ready to move.

"No opening to your ribcage," said Brino. "Right?"

Tom nodded, waiting.

"But let's work the angles."

There was a thud against Tom's floating ribs, and he forced himself to stay upright, exerting breath control.

Where did that come from?

"Nice," was all he said.

"See?" Brino moved slowly this time, showing him. "Fluid and deceptive: finding the opening."

From Brino's line of sight, Tom's guard should have closed off the gap . . . yet Brino's leg unerringly coiled and thrust, foot somehow shooting up *between* Tom's arm and torso, reaching the target.

Tom backed away before he spoke.

"You have a 'trope which can teach that?"

"You can already do that." Brino's smile was beatific. "We can just open up the possibilities of your own perceptions."

"Let me think about that."

The nausea hit him two strata from home.

Home? His palace, his—*Sweet Fate!*

Bad cramps were clenching his intestines. He was in a wide cargo-access corridor, and he had to stumble past heavily laden smoothcarts, searching around the hong's bays, until he found the servitors' washrooms.

Ignoring a startled exclamation from a liveried cargo-loader, Tom rushed inside and vomited into a red-enamelled sink.

What's wrong with me?

But a part of him knew: as he had left the Kilware Associates tent, the shaven-headed man, Brino, had bowed too low, in full acknowledgement of Tom's rank.

I refused the logotrope. But somehow—

A jangled lattice of red light fell across his vision; a thousand fingernails clawed across his skin; strange kinaesthetic waves danced through his skull.

Pain . . .

How had they achieved it? Anaesthetic nanodart? Some form of inductive coding, using resonance to reprogram the femtocytes already inside him?

Regardless, the waves of agony swept through him, a logotropic tide of neural disruption.

In all the pain, there was one constant: it was his left arm, finally, the unchanging burning which could never be overridden, that gave him something to cling on to.

And then it was past.

He slipped out of the hong before its steward and his watchmen could arrive. Though he had his thumb ring, Tom did not want to fall back on his authority unless he had to.

Wouldn't want them to think their Liege Lord was just an ordinary human being.

At a clothing shop, he used an anonymous cred-needle to buy a new cape, dark blue and unhooded, for twelve coronae. He dumped the old, tattered cloak—now stained and unpleasant—in a reclamation vat.

Looking more respectable, he found a small daistral house, and took a seat among flowering potted trees which overlooked a broad piazza. Above, the ceiling was an ochre mosaic among azure inlays.

The drink and a small pastry began to revive him.

"Thank you." He smiled at the pretty servitrix and she bobbed him a curtsy.

Her sidelong glances, as she bent to clear and polish a nearby table, made him wonder: did she think him a half-rich freedman, a hong-owner's son perhaps? Or—

Hands wringing, endlessly.

It was something about the girl's polishing motion, the way she twisted the damp cloth . . .

Hands.

Like the old woman, the would-be thief who had rubbed her hands together, stung endlessly by the membrane toxins which guarded Kilware Associates' goods.

Like Mother . . .

In a moment of intuition, Tom realized: Mother, too, had once been burned by whatever pain-gel was in the membrane. Somewhere, at some time, she had stolen, or attempted to steal. To support a dreamtrope habit?

Always, under stress, she would wring her hands like that . . .

But you had to pay, normally, to get the antidote. That's what Brino had said.

How did you pay, Mother? What were you forced to do, to atone for your crime?

And Father's defensive words to Trude: *"She was down on her luck, that's all."* Wasn't that what he had said?

Red lines pulsed across his vision as he stood.

Breathe . . .

Regaining control, he credited the daistral shop with a generous tip, and walked on. Heading for his palace, where his servitors would be glad—he hoped—to see him. Then to send some of the palace watchmen downstratum to find Kilware Associates.

The watchmen would be out of their depth if it came to violence. But Tom was sure that Brino and all trace of the weapons emporium would be gone by the time they arrived.

But a dizzy spell hit him, doubling him over.

"Are you all right, sir?"

Tom allowed himself to be taken back into the daistral shop, sat down in a quiet corner, and plied with analgesic. Someone fetched a diagnostrip which oscillated wildly, unable to pin down symptoms—much less form a diagnosis—and finally tossed it aside.

They settled for the restorative powers of simple broth, and finally allowed Tom to doze in a chair. It was when he saw them moving chairs into the inner chambers that he realized the entire working day had passed, and they were closing up.

"No, no." They refused additional payment, beyond that for broth, but Tom made note of their name: the Dancing Bee. "You take care of yourself," they said. "Come back and see us."

Smiling, Tom agreed that he would.

Death came in the dark.

His running-gallery had been deserted. Even the kitchens—barely lit by two glimmering glowclusters—had no staff, and Tom had helped himself to a small piece of fruit tart from a procblock, and taken a cup of sweet mint daistral.

Afterwards, he had walked, pleased by his ability to take a solitary tour, among his rudimentary art collection: primitive flatpaints, rhythmic dust-sculptures mutating in their lev-fields, musical self-composing interference patterns made visible by thermal imagery.

Still not sleepy, he headed for the conference chamber, where he could find the crystals he had been working on. He was humming to himself as he slipped off his cape and stepped through the membrane—

Scarlet arrays slatted into place across his vision.

—there: one man in the shadows, almost upon him—

Waves pulsed across his skin. The darkness was pitch black.

—from left and right; Tom leaped forwards but *there was another one* rushing him—

Faint silver glimmer of eyes, half-glimpsed.

—and he moved faster, avoiding, spinning, but *there were seven attackers* and footwork could grant him only milliseconds—

They were using corneal smart-gel, photomultiplying and IR-sensitive, but it didn't matter because Tom's entire skin and body were a sensory organ, creating a doppler-map in three dimensions. He *felt* attack-vectors as proprioceptive flow.

—and a heel-kick stabbed close to Tom's spleen—

Sweeping block, without looking.

—with follow-up hook-punch.

The man was big and murderously fast, punching for Tom's throat, but as the hand came close, scarlet spots sprang out across the man's inner forearm—*targets*—and Tom went for the lung-8 point over the radial nerve, elbowed the radiobrachialis and whipped a sword-hand strike against the carotid sinus, and the big man dropped.

Pause.

One stumbled, but—glint: *watch out!*—another, bringing a graser rifle to bear—

Crescent kick, deflecting the weapon, then Tom concentrated on limb destruction until the rifle clattered to the floor. Hip-throw.

—and the other four were dangerous, moving in pairs: trained attack team—

Overdrive. Pure Zen. He rolled over the glass conference table, using the environment, driving off the wall.

—lattice blade crackling—*arm, burning*—very close—

Tom's kick took out the knee with a crunch as he tangled the man's arms together, twisted, whipped his leg up high and dropped an axe-kick.

—three left—

Sidestepped as a graser beam split the air apart—*move now*—and he dropped low, grabbing the weapon as he shoulder-barged—left stump good for something—tossing the man against his comrades.

—one man in the clear—

A spinning kick faster than thought, and he was down.

—but three were still moving on the floor, scrabbling for weapons—

And Tom's motion became a blur as he darted among the shadows, striking out, choking, until seven shadowed lumps lay motionless.

Victory.

Sudden bright lights sprang into being as the door membrane dissolved and glowclusters blazed with full intensity. Squinting, Tom froze as four mirror-visored troopers entered, rifles locked on.

But their officer was dissolving her visor, looking at him with clear grey eyes. She frowned.

"I know you."

42

TERRA AD 2123

<<Karyn's Tale>>
[10]

An unmarked skimmer picked her up at the *pension* (which was quaint, overdecorated in the alpine mode, with precise cuckoo-clock charm), and dropped her off at the lakeside, far from habitation, where waves gently lapped against the deserted shingles. Then, in less than a minute, unseen endothermal filaments created an ice bridge, greenish blue and solid, arrowing across the surface. Karyn had walked perhaps ten precarious metres from shore when a bullet-sub surfaced, and its uniformed crew waved her aboard.

The ice bridge was already dissolving as they sank beneath the waves.

"Isn't there a public-access tunnel?" Karyn asked, made nervous by the apparent subterfuge.

"Closed for inspection."

Have I overplayed my hand? After the flurry of h-mail—denied requests—had she hinted at too much?

Her paranoia intensified as they drifted closer to the crystalline complex which was Genève-sous-Lac.

After docking, she was taken to an empty waiting-room, and left alone. One wall was convex, transparent, looking out upon the clear, dark waters. Small white-and-gold fish nibbled at it.

Damn! She paced restlessly, then forced herself to sit. *What the hell am I doing here?*

Her leverage, for the forthcoming meeting, was in the handful of crystalline splinters tucked away in her jumpsuit's pockets.

Decision.

Risk everything.

To save Dart, she had to be prepared to throw away their only chance.

"Frau Doktor Schwenger," said an automatic system in English, "will see you now."

"*L'affaire,*" said Karyn peevishly, "*est dans le lac.*"

Colloquially it meant: everything's a mess. The AI made no reply.

A holo arrow indicated the way she should go. Reluctantly, Karyn stood again and followed; the arrow moved, projectile-like, ahead of her.

Doktor Schwenger's suite spectacularly looked out upon the lake's bed: low lighting glittered on quartz insertions, and shadows played among tendril-like aquatic plants which Karyn could not have named.

"Sit down." Schwenger was small and blonde, and wore her authority easily. "Please."

"*Vielen Dank.*"

A small smile crossed Schwenger's face. "*Sie haben aber viel gut Deutsch, nichtwahr?*" Karyn shrugged, as Schwenger added: "*Wir können uns auf irgenden Sprache unterhalten.*"

"*Also gut,*" replied Karyn. "But I bow to your superior command of English."

"So." Schwenger's smile was a little too quick.

I shouldn't have conceded that, was Karyn's first thought. But her aikido training gave her deeper insight: *I need to blend and flow, not score points.*

"Thank you for seeing me so quickly, Doktor Schwenger," she said. "You must have a busy schedule, as do I."

A tiny frown. "I understood you were on leave."

Disingenuous: Schwenger would not have rearranged her schedule to meet a mere Pilot Candidate without suspecting something.

"Some PR matters." Karyn tried to appear nonchalant. "An interview with TechnoMonde Vingt-Deux. Other things."

"Unusual, for a Pilot Candidate."

Ice-blue eyes. A disconcerting hint of ironic smile.

"Isn't it?" Karyn nodded. "I was hoping to talk about the *projected rewiring* of my nervous system."

Schwenger was very still.

Zero points for subtlety, McNamara, Karyn told herself. *But at least she's got the message.*

"In what respect?" Schwenger asked quietly.

What Karyn really wanted was all-out search-and-rescue, using the entire fleet; but no amount of leverage would give her that.

"Bringing forward my Phase II." Centring herself, Karyn added: "And giving me the next new ship."

Frau Doktor Ilse Schwenger was a divisional director, with board-level responsibility for the Commissioning Programme. She could do this.

"That would not be very easy, as you must appreciate."

Atemi is 90 per cent of aikido, O-Sensei Ueshiba had allegedly once said. The founder of that most gentle of arts knew when to blend and when to strike.

Show her.

Nerves screaming—flashes of Dart: alone and dying—Karyn laid out the crystal shards upon Schwenger's desk, knowing that in the next few seconds her own career in UNSA might be over.

Blue toroid, engineered foetus. Blurred text and graphs.

Damn the career. But Dart needed her.

"Low-res images," murmured Schwenger, as she slid each fragment in turn through her desktop's lasing slot. "Hard to make out detail."

The last image hung there: actinic blue.

"Not in the original crystals."

Tear the corner off a photograph. In that corner, one has a small piece of the picture. Any piece of a still hologram, though, contains the whole solid image: the smaller the shard, the lower the resolution.

"Who has the crystals?" Schwenger's eyes were glacial blue. "You or TechnoMonde Vingt-Deux?"

She knew, all right. Schwenger had hardly had to glance at the images to understand what they were.

What should I do?

One option: play hard to get. The other—

Gamble.

"They're in my room at the Gasthaus Irving, in Lausanne. Can you send someone to pick them up?"

Schwenger frowned, then nodded agreement.

"Let me call the reception desk there." Karyn waited for Schwenger to hand over control of the desktop holo, and made the call, authorizing UNSA personnel to visit her room.

I hope I'm doing the right thing.

"The crystals are time-stamped and logged," Karyn added, closing down the comms display. "Along with the camera. Full set. Nothing missing. No duplicates."

The Frau Doktor made the arrangements for pick-up, closed the call, then opened up a second session. But she minimized and silenced the display, then clasped her hands and looked directly at Karyn.

"Thank you, Pilot Candidate McNamara. We appreciate your co-operation."

"Just doing my duty: we can't let misguided UNSA personnel put our public standing at risk."

"I agree with you, of course."

"Sheer good luck I found out about them . . . You know, I take my career very seriously." Meaning: she was prepared to throw it away, if she had to.

The slightest narrowing of ice-blue eyes. "That's good, Pilot Candidate. How are your plans progressing?"

"I'm speaking openly"—both of them smiled at that—"when I say how much I hope you'll change the new vessel's mission profile. As well as put me on board, of course."

"You're referring to Pilot Mulligan." It was as though a mask had dropped: Schwenger's concern looked genuine. "An effective rescue mission, though, given the timescale—"

Before Dart's ship disintegrates. Karyn knew what she meant.

A subtle hand gesture, which Karyn almost missed. Then Schwenger leaned forward: "Officially, I accept that there are no additional copies of the stolen data. But this is off the record."

She's switched off a holo-log. Everything had been recorded, until now. Assume trickery: a second holocamera might exist.

"Your price for silence," Schwenger demanded, "is this assignment? Am I correct?"

"Yes."

"Even if—"

"It's not futile. Please look at this." Karyn handed over a crystal: the projections which she and Chojun Akazawa had laboriously put together.

Holo, blossoming.

"Please." There was no disguising the desperation in Karyn's voice as she begged Schwenger to believe the data. "See here." Her finger traced a trajectory through a twisting manifold: a representational phase-space, not physical mu-space. "It's a kind of reverse relativity: I can reach Dart in minimal time, according to *his* timeline, by following this subjectively longer geodesic."

Schwenger shook her head, but Karyn could see that she was following the technical argument, gaze skimming across numeric dataflows. "Dangerous," Schwenger said.

"Feasible."

"Yes." Schwenger leaned back in her chair.

"Yes, you think it's possible? Or—?"

"The mission profile's changed, as of now." Schwenger's control gesture magnified and unfroze the suspended comms holovolume. "Fully urgent, Willi. We're changing the new vessel's mission profile." Muted sounds from the holo. "We'll need field enhancers, details to follow. Bump the current Pilot off the list. We're going with Pilot Candidate McNamara."

The conversation became silent. *Anti-sound protection*, Karyn realized.

Then: "Downloading the annexe now. Endit." Schwenger cut the comms session and ejected a small wafer from the desktop. "Sign this, please."

She held out the wafer.

"What is it?" Karyn took the wafer, holding it by the edges.

"An addition to your contract of employment. It makes you part of Project Rewire, and binds you to the terms of its non-disclosure agreement."

"But—"

"But the project originators are going to get into a lot of trouble— off the record." Schwenger leaned back in her chair. "Nevertheless, I require your acceptance."

"OK." Karyn agreed via voice and thumbprint.

"You can read it first."

"Not necessary." Karyn placed the signed wafer on the desktop. "Thank you. I'll cancel my interview with—"

"Please don't. A personal contact with a major NewsNet could be very useful . . . so long as we keep sensitive information out of the frame."

"I'll do that." *And I'm in a lot of legal trouble if I don't.*

The price she had to pay.

"There'll be some senior board members stepping down shortly." Schwenger tapped a crystal shard. "Opening up interesting opportunities."

Your rivals, about to fall.

"Foolish of them to sponsor such a misguided project," Schwenger added. "Interesting coincidence, that I should be the one to learn of it."

Coincidence, right.

Karyn said nothing. Blend and flow.

"You wouldn't ever try to move against *me* this way, would you, Pilot Candidate?"

Karyn bowed her head. "I wouldn't dream of it, Frau Doktor Schwenger."

Short silence.

Then: "Please, Karyn"—a smile lit up the blonde woman's face—"call me Ilse."

<<MODULE ENDS>

43

NULAPEIRON AD 3413–3414

It took a full Standard Year.

The five sigmas are: speed, strength, stamina, suppleness and skill. Maestro da Silva's dictum. *But speed, Tom, will serve you above all else.*

Tom wondered, though, whether the maestro would approve, even in the smallest way, of Tom's using his flow/focus skills, his phi2dao tactics, to plan assassination.

Father. Mother . . .

He allowed himself to think of his mother more often now. At any time in his investigations, he might come across mention of her.

But it did not happen. She had meant nothing to the Oracle. The destruction of Tom's family had been an irrelevance, not worth recording in official data.

Even I can affect others' lives now, without meaning to.

Not just collaterally: there were the seven injured troopers who had mistaken him for an intruder.

The demesne's capital funds covered their medical care. In the end, thank Fate, none of them died: two had inhaled blood and undergone cardiac arrest, but were successfully revived. All seven received post-trauma counselling. Tom offered to transfer their allegiance back to Lady Darinia, or to any Lord needing subjects with their (highly desirable) skill-set. They all refused.

The troopers were reassigned; two of them became team leaders under the new structure put into place by Tom's security chief, Captain Elva Strelsthorm.

"I know you," she had said to Tom, entering the conference chamber where the injured men lay.

It had taken little prompting—Elva's visual memory being apparently near-eidetic—to recall the frightened boy hiding in a dark storage alcove, between the dripping mop and broken-down cleaning-drone.

"Your eyes haven't changed, my Lord," she told him, after the medics had departed.

Elva had gained maturity, too. The twenty-something proctor who had come to Tom's family dwelling was now almost ten years older: easy with command, well organized and disciplined. She cared about her troopers' well-being—as Tom observed over the coming tendays—and it showed in the automatic respect they accorded her.

Between her and Jak, Tom was able to delegate most of the day-to-day running of his realm. Felgrinar was theoretically at the same level—part of a triumvirate subordinate only to Tom—but in practice was guided almost entirely by Jak's (and sometimes Elva's) suggestions. Felgrinar's disposition improved, and it began to look as though the demesne's budget, at least in the Primum Stratum, was going to show a positive balance within three SY: earlier than estimated.

A truecast—if there were any available to cover fiscal analyses of a minor realm such as Tom's—could have delivered a guaranteed-accurate prediction. But Tom steered clear of Oracular output.

Call it superstition; call it fear of entrapment by paradox. But he *had* to work in ignorance of his own eventual success or failure.

More than that: if he truly succeeded—or even failed, in a spectacular fashion—in killing Gérard d'Ovraison, then there were still about five thousand Oracles in the world. Others who could form truecasts, possibly *had* formed truecasts years ago, depicting the event.

If they had, it was a secret from Tom, even with his noble-house access. Because there were other levels to which he had no authority?

Or because the Oracles censored themselves?

In a sense, it freed him. Ignoring paradox, except when it served his tactical approach, he worked as though only security forces, without Oracular assistance, existed: in secret, with great care, drawing up his lonely plans.

At first, it seemed as though it would take forever. Then, when he had the basic concepts straight, he estimated a few tendays at most.

After heartbreaking effort spent on his proof-of-concept project, based on truecasts and newscasts about Duke Boltrivar's demesne (to choose a topic not entirely at random), Tom realized he had to throw away all his work and start again.

Though the simulations worked, they could not create an entire fictitious world. His design paradigm was wrong. The only solution was to conceive every single facet *from the start* in terms of infinite-dendrimer autoreflexive processing.

Then it became feasible . . . in principle.

Other preparations: the physical conditioning, the climbing, the times spent immersed in Karyn's Tale beneath blue skies and grey, desensitizing his acrophobia and agoraphobia.

And it took an entire Standard Year.

First, the triple-shielding of his study. Elva said nothing as she oversaw the threading of dumb caging and smart interference-emitters throughout the quickglass inner walls.

You don't talk much, Elva, thought Tom, watching her at work, *about the things that matter.*

Layers within layers of security. For her sake, in case he were caught, it needed to be obvious that he was working alone.

They did not talk much of the old days, but her presence sparked a re-evaluation in Tom's mind: of Trude's strange manner, her trips to far places (by the market's standards), and her anxiety (and mysterious hooded companions) when he had told her of the questing Jack's proximity.

Had Elva ever known Trude? They had met—had talked, after Father's funeral: Tom had seen them—but did they actually know each other?

He did not ask.

Nor did he mention his unwillingly loaded tacware, though he asked her to investigate the strange weapons emporium.

"No trace of Kilware Associates," reported Elva, on her return from downstratum. "Never mind this Brino feller. I could contact Lord Shinkenar's proctors—"

"Never mind," said Tom. "Let's forget it, shall we."

More suspicions.

It was the way Brino moved, the quiet confidence with which he held himself . . . Tom wondered whether he had, for the second time in his life, met a Pilot.

But I couldn't have risked revealing the comms relay.

"All finished," Elva said in the same meeting. "Your shielding, I mean. We ran the final tests this morning. Not a peep escaped."

"Not bad." Tom was impressed with her rapid progress. "Not bad at all."

Coincidence, too, that Dervlin's fighting style held something of the fast, flowing multiple-strikes-per-second method of the Pilots?

And wasn't Dervlin an old friend of Trude's?

Forget it. Tom opened up the stallion talisman and removed the capsule. *Let's focus on the objective.*

With the shielding in place, it was the first time Tom, ignoring the download needle, had openly prised apart the nul-gel coating, revealing the crystalline comms relay which had lain hidden for nearly a decade.

"Logon," he said. "Ident: pi sigma three cee-cedilla nine eight nine slash Petra deVries. I'm her proxy."

Strangeness.

Gripping the arm of his chair, he plunges into vertigo.

Golden light, burning.

Snowflake?

For a moment, he sees the small, scarlet, stellated shape slowly revolve—then the labyrinth crashes into being.

Cubes of blood.

But each cube is also—somehow—an endlessly branching snowflake in three—no, in many—dimensions. He leans close to one, and it explodes into detail: an entire infinitude, an apparent universe of complexity.

Sweet Fate . . .

He had hoped for a mere comms interface, but this is so much more: it is everything.

Blood-snow in the golden sea.

Multifractal cellular automata.

Shimmer and coalesce: patterns form as they learn from him and he adapts; the system's matrix-factorization maps eigen-functions from Tom's brain to mu-space processor-architecture; gestalten-integration solitons pulse between continua.

Limited-diffusion aggregation patterns coalesce, like lightning around seedpoints, forming complex structures.

Low-level tools at first: simple Turing-machine complexes, gently introducing him to their operations.

Then the hints of gleaming vistas beyond, of the logic-beyond-logic that is possible in this universe.

He can work with voice and image; touch and motion; thought and dream: can simulate an atom or a human being . . .

Did you want me to use this—he addresses the dead Pilot rhetorically in his memory, careful not to let the tools pick it up: he does not want her replicated virtually here—*just to ask off-worlders for help?*

Slatting into place all around: blood-flakes representing ever more powerful mind-tools, in a phase-space based on hardware he can never directly experience—an infinite-capacity processor somewhere in mu-space.

If he had the intellectual capacity, he could create his own virtual universe . . .

But there is no need for that: just one Oracle's future to model.

Golden light.

Strange patterns sweeping through the tessellated automata, the multifractal blood-maze, the impossible-perspective tool-shapes revolving close by . . .

For a second, for eternity, he regards a system beyond limit: a processing-space where even the laws of logic may be transcended.

"Enough."

Shuddering, withdrawing, until the interface is the lightest of touches, and the tool-infinicons respond only to concentrated, directed, conscious control.

He started work.

In the guise of helping Elva—and of interest in the tech for its own sake—he learned as much of security protocols as he could. For all the strange self-referential, infinitely recursive functions he was designing and running, it was low-tech physical logistics and tactics that could trip him up.

One piece of luck: overhearing a conversation between Jak and Elva set Tom to tracking supply routes. Lord Shinkenar, in the neighbouring demesne, shipped supplies for Oracle d'Ovraison's use. He was a middleman.

The goods went via cargo train, passing through the sixth stratum of Tom's demesne without stopping, and passing through sealed tunnels—inaccessible from any form of side corridor or access shaft—through seven demesnes and into the next sector.

And somewhere in the unmarked volumes between sectors, the train made a stop which was not recorded on any manifest, nor reproduced on any order which Tom could access.

✧✧✧

He stepped up his training.

Free-climbing around his practice chamber; sparring with surplus mannequins bought from Lord Takegawa's military academy; running endless lengths of his deserted gallery.

The translation algorithms took three times longer than he had estimated, but then he was able to feed real newscasts and truecasts into his multifractal simulated world.

Then changing, extrapolating . . .

Imperfections twisted the models, so that occasionally they became weird rides through nightmarish dreams: impossible events played out against collage landscapes.

But the models ran, and that was a beginning.

He ignored Sylvana's invitations to visit, and—guiltily—a query from Avernon, wondering why Tom had published no work.

Tom composed a reply—*Because I've ignored orthogonal-component matrices in favour of a multifractal-function approach which reifies algorithms in mu-space in no time at all*—and deleted it without sending.

On occasion he sparred with some of Elva's troopers, but they were nervous of him. He was their Lord, after all.

The mindless sparring-mannequins had no such inhibitions.

One of his small side excursions into the Pilots' structured knowledge domain scared him. *Many Terra-sized planets*, he read, *exist in "interstellar" space. Six were found in the Sol system, only in the twenty-fourth century.* A chill spread through him. *Thrown far away from the accretion centre at formation, averaging only 30K in temperature, nevertheless radioactivity (and resultant vulcanism and storm meteorology) provides surface conditions allowing water oceans . . .*

It took several days of research to determine—to Tom's relief—that Nulapeiron, like Terra, orbited normally around a star.

Finished.

Memories.

Immensely old, the white-haired Oracle lies dying. Sunken flesh: wide-boned shoulders are the only hint of former power.

All around, servitors and Lords stand with heads bowed, silent and respectful.

Perceptions, carried back to earlier times.

The final newscast—a memory transmitted to his youth, as entropic time-flows—flickers out.

Boundary condition.

The last moment of awareness, as the old man dies.

The simulated lifetime was complete.

After all this work. So hard—

It was an end, and a beginning.

Tom lay down on the floor of his study, and wept.

The next day, he used a fine glass clamp, extruded from his desktop, to hold the comms-relay crystal. Awkwardly, he pushed the nul-gel coating back into place around it.

He split his talisman and inserted the crystal.

"Fine workmanship, Father." Tom sealed up the stallion, hung it around his neck. "You did a good job there."

That night, he donned a jumpsuit, fastened a small pack against his lower back, and tugged a long, black cape around his shoulders.

Stepping quickly from his bedchamber, he almost bumped into Elva, who was performing one of her solitary impromptu patrols of the palace.

"Oops! Sorry, Elva."

"It's late, my Lord." She looked at him closely.

"I'm going to my study: it's out of bounds to everybody for two days. I've a long test-run to perform."

"My Lord." Elva bowed, used to Tom's locking himself away from the world.

But he only went into the study long enough to crank up holovolumes displaying various corridors within the palace.

Checking that his route was clear, he activated the false-image feeds.

Then he slipped out into the corridor, threw his cape back over his shoulder, and began to run.

44

NULAPEIRON AD 3414

His first thought had been to infiltrate the tunnel somewhere in his own realm, cause a temporary stop—a small rock slippage, perhaps, which the automated graser torches could have dealt with—and make his way on board. But it was too risky, in terms of later investigation.

Ideally, this supply run should be, and should be recorded as, an utterly normal affair.

It was not a complete coincidence that Lord Shinkenar's demesne should be the local point of supply for the Oracle: they were all, in some sense, part of the local nobility.

From his palace Tom went down, first of all, as far as the fifth stratum. Then a slow jog to the border, to a well-chosen point where both his demesne and Lord Shinkenar's bordered on unreclaimed caverns.

He slipped past the natural scree which he had surveilled routinely for five tendays, through a twisting narrow tunnel, into a broader thoroughfare which led to a warehousing and distribution district.

There, he became part of a crowd, taking the spiral steps down to the trading district in the stratum below. Late-shift workers, heading homewards.

"Be glad to get to my own crib."

"Don't blame you," muttered Tom.

"Soddin' Klinwald gave you a hard time, too?"

"Bastard." Tom nodded, then turned off from the main group, trailing three men who walked separately, not talking.

As soon as practicable, he sidestepped into a small alcove and willed himself into total stillness.

His thumb ring got him through the loading-dock's scanfield. The tricky part was coding it to backout the log entries in the security journal, so that his ID would not appear.

As scheduled, black rubbery cargo pods were stacked on the dock: two-metre spheres with stubby legs. Tom reached into the pack at the small of his back and drew out his redmetal poignard.

Crouching down by the nearest lone pod, Tom checked the destination—Oracle d'Ovraison's dwelling—then slit open the outer casing. He was in luck: the contents were small, soft packages, dried gripplefruits and wiklanberries.

In the tunnel through which the cargo train would come tomorrow, there was a faint rustling. Smiling grimly, Tom took the food packages into the tunnel—it took twelve trips in all—and left them, opened, for scavenging ciliates.

He could hear the pattering and rustling, the tearing of wrap-fibre, as he sealed himself into the cargo pod, fitted the low-tech resp-mask across his face, and curled up in the darkness.

Movement.

Oscillation from side to side. Then he found himself turned upside down as the cargo pod changed from walking to rolling.

Tom braced himself, still slipping as it rolled up an incline—cargo ramp—and came to a standstill. With a crick in his neck, Tom shifted around to regain some degree of comfort.

A low vibration. Moving off. The huge cylindrical trains—often kilometres long—had no acceleration to speak of. They did, however, keep that acceleration applied for a long time: by the time half an hour had passed, its velocity was huge.

He tried to sleep, but failed.

Instead, his eyes were gritty with tiredness when, hours later, the train came to a stop.

There were no voices to be heard as the cargo pod moved. Insulation again, or just complete automation? There was no way Tom could open the pod wall to check.

Rolling. Finally, a shuffling into place.

Then the inchoate roar of powerful engines. Even inside the cargo pod, Tom's whole body shook.

Finally, the stomach-dropping sensation of vertical acceleration, as he and the cargo pod hurtled upwards.

The ascent seemed to last for ever.

Move it.

He tried the poignard, opening a slit, but the pod was part of a formation, a three-dimensional lattice filling the darkened cargo hold. He could see out, with the help of a tiny glowglimmer, but he could not leave the pod.

The hold's air was cool. The pressure seemed normal.

Tom tried to hold the opening, but there was a sudden shift in attitude, and for a moment Tom floated free, completely weightless—

I'm truly airborne.

—as the cargo shuttle arced into a parabolic trajectory, high above the surface of Nulapeiron.

45

NULAPEIRON AD 3414

It fell away beneath him.

Watch it! Crimping his fingertips against the hold—no more than a tiny bump in the stonelike material—he leaned out against the hold, toes against the slope.

It fluttered, batlike: his discarded cape fell downwards after the departing shuttle, and was gone.

He was clinging to the outside of a horizontal stone ring perhaps ten metres in diameter. Below, the lev-drive's collimating shaft pointed downwards, to the distant landscape.

Landscape!

For a moment the nausea caught him and he clung tightly to the face—*Danger! Don't forget what you've learned!*—almost catapulting himself into space until he forced his breathing under control and— *look at the face*—leaned outwards, so that his fingerhold was an axis, torque jamming his toes against the rock.

Floating, three thousand metres above the surface.

Horizon.

For the first time in his life he could see a true horizon, lemon skies and dark-brown clouds above a variegated landscape: dark, distant purple mountains; here and there, silver-grey lakes flashing in the sun; and, beneath Tom, the rust-and-teal patchwork of moors and fells. The air, even this high up, was heady and pure.

But palpable. Winds buffeted him as he began to climb.

Getting inside with the cargo had never been an option: he would have been sliced apart by the transfer system. Instead, he had exited via the auto-shuttle's maintenance panel, clung to the outside hull, then shifted onto the ring structure as the shuttle disengaged and fell back in a controlled glide towards the ground.

His breathing was normal. He tossed his unnecessary resp-mask into the void. *I'm ready.* Breath control. Believing in himself. *I've trained for a year just for this.*

More than that. His entire life since leaving the market chamber had been a preparation for this moment.

He had the strength, the will, to make it.

Tom began to move.

The ring extended upwards, sheer, just for a few metres. There, it merged into the convex surface of the sphere.

That was the bad news. A huge overhang which bellied outwards like an immense curved cliff—decorated with hundreds of thousands of carvings: gargoyles, labyrinthine knotwork, terracotta-like tableaux—and was going to take hours to climb.

Tom Corcorigan, tiny and insignificant, clung near the lowest point of a vast stone sphere, a kilometre in diameter, which floated above the surface of Nulapeiron. Intricately carved, from a distance it would look like a fuzzy stone ball, from whose apex a stream of creamy clouds endlessly spewed.

It was a terraformer sphere, one of thousands in Nulapeiron's skies, and it had floated here for over six hundred years.

And, two decades before, Oracle Gérard d'Ovraison had made it his home.

Hanging underhand, using both feet in a double toehold around a gargoyle's head, Tom hung: resting briefly.

He was sweating inside his jumpsuit, but not too much. Nicely supple. In the shuttle, trapped within the cargo pod, he had not been able to warm up properly, but no strains had occurred.

He checked the next section, visualizing, then climbed onwards, solving the problems with fluid grace.

His personal climbing-style included techniques all his own—stump-jam and stump-hook often came into play—but sometimes he had to rely on three-limb power moves. Rocking up to a high step, letting go with his one hand, then boosting upwards to find the next handhold, with zero margin for error.

Fist and stallion.

Dervlin's old Zen Neuronal Coding refrain kept him in the groove, flowing with the spatial rhythm determined by the convex rockface.

And stretch . . .

Suppleness was a cornerstone of his style, as he moved spiderlike upwards. Belief in himself, and precision of technique, mattered more than strength: no-one could use power alone to climb like this.

In rough terms, a strictly vertical climb would be a quarter of a great circle: say eight hundred metres. His angled route—sometimes backtracking—would be nearer a thousand, to reach the terraformer's equatorial rim.

Long moves, keeping his body close to the overhanging face, dropping one knee inwards to increase his reach—*keep the flow*—working the surface.

Getting tired.

He hung in the frog position, fingers hooked around a small knot pattern. Soon he would need somewhere to take a longer rest.

Below, empty space filled the long three-klick drop to the distant ground.

Not empty. A tug of wind nearly snatched him from his handhold. *Turbulence . . .*

A term from ancient philosophy, before Fate became hardwired in men's souls.

Jam and smear, he told himself, walking his feet across a nearly featureless stretch of grey rock, relying on his climbing-slippers' friction.

Time to rest.

Then he found a wide crack—a chimney formed between two

panels of intricate mazework—jammed himself in using counterpressure, and relaxed as best he could.

Destiny! This is hard.

But he had never thought it was going to be easy.

No attack drones came hovering; no troopers rappelled from above, grasers pointing; no defence fields activated, throwing his lifeless body from the terraformer sphere.

Thank Fate.

But there were more subtle dangers involved in confronting an Oracle who knew his future . . . or thought he did.

Tom was doing horizontal splits in mid-air, stemming the gap between two encrusted ornamental knots where it widened to over a metre and a half. He was so warm that the stretch came easily; he let go with his hand, to rest it.

Reach and pull.

At the climb's start, Tom had been climbing out under a virtually horizontal overhang. Now, as he proceeded up the bulging rockface, the gradient lessened, but the need for constant counterpressure remained as his fatigue grew. The chances of a fatal slip were increasing.

Halfway to the equatorial rim, where the slope was forty-five degrees, he hit a smooth patch which he could not manage. By the time he made it back to a safe position, all three limbs were trembling.

Fist and stallion.

Pain shot through his fingers as he crimped onto a tiny hold—*Father's knucklebones, falling into the acid vortex*—but he forced himself through it, in too precarious an intermediate position to allow a stop, and continued moving.

Wispy grey clouds floated below him, partially obscuring the distant ground. He shivered, only partly from the lowering temperature.

Drops.

He was climbing quickly now.

Raindrops.

He was almost floating up the rock, a problem-solving machine incapable of feeling. He had been climbing for over three hours.

Nearly there.

And then it hit.

The full blast of the rain hammered against him, and already the rock was becoming smooth and slippery. Above him, just two metres above, the rock jutted out horizontally.

Two metres, that's all.

The equatorial rim.

But it was smooth underneath, with no holds, and Tom was using a one-finger hold with his flexor muscle starting to burn.

Move.

It was a ballistic throw with no possibility of retreat, launching himself into space—*reach!*—and grabbing onto the very rim.

Do it now.

For a few endless seconds he hung there from his handhold, just the strength of his crimped fingers separating life from death, and then he swung his foot up higher than his head, finding purchase and hooking in with his heel.

Now.

Rain in his eyes, and he swung quickly, bringing the other foot up.

He was upside down, feet higher than his hand, but he only had seconds as the rock turned slippery—*pull*—and then he was upright on the rim.

The nearest drop-bug opening was close, and he traversed the gap quickly—*watch it*—slipping once in the driving rain. In a moment his fingers were on the opening and he swung himself inside to safety.

He was in a tunnel three metres wide, arrowing into the terraformer's interior: horizontal exit tube for an emergency drop-bug. But a membrane stretched across the tunnel, a metre inside; he could not enter this way.

He lay down on the hard floor and began to shake.

Shock, he told himself.

His rational self was disconnected from the physical organism: he could only observe as his body shook, as though in seizure.

He awoke.

It still seemed strange, in retrospect: his inability to control his trembling body. But eventually the tremors had lessened, died away, and he had slipped into anaesthetizing sleep.

Now he undid the compact pack at the small of his back, drank from its flask of electrolyte-replacement fluid, chewed his tasteless hi-carb wafers, and felt his wakefulness and sense of energy return.

Outside, the rain had stopped falling. A fresh breeze wafted around him in the horizontal tunnel; outside the sky was a deeper yellow, tinged with purple at the horizon. Clouds were a murky brown.

Time to get moving.

He did not bother examining the internal membrane which led to the terraformer's core. Had he carried any smart-tech capable of disarming it, sensor webs would have detected his presence before now.

He discarded his pack and all its contents save for the most important item: the long, sheathed redmetal poignard, which he fastened horizontally against the small of his back. Touching his stallion talisman through his jumpsuit as if for luck, he leaned out of the opening, looked down once at the patchwork landscape far below, then swung himself outwards and began to climb once more.

$$\diamond \diamond \diamond$$

Winds had mostly dried the rock, but tiny cracks and holds remained slippery so he had to be careful. But he was now on the upper hemisphere, travelling easily, and the higher he climbed, the more gently the surface sloped.

Where the face was worn, he traversed easily, almost walking upright across the slope, until he found a tall tableau surrounded by worn gargoyles, and quickly ascended.

As he neared the apex, he could see the creamy gases spewed forth from the top, forming a thick horizontal layer which dispersed far from the terraformer. For a moment he stopped, wondering whether the air would remain breathable, but there was no choice—had been no choice since he entered the cargo shuttle—and he continued up the easing slope until he reached a balustrade.

He hopped over and was on solid, horizontal ground: a ring-shaped balcony which ran all the way around the sphere, close to the top. Above, the ornamented output-stack grew upwards, and emulsion-thick creamy gases belched and poured upwards and streamed away into the atmosphere.

The arched entranceway to the interior was marbled, inlaid with platinum, and the hall inside seemed spacious. There was no membrane. Neither the ozone smell nor the skin-tingling ionization which might denote a sensor field. No troopers on guard.

Moving softly, Tom crept inside.

Gleaming floors. Beyond, shadowed spaces, and the echoes of a conversation, voices raised, which might have been an argument. Even after all these years, Tom recognized the man's distinctive baritone.

Gérard d'Ovraison.

The other voice—a younger man?—abruptly turned to silence. *Oracle.*

"I'm here," Tom whispered, in a voice which was hardly his own.

The big, broad-shouldered man walked into the hall in which Tom stood. He stopped, regarded Tom, and smiled; his teeth were very white.

Scarlet pinpoints of lights seemed to spring out across the square-jawed, bearded, handsome face; the muscular neck; and across the fine turquoise and white garments. Attack points, delineated in virtual light, while kinaesthetic tugging sensations mapped all the strike-vectors which Tom might follow.

His hand itched to drive into the carotid sinus, to whip edge-on against the laryngeal cartilage and watch the Oracle inexorably choke to death.

The pulse pounded in Tom's ears as d'Ovraison finally spoke.

"Greetings, Tom." Again, the easy smile. "Would you believe . . . I've been expecting you."

"Of course you have," said Tom after a moment. Every sense was keening: even the hairs on his skin seemed to pick up vibrations, searching for danger.

"I have been, and often will be, aware of this discussion we're having now." The big man pushed his cape back over one shoulder.

Tom circled.

The Oracle turned easily, keeping him in sight.

"Must be a tired dance for you, Oracle."

An unreadable expression clouded d'Ovraison's eyes for a moment. Then: "How I've looked forward to your saying that."

Tom smiled appreciatively, but answered: "Your lies lack conviction, Your Wisdom."

"Shall I tell you how this conversation ends?"

Icy fear gripped Tom, remembering how the last prediction had fulfilled itself.

Father . . .

"It should have started"—Tom slid the poignard from its sheath—"with your calling the guards, or activating smartmists. But it's too late now."

"I don't think so."

The Oracle retreated before Tom's advance, but there was no fear in his eyes. Only a strained resignation—just for a moment—and a hint of ancient weariness. Then his urbane charm returned.

"There's no need"—smoothly—"for physical action. I've always known, you see, that you'll not be able to resist seeing her."

Tom stopped, crouched in cat stance: defensive, but ready.

"She's this way." A brief smile in the broad beard. "Follow me."

Cape swirling, the Oracle turned and stalked away down gleaming flagstones, turning into a spiralling ramp, descending farther into the terraformer.

Initiative lost, Tom could only follow.

Ovoid, sapphire-blue crystal shell, cradled in a sweeping frame of gold which curved up into a canopy and was everywhere encrusted with baroque carvings, inlaid with strange minerals in which glimmering fires danced and moved. The great sculpture was the chamber's focus: all around, sweeping buttresses and the stellate ceiling and concentric white-and-blue flagstones centred upon its structure.

As Tom drew near, the air became chill. Beads of moisture dotted the ovoid crystal, blurring the shadowy form inside.

Cryosarcophagus.

"You dare—" Tom leaped forwards, poignard raised high for a sweeping cut, but the Oracle's motion was a subtle avoidance, as though he had known *exactly* how Tom was going to move, and then blue sparks in one of the Oracle's ornate finger rings were answered by a blossoming of holovolumes all around the majestic crypt.

Focus.

But his peripheral vision was already on the status displays, the slowly moving and static manifolds, the lattices of digits in which changes dripped only slowly, here and there.

Only angiological data flowed, represented at branching levels from arteries/veins down to capillaries and sinusoids: differential gradients cycling through changes.

So much of the rest was flat-planed: in the cortex, superolateral/medial/basal surfaces were devoid of signal; in each half of the midbrain, shallow electrical tides swept crus cerebri and tegmentum; only deep in the rhombencephalon was there true activity.

"You said she was alive."

"Did I?" said the Oracle, and the sadness in his voice washed through the room, lingered when silence fell again.

I don't know. Uncertainties mixed in Tom's mind. *I thought you did.*

"The machines," added the Oracle, "keep her body running. Only the higher functions are long gone."

"I can see that."

Mother!

"She's been dead for seven years."

Wiping away condensation, he saw: high cheekbones, flawless skin, full rose-pink lips hinting of overbite. Eyes closed. Vibrant cupric hair.

So young.

How old could she have been when Tom was born? Arrested in death, she looked no more than ten years older than he was now.

"Death is the full stop"—Gérard's smile was scarcely human—"at the end of a life sentence."

He gestured a flat-text holosheet into being, in case Tom had not understood the reference. Then *with no gesture from the Oracle* every holovolume collapsed into oblivion.

Ancient, banned tech: Virtual Synaptic Interface. Direct neural control of the terraformer's systems.

New displays sprang up.

"Actuality, Tom."

Newscasts and truecasts.

"One spends so much time," added the Oracle, "just passively absorbing, watching the events of real peoples' lives."

Displays, analyses.

Political speeches. Convocations, ceremonies. Criminal courts, servitor executions, mumbled public confessions. Rallies. Military action.

"How dreadful for you."

A hundred shades of liquid light reflected on that blue crystal carapace.

Again, the hint of inhuman cold in those piercingly intelligent eyes. "You might dread it, my young friend. But you'll never understand it."

Tom tore his gaze away from the crystal-and-gold sarcophagus.

"Let me try."

"I don't think—"

"Your consciousness, poor Oracle, bounces up and down your timeline: you make a living by reporting newscasts you "remember" seeing in the future. The same future which traps you, always."

"If you could remember"—ice, colder than the cryosarcophagus, in his voice—"the moment of your own death, your . . . outlook, too, would change."

Tom looked down at the poignard in his fist, then stared into the Oracle's eyes. "I foresee *your* death."

"Many years from now." Old pain; an undertone almost of wistfulness. "Long after you, Tom."

Stepping forwards, watching the attack-point overlays spring again into his vision field, holding his weapon's hilt lightly but firmly.

"You can address me," Tom said, "as Lord Corcorigan."

Stepping away, stepping *through* the muted moving holodisplays—the Oracle's broad shoulders and handsome face just for a moment in the centre of swirling floodwaters, a child's outflung hand—he retreated to a buttress, leaned against its plunging arc.

"Recognize that?" Tom gestured.

"Yes, I—" A frown, then: "Duke Boltrivar's realm. A flood. Has it happened yet? Or is it yet to come?" A half-laugh. "My perspective is a little different from yours."

Now.

"You're dead, Oracle."

Tom lunged.

"Sorry, Tom. Procedure: execute." Again, the Oracle subtly moved, and Tom's momentum took him sailing past but he stopped and whirled in time to hear: "Duration, two minutes."

Melting . . .

He was ready to strike again but the motion caught his attention and he froze, watching as the crystal liquefied and *flowed*, melting into the great golden sculpture which cupped the cryosarcophagus.

A wash of frigid air.

Sweet Fate! Impossible—

Slowly but deliberately, his dead mother sat up in the sarcophagus, turned and opened wide her eyes as blue as Terran skies.

"Tom?"

She focused. Her voice, petal-soft, was as familiar as breathing.

"Is that really you?"

46

NULAPEIRON AD 3414

Abomination!

Diaphragm paralysed with shock, Tom forced himself to speak.

"How are you doing this?"

Ignoring him, the Oracle stepped up beside the sarcophagus. "Don't bother getting up, my love." He took gentle hold of Mother's hand.

Madness. I can't be seeing this.

Blue/gold, the white/blue floor, all seemed to swirl; blood-rush filled Tom's ears.

"Would you believe"—d'Ovraison's voice was distant—"by force of will?"

Breath control.

"Not really." Forced urbanity.

Mother's beauty was palely ethereal. Held on the point of death, reawakened for odd moments of the Oracle's life? Or was there something else?

Fist and stallion.

Tom fought to regain his focus.

"Ranvera." The Oracle could look only at her. "Ran, my love."

"Gérard."

The sweet softness in her voice, directed at her husband's nemesis, washed over Tom, bathing him in icy hatred.

I'm going to kill you, Oracle.

Now he could do it. Sighting in on the targets, going from radial to common carotid in one arcing motion—

"Oh, Tom. Whatever happened to you?"

"Mother?"

He stopped, mind racing. Could this be illusion?

"All grown up, and handsome, too. Do the girls—?"

"Mother." Harshly. "Has this one"—indicating d'Ovraison with his poignard's point—"told you what happened to Father? What they did to me after he died?"

"Died?" A dreamy frown. "Davraig died, too?"

"Don't tell me you didn't know."

"It's not so bad . . ."

"*What?*"

"Dying . . . Just a black tunnel, and you fall in. That's it."

Gérard, with exquisite gentleness, touched her cheek.

Breathe.

Tom struggled for self-control.

Just breathe.

Focus.

"It's only dreamtrope addiction." He stepped back—making room, so that the Oracle could not reach him when the process began. "Her long memory lapses. Picking up the threads of a days-old conversation as though no time had elapsed. Did her insanity make her more attractive to you, poor Oracle?"

Rage flashed in d'Ovraison's eyes.

Scored a point.

Tom sensed Mother's presence, the hint of her perfume on the chilled air, but his attention now was all upon his enemy.

"Poor, trapped Oracle," he continued. "Unable to stay in the normal flow of entropic time. Do you envy us that much? Matching your fragmented consciousness to the symptoms of her illness?"

D'Ovraison's big hands bunched into fists.

Mother spoke. "No, Gérard." Trembling, covering the Oracle's hand with hers, she added, "You promised, my dear."

"I did, my love. Don't worry—"

But the tiniest of frowns had appeared between the Oracle's dark eyebrows.

Mother . . .

Tom pushed the thought aside.

He unfastened his jumpsuit, descending to one knee, as though genuflecting. He placed his redmetal poignard on the floor and unlooped his talisman.

"Fine workmanship, don't you think, wise Oracle?" Placing the stallion on the floor. "My father's work. Remember this, Mother?"

And I remember the Pilot. Did she know what she was giving me?

"Maybe. I'm not—"

But Tom was already forming the control gesture, causing the stallion's two halves to neatly fall apart, revealing the nul-gel capsule.

Did she think I would just communicate with other worlds?

"Watch, now." The poignard's point neatly sliced open the gel, revealing the crystal. It sparked with blue light.

But those processors can do so much more.

Every holodisplay in the wide chamber suddenly went chaotic, rippling with wild hues, tripping kaleidoscopically through the spectrum.

"What's happening?" The Oracle's voice faltered.

"Download," said Tom tersely. But control tesseracts told their own story.

In realspace, logic itself is incomplete . . .

"I don't—" The Oracle stopped, entranced, as displays pulsed hypnotically.

. . . constricted by Gödel's theorem: truth is not always provable . . .

"Your life, poor Oracle, is but a dream."

. . . but in mu-space, in its infinite reflexiveness . . .

Logotropic interface.

. . . all may be proven . . .

The crystal was already broadcasting standard strobe codes, but a parallel task searched for other means, locking on to the VSI implant and suborning that, also.

. . . and anything at all may be simulated . . .

Dropping Mother's hand, d'Ovraison backed away, his wide, powerful shoulders hunched with uncertainty. "Don't . . . understand."

. . . even . . .

Direct rewiring: subverting the Oracle's own femtocytes.

. . . an Oracle's . . .

"Everything from this point in time is just a model, a simulation. *My* universe, Oracle. All your future memories consist of images, sensations, which I've designed."

. . . life.

The crystal broadcast the new code: rewriting molecular configurations, potentiating memories of future events which would never occur.

"Impossible."

I'm rewriting your mind—

D'Ovraison gave a frightened glance sideways. Mother was sinking back into her sarcophagus.

—and you know it.

"It's already happened."

"No . . ."

But it had.

The final newscast—a memory transmitted to his youth, as entropic time flows—flickers out.

Boundary condition.

The last moment of awareness, as the old man dies.

In an infinitesimally short period of time, d'Ovraison's *entire memories of the future beyond this moment* had been written logotropically into his brain. All his future perceptions were the product of a multifractal-modelling simulation.

Even the memory of his distant, future death—due to old age—came from Tom's imagination.

All your predictions . . .

The big man shook violently as tympani-potentiation took hold and the new memories coalesced.

. . . and all your imagined future . . .

The simulated future newscasts were not random predictions. They were based, as much as possible, on the truecasts of other Oracles, for consistency.

. . . are just a mirage . . .

Poor Oracle.

. . . of my devising.

That fiction included algorithmically incompressible processes: impossible, in realspace, to simulate—quicker to let them actually occur. But Tom had broken free of the universe's constrictions, penetrated the ur-logic of infinite mu-space.

"The memory of this event," he told d'Ovraison, "will not spread back to other parts of your timeline. For a few short seconds, you're going to be almost human."

The Oracle was in a new future, one he had never seen.

Interface.

The real future.

"This can't be."

Maybe.

Tom clasped both crystal and poignard in one hand, and slowly stood.

But I'm changing your Fate, Oracle.

Blue fire rose up around him as he stepped forwards, and he halted.

What's happening?

It was as though the air resisted him.

He forced one pace. Then another.

"Just another . . . paradox . . ."

I don't understand.

Another.

But I won't let it stop me.

Tom pushed himself through rising blue sparks. Unexpected: in one sense he had altered the Oracle's future by a mere programming trick, rewriting his perceptions.

But this resistance, as though *realspace itself* was pushing against his alterations . . .

He pushed on.

This moment, planned in advance, had been a stopping-point when Tom had first devised the strategy. How could the Oracle not "remember" the future alteration of his own mind?

But the memory would indeed be wiped out—by trauma—since *the Oracle himself* had not expected to die, not for many years.

As Tom pushed through another barrier of intensity, a grimace-like smile tugged at his lips: a new paradox.

Poor Oracle.

Doomed by his own perceptions.

Another step.

Infinite instantiations, now over.

No simulation: this was reality.

"A gift, Oracle."

Crackling energy, spitting through the air.

Don't stop now.

"Your first—"

A *new* reality.

D'Ovraison's eyes were wide, frozen.

"—ever—"

A cobra's prey.

"—surprise!"

And the final barrier of blue flames and sparks gave way as Tom rushed forwards and thrust under the Oracle's left arm—his own non-existent left arm burning white hot with hatred—stabbing through the armpit, twisting downwards, burying the poignard to its hilt.

Done it!

The Oracle fell.

Tom watched him writhing, struggling: like a stranded fish gasping at the air, smearing scarlet on the white/blue floor, reaching ineffectually for the embedded weapon, eyes popping, drowning in his own blood. He *mewled*, a strange eldritch cry.

But the Oracle Gérard d'Ovraison was a big man . . .

Vengeance.

. . . strong and powerful . . .

Fist and stallion.

. . . and took a long time to die.

The crystal seemed fused and lifeless, but he reinserted it inside the stallion anyway, and looped the whole thing in place inside his jumpsuit. Then he tugged the poignard free. It came out with a wet, sucking sound; he forced it into its sheath.

Tom gestured, and a small control display flickered into existence. At his summoning, a swarm of microdrones floated into the chamber.

Gesturing rapidly, he forced them to begin execution of their housekeeping routines. He was careful to use only some of them on d'Ovraison's body, disabling safety med-alerts, working on surface decontamination only. The others went to work on the chamber itself.

With luck, they would destroy all forensic traces before anyone realized what had happened.

Then there was nothing more he could do to avoid the thing he was putting off.

Mother . . .

It was as though another barrier prevented fast movement; but this one was purely imaginary.

Have I killed you, too?

But even as he leaned over her, Mother's lifeless form gave a low gasp—holovolumes flickering all around—and, almost creaking, her head turned. Eyelids half opened, but the eyeballs were upturned and milky.

"You . . . think . . ." Rasping. "Did not . . . know."

Hardly a human voice.

"Corduven . . . will kill . . ."

Oracle.

"Love you . . . Tom."

"Mother!"

Flatplane.

*** AGONAL TRANSITION ***

Had he talked to Mother or the Oracle? Or some superposition of both?

*** PATIENT DECEASED ***

"NO!"

Fine mouth falling slack for the final time.

Not again. Not another death.

Glowing blue.

Gripping the edge of the sarcophagus, he watched azure fluid—glowing, fluorescing with inner light—spill slowly from her mouth, her ears, and pool inside the sarcophagus.

I've seen this before.

But the glow faded to a faint glimmer, and then it was gone. The fluid was matt and lifeless, and after a while something stirred inside Tom and he backed away from his mother's corpse.

Time to go.

47

NULAPEIRON AD 3414

"My Lord?"

Tom could hear her, but it was of no import.

"Can I help you, my Lord?"

Black despair.

He was slumped in his chair, brooding behind his quickglass desk, surrounded by the rows of crystals—so much accumulated wisdom—which adorned his study.

"Tom!"

Such familiarity penetrated his heavy mood.

"Elva? How are you doing?"

Not even Jak would have dared to use his first name, but Captain Elva Strelsthorm was fearless.

Blood on his hand.

"I'm fine, my Lord. It's your welfare that concerns me today."

Not literally: he had wiped it.

"I've never . . ."

After the Oracular inkling of his own death: his ultimate Fate.

". . . been better, Elva."

Remembering the apparition, no, the actual experience of *walking out of the chamber, turning his back against both corpses, shuffling out onto the parapet. Nightfall.*

He had never seen true night before, but this was it: darkness shrouding the world. Cold winds. Purple/white lightning spat, and solid curtains of rain smashed against the stonework, spattered him with silver ricochets, blinded him with its force.

And he felt torn apart—a literal separation—as some part of him climbed slowly onto the slippery balustrade—thinking: journey's end, at last—and launched himself into the void, falling down through the biting air, paralysed by windrush, scream lost amid the slipstream, plunging to oblivion.

"I've never seen you worse, my Lord. And that's the truth."

Heart pounding, he dropped back onto the balcony floor, drenched with fear-sweat as well as rain—asking himself endlessly: what happened?—trying to convince himself that it was hallucination, brought on by shock.

Or had he glimpsed—felt, touched, smelled—another reality, an alternative world where he threw himself into nothingness, welcoming death as the closure of life suddenly devoid of meaning?

Did he know less of the nature of time and Fate than he thought?

"Perhaps, Elva. Perhaps so."

He returned to the chamber then, trying to ignore the pitiful remnants cupped in the golden framework, and the Oracle's lifeless, collapsed remains upon the floor. Three microdrones were already working their way like scavengers across his clothing, his gaping wound.

The systems told him the terraformer's complement of guards: over a hundred armed troopers, nearly thirty ancillary staff. Too risky to descend into the terraformer's interior.

So he ordered a femtofact-mesodrone to extrude braided polyfilament, used the golden framework of his mother's bier as a tether, and went back out onto the storm-swept balcony.

"My Lord, I've fetched a visitor for you."

Was this the same conversation? Or had time elapsed?

"I don't want to see anyone."

"But—"

"Thanks all the same, Elva. But that's an order."

The long dangerous rappel down the curved exterior. It was the best part of a thousand metres: easy enough in dry conditions, taken at an unhurried pace; dangerous as Chaos right now as he jumped and slid along rain-slick stonework, braking the filament by friction round his waist and bare hand, near-sightless in the darkness and the pounding rain.

"Tom . . . ?"

A different voice.

Finding the equatorial rim, clambering along it on hand and knees until he reached an opening, then the precarious lowering of himself, fingers crimped on wet stone, and swinging into dry safety.

No choice then but to plunge through the membrane, hoping it would do no worse than sound alarms. Sprinting, crouched over, into the interior.

"Thomas Corcorigan . . ."

Into a wider space—drop-bug launch-cradle—but a Jack—not Jak, his friend: but a dermawebbed Jack with microfaceted silver eyes and white sparks of liquid light playing across his skin—leaped forwards, weapon-system powering up, but Tom was fast, very fast, and then the Jack was down and blood was pooling—dark, almost purple: another death—on the ceramic floor.

Flash image: dead feline, neko-kitten's mother.

". . . What do you think you're playing at?"

Then throwing himself into the drop-bug and shouting: "Go!" Mallow-like cocoon pressed against him as the bug sealed itself and launched.

There was sickening acceleration, a distant thump, then the free-floating parabolic descent, the final roar of simple chemical jets, the cushioned impact.

"Trude?" When he looked up from his desk, he felt for the first time the cold tears which had tracked down his cheeks.

The long trek on foot, just to make distance across the dark landscape.

A fitful rest.

Then magnificent dawn, painting the sky pale yellow streaked with lime, white sunlight sparking from the launch site's membrane. No people, only dumb equipment, so he could make his way inside and climb down into Nulapeiron's depths, away from the unnatural spaces and the skin-burning elements.

Finally, the long run—journeying on foot: an ultra-endurance event such as he had never imagined—using glimmerglows stolen from the cargo-shuttle launch site to illuminate, pitifully, his path along the dark tunnel, expecting at any moment to be struck by a hurtling cargo train, spattered, smashed out of existence.

Part of him longed for that. But part of him wanted only to run, and keep on running.

"What are you doing here, Trude?"

That familiar old face: more wrinkled now, and the once grey hair was mostly white, but it was bound by a familiar style of mandelbrot scarf and her sudden smile had not changed at all.

Running . . .

"Tom, Tom. What have you been up to?"

A wan smile beneath his cold tears. It had been so long . . .

Run and never stop.

"That's easy. He's been—"

It was Elva who spoke, standing behind Trude, hands clasped lightly in front of her but ready for action, her wide shoulders relaxed.

"—killing Oracles."

Small blind ciliates, scurrying.

"Procedures and protocol?" asked Elva.

The thing was huge: scorched and blackened, part of its thorax overhanging a shadowed crevasse in the natural cavern's floor. Tendrils hung in catenary arcs, their end-pads still fastened to the walls and roof as they had been at the time of the attack. Or accident, if that was what it had been.

How did she know?

One tendril lay coiled and broken like dead rope on the ground.

How did Elva know about the Oracle?

"Poll-and-acknowledge are alpha-hash-standard for today." Trude's voice was matter-of-fact. "Scatter-pattern beta if anything goes wrong."

A lone ellipsoidal ciliate queen—half the size of a man's leg, with several fingernail-sized males clinging to its mottled carapace; its brushlike hair-legs rippling—scuttled down the wide hanging tendril from the wrecked arachnargos body. It headed for the quiet shadows.

"I'll go first." Elva crossed over to the arachnargos and went inside.

Trude reached out for his arm but Tom ignored her, keeping his cape wrapped tightly around himself.

What am I doing here?

Elva leaned out of the gaping wound in the bulbous thorax, inserted thumb and forefinger in her mouth, and gave a low, piercing whistle.

"Sophisticated signal code." Tom tried for irony, but his heart was not in it.

"Whatever works." Trude patted his arm.

"How long have you known Elva?"

Trude's lined face was half-hidden in the gloom.

"A while."

Since the days when he lived in the market? Tom shrugged, inside his cape. They wanted to be secretive; he would not concern himself.

Scarlet smeared across the white/blue floor . . .

The connection between the market-dwelling stallholder's son and his present self seemed tenuous: a distant, fragile thing.

The only way in was to clamber along the one loose tendril and swing in through the opening. For a moment, hanging over the long drop, he felt an almost overwhelming desire to throw himself off—

"Tom?"

—but he saw then that Trude was unsteady on her feet, and he helped her through the dark opening into the wrecked arachnargos. He followed her inside.

Shadows.

Waiting for his vision to adjust, Tom kept his eye-focus soft: twelve shadows against the background gloom. Discount Trude and Elva; but the others were potential enemies.

Something stirred inside Tom: a gathering of interest, or the awareness of danger.

Too soon.

Deep inside, his nerves were silently whimpering.

A tiny glowglimmer, trapped in a collimating tube, lowered itself from the ceiling. Its low illumination was directed at him.

"Who are you?" he said.

The shadow-shrouded figures were bulky and shapeless: wearing voluminous capes, baggy hoods drawn forwards. A natural precaution.

A moist smell lingered in the air.

"You'll forgive us"—softly spoken: a young man's voice, possibly Zhongguo Ren—"if we're a little reticent on that point."

Someone sneezed, and murmured an apology.

"This meeting wasn't my idea." Tom kept his tone neutral.

One of the figures leaned forwards and muttered: "*Dyestvityelna, rezap proroka?*"

"Yes, he did," said Elva. "Stone dead."

Tom looked at her, surprised.

She shrugged. "My accent's terrible, but I understand the basics."

"Exactly how?" one of the others began, in a deep baritone. Then, "This is ridiculous." He lowered his hood, revealing blocky features beneath cropped white hair. "Exactly how did you achieve this particular termination, Lord Corcorigan?"

Tom shook his head.

"A trick?" someone asked. "How do we know it actually happened?"

Another man drew back his hood. Narrow face, dark-brown skin.

Tom, recognizing the bright-yellow tattoo on forehead and cheek, cast his memory back for the name. "Dr Sukhram. My regards, sir."

He bowed, equal-to-equal.

The doctor hesitated, then returned the gesture.

"This is a little theatrical," said the white-haired man, "but you can refer to me as Sentinel. It's a reasonably appropriate codename."

"I won't ask why." Tom looked around at the others. No more impulses to reveal themselves.

"Anyway." Sentinel leaned back against a grime-streaked bulkhead. "The security networks confirm the kill. In fact, the covert channels are buzzing with the news."

He looked at the hooded man who had expressed doubt; the man abruptly nodded.

"But why"—Tom heard the slightest tremor in his own voice—"do you identify *me* as the killer?"

There was silence for a moment, then Elva said: "Don't worry, my Lord. Not from evidence at the scene: I don't know anything about that. Just observations in your own demesne."

So I didn't leave and return undetected. Nicely done, Elva. Perhaps he should have been glad she was so thorough. *But you've told these people all about me.*

A betrayal? It didn't seem that way.

"So who are you?" He made it a general question, but it was Dr Sukhram who cleared his throat and answered: "An umbrella organization, of sorts. LudusVitae, when we need a name. Something of a loose alliance, with not entirely common objectives—"

"But we agree"—a woman's voice, harsh—"that the use of Oracles must stop."

Waves of tension, criss-crossing the darkened cabin.

Sentinel said: "Some of our more, ah, *progressive* colleagues favour radical redesign of social structures. But, frankly, there are thousands of demesnes in the world, and not all of them even have Lords, as such. So a global—"

"You won't find many deep strata"—low voice: coarse accent but clear articulation—"without widespread support for total revolution. I'm talking about a worldwide change in—"

"Please." Trude held up a hand. "This isn't why we're here."

"Agreed." Sentinel squeezed his eyes shut briefly, as though in pain. Then, "We're more than a debating society," he said.

Uneasy, not trusting these disorganized strangers who held his life in their hands, Tom remained silent.

Somebody shifted position, and red dots sparked into being across Tom's vision field, as kinaesthetic awareness slotted attack-vectors into place.

"Frankly—" Sentinel began, but stopped as Dr Sukhram cut in: "My Lord, whatever technique you used to circumvent an Oracle's awareness . . . With such a method, the debating could end. What we need is direct action."

And you're a healer? But Tom had the patience of discipline, and still he said nothing.

"Mister Cor—" Sentinel hesitated. "I mean, my Lord . . ."

Of course. They've never had a noble among them.

". . . Oracular domination is a crime against humanity. The only way—"

Tom: "They haven't done anything to me."

Shocked silence.

Then, "But you killed—"

"That was personal."

Tom withdrew.

They can't give me up to the authorities. They'll have to kill me themselves.

He stepped outside the cabin, then sat down carefully, cross-legged, on the wide tendril. Pulling his cape close, he leaned back against the besmirched, burned hull.

If they can—

But here, in interstitial territory, there were no sensor webs to detect energy weapons or femtotech. Fate only knew what armaments the conspirators were carrying.

Trude and Elva were his friends, but how much did that count for?

Shadows lay below, dark and inviting. A twitch of the muscles, a drop of a few seconds, and it would all be over—

I wonder what they're saying, inside.

Perhaps they could control their disappointment in him. There were raised voices, but he could not make out the words. Then a low muttering.

But what shall I do now, Maestro?

He addressed his thoughts to the inviting shadows.

In a sense, it was the same dilemma which had accompanied his taking possession of Corcorigan Demesne: the choice between a life of scholarship and ease, or determined vengeance.

Father . . . I wish you were here.

Even after all these years.

I miss you.

The ascension of Tom Corcorigan to Lordship: if only Father could have seen it!

What should I do?

But the paradox was not lost on Tom. It was Father's death that had uncovered buried strength: the power of hatred.

And there are five thousand Oracles still in the world.

There was a long, still moment, during which no stimulus intruded into Tom's awareness. Blank, dark; silent.

He was not conscious of making a decision, but he found himself carefully standing—with precise technique, getting up without using his hand for balance—and letting out a long, calming breath.

Then he turned and re-entered the darkened arachnargos cabin.

They were scared. *Scared enough to be dangerous.* Even with their hooded figures shrouded in near-darkness, the tension in their bodies hung like black knots in the air. It struck Tom's deep physical awareness; *wu shu* practitioners, like the Strontium Dragons' warriors, would think of it as disrupted *ch'i*.

With one's dream in sight, just within reach . . . overwhelming fear is the natural response.

But this is my time. It was the thought that had sustained Tom before, on taking possession of his realm, giving the strength to avoid easy choices.

"You'll have to explain the technique again," said a woman. "How exactly does simulating an Oracle's future allow you to—?"

"Never mind." It was Dr Sukhram who ended the discussion, chopping the air with a decisive gesture. "We have empirical proof, don't we? The details are for later."

A pause, then scattered nods of agreement.

Looks as though I have to do it.

Having done it once . . . would that make the next one easier? Or harder?

And committing my whole life to eradicating the Oracles . . . But what else would I do?

He felt as though the decision had been made for him—No, that wasn't right. As though there was *no* choice to be made. No alternative. There was a rushing sound in his ears, and he felt for a moment as though he was swaying. Then he refocused on his surroundings.

"—actually need their deaths?" Sentinel was saying. "If we discredit the truecasts, so true cannot be distinguished from false, should that not be sufficient?"

Elva spoke up. "There must be some critical number we need to, ah, take down. My Lord?"

"Take down, yes." Tom smiled, grimly. "Subvert or kill. Whatever we need to do."

He saw the sense of commitment settle upon the group.

In Sentinel's eyes was a new glimmer: empty dissent could now become effective action.

"You can help, Lord Corcorigan, to bring freedom to the world."

A bitter, cynical laugh rose up inside Tom.

Me? Freedom?

He could not have come this far without gaining some self-knowledge. The Tom who might have spent a lifetime engaged in logosophical analyses of Avernon's metavectors . . . that Tom no longer existed.

"Who better?"

His previous ennui dissolved as his nerves once more tightened and his inner strength returned.

The power—

For the real Tom knew, finally, that civilized society was not for the likes of him.

—of hatred.

48

TERRA AD 2123

<<Karyn's Tale>>
[11]

"When's it going to happen?"

Anne-Marie's eyes shifted randomly. Barney, the dog, raised his muzzle to follow the arcing trajectory of the taxi as it lifted into the grey-clouded sky.

"This afternoon." Karyn looked down and patted Barney's head.

"How quickly? No, don't tell me." Anne-Marie's smile appeared mirthless. "Distance is a strange concept in mu-space. You'll reach him in time."

"God, I hope so." Though it was warm, Karyn shivered. "They're going as fast as they can. Viral insertion today. Fly to Phoenix late tonight." More jet-lag. "The rest starts tomorrow."

"How accurate—I mean, do you know *exactly* where he is, in mu-space?"

Hefting her bag, Karyn began to walk: whether she or Barney moved first, it was impossible to say.

"Near as damn it."

The soles of Karyn's boots were silent on the piazza's green and orange tiles, but Anne-Marie knew exactly where she was.

"My place first," said Anne-Marie. "Lemon tea, almond cookies. OK?"

"Fine." Karyn blinked away tears.

What's wrong with me?

But Anne-Marie must know she was crying. Even Barney, catching the confused vibrations, stared up at Karyn as they walked.

Next morning, early, she bowed in, took the wooden sword—the *bokken*—from its rack and began her solo *suburi* exercises, cutting the air and thrusting towards imaginary opponents.

Trying to feel expansive, to make the empty dojo her home, she moved faster while feeling everything slow down. She did not think: movement just happened. Neither jet-lag nor lack of sleep hindered her.

"Good."

Sensei. Mike.

She knelt and bowed, then gave him the gift of a flowing attack, sword hand arcing towards his forehead. Sensei blended with the motion, entered, and she rolled through the air, scarcely feeling the mat's touch as she regained her feet.

"Something different today," said Sensei a little later, pinning her with *ikkyo*, "about your spirit."

"I know."

Too soon for the nanocytes to have begun their work.

"Something . . . joyful."

Truly, she almost floated through the throws.

When the training-session was over, she headed for the changing-room. She tugged off the baggy black split-skirt *hakama* and white *gi* jacket, folded them and placed them in her bag. Wearing just a white T-shirt and trousers, she looked towards the showers, frowned—then suddenly the paroxysm hit her and she was inside a toilet cubicle and vomiting as though she were about to die.

It looked like some sort of mothership: transparent-hulled, spawning strange tangled exploratory vessels with missions of their own.

"This is fuckin' criminal."

The smaller ones were waldophages, borne to their target sites by the nanovector. Already they were unfolding their monomolecular arms, ready to perform the most intimate of surgical procedures: laying new substrate, extruding RNA-precursors ready to duplicate existing neurons, manufacturing Cooper-pair qubit-gates when merely rewiring the existing cortical connections would be insufficient.

"Nice bedside manner, Doc."

The grouping in the image was one of hundreds of thousands inside Karyn's nervous system. Already the examination room's angles seemed to twist and shift through odd perspective changes, light transmogrifying from normal hues to greys and indescribable not-greys.

Too soon. Hysteria, that was all. It would be days before such coherent macro-effects would become manifest.

"Not you," the chief medic growled, then wiped his bushy moustache with the back of his hand. "Damn it, you didn't know, did you?"

Karyn started to rise and he pushed her back down. She was surprised: at his action, and that she did not rupture the limb at wrist, elbow and shoulder as she had been taught.

"Fran! God damn it!" The medic angrily stabbed a finger over a sensor pad, but another medic, a woman, was already rushing in.

"What's up?"

"Check this."

Pulsing holo. Abstract phase-space; text sheets abbreviated in codes Karyn did not recognize.

"I don't suppose either of you wants to—"

"Shit!" The second medic, Fran, gave Karyn a startled look. "Confirmed, confirmed," she muttered, then said to Karyn: "You underwent Phase II in your condition?"

"What cond—?"

"She doesn't know." The chief medic lightly touched Karyn's shoulder. "Do you, darlin'?"

$$\diamondsuit \; \diamondsuit \; \diamondsuit$$

Karyn closed her eyes, and forced out a long slow breath. If the nanoviral insertion had failed, then Dart was dead. That was how serious the matter was.

"That's right." The woman, Fran. "The normal procedure would have caused you to abort, regardless." Grim anger tightened her voice. "This was done deliberately."

Abort?

"You don't mean that literally," Karyn said, but dismay was already rising inside her.

"You're pregnant, darlin'." The chief medic, walruslike with his big moustache, was serious now. "There's no question of it."

But Fran was staring intently, manipulating auxiliary displays. "Secondary concentration, just here." She pointed. "Can we rotate and magnify?"

Stomach-churning sensation as a galaxy of light-points swirled and grew larger.

Dart . . . We're having a baby.

Stupid way to think.

"Bastards." Fran, softly. "God-damned bastards."

"There are still choices." The chief medic took a deep breath and looked at Karyn. "We can—"

"Stop. Don't tell me." Karyn sat up on the examination couch, pushing away their hands.

"But the baby—"

Shifting overlays, a hundred shades of blue. Tiny shape: hardly recognizable, but Karyn knew it for what it was. At one end, a cluster of white sparks of light.

"The nanocytes are in my baby's brain. Aren't they?"

Project Rewire.

And she had signed the contract. But that gave them no defensible right to—

Fran's face was white, pinched with fear and rage. But the chief medic slowly nodded his head. "They can't be nondestructively removed. It's already too late for that."

"I'm another experiment." Swinging her legs off the couch, and standing up. "Wonderful."

"I don't think you should—"

"*I have no choice!*" Karyn's voice bounced back off the walls, a screeching echo. "Whatever they've done to me, I have to complete the mission."

"Agreed." The chief medic held up his hand as Fran started to protest. "But when you return, if you decide to take legal action, I will testify on your behalf."

Fran mutely nodded her support.

"Thank you. If you could just give me something for the sickness?"

"No problem." The chief handed over a dermastrip.

She was halfway to the door when a sudden realization hit her: "The baby. I mean, the embryo. They wouldn't—"

Unable to continue, she could only watch as the two medics grimly checked their displays. Fran accessed the pan-UNSA Pilots' database, quickly sifting data.

Then a sudden grin split her face.

"Fifty-fifty," she said. "You and Pilot Mulligan. DNA match, everything normal."

Except that nanocytes are rewiring my baby's nervous system.

"Thanks." Karyn nodded to them both.

She left the med-centre and went out into the scorching heat of an Arizona summer morning. One of the passing medics wore a T-shirt with *two holo-skeletons, lying on a strip of parched red sand apparently extending into his torso, and projecting half a metre in front of him.*

As Karyn passed by him, her proximity activated the garment's audio and holo-motion—*one skeleton turning its skull, saying to the other*: "BUT IT'S A *DRY* HEAT"—echoing the tourist-board enticements to visitors.

A strangled sound halfway between a laugh and a sob rose inside her.

At the end of the long, white runway, rippling in the furnace-hot air, the domes of Phoenix LaunchCentral stood clean and massive, strong, mirror-bright and totally impersonal.

<<MODULE ENDS>>

49

NULAPEIRON AD 3414

"Are we softworms or are we men?"

Angry mutterings among the ragged crowd. There were stevedores and labourers of every kind, big forearms and big bellies or else skinny, like ferrets. Black-skinned or white, they were mostly stained with grey grime.

"What about women?" called out a big woman, arms crossed above her mighty bosom. She was as brawny as many of the men.

"Yes, please," someone said, and laughter rippled through the gathering.

Tom smiled from his vantage point: a tiny alcove, once used to hold a statuette; only its broken base remained. The alcove was high up, just below the groined ceiling. The stone felt greasy with moss and mutated fluorofungus.

"OK, OK." The speaker—the authorities would term him a rabble-rouser—held up his hands, allowing the amusement to peter out. "Brothers . . . and *sisters*"—hoots of laughter—"all of us: we're humans, and therefore we should have our dignity, our pride. But do our masters grant us that dignity? Do they?"

Mumbled negatives among the crowd, but not boisterous, not now. This was striking too close to home.

Below Tom, hanging in mid-air near the wall, was one of his first attempts at seditious verse:

For freedom's curse
Could not be worse
For Oracles, or then for me.

The slaves he whips
Inconstant rips
For darkness' sake, will always be.

But Chaos waits
Beyond the gates
Where Oracles no longer see.

The tiny holocrystal projecting this poem had been in place for several days. The script was in large, simple tricons, and the colour-coding was garish, but it had a dual purpose. The shading was a gen-erally recognized code which proclaimed the public meeting here, at this place and time.

Similar verses were scattered around the locality: twelve strata down, just inside the border of Lord Shinkenar's demesne.

If the mass of people are illiterate, Tom wondered, *then why are they affected so by poetry?*

Perhaps it was just the times, the choice of subject matter. Or maybe the nobility underestimated the populace.

Reflexively, he reached for the stallion talisman beneath his jerkin. It was there, but empty: the comms relay was back in his study. Trusting Elva's security routines implicitly. Technicians were working ceaselessly, in shifts around the clock, in chambers with no dark periods (like Lady V'Delikona's realm), to restore and duplicate its capabilities.

Whatever had happened on the Oracle's terraformer sphere, it had left the crystal blackened and only partially functional. The basic comms frameworks were there, but they would not activate. Karyn's Tale was inaccessible—though he still had the previously downloaded modules—and only a hint of its vast processing powers was available.

For all the tech-talk of exaqubit architecture and hectoday-long reverse-engineering analyses, it was just one small crystal they were trying to take apart. It seemed that building the requisite toolkits would be the hard part of the project. Regardless, the regular brain-storming discussions were surprisingly enjoyable, though Tom knew none of the technicians' names. That was one of the simpler precautions taken by LudusVitae cell members.

Tom adjusted his position in the high alcove. The greasy stonework felt cold.

"And how many hours do you work every day?" The speaker, down below, singled out someone in the crowd.

A *plant*, Tom thought, gathering his tattered cloak more tightly around his hunched body.

"Too many!" was the shouted answer, and other voices rose in angry support.

"And will we present their Lordships with our demands?"

"Aye!" Mutterings. "*Demands . . .*"

But there was jostling at the back of the crowd, a ripple of push and shove, and then Tom could see the uniforms. Some of them were civilians with only diagonal black sashes to identify them.

Not regular militia, those others. Professional thugs, armed with staves.

They used a wedge formation to force their way into the crowd's centre, while a small group circled the dank chamber's edges, trying to cut off the speaker's escape.

Most fled, but others fought, and there were cracked heads and streaming blood on both sides as confusion reduced them to a milling mass of bodies. The speaker tried to fight, but some of his own followers pulled him away and bundled him off to a dark side tunnel.

Damn them!

But it was not entirely unexpected, and there was nothing Tom could do to help. He was more useful to LudusVitae alive and free, and the numbers were too great: no matter how skilled he was, eventually sheer weight of numbers would press him into a corner and then he would be done for.

But he was afraid; and part of him wanted desperately to confront that fear.

Soon the chamber was deserted, save for the few wounded who had not been arrested. Moaning, holding foreheads or bloody temples. Two were lying still.

Damn them to Chaos.

It was a long time before members of the local populace—not organized: in twos or threes, looking for relatives—came to take away the survivors. One of the prone men had partially awoken, and began to moan incoherently as they carried him away on a blanket used as a stretcher. The other did not react as he was dragged out.

When the chamber was empty, Tom swung himself out of the alcove and climbed down the rough stone wall.

"My Lord?"

He span, hand ready, lowering into a crouch.

"I'm just a messenger." A small oriental youth bowed. "Did you see the action? It was quite a beehive of activity."

"No-one managed to block the incursion."

"Just so. Will you follow me, please?"

Beehive: block. Today's general-intro code.

"Where are we going?" asked Tom, but the youth had already turned his back and slipped into the shadowed corridor from which he had come.

Silently, Tom followed.

Cream-walled halls, square pillars with inlaid gold. Spreading green ferns at their bases. Soft music playing.

They were three strata up from the trouble scene, and the atmosphere could not have been more different: calm and prosperous. Not bad for the Nonum Stratum.

The youth's travel-access had been sufficient to get them both through the ceiling hatches. Tom's own control codes were not required, and he noted this. It signified a cell with significant resources.

Golden lev-platforms; merchants hawking fine pottery. A small amount of licensed smart-tech: moving figurines, self-composing music-crystals. Tom would have liked to stop—all pleasurable music is based on the constant $1/f$ parameter, but the annealed-transition algorithms sounded particularly interesting as a complex piece shifted from adagio to allegro—but a discreet establishment, blocky golden lion statues guarding the entrance, was in front of them.

Inside, a faint smell of incense hung in the air.

"Please wait," said the youth, bowing. He stepped through a membrane.

Cool and shadowed. Long displays of jewellery, infocrystals, statuettes. Bladed weapons which looked purely decorative: flexible blades, bright scarlet tassels.

Some customers quietly browsed. A lone woman, a couple holding hands. Two slender youths, in identical black silk tunics, waited patiently for any summons to help.

"How much is this?" The woman, holding up a flat octagon, decorated in red, gold and green, in which a round silver disc was embedded.

"The *pakua* mirror? Did you want it blessed?"

"If it can be done now. How much does it cost?"

"Master Tang has a couple with him at the moment: a geomantic consultation . . ."

Tom tuned out their conversation, only half listening as the fee structure was explained: the amount being whatever the woman could afford, provided certain numerologically significant digits appeared in the final sum.

He took down a chain-whip from the wall and weighed it in his hand: surprisingly heavy. He remembered the *wu shu* demonstration, so long ago, when Zhao-ji's people came to the caverns near the Ragged School.

A lifetime ago.

"We are all living in the dragon's veins." One of the oriental youths, addressing Tom.

"I've always thought so."

"Master Tang will see you now."

Rising straight up through the floor via a circular membrane, a young couple bearing scarlet-wrapped packages bade farewell to the youths, who returned the gesture: left hand clasping right fist, a short courteous bow.

"This way."

Tom replaced the weapon and followed the youth to the room's centre, tensing slightly as the membrane liquefied and elongated, slow and viscous. It lowered them into a basement chamber, then slurped back into position, regaining its original shape.

"Lord Corcorigan." From his seated position, the man bowed.

"Master Tang."

"We are honoured. Please"—indicating a chair of square design—"take a seat." Master Tang clapped his hands, and the youth hurried off through a side membrane.

Tom waited.

"I'm so sorry," Master Tang continued, "that our poor establishment cannot match the standards you are used to."

"I'm glad to be here."

If only you'll tell me why.

"Thank you. Please, my Lord . . . If I make any errors of protocol, be assured that no offence is implied. It will be just unfamiliarity with noble ways."

Tom bowed, hiding a smile. It was the apology he should have made, and he wondered how many rules of etiquette he had already broken since entering the chamber.

"In the interests of mutual understanding," he said, "let us forgo embarrassment. If we spell out intentions and agreements in detail,

explained simply but without assumptions about each other's infer-
ences, then we should avoid any problems."

Master Tang's sudden laugh echoed back from walls and ceiling.
"In other words, my Lord, you'd like me to get to the point."

Tom smiled. "If you like."

"But not before we've had some daistral. Ah, Younger Sik-chun."
He beckoned to the youth, who had reappeared with a laden tray.
"Thank you."

The youth held the tray at knee-height between Tom and Master
Tang, then let go. It remained floating in its lev-field. He poured daistral from a pot into two cups, then bowed and exited.

"An old friend of yours, Siu Lung"—Master Tang took a sip—
"sends his regards."

"I'm sorry, I don't—"

"Little Dragon is his commonly used name these days. It was not
always so."

Zhao-ji. His old friend.

"Is he well, Master Tang?"

But it was a decade since Tom had seen him, and this meeting was
about more than lost friendship. And why was it taking place now, in
particular?

"He is ranked *sheung fa*—Double Flower—and that is high indeed,
my Lord."

Tom looked at Master Tang directly. "Only four steps down from
Dragon Head, the *lung tau* himself. I'm very impressed."

Master Tang, too experienced to show surprise, nodded. "So am I,
my Lord."

"May I enquire as to the society's name?"

There were many, and Tom knew only a few of their names.

Master Tang said nothing—

Crimson, curling creature, wings unfurled, breathing fire. Bulbous, intel-
ligent eyes.

—but smiled as Tom rocked back, startled by the near-subliminal holoflash.

Recovering, Tom bowed. He had heard of the Strontium Dragons, possibly the most powerful syndicate in this sector. But its boundaries did not stop there, and it had links and alliances to societies in far-flung demesnes.

Most of his information came from Elva's tendaily security briefings. For the first time, he began to appreciate just how detailed and professional her analyses were.

Biding his time, he picked up his cup and drank some daistral. "Very good." He sat back, savouring the taste.

Master Tang remained silent.

We could sit here all day, without another word. But it would not do to betray a lack of control.

In Tom's first meeting with LudusVitae, in the abandoned arachnargos wreck, there had been one oriental man at least. Another member of the Strontium Dragons?

Finally, Master Tang turned and looked at the side membrane just as the youth, Younger Sik-chun, returned bearing a black-lacquered box.

Sik-chun relinquished his hold; like the tray, the small box floated. As before, he bowed silently and left.

"Earlier this year"—Master Tang's dark eyes glittered—"an untoward event occurred on a terraformer sphere, high in the atmosphere."

Tom's body readied itself for combat. But he could sense the waves of spiritual strength, of *ch'i*, emanating from Master Tang. His body, too, showed the paradoxical relaxed tension of a prepared warrior.

"Indeed."

"Such an unnatural environment, do you not think, my Lord? However—"

Yes, get to the point.

"—a lone assassin carried out a startling crime. As you can

imagine, proctor and astymonia investigations since then have been both thorough and widespread."

Fear crawled across Tom's skin.

He knew from Elva's summaries that security forces of all descriptions were clandestinely hunting, primarily in this sector, for Oracle d'Ovraison's killer. It was not a very public inquiry, for revealing the fact of an Oracle's murder might perturb the status quo, but it was indeed a thorough one.

I'm vulnerable.

Too many people in the LudusVitae organization knew about him. Yet he had thought himself safe . . . unless one of those people was undercover, a paid informant.

But here was a different motivation. If the investigations were so wide-ranging that it was affecting the syndicate's less than legal activities, then it would make perfect business sense to give Tom up to the authorities.

"I can imagine." He kept his voice level, disinterested.

"Can you, my Lord? Every single cargo pod, every shuttle, torn apart in the search for forensic traces. And, above . . ."

Cold, now. This was worse than he had thought.

". . . drones scouring the landscape. The best technicians analysed the crime site, autopsied the victims."

Mother.

"After the bodies' dissolution, though, it became possible to amend the DNA-profile record of one of the victims. It seemed the expedient thing to do." Master Tang raised his hand. "And some discarded personal effects were discovered."

He waved his hand, and the floating black box opened.

Two tiny objects, in an area of hundreds, maybe thousands of square kilometres. The search was *that* detailed?

"They were eaten away by acid." Master Tang was referring to the self-destruct capsules embedded in both cape and mask. "Almost totally."

Scraps of rag, twisted pieces of shrivelled membranous film. *Blackmail*.

"What is it," asked Tom carefully, "that I can do for you?"

He waited, every sense alert.

"Oh, no." Master Tang feigned shock. "Please"—pushing the box gently in its lev-field, towards Tom—"this is for you. All that remains. Think of it"—very formally—"as a gift, my Lord."

A trap? Am I under surveillance of some sort?

But taking the box was not an admission of guilt . . . though not reporting it to anyone later would be.

Tom gently closed the lid, tugged the box from the field and placed it beside him on the chair.

"If I can be of any assistance, Master Tang . . ."

"Perhaps, under the aegis of LudusVitae, my Lord, it might be possible that your group and ours could work more closely together. In areas of specific expertise and tactics."

"May I speak bluntly? Anyone with contacts inside such an investigation has no need of assistance."

"Perhaps so."

"Using contacts, though, who might talk to their superiors—among the proper authorities, I mean—at any time."

A tiny shake of the head. "Our people are not known for lack of loyalty."

"No—"

Remembering: *the girl, Feng-ying, bowing her head as the white explosion came.*

"—I suppose not."

Master Tang stood.

Puzzled, Tom followed suit. "Do you have details of the . . . areas of expertise we're discussing?"

"Oh, no." Again, the feigned shock. "I am not important enough to go into such weighty matters, my Lord."

Picking up the black box, Tom gave Master Tang his most courteous bow. "That surely cannot be the case, most esteemed Master Tang."

The youth returned to the room.

"Ah, Younger Sik-chun. Please escort his Lordship out."

50
NULAPEIRON AD 3414

"Heptomino One, advancing."

The blue dots moved through the semi-transparent tubes: shaded amber in their current position, but dangerously red nearer their destination.

"Heptomino Two. Stable."

Another pattern, deeper blue: cobalt, perhaps. The dots were moving, but holding the same general position.

"Acknowledged. Tumbler, are you holding?"

Third pattern.

"All quadrants secured."

"May I?" Tom leaned over Skolnar's shoulder, indicating a triconic lattice.

"Go ahead."

He pointed, and the information unfurled: durations and vectors, battle plans and probability-weighted contingency tactics, dependencies and alternatives mapped in detail.

Behind Tom, Elva murmured: "Too far."

They were in a wide, elliptical chamber with outward-curving walls: pink-white nacre, which under ordinary circumstances would have shimmered; tiny silver-winged statues in decorative nooks. Normally genteel-looking, the place was shrouded in shadows, glowclusters deactivated. Around the room's edges, seven, no, eight support staff moved, working at their displays. None of them paid attention to Tom.

He checked the teams' itineraries.

"For Fate's—" he began, but stopped as he realized that Skolnar, pale and intense, was concentrating on his eyes/ears-only data being lased to his retinae, coherence-resonated on his timpani.

Tom's eyelids flickered.

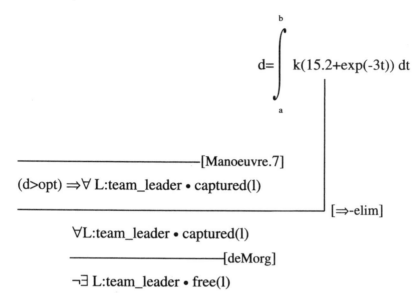

$$d = \int_a^b k(15.2 + \exp(-3t))\, dt$$

———————————————————[Manoeuvre.7]
$(d>opt) \Rightarrow \forall$ L:team_leader • captured(l)

——————————————————————— [⇒-elim]

$\forall$L:team_leader • captured(l)

————————————————[deMorg]

$\neg\exists$ L:team_leader • free(l)

Fragments of Sun Tzu's *Art of War* flashed in his mind's eye, triggered partly by intuitive understanding, partly by the beginnings of a metavector analysis which mapped real-world attributes quantitatively into tactical predicates.

"You can't afford to lose all three team leaders," he said.

Skolnar turned round and glared. "We won't."

Tom glanced at Elva. She knew: they had advanced too far, too fast.

It was Tom's first chance to observe command-and-control on a paramilitary op, and so far his reaction was ambivalent. The comms links seemed first class—femtosecond-bursts of minimal data, by line-of-sight, then bounce-relays—but the intelligence background info's validity was unknown, lacking probability analysis, while the actual manoeuvring was without finesse.

The teams had two objectives between them: to duplicate arach-nargos-manufacturing femtospores from the growth site, and plunder the business-history archives for shipment data. Twin targets alone suggested high-risk complexity.

Tiny white spheres bloomed in the display.

"Security forces," said Elva.

Not like you to mention the obvious.

It was a sign of her nervousness.

Tom had not met Skolnar before, but he shared Elva's lack of confidence in him. In the display, there were white clusters above and below the target volumes, as well as on the flanks. Some tunnels were still clear. But were the apparent escape routes real or decoys?

"Rajesh is in the relief group." Elva pointed to a small, blue cluster off to one side, waiting to move in and help the primary teams to escape. "With six Brown Panther enforcers."

"Raj—? Oh, Dr Sukhram. Fate."

Confused voices echoed in the elegant chamber, a cacophony of tactical confusion as all three teams came under attack at once.

"Heptomino Two, executing gamma-reversal."

"Tumbler, we're under—"

"Heptomino One, it's not looking—"

"Fate damn it!"

"—heavy fire, returning—"

"—not have the objective. Repeat. Objective not attained."

"Tumbler, Tumbler." Skolnar. "Move to your—"

Skolnar choked as Tom's fist, gripping his tunic, twisted his collar into a tourniquet-like hold.

"Cut comms," Tom said.

Skolnar's eyes bulged. Some of the support staff reacted as Skolnar struggled futilely, but Elva was faster than them all. Graser pistol out, she gave the order in a calm, icy voice. "Do what he says. Cut it."

Comms fell silent. The tactical holodisplay shivered into stillness.

"Ah," Skolnar gasped as Tom released his grip.

"Sorry." Tom shook his head. "I had to get your attention quickly."

"Mad bastard . . ." Rubbing his throat, Skolnar glared at Tom, then looked around for support.

"Your communications were compromised." Tom gestured at the display. "Couldn't you tell?"

"What?"

"The security forces were too well co-ordinated, and they shouldn't have anticipated Heptomino One's manoeuvre."

Still holding his throat, Skolnar shook his head and waved the support team back to work, though the update-feeds were gone. But some of them, galvanized by Tom's words, were already delving into tac-modelling phase-spaces, working furiously.

"How could you tell?" Skolnar addressed Elva, who was returning her graser pistol to the sticky-tag on her hip.

"I couldn't."

"But—"

"I trust Tom implicitly." She looked at Tom and shrugged.

Progress on the egalitarian front. Tom would have smiled, but he was carefully watching Skolnar. *First time Elva hasn't used my title in company.*

"Without comms, they'll revert to working as autonomous cells," he said to Skolnar. "Am I right?"

"Er, yes. That's standard."

"Good. Then they'll have a chance."

Elva was examining the static complex of mapped tunnels and caverns. "What about Rajesh's group? Any way we could give them coded instructions to help the others?"

Skolnar span in his seat, looked intently at the schematic, then at Tom.

"I want them back alive." He swallowed, his expression serious. "Tell me what to do, Tom, and I'll do it."

"Well"—Elva gave a half-smile—"that's a start, anyway."

Blood-red arterial transparent tubes hung in the vast cavern system. Tens of kilometres in extent, the ceilings glowed skylike, peach and orange. Here and there, great sweeping pillars of cream and gold connected ceilings to cavern floors.

Free-floating drones looked like insects. In the transport tubes, dimly glimpsed shadows moved.

"I like it here," Tom murmured to Elva.

"Very impressive." It was Elva's first visit to Lady V'Delikona's demesne. "Oh, here comes Jak. I'll cover for you while you're gone."

They were on a wide balcony, halfway up the statuette-encrusted cavern wall, overlooking a small piazza across which several Lords and their retinues were walking briskly.

"My Lord?" Jak seemed slightly out of breath. "I've done my prep for the trade meeting, but I'd rather run over my conclusions beforehand."

"I trust you, Jak. Go with your instincts."

"But—"

"Just a quick look." Tom was wearing a heavy silver bracelet. He held out his hand so that Jak could insert an infocrystal into the bejewelled socket. "This is your summary?"

The triconic lattice was small, and Tom scanned rapidly, drilling just one level in on each major point.

"Looks good to me." He gestured the display away, and held out his hand for Jak to remove the crystal.

"I'm a bit unsure about the presentation . . ."

"You've got Felgrinar, haven't you? Elva, why don't you attend as well? Offer some moral support."

"My Lord."

Tom nodded in dismissal then, and watched as Elva and Jak went inside together. The corridor, glowing gold and royal blue, led to a suite of conference halls. Though he had missed this year's Convocation—and the first anniversary of his elevation to Lordship—Tom had no real excuse for missing these local-demesne discussions. They were much smaller than a Convocation; still, there were plenty of people around. A short absence would not be noticed.

He used a servitors' tunnel, moving quickly, to head out of the conference complex. As he walked, he took off his brocade-trimmed cape, reversed it, and fitted it once more around his shoulders. It was now dark grey and a little shabby.

Tuneable smartfabric would have been easier, but he could not take the chance of a sensor web noting the presence of smart-tech.

Crimson wings unfurling, flames licking—

Holoflash. He stopped abruptly.

He had come out into a labyrinthine knot of spiralling ramps and transparent-walled tunnels in which stevedores and cargo pods and drones moved through an intricate dance of loading and unloading, departing and arriving. Beyond a small group of people, a lone woman watched silver ovoid cargo vessels being kicked from launch platforms into scarlet-filled transport tubes. Like pulsing blood, the scarlet fluid spat the transport vessels along the tubes.

She moved only slightly, but Tom picked up the gesture and walked up. He stopped nearby, head turned away from her.

"To your right, high up," she murmured, "there's an arrival."

"I see it." The shadowy outline was sliding into view.

"Take a stroll up that ramp"—the tiniest motion of her chin—"to watch. It's due to depart empty. Be on board."

"I—"

But she had already turned away and was walking with tiny, mincing steps towards the nearest exit.

Clangs and shaking. Tom sat with his back against the wall, arm clenched around his knees, hoping this was not going to be too rough.

Jolt. Then a rocking sensation as the cargo vessel stabilized in the flux, followed by a sudden tug of acceleration which rolled Tom over like a lightball.

Then the trajectory smoothed out, and Tom laughed out loud, surprising himself.

The invitation, sent to the higher echelons of LudusVitae but specifying Tom by name, had followed soon after the botched attempt at raiding the arachnargos-manufacturing complex. Though the mission's objectives had not been achieved, Tom's primary goal had: every cell member had returned alive.

Not a deliberate test, of course, but his performance seemed to have triggered some decision among the Strontium Dragons' unknown leaders.

Abrupt deceleration. Tom tumbled, unhurt, across the cold deck. Then a side hatch melted open. Cold air flooded in.

He had been half expecting to exit straight into the red transport fluid, but this was an ordinary-looking depot: devoid of people, perhaps two dozen vessels being shunted into or out of tangled tubes. Stepping out, he brushed off his cloak as the vessel behind him sank back into its tube and moved on to a holding-volume.

There was a soft whisper of sound and Tom turned.

Ten tunnel-fighter types. Shaven-headed and stocky, or slender with triple-braided hair, all had the stony expressions of syndicate footsoldiers, or 49s. At their rear stood an older man with short-cropped grey hair, a dark scar across one cheekbone.

One of them, eyes half-lidded, clenched his callused fists. Dying to try out for real the techniques he had drilled in for years.

Primary target.

Immature and uncontrolled: Tom would go for him first. But the grey-haired man looked calm, almost dozing—real trouble. No illusions here. Tom could not defeat the whole group.

The grey-haired man moved. "This way, please."

"After you."

"Hello, Tom."

The slender, somewhat frail-looking figure on the chair had long hair and a narrow black moustache, but recognition was instantaneous.

"Zhao-ji!"

They clasped wrists.

Zhao-ji's eyes were as dark and fearless as they had ever been, and his grip was surprisingly strong, given his appearance. But Tom was aware of his own greater strength and physical ability, and a little ashamed of his surge of pleasure.

A chair moved into position for Tom, but he ignored it as Zhao-ji spoke. "Someone special to see you." Zhao-ji gestured, and there was a hint of sapphire blue glowing inside his left wrist, on his prominent veins. He tugged down his cuff.

Slowly, from a curtained alcove, a golden filigree cage floated into the chamber.

"Oh, my Fate!"

Inside the cage was a white neko with sea-green eyes, large and comfortable. The filigree wound itself back as Tom reached inside. "Paradox! How are you, boy?"

The feline blinked lazily as Tom rubbed behind his ears.

"Just so you know," said Zhao-ji, "that he's been in good hands."

"I can see that." Tom grinned as Paradox purred: a soft steady motorlike buzz deep in his throat.

But we're not just old friends, Zhao-ji and I. He withdrew his hand; the cage closed up. *This is a negotiation, and we're just beginning.*

"The last time we were supposed to meet, I got a little held up."

Zhao-ji could not help glancing at Tom's left shoulder. "We heard about it. Petyo—remember him?—knew you'd been captured. He had some pretty scathing things to say about Algrin, as I recall." He looked carefully at Tom, as though worried about giving offence. "Uncle Pin tried to use his influence, but with a Lady decreeing the sentence . . ."

"I know." Tom sat down in the vacant chair.

"He did try, though. Used up a lot of *guanxi*."

Debts of honour: Tom recalled the term from evening conversations in the Ragged School's deserted dorm.

Zhao-ji shifted position, and again Tom caught a glimpse of shining blue inside his wrist.

"I wonder"—Tom leaned back in his chair, casually crossing his legs—"how Kreevil Dilwinney fared."

Trapped in the floating blue liquid; tendril growing from his body—

A small smile grew on Zhao-ji's face.

"You've grown subtle, Tom, over the years. Kreevil . . . I do know how Petyo fared."

"Thank you, my friend. What happened to Petyo?"

"He worked for us . . . until he chose to forget his obligations."

Tension tightened inside Tom. "I sense that you, too, have achieved a great deal."

"And now we have a chance to work together."

A short laugh. "Who'd have thought it?"

"It's something of a paradox"—Zhao-ji smiled briefly—"that we, you and I personally, can achieve so much. Neither you nor I have that much power inside our respective organizations, but we can influence them enormously."

Meaning . . . what? That Tom could help Zhao-ji achieve his ambitions?

No. More to it than that.

"You know our traditions, I gather," Zhao-ji continued. "At times, when it becomes necessary, open warfare—or something close to it— must be engaged in."

"When defeat is otherwise inevitable."

"Or when the chance of victory is high."

Tom nodded. "You think something major is going to happen?"

"Don't you?"

Silence.

From his cage, Paradox complained: *mrrghaow*.

Zhao-ji snapped his fingers as two hard-eyed youths entered. "Take Paradox out. Give him fishblock and cream."

The youths left with the cage floating between them.

Tom watched them leave. "You can't take a chance on his getting loose?" Not quite a question.

"Not here. In . . . At home, he has the run of the place."

"Ah."

"Not that he runs much nowadays. Getting lazy. Not like you, I hear."

"Maybe." Tom sat upright. "So what would persuade LudusVitae that your people should play a greater role in any . . . forthcoming action?"

"Information."

A pause, waiting for Tom to ask: *What kind of information?*

When he remained silent, Zhao-ji nodded, carefully adjusting his cuff, and said, "We know where the Oracles come from."

51

NULAPEIRON AD 3414

"Strangle me."

The woman went for the small man's collar, arms straight as she applied a loose grip.

"OK, like this." He hooked his arms around hers in a complicated motion and twisted; her hands lost their grip. "Then elbow." He turned and leaned sideways for the strike.

"Hey, that's pretty neat."

Tom, watching, shook his head.

That could get you killed.

They were in a wide white marble chamber, and the outlying corridors were guarded by Zhao-ji's people. The man and woman were part of LudusVitae.

"I like this one, too," said the small man, leaning forwards from the waist for a flowery elbow-block. The technique was from a traditional form, but sloppily presented, its meaning misinterpreted.

"You interested in this stuff?" The woman was looking at Tom.

"Er . . ." He checked the shimmering entrance membranes. No-one arriving. Just the three of them here, early for the meeting.

He chuckled. "You could say that. Look." Standing in front of the man, Tom curled his hand around the back of the man's neck. "If someone grabs you, it's not static." He jerked forwards. "It's to pull you onto a head-butt or a knee."

"When I was in school"—the woman looked offended—"and one of the boys, a lightball player, grabbed me—"

Tom stared at her, and she fell silent.

"You grab me," he said to the small man, and whipped his elbow up between the two arms, right on the point of the fellow's chin.

"Chaos!" The woman.

"Just hit him," said Tom, "as the hold's coming on. Fast and hard. Keep it simple."

"Fate! I'm glad I never did grappling, then." The small man scratched his head. "Grabs and chokes obviously don't work."

He still hasn't got the point.

Slap of his hand, spinning the small man sideways, hooking around the throat, thumb inside the man's collar.

"If I'd hit here"—Tom tightened his grip: radius bone against carotid artery—"you'd have been out. Forget about struggling for thirty seconds, or even three. Do it just right, and the strangle's instantaneous. Otherwise"—kicking the back of the left knee, lowering gently—"you take him down, put one knee against the spine . . ."

When Tom released him, the small man stepped back and bowed, followed hastily by the woman.

"Could you show us that again, my Lord?"

They talked afterwards about some of the myths of Terran martial-arts history; Tom kept mostly silent and did not disabuse the other two of their delusions.

"Imagine," said the small man, whose name was Tarmlin, "the Okinawans smashing their invaders' wooden shields with a single punch . . ."

The sort of stupid story that gives the martial arts a bad name.

In the Philippines, Magellan was killed by a native using the indigenous Filipino fighting art—but by the time that art became known to the outside world, its name was escrima, and its terminology was in the conquerors' language.

The Okinawans, creators of karate, were invaded many times. The Shaolin temple was destroyed by soldiers. Brazilian slaves formulated capoeira: deadly when used by individual masters—but the slaves remained in chains.

Mostly, Tom thought, it was the Golden Age myth: that pre-nan-otech man was a warrior. Fighting tales of the third millennium were both stranger and more likely to be true, but early stories of uncorrupted, natural humans held a mythic power.

But that's not how we'll win, he realized. *Not hand to hand. There has to be a better way.*

Taut, pale skin; hooked nose; white hair. A difficult face to read: was the hair prematurely white, or the skin unnaturally taut?

"Viscount Vilkarzyeh." He bowed to Tom.

"Lord Corcorigan." Tom's bow held a questioning nuance of insincerity, mocking their noble rites under these circumstances. "Originally of Lady Darinia's demesne, in Gelmethri Syektor." And, speaking in Laksheesh: "You're from Bilkranitsa?"

"Very astute, old chap. Follow me, why don't you?"

Vilkarzyeh passed the two cell members without a glance, but Tom bade them farewell.

"We'll keep practising," said the small man, Tarmlin, with a grin.

Through a circular pink-tinged membrane, and along a short, white, round-walled corridor. Tom's skin tingled—*scans of some sort*—then a golden disc-door melted open, and he followed Vilkarzyeh inside.

It was a hall of twisted spaces, real and holo intertwined: curling walkways, Escher ramps, impossible polygons. In its centre, a small area of geometric sanity held a square conference table and a dozen lev-chairs.

Zhao-ji was already sitting there, pensively stroking his moustache. Two black men, both strangers to Tom, sat facing Zhao-ji.

"Sorry we're late."

The woman's voice was from Tom's left. He turned. She had pale, freckled skin and one good eye; the other was totally green-blue and beautiful, but nonfunctional. Her hair was a deeper auburn than he remembered.

"Arlanna!"

"Hello, Tom."

She was the first person, of all the old acquaintances he had encountered since his ascension, to use his forename without thinking.

"Great Chaos, Arlanna! How long ago were you recruited?"

"Before you, probably." A big grin. "How the Randomness are you?"

"I don't know." He shrugged. "Fine, I suppose."

"Hmm. Must be a strain, keeping a demesne running and doing all this."

"I've got Jak helping me."

"Ah well." Laughing. "You'll probably make a profit, then."

"Probably."

Tom noted peripherally that Vilkarzyeh was watching them closely. He would have to learn more about that man.

"You're taking an awful risk, Tom." Arlanna frowned.

They were all seated now. Twelve LudusVitae members, all of them in the upper echelons of that organization or else high-ranking representatives of one or other of the member societies. Only Tom and Arlanna were there purely as strategic advisers, without cell networks under their direct command.

"He's not the only one." Vilkarzyeh. "Turning a blind eye to the Strontium Dragons' activities is one thing—"

Arlanna froze, but Vilkarzyeh did not even notice.

"—but this is infinitely more risky, for a Lord."

So why are you here, then? Tom wondered.

Vilkarzyeh stopped, then addressed Tom directly, as though guessing his thoughts. "But I have my reasons, as you do."

"Time, I think, ladies and gentlemen," said Zhao-ji, "to begin the technical presentation."

Spheroid of pearly light, stretched out teardropwise at two horizontally opposite points.

It looked familiar: almost identical to the cosmic model Tom had displayed over a year earlier, before the Convocation's Review Committee.

"I know"—Zhao-ji gestured, magnifying the holo—"that cosmology is not normally on the agenda." He paused. There was some polite laughter around the table. "But we need to establish a—how do I put it?—a conceptual background."

Tom watched the others; their attention was focused on the holo.

"This point represents the big bang." It flared briefly red as Zhao-ji spoke. "The other end is the big crunch."

Frowns of concentration around the table.

"Pretend that the visible universe is a flat disc instead of a solid volume: then we see the disc expanding with time, starting at a point—the big bang—and reaching a maximum size here."

A vertical red circle ringed the spheroid, was gone.

"Then the cosmos shrinks inevitably to the big crunch, but with time reversed. That's been known for a thousand years."

Vilkarzyeh nodded impatiently; the others remained still, intent.

Tom had expected them to start growing bored.

"As Tom would put it"—Zhao-ji nodded in his direction—"it's as though there are two big bangs which meet in the middle, since both halves of the life cycle experience entropic time flowing towards the midpoint."

Again, the vertical red circle.

Zhao-ji seemed to know the contents of Tom's presentation to the Review Committee, and Tom noted this. Was he deliberately letting Tom know how deeply Strontium Dragons' links were embedded in noble society?

Plans within plans, my friend?

"So, the interesting part," continued Zhao-ji, "is the midpoint itself. In the real universe, it's the moment when it has expanded to maximum size. But just how, exactly, does time reverse itself?"

Suddenly Tom's attention was riveted.

This is new to me.

Zhao-ji: "Does time somehow flip over *at the same instant* throughout the universe?"

Tom's skin prickled.

What does a criminal society know of this?

As Zhao-ji gestured—once more, a glimpse of searing blue inside his wrist—a central vertical slice of the holovolume was highlighted.

Points of light sparkled.

"Or are there singularity seed-points from which the reversal spreads out rapidly, engulfing the cosmos in a storm of time-reversal?"

Yes, thought Tom. A *null-time transition boundary, with scattered bifurcation points, breaking the symmetry* . . .

Arlanna cleared her throat and spoke. "Sir? This is trillions of years into the future, isn't it?"

"Oh, yes." Zhao-ji wiped the holo from existence. "What I really want to talk about"—he tugged unconsciously at his moustache—"is Oracles."

He gestured.

Blue tracery: eldritch fire, spreading both ways in time. In neo-tubulin microstructures, quantum waveguides pulse around bichronic lenses . . .

Metavectors track emergent neural properties—consciousness, scattered across time in randomly sequenced blips; the sanity-twisting mindset of an Oracle.

For a long moment, the chamber was silent. Around the conference table, the LudusVitae officers could only stare at the analysis: their enemies made manifest before their eyes.

"There is a great deal," Zhao-ji finally added quietly, "that we don't understand. Oracular brains embody negentropic time, yet contain its cascade effects."

The holo winked out of existence.

"Shall we take a break?"

"How do you know all this?" asked one of the senior executives, after they had reconvened.

Zhao-ji merely shook his head. But Tom could guess, at least part of it.

The glowing blue fluid, the stuff Kreevil was immersed in. Tom remembered the sapphire flashes at Zhao-ji's inner wrist. *It's part of the process, and the Strontium Dragons deal in it, somehow.*

"How does this help?" Vilkarzyeh looked at Tom. "You already know how to deal with an Oracle."

"One Oracle, yes."

Arlanna was staring intently at Tom with her one good eye.

Does she know I killed Corduven's brother?

"We'll have to move," said Zhao-ji, "against all of them simultaneously. We—the Strontium Dragons and our, ah, associates—can provide detailed information on their locations."

Really?

But the group's attention was gathering on Tom now. Until this moment, he had felt out of place and somehow unprepared. But, for all their years of planning, their shadowy extended organizations, none of them had achieved as much as Tom.

I did what they've only dreamed of.

Suddenly, everything seemed to settle into place.

"Many Oracles," he said, "are scarcely able to pull into normal timeflow at all. They spend their lives watching newscasts—which they reproduce as truecasts in earlier times—largely passive. On the other hand, they tend to have larger staffs . . . They're still the lesser danger, though."

Arlanna spoke up: "You, ah, somehow create a false future for them, is that right?"

Tom smiled. "Essentially, yes. False memories: from the cut-over moment, all of their future memories will be false."

"Then we can do anything at all with them. Is that right?"

"Yes, that's right."

Scarlet, smeared across blue and white.

"So we don't necessarily have to kill them. We can be"—Tom noted the frowns around the table, but pressed on—"more humane than that."

Father, a grey and empty husk . . .

"Humane?" It was a hatchet-faced woman who spoke.

"We have that option." Tom let out a long breath. "That's all I'm saying."

I'm not the only one who's suffered because of Oracles.

"These more passive Oracles . . ." Zhao-ji's tone was contemplative. "We only need to take control of what they see, is that correct?"

Tom smiled. "Absolutely."

"*Only* take control—?" Vilkarzyeh shook his head, but he was smiling. "That probably involves kidnapping; taking the Oracles, drugged, to exact reproductions of their previous environments. You didn't say it would be easy. I'll grant you that."

Zhao-ji inclined his head, saying nothing.

"And the others?" Arlanna.

"We use," said Tom carefully, "the method I employed against Oracle d'Ovraison."

Everyone in the room grew still.

He could see the realization on their faces, sinking truly home for the first time: *This man has killed an Oracle.*

"A fictitious future, lasting many years . . ." It was a round-faced black man who spoke. "And consistent with previous reality. How can this be?"

There were nods around the table.

"They have a point, Tom." Zhao-ji leaned forwards. "Not even femtotech can give you that kind of processing power."

Is that why you want to help? To find out the secret?

But this was the moment to reveal all, or turn away from the whole enterprise.

Very well.

"The equipment I used was damaged," Tom began. "We'll need a lot of resource to repair and duplicate it."

"That doesn't explain—"

Talisman.

Slowly he reached inside his tunic, and drew forth the stallion his father had crafted. All around, the air seemed to crystallize into solidity.

Gesture, and it fell neatly into two halves.

"The coating"—he picked up the comms relay between thumb and forefinger—"is nul-gel. The crystal was given to me by . . . by a Pilot."

They stared at him.

Chaos. After all this time—

Inside, he shivered: revealing the secret he had kept close, always.

"In mu-space," he added, "we can run any simulation we like."

Commitment—Fate! Am I doing the right thing?

Arlanna was the first to speak.

"How long before, ah, before we can use this stuff?"

At least one person believes me.

The others looked stunned, even Zhao-ji.

"Two years," said Tom, "and we'll be ready."

52

TERRA AD 2123

<<Karyn's Tale>>

[12]

Ten days.

Ten long days, from the news of Dart's micro-buoy to the final interface. Seven days for the viral rewire to perform its transformations; during the first five, Karyn continued to work on the visually based simulator, but by the end her vision grew wild and hazy. When training became impossible, she shut herself away to meditate, waiting for the process to end. Trying not to think of the innocent embryo growing inside her.

On the seventh night they removed her eyes.

They inserted silver sockets as replacements, but these would be nonfunctional outside her mu-space vessel. In the meantime, she had to wait for them to heal.

Even with nanocytic healing agents, it was not until the eighth night—while Karyn exerted all of her self-discipline not to explore the metal implants with her fingertips—that the sockets were ready for interface.

They led her in darkness—only the cool air, with a hinted scent of distant mesquite, told her that this was true night, not just the endless night of blindness—to a waiting TDV. Then the short drive, breeze tugging at her hair, across the runway to her waiting vessel.

Sure hands guided her to the lift-chair; there was no vertigo as she was swung high up into the air, then slowly lowered through the opening on the ship's upper hull.

In the eyes of her imagination, the ship existed: a silver, delta-winged bird, poised upon the runway, ready to lift.

Hands and robot arms fitted her into the command couch. A soft hum sounded, then a click as high-bandwidth bus-fibres were plugged in, where her eyes used to be.

Faint mist of mathematical spaces, of shadowy geometries beyond sight.

"I'm ready," she said.

But it took two more days.

Two more days of lying there, without privacy when she had to use the attached waste-tubes, waiting while the diagnostics ran and technicians jostled her and monitored her reactions when she slipped into the migraine-inducing hallucinations of billowing phase-spaces.

Finally, someone leaned in and touched her shoulder.

"Ready to fly, ma'am."

As dawn rose, Sensei was standing at the runway's edge, praying harder than he ever had before in a long life of self-discipline and worship.

Burnished fire dripped along the silver hull. Beside him, Anne-Marie held his arm for support, her head still and rapt as her dog's, staring at the same thing: *Karyn's ship*.

"Systems check OK," said a lieutenant, as transparent blast shields rose up before them. "She's going now."

Reaction burners banged into life, the silver ship shuddered, released brakes and hurtled down the runway, lifted its nose, then arced upwards into the air, high, and sped into the clear sapphire sky.

They watched the holos as satellites tracked Karyn's trajectory. Unbelievably soon, the ship rose through purple darkness at the atmosphere's edge and burst into the high-contrast blackness of interplanetary space.

Then it rippled, miragelike, grew twisted and knotted through impossible shifting angles, shrank to an infinitesimal silver point, and was gone.

All the time, during simulation training, she had been pushing the insertion angles to the limit. In mu-space, a vessel became a solid projection, a volume shadow of the realspace object, protected by its event membrane from the chaotic effects of fractal time.

Now she was doing it for real.

Ignoring optimal safety parameters, Karyn pushed it to the maximum. Relative to the size of Dart's vessel, Karyn's ship became a tiny thing, a silver insect speeding through the golden void.

She was minimizing the journey's duration—from Dart's point of view. Trawling through a different context, a different level of size, her voyage, subjectively, was paradoxically longer.

Her trip lasted thirty-three weeks.

Internal robot arms manipulated her limbs, electrostimulation worked the muscles; internal manifolds and scrolling digits, in her augmented non-vision, monitored the embryo in her womb.

If there had been passengers aboard, they would have been anaesthetized: no-one, even protected by the vessel's event membrane, could survive mu-space's mind-bending perspectives. But the baby—

Scarlet-analogue flashed across her non-vision as proximity sensors blared.

Destination achieved.

His ship was bronze.

++ COME IN, DART. COME IN. ++

No surprise: she had chosen that exact hue as one of her colour-simulation calibration points.

++ DART, PLEASE . . . ++

But this was not how she had visualized his proud winged ship—impaled by fractally branching tendrils of scarlet and purple lightning, which coruscated endlessly across the hull's event membrane, brightest at the points where it was beginning to bore through.

KARYN? IS THAT YOU, BABE?

++ DART! ++

If she'd had eyes, she would have wept.

Subjective time passed.

I DON'T WANT YOU HERE.

As she drew closer, the bronze ship grew huge, hundreds of times her size. Manoeuvring was tricky, as she avoided questing tendrils of lightning.

++ TOUGH. I'VE COME A LONG WAY. ++

Just to get you, she meant, but her concentration was divided now, and communication was hard.

Her ship juddered as the enhanced field generators came online. The event membrane shivered across her hull, and her senses spun as resonance effects perturbed her sensors.

OK, TELL ME WHAT YOU'RE DOING.

++ ENHANCED EVENT MEMBRANE. ++

She dipped and twisted her vessel, evading the scarlet lightning.

++ GET READY. WE'RE GOING TO MERGE MEMBRANES. ++

SOUNDS GREAT, DARLING.

Drawing close.

++ INITIATING. . . ++

Contact.

Black light pulsed and waved across their conjoined vessels: the tiny silver form of Karyn's ship, the massive bronze of Dart's.

GIVE ME AN INTERFACE.

Karyn checked progress before replying: ++ OPENING INFOFLOW. MAKE IT TWO-WAY, BABY. ++

She needed to know the exact figures if they were going to throw off the energy pattern by their parallel efforts.

JESUS CHRIST!

Inside her Pilot's cocoon, she might have laughed.

++ HEY, DART. YOUR DAD'LL REPLAY THESE LOGS SOME TIME. ++

A silence, during which Karyn nervously noted the lack of progress in the membrane-strengthening procedure.

Then Dart's reply came: ## YOU'RE PREGNANT, SWEETHEART. ##

Cursing herself for not realizing that he was going to see *all* of her internal dataflow, she sent a brief acknowledgement code.

No time for anything more. A tiny scarlet tendril was playing about her own ship's hull.

YOU SHOULD HAVE TOLD ME.

A pause, then: ++ DART, I LOVE YOU. BUT I'M BUSY RIGHT NOW. ++

I KNOW.

Her attention was on the turbulent stream of rushing data. Dart would be doing the same thing.

IT'S NOT GOING TO LET ME GO.

Another tendril on her hull, joining the first. Then another.

Questing: not blindly, but algorithmically driven. Shifting frequencies, searching for pseudo-quantum tunnelling across the event-membrane barrier, to drill into her vessel and tear it apart.

++ THE HELL IT ISN'T. ++

A fourth tendril.

More. Homing in, like an immune response against an invading pathogen.

And, across the body of Dart's ship, the lightning's insertion points were growing *brighter*, not weaker, as the field generators red-planed into max output.

Sickened, she checked: it was the only interpretation.

Her arrival had *stimulated* it, if anything. Given the energy pattern more data to work with.

++ IS IT ALIVE? ++

Status flags tripping everywhere: it was almost through. Ready to tear both ships apart into total dissolution.

I DON'T THINK SO. MAYBE.

Then, after a pause: ## KARYN. YOU HAVE TO LET GO. ##

++ NO CHANCE. ++

Glowing figures, highlighted as Dart pinpointed the intensity manifolds and sent the data back to her.

IF YOU STAY, IT'S GOING TO GET ALL OF US. ALL THREE OF US.

The data hung in her awareness. Desperate, she searched for counter-strategies.

LET ME GO, KARYN!

Breakthrough threshold. As the shared membrane around both vessels began to split, a peripheral-data phase-space, at the edge of Karyn's internal awareness, flared with authority-adoption commands.

++ DAMN YOU, DART. NO. WE'RE GETTING OUT OF—++

But she had not reckoned on his expertise. While she had been reconfiguring the output characteristics to suit the lightning's interference mode, Dart had been picking control codes from her comms protocols and forming his own instructions.

Sudden pain tugged through Karyn, and for a moment she thought the lightning had drilled through, but then she realized.

Contraction.

KARYN. ARE YOU ALL RIGHT?

She nearly laughed, but another contraction rippled through her womb.

++ TOO EARLY, DAMN IT. IT'S TOO EARLY! ++

Op-codes streamed through her input buffers, unidentified until it was too late. Dart had control.

I LOVE YOU, KARYN.

Waves oscillated across the black field as he triggered the power-down sequence.

++ DART, NO. I—I LOVE YOU, TOO. ++

Datastreams froze. Ships, membranes, pulling apart.

LOOK AFTER OUR DAUGHTER. I—##

Separation.

For a moment, tiny tendrils still played about her own ship, but then the explosion came.

Dart's vessel blew apart into a million fragments.

Her last sight, as she triggered reinsertion, was a cloud of sparkling bronze motes, twinkling in a sea of golden light.

A strange feeling of euphoric warmth, of loving benediction—

Then the scarlet lightning released her, and the vision was lost.

Realspace.

It was dark outside but her attention was turned inwards. The baby should not have been ready to be born.

Position warning.

The internal systems were not designed to help a pregnant woman give birth; that was as helpful as the scan routine could be. Redirecting the resonance imagers from device-monitoring to herself, she could see the problem: the baby was twisted around, sideways on to the opening cervix.

Breach birth.

No problem under normal circumstances, but there was no way to stop the birth process once it had reached this stage. With her mind torn apart in confusion, Karyn could not have re-entered mu-space, much less navigated her way homewards.

Happening now.

There was only one thing she could think of, and she did it. The internal robot arms pulled the cocooning material back from her abdomen.

Careful . . .

She screamed as the arm's laser bit through her belly, peeling skin and striated muscle apart.

Pain!

Then two more arms dived into her womb and gently, gently pulled the struggling baby free. But the robots were already under their co-processors' control.

Karyn's consciousness disintegrated.

<<MODULE ENDS>>

53

NULAPEIRON AD 3414

Slowly at first, it began.

Strontium Dragon trading-visits. Recruitment fairs: a natural cover, organized for the most part by Jak—who did not know of their true objective—since the economic viability of the still-young demesne was obviously of high concern. And seminars: Tom wanted publicly to encourage education among freedmen, and bringing in outside lecturers and technicians was a part of that.

It began as a trickle, but soon there were nearly three hundred technicians and scientists working in secret teams on the Tertium Stratum. Administration and security procedures were handled by Elva; Tom himself sat in on the major technical briefings.

Such a waste.

Every time he left an arduous session, exhausted, he thought the same thing: here were a couple of dozen alpha servitors and freedmen—even a few low-born citizens—who could have been Lords under other circumstances.

But the atmosphere was electric: for the first time in their lives, these young men and women were being given the chance to stretch their intellectual talents to the utmost. When he could, Tom spent time preparing eduthreads and logotropes, to help feed their frenzied, voracious appetites for learning.

He remembered his first trip to the Sorites School, seeing the scholars and thinking: *You don't know how lucky you are.*

"Recruitment," said Elva during a security briefing, "will make or break us."

It was true. The more people they took in, the greater the chances of a misplaced word or even malicious informing.

And, at a later meeting: "I think we need to bring Jak in on this, my Lord."

"Are you sure, Elva?"

"I've been sounding him out subtly for a long time, and doing background checks. Don't you agree?"

Tom looked away. "We never really discussed politics."

He made occasional trips to other demesnes, to various secret locations of training-camps and LudusVitae-controlled communities. Whenever he could, he joined in the close-quarter-combat training-sessions, either as a student or, increasingly, as a guest instructor.

In the latter case, they always applauded when the session was over.

His expertise was strategic and technical—at home, his Ludus-Vitae role was technical project management, more than anything—not command. No action cell reported to him. Yet he visited every command group in the sector, and several outside the borders.

"The Planning Council," said Vilkarzyeh during one pan-sector strategy briefing, "has great plans for you, Tom."

"I don't think so, Alexei." By now, they were on first-name terms. "But thanks for trying to cheer me up."

Yet it was noticeable that Tom saw more of the organization than possibly any other member. For sure, it was an advantage: his detailed mental map of LudusVitae in this sector was vital to his strategic models.

There were internal wrangles and power struggles in the Planning Council and other echelons, but Tom always held himself aloof.

"But that's what makes you popular, my Lord," said Elva as she escorted him home from one meeting, with a dozen fanned-out troopers in plain clothes covering the corridor ahead and behind. "The way you don't get involved in their stupid chest-pounding."

"Politics. That's all I need!"

And Elva laughed. "Everything we do is politics."

Later that night, after Tom had run his usual twelve kilometres and returned to his study for private work, she asked to talk to him.

"What is it?" he said as she came through the membrane.

"You know the MetaConvocation?"

"Well, yes." Before assuming Lordship, he had never heard of it, but he knew now: from each Convocation, annually, delegates were sent to a global MetaConvocation. Not every demesne, but certainly every sector, was represented there. "What of it?"

"This year's event will be in Bilkranitsa Syektor, did you know?"

"I hadn't thought about it." Tom frowned. "I guess I'd heard. Is that important?"

"It's where Vilkarzyeh's from." The tone in her voice indicated her dislike.

Tom leaned against his quickglass desk; it reconfigured to accommodate his weight.

"I don't see—"

"Vilkarzyeh's going to propose you for some sort of regional-delegate position."

"Well . . ." Tom shrugged. "Alexei's trying to do me a favour, I guess. But I'm not sure I'd have time, even if he could swing it."

"He'll swing it, my Lord," said Elva, "if it's important enough."

"Probably." Smiling, to take the sting from his words: "What are you really talking about?"

"It's the Planning Council who want you to take the post."

Tom stared at her. "But why?"

"When the Prime Strike happens"—the provisional codename for Nulapeiron-wide action, still the best part of two years away—"they're going to want an official ambassador."

"But . . . Going public. That hasn't been discussed."

"Not by us, it hasn't." Elva crossed her arms. "And that's my point."

Gold and scarlet: the tricons and network, suspended in mid-air, shifted softly. It looked intricate and static, but that was an illusion.

"Moneylenders?" said Tom. "And cargo hongs?"

The Zhongguo Ren, one of Zhao-ji's lieutenants, nodded. "Not our own hongs, of course."

"Of course not."

Armed robbery. But the money was needed to finance operations. Even if the few noble members of LudusVitae—and associated organizations—could afford to bankroll everything, the massive movements of money would be noticed and tracked, sooner or later.

Vilkarzyeh crossed the control chamber and joined them. "The first raid's due to start."

"Hmm. Thanks, Qing."

The oriental man bowed, hearing the dismissal in Tom's voice.

"There won't be much tac-feedback. That's due to you, of course." Vilkarzyeh smiled. "Though, with you here, we'd probably know soon enough if the authorities had our comms tapped."

"Best to remain undercover."

"Naturally."

"I mean, completely unseen."

"Ah." A knowing nod from Vilkarzyeh. "Elva Strelsthorm has been digging, has she?"

"I don't know what you mean."

Vilkarzyeh pretended to watch the tac-display.

"It's true," he said, "that we've never gone public before. But after Prime Strike, that will be the time to present our terms."

"Maybe." Tom had not planned beyond that point.

"Definitely. And who better than Lords with official recognition? Lords who understand the noble ways of thought."

"You and me, you mean."

"I see myself as your lieutenant, Tom."

No, you're setting me up for a fall.

The young Zhongguo Ren, Qing, was in earnest discussion with the support team. Then he nodded, tapped one of them encouragingly on the shoulder, and headed back towards Tom and Vilkarzyeh.

"Thank you, Alexei." Tom tried to keep his voice sincere.

A fall. And then you'll take over, and leverage that into leadership of the Planning Council.

Qing: "Pentomino Two and all three Gliders report success. Minimal casualties."

But I've got two years to prepare for you.

Aloud, Tom said, "Minimal casualties?"

Vilkarzyeh shrugged. "We're going to war, Tom. I thought you'd realized."

"Oh, yes." Tom stared at the tac-display, seeing nothing. "I knew that when we started."

Many nights he awoke with purely imaginary triconic lattices fading before his eyes. Though he would have run earlier, he would go again: tearing along deserted tunnels as though devils were at his heels.

If he was away from home, undercover in some strange demesne, he would unroll his flat running-pad and run—alone in some strange chamber—automatonlike on the spot, eyes set to infinity-focus.

He travelled anonymously to many demesnes, met hundreds of people, losing track of where he was. When he could, he listened to individuals' stories: the draper whose mother died of a curable wasting disease, unable to pay for treatment; the astymonia sergeant whose sister had been taken by an Oracle's entourage; the old couple who had lost four sons in the Belkranitsan food riots. The schoolteacher who cried as she recounted the conditions of her young pupils' lives. The young men and women with clenched fists and fire in their eyes as they talked of strikes broken by deadly force, families evicted at graser point, of enforced bans on education.

Then Tom would leave behind copies of his poems, designed to stir the populace to rebellion.

A pitiful effort.

A chime. It was late evening and Tom was at home in his own demesne; as usual, he was in his study.

"Come in," he said.

"My Lord." It was Elva. "I don't suppose you fancy going to a wedding?"

There was an outstanding invitation to which he had not replied: Lady Sylvana was throwing a party; it was the third such invitation and it was probably time he went.

As for the wedding, that was the day before: ten strata down, in the same demesne, Elva's brother was getting married to his long-time fiancée.

Tom had not even known she had a brother.

"It'll be strange," he said, "going back to Lady Darinia's demesne."

"A homecoming, my Lord?"

"I guess so."

Although it was contrary to normal policy, Tom had asked Jak if he wanted to come along—but Jak was too busy on the tax-regulation reforms, running committees which in other demesnes would have been presided over by their Lord.

One had only to glance at warehousing and distribution revenue to see just how diligent Jak was in fulfilling Tom's fiduciary duty. Had they not been diverting funds to LudusVitae, the demesne would have shown an amazing profit for its first year.

Two arachnargoi, rented from a hong in Lord Shinkenar's realm, hung stationary in the high-ceilinged inner court of Tom's Palace. Small cases were being drawn up into the thoracic cargo holds.

"Definitely going home in style, my Lord." Jak was there to see them off.

"I'll say."

Elva gave Jak a brief hug.

Then, catching the eye of one of the loading-crew, she went over to talk to him.

"I'm off. Take care of my realm, Jak."

Tom grabbed a slender hoist-tendril, and it drew him upwards. He grinned as he saw Elva give the stevedore a goodbye kiss.

Good for you, Elva.

She glanced upwards, saw Tom looking, and shrugged. But her cheeks were faintly pink as she caught a tendril and ascended after him.

Inside the arachnargos, he helped her onto the cargo hold's catwalk.

"True love?" he murmured.

He could not help laughing as she blushed bright red.

Immersed for so long in deadly plans, Tom found it hard to think of ordinary life proceeding as usual: marriages and funerals, everyday employment, shopping—*damn, I didn't buy a present*—and the trivial, bickering arguments and off-the-cuff humorous pleasantries which made up a normal day.

"Hey, not bad!" Elva was riding up front with Tom.

"Oh, of course." Tom looked out at the great, square-cross-sectioned thoroughfare: its white and pink marble, its massive floating sculptures. "You haven't been here before. This is Rilker Broadway, named after her Ladyship's father."

It was Elva's home demesne, but the first time she had travelled through the Primum Stratum here, and her eyes were wide in amazement.

When they alighted at the Palace, there were twenty servitors to lead the way. Tom recognized none of them.

What do they think of me?

Servitor-impassive expressions hid their thoughts. He wondered, as they walked on foot through the familiar plush corridors, whether the servitors knew he had once been one of them.

The walls became nacreous, more opulent, as they came to the inner Palace.

Shimmering.

Just for a moment, a faint ripple—as though of recognition—passed across the nearest wall, and was gone.

Tom smiled.

His party numbered ten: himself, Elva, four of her troopers, two servitors and two servitrices in the Corcorigan livery. The guest suite was big enough for all of them. It was unusual, though not unknown, for servitors to remain in the same quarters as their masters.

An invitation tricon was hanging, magnified, at the antechamber's exact geometric centre. Tom pointed: unfurling, it gave details of a small gathering to be held late tonight, in the ballroom near Lady Sylvana's apartments.

Sylvana . . .

"It's time, my Lord." Elva.

"Let's go."

One of the servitors handed Tom an old cape, and he pulled it on. Pausing by the door membrane, he laid his palm against the wall and said, "It's good to be back."

Then, ignoring Elva's questioning look, he went out into the corridor; four troopers hurried out into protective formation.

"I don't suppose Trude will be there?" He had not seen her since his recruitment into LudusVitae.

Elva shook her head. "Not as far as I know."

Reaching the Palace boundaries, they entered a round, bronze-panelled, flat-ceilinged chamber. Tom used his thumb ring's control codes, and the entire floor slowly revolved, corkscrewing downwards.

It took a whole minute to descend to the Secundum Stratum.

"Well, that was different."

Tom chuckled as he led his party out into a rich-looking corridor. Though smaller than a typical counterpart above, it was nevertheless panelled in dark red mother-of-pearl, with glowing surrounds. It was as rich as any part of Tom's palace.

Elva and all four troopers took off their uniform tunics and reversed them, displaying motley patterns. Each garment was different; all were fluorescent and garish. Two troopers shook out bright lightweight half-capes and draped them around their shoulders.

Startling, but an effective disguise.

Tom took off his thumb ring and tucked it inside his waistband, though he would need it for the floor hatches. Normally there were few security checks on descent—none on lower strata—but he was using noble-house privileges: allowing his escort to carry pocket grasers, on Elva's insistence.

There was less anonymity this way, but he could always justify a nostalgia trip.

"Now we look more like a wedding party," said Elva.

But, as they walked, her four troopers constantly scanned their surroundings—guarding their legitimate Lord and senior LudusVitae executive officer—and their hands stayed close to their weapons.

Five strata down, they stopped in a market chamber while Tom paid too much—unhesitatingly crediting the merchant with an amount which would have kept Father in profit for half a year—for a decorated goblet.

"You think that'll be OK?" he asked Elva, as the merchant's young daughter wrapped the goblet.

"Perfect, my—My brother will love it."

"Good."

Later, as the six of them descended once more, Tom said: "I don't even know your brother's name, nor his fiancée's."

Elva held out a tiny tricon woven from copper and tin: an invitation. "She's Trilina U'Skarin. My brother's Odom Strelsthorm."

"U'Skarin?" Tom frowned. "Isn't that Arlanna's family name?"

Elva had not known Arlanna during Tom's servitor days, but the two women had attended LudusVitae security briefings together. "They're related. Second cousins, I think."

"If she's going to be there, we could all have gone down officially."

"She isn't," said Elva. "Arlanna's not going."

"Oh. Families." Thinking: *Mother.* "Or was it Sylvana, not granting leave of absence?"

Elva looked as though she was going to say something, then shrugged.

Up ahead was a busy crowd, and the corridor was narrowing, so Tom let the troopers lead them through a small Aqua Hall—floating copper sculpture, water fountains, citizens queuing with empty containers—and out into a dank side tunnel.

Tom: "So why isn't Arlanna going?"

Elva mis-stepped into a puddle, and splashed dirty water.

"Because—" A short exhalation. "Because I told her you're going to be there."

"What?" Tom stopped.

One of the troopers span, expecting trouble. Then all four took up static formation, scanning the deserted tunnel.

"At the last briefing," said Elva. "I told her."

Tom shook his head. "I didn't think Arlanna hated me. Have I—?"

"She's got strong feelings for you." Elva tilted her squarish jaw upwards. "But not hate."

It took him a moment.

Then, "I'll be heisenberged," Tom said.

Elva looked at him.

"True love, my Lord?"

54

NULAPEIRON AD 3414

Butterfly wings, flapping. Turquoise and gold, five metres across, beating steadily above the archway.

"Not bad," murmured Tom.

"For this stratum, anyway." Elva.

They went inside, keeping to the semi-ovoid chamber's rear. All the guests were standing: it was the Laksheesh-Heterodox tradition.

A chanting began just as Tom caught a glimpse of short red hair in one of the front rows. A wide-shouldered man. Tom stood on tip-toes, and was certain.

Dervlin!

It had been so long. They had met only on a couple of occasions, but those had been turning-points. Images and questions span in Tom's mind—from memories of the post-funeral meal, to Zen Neuronal Coding.

But the priestess was entering, flanked by attendants—and the whole congregation bowed as the betrothed couple stepped up onto twin floating obsidian discs.

"*—to bind each to the other, meld two into one—*"

Reviewing old memories. So like the dead Pilot's, Dervlin's flowing fighting-style.

"*—since birth until this moment, separate twines—*"

And questioning his remembrance. Why would Pilots out of legend be interested in this world?

"*—swear before Destiny to hold this truth—*"

And what of the Oracles' origins? Even with the Strontium Dragons' help, LudusVitae had only hints to work on.

"*We do.*"

For that matter . . . was Karyn's Tale literally true? Or did the crystal's ware rewrite itself, for its own purposes?

"—*may kiss*—"

Smell of incense. Happy applause.

Rustle of purple silk. "I wanted to thank you." Hands in a mudra of benediction.

From the doorway, one of Elva's troopers gave a slight nod in Tom's direction, wanting to talk; but Tom could not get away just yet.

"For what?"

The priestess had headed straight for him as the rest of the congregation began making their way to the post-ceremony reception.

"Helping me to regain my faith."

"I don't—"

And then he recognized her: the young priestess who had been with her senior, the Antistita, when Father was dying. And at the funeral.

"When your father died, I had been undergoing a crisis of conscience—and confidence, I suppose—and then the Antistita knew, just knew, when it was time for me to . . . see you."

There were lines on her face now, from the constant strain of ministering to the faithful: an endless series of traumas. Tom wondered how many parents, how many children, she had seen die since then.

"I'm honoured"—Tom bowed formally—"to have helped in any way."

She turned to follow the general movement then, and Tom walked alongside, but dropped away as the plainclothes trooper drew near.

"Thought you should know, my Lord—astymonia patrols. Three teams in the vicinity."

"Keep alert."

Up ahead, the priestess's two assistants now flanked her. Tom smiled to himself, very slightly, and headed towards the reception chamber.

Away from the ceremonial chapel—built by the donations, Tom noted, of people who had practically nothing of their own—the decorations were simpler. The reception's door was a plain ochre hanging, more like a private dwelling.

At least they believe in something.

Running footsteps and he turned, crouching.

"I told ya we was late!"

His plainclothes trooper bodyguards were moving from their posts, but Tom motioned them back with a subtle hand signal.

"Your bleedin' fault."

"But you said Trindle Chamber, so that's where—"

The trio, puffing, came to a sweaty halt in front of Tom.

"Mind out, mate," one of them said. "We're goin' in there."

The short one had a small paunch; the thin one was prematurely bald. But it was the third who caught Tom's attention: burly, potbellied, purple birthmark splashed across his face.

Stavrel.

Even before Algrin and the Ragged School, there had been Stavrel to make Tom's life miserable.

"You two"—Stavrel addressed his companions—"go get some grub for me."

"All right, Stavrel, mate."

The two went inside.

"I know you." Stavrel.

Astounded, Tom realized that the two men who had gone inside might be Padraig and Levro.

"That's mutual," said Tom. "Sadly."

"What're you, then? Freemerchant?" A smirk. "Who'd ya bugger to get that, then?"

The same old feeling prickled up Tom's back.

"I tell ya." Stavrel wiped the back of his hand across his nose. "I heard you been learnin' how to fight. So you can defend yourself from me, eh?"

He knew of Tom's training, but not his rank. Twisted rumour, or mistaking Tom for someone else?

Involuntarily, Tom smiled.

I don't believe it.

It was a very gentle smile. It was as though all his birthdays—and Anniversaries of Elevation—had come at once.

"You little—" Stavrel's voice faltered.

Red lights, but Tom blinked them away, not needing the tacware's overlay.

"Er, well then . . ." Stavrel's gaze broke, eyes shifting to the left. "I better find my mates."

Tom stood aside and let him pass.

After a few moments, one of the troopers came up.

"I thought you were going to kill him, my Lord."

Tom shook his head.

"It wasn't necessary."

"Dance, my Lord?" It was the bride, Trilina, eyes modestly downcast but cheeks flushed with happiness.

"My pleasure."

Tom followed her out onto the circular dance floor. He had been looking for Dervlin—that shock of cupric hair should stand out in a crowd—but had seen him nowhere.

With athletic abandon, Elva was dancing a reel with her brother Odom.

"Thank you for coming, your Lordship—"

"Call me Tom. Please."

There were scarlet ribbons in Trilina's hair and wound around her sleeves; Odom wore crossed sashes of the same material.

"Great ceremony," Tom added, joining in the dance.

The tune was a complex reel, played by the chamber's in-built system, and it took Tom a while to recognize the refrain: "The Borehole Lilt," embellished.

"Are you OK, my—Tom?"

"Just tired. I think I need to sit down."

Too many memories.

Tom bowed and left her. He took a glass of sparkling water from the buffet table, and went to stand by himself against the stone wall.

For a while he was content to watch the dancing, but then the music died softly away, and the guests clapped as Dervlin, appearing from behind a brocade-edged arras, ascended the small stage.

Fate, Dervlin! We've a lot to talk about.

"I've just got a short speech to make—" Dervlin pulled out a huge mock infocrystal from his pocket and pretended to load up a display as laughter rippled around the chamber. "Since I've known Odom for many years, and there are a few things about his early life he may not have told the lovely Trilina . . ."

Hoots and guffaws.

". . . when the five Tildrilli sisters took him to see their tunnel . . ."

A *bit near the knuckle*, thought Tom, but laughed along with everyone else. He fetched a second glass of water.

". . . or the time he—"

An amber beam split the air.

Then a massive thud.

What's happening?

Explosion.

Its percussive wave smacked Tom flat against the floor.

Dust clouds billowing. Screams and low moans.

"My Lord!"

Hands pulling him upright.

"What the Chaos—?"

Sore cheekbone. Warm blood, trickling.

"Come on."

Slipping on ceramic shards underfoot, sliding on rubble.

"I'm OK." Recovering, he pushed the trooper's hands away.

"It's Jivrin." The trooper pointed to a ragged body, opaque eyes staring sightlessly. One of Tom's men.

I didn't even know his name.

All around them, people were running in random directions, yelling, or cowering silently upon the floor. Tom pulled his cloak across his face, trying to filter out the choking dust.

A wide-shouldered figure stepped easily across the rubble, a child under each arm.

"Dervlin! I've been wanting to—"

"Young Tom." A grim smile. "All grown up . . . Here. You'd better take these kids."

From outside, distant shouts. The sizzle and crack of graser fire.

"What's happening?" Tom took one of the children, a small girl, by the hand; the trooper scooped the other child up into his arms.

"Our people are holding them back. Militia raid."

Coughing, Tom looked out past the scorched hanging, but the corridor was still clear.

"Right." Tom glanced around the chamber: amid the confusion, there was a general scramble now towards the chamber's rear.

"Get going, Tom. We'll catch up on old times later."

A tiny floor-level opening. It must lead into a service shaft: people were already crawling through on hands and knees.

Tom said, "How many action-trained cell members do we have?"

An agonizing scream from outside, suddenly cut short.

"There is no *we*, laddie." Dervlin took the dead trooper's— Jivrin's—graser in his right hand; in his left, he carried only a monographite drumstick. "You're getting out of here."

Soft whimperings from the shocked and wounded.

Tom unclasped his cape and threw it aside.

"I'm going to—no, thanks." He waved away an offered graser as his other two troopers came up. "I don't like the noise they make. If you lay down covering fire"—he pointed—"I can make it outside to that side tunnel. From there I can circle round, with luck."

The two young children whom Dervlin had rescued blinked, wide-eyed.

"You don't understand, do you, boy?"

Stiffening, Tom looked up at Dervlin. Despite the blistering sizzle of renewed graser fire outside, he almost laughed: no-one had spoken to him like that for years.

"You might be their target, Tom. Hadn't you thought of that?"

Ice across his skin.

This is my fault?

But it might be true. The militia's intelligence could be partial: perhaps they knew that a ranking executive officer of Ludus Vitae, carrying priceless strategic plans in his head, was in the vicinity . . . but *they did not know who he was.*

Suddenly, travelling under less than complete anonymity seemed a stupid idea.

My fault.

A corollary: Dervlin knew everything, including the local situation. In his judgement, Tom had to flee.

Good enough.

"We're going." Decision made, Tom again took one child's hand. "You three are coming with me. Is there any ID?" He looked down at Jivrin's body. "We'll take him with us."

"No, I'll deal with him." Dervlin. "Hurry now, lad."

"I—Take care, Dervlin."

"Go on."

Then Tom was rushing across the chamber, towing the little girl, while his guards kept in formation around him, one of them with the other child cradled against his tunic. Ahead, by the low exit, Elva was pushing people through the opening.

Triple beams spat and bodies fell.

Fear bathed Tom in sweat. Shame pulsed inside as he crouched down at the tiny exit.

"Elva, you have to come, too."

"My Lord, I—"

"We can't risk your being identified."

The bride and groom were already gone. Tom had caught a glimpse of tattered gown, scarlet ribbons flying, as urgent hands pulled them into the escape shaft.

Sizzle, crack of graser fire—yelling—inside the chamber now.

When he looked back, Dervlin's face was bathed in bright blood but he was returning fire.

Move it!

Tom was galvanized into action, scooping up the little girl, ducking down and scrambling through.

Hurry.

He carried the child into the grey, dusty horizontal shaft as fingers of light flickered, questing—*very close*—and he could smell his own hair burning.

"Look out!"

Save the girl.

Then they were upright in the shaft, running—it was high but narrow, their shoulders brushing the walls—but up ahead orange light cut *through* the wall, and a figure dropped in a flurry of rustling purple silk.

Precious bundle.

Run!

Tom kept the little girl tight against his chest as he jumped over the dead priestess's form and kept running. Behind him Elva shouted to the troopers.

Choking now, vision obscured by dust, Tom half stumbled—*don't drop her*—as they came into a wider, broken-floored space. Service-shaft intersection: eight tunnels met here, and people were scurrying in all directions, splitting up.

"Second right!" yelled Elva, and Tom leaped into the shadowed tunnel's mouth and began to sprint.

"OK soon, sweetheart," he said to the child.

Faster now.

It was a good choice. Dark, with puddles underfoot, but this tunnel's floor was relatively unbroken and the air smelled cleaner as he poured on the speed.

No time to glance back, but footsteps splashed and thudded behind: they were keeping up.

The young girl he was carrying made no sound.

Don't be afraid.

"My Lord—"

Faster.

"Can't keep going . . ."

He slowed, stopped. Looked back.

Elva was bent over, clutching her side.

"Just a . . . stitch, my Lord." Her face was wan, illuminated by sickly fluorofungus clinging to the damp wall.

Don't worry, little one.

The three troopers came splashing up behind her, then turned and went down in the puddles on one knee, chests heaving, grasers pointing back the way they had come.

Just a moment's rest, and we'll continue.

Then Elva, trying to control her breathing, was saying, "I'll take her, my Lord."

Other hands steadied him as he swayed. "No . . ."

Taking the girl.

No.

Suddenly, he pounded the wall with a hammer-fist.

"NO!"

But they found an alcove, and Elva gently laid the dead child down. Eyes closed, as though sleeping.

"Come on, Tom." Elva took his sleeve. "We have to carry on."

55

NULAPEIRON AD 3414

They were waiting for him in the Palace.

It's all going wrong.

"If you would follow me, my Lord."

The alpha servitor and his attendant betas bowed low, then walked ahead of Tom and his group, leading the way—*you think I don't know this place?*—along an eggshell-blue and yellow corridor which Tom had walked a thousand times before.

"They're all inside." Gesturing with a white-gloved hand towards the shimmering white/gold membrane. "And the others?" Raised eyebrow, asking Tom what Elva and the three men should do.

"Show them to my suite."

"Very good, my Lord."

Tom slowly exhaled. The membrane slipped softly across his skin as he stepped inside.

Lacking clean-gel, they had washed using water stolen by Elva from a restaurant kitchen—wasting a precious resource—but Tom thought he could still smell burning, even above the clean yet musty smell of his new clothes. The garments had come from a small marketplace and been legitimately paid for by Elva, whose original outfit had been comparatively unmarked, while Tom and the three troopers remained hidden.

"Tom."

"My Lady." He smiled. "Sylvana."

He felt disadvantaged: skin scaly with old sweat, fifth-stratum clothes—pale yellowish pink and burnt orange predominating—and exhaustion weighing him down.

"It's good to see you, Tom."

By Palace standards, the chamber was modest. Round, low-ceilinged, in scarlet encrusted with gold. Some twenty nobles were in the room, in small groups of three or four, attended by only three alpha servitors.

"I'm looking forward to the big party."

"Me, too." Sylvana took his arm, and the thrill washed through him, even in his condition. "Though this thing here is not quite the happy affair I'd hoped."

Lord A'Dekal, white-haired and frowning, tracked Tom's progress across the room. But, behind him, Lady V'Delikona's eyes twinkled as she caught sight of him.

"Is that Lord Corcorigan I see over there?"

"The same, ma'am." He hurried across, bent over her offered hand and kissed it.

"Delighted, old chap"—A'Dekal's tone was frosty, conspicuously lacking delight—"that you could make it."

Danger here. Did he suspect where Tom had been?

"We were discussing the latest outrages." Another Lord, whom Tom did not know. "Three robberies in the sector this past tenday, and some kind of disturbance today, in this very realm." Sipping clear wine, he added, "Down below, of course."

"Of course," murmured Tom.

"What do you think we should do, Tom?" asked Lady V'Delikona seriously. "About these terrorists, I mean."

"Does anyone"—he put the question, knowing the answer—"actually know what they want?"

The unknown Lord snorted, and Lord A'Dekal said: "Brigands, pure and simple. We should sweep through the place with full military forces. Through every single stratum of every single realm, if we have to, until we clear the devils out."

"Easier said than done, I think," Lady V'Delikona replied before Tom could.

Control your anger.

But that, too, was more easily said than done, and bright-red target spots leaped out across A'Dekal's skin—*limp body, Elva lowering the lifeless child*—as Tom felt the growing pressure inside him to strike out and kill.

"—is why," Lady V'Delikona was saying, "I especially asked for you, Tom."

"I . . ."

Control.

". . . thank you, of course."

Breathe, relax.

"I would say"—A'Dekal's tone was clipped—"you could bring a unique perspective to the team, Corcorigan."

Tom bowed slightly, as though that were a compliment.

"Define for me exactly," he said carefully, "this team's objectives."

"A think-tank," said the unnamed Lord, as Lady V'Delikona nodded agreement. "To advise on counter-terrorist strategies for the entire sector."

Chaos!

"For brainstorming sessions only, I take it?"

"Oh, no. With a large budget and the ability to initiate projects."

Projects. That could mean anything.

"Any military involvement?" Tom asked.

"The overall responsibility, of course"—A'Dekal—"rests with the military. But the group will be presided over by a high-ranking officer; that's a measure of our serious commitment."

"And who will—?"

But another group of Lords was approaching, and at their centre was a gaunt, blond man with taut skin, pale in contrast to his dark grey military uniform.

"Lord Corcorigan"—A'Dekal fingered his white beard as he spoke—"may I present General Lord Corduven d'Ovraison."

"Good to see you, Tom." The others had left them alone for a time; it was just Tom and Corduven. "Shame about the circumstances."

"Just what I was thinking."

Every now and then Corduven and Sylvana crossed glances, then quickly looked away.

"Did you ever study tactics," asked Corduven, "with Maestro da Silva?"

"Er . . . A little. It was mostly physical training."

"Pity." Corduven took a slug of the pale-green spirits he was drinking; it had no discernible effect. "Those bastards are experts at guerrilla warfare. Small action groups, largely autonomous."

"I didn't realize . . . The last I heard, you were at Lord Takegawa's academy."

"Hmm." Corduven held out his free hand, as though checking its steadiness. "That was where I started, for sure."

It correlated with Tom's first impression: that Corduven's self-control was massive, but his nerves were wound tightly, close to the limit.

What have you been doing, these last few years? It was a reasonable thing to ask, so he put the question aloud.

"I've been in Sector Vilargi, near Kranitsia. It's something of a hot spot."

So that was you.

As the campaign to steal more funds had increased, there had been one demesne in particular where the authorities' countermeasures had proved successful: blowing courier lines, taking out a supra-cell briefing-group, infiltrating the local LudusVitae apparatus and dismantling it from within.

That was the tactical summary: in human terms it meant more

orphaned children, screams from isolated chambers as the inquisitors went to work, and the endless paranoia of neighbours watching neighbours, alert for betrayal or the opportunity to betray.

"Hence the rapid promotion?" asked Tom. "It's still an amazing achievement."

"Thanks." Corduven drained the glass and put it down. "But I'm looking forward to getting things moving here. And I'll tell you—I'm glad I've got someone I can trust. A friend."

For a moment shame flooded through Tom.

"I have to go now, Tom. But I'll see you at the ops-initiation meeting?"

"Let me know details, and I'll be there."

They clasped wrists.

As Corduven left, Tom noticed how the gazes of all five Ladies in the room followed him. His pale, drawn intensity seemed to fascinate them—even Sylvana.

"You knew him when you were younger?" It was Lady V'Delikona, coming to talk to him, waving away the other Lords.

"Yes, I—We knew each other as well as could be expected, given our stations in life."

He always treated me as an equal.

"That's very unusual," said Lady V'Delikona, though the same could be said of her own encouragement, her friendship.

"I know."

"He's changed a great deal."

"Yes, I . . . I know what it's like to lose a family member young."

Corduven, what have I done to you?

"You're a good man, Tom Corcorigan."

No, I'm not.

56

METRONOME STATION DELTA CEPHEI AD 2123

<Karyn's Tale>

[13]

Steady beat.

The workroom was long and curved, dimly lit on this shift. Only one person was on duty, Dorothy Verzhinski, and her booted feet were up on her console as she leaned back in her chair reading a hardcopy book: *Anna Karenina.*

Background stimuli fade into the environment, in audio as in the other senses. The pulsar's steady beeping had been a part of Dorothy's world for so long that she no longer noticed it.

BEEP-beep BEEP-beep BEEP-beep—

"*Bozhe moi!*"

She knocked the book aside, swinging her feet to the deck as the signal changed. She'd tipped her mug and cursed again as she wiped coffee from the controls, stabbing at command tabs.

"*Waaaah!*"

"Impossible." Tracer codes oscillated across her display.

She punched up a comm session.

"Shuttle Two. How's it goin', Dorothy?"

"Wait till you hear, Jean-Paul. I've got a distress call."

There was a moment's silence.

"Out here? Are you feeling all right?"

By "out here" he meant medium-range orbit around Delta Cephei. Shuttle Two was laying out a long chain of research satellites; the other shuttles were, like Dorothy, safely on board Metronome Station.

Lifeless space stretched in all directions, more desolate than humans had ever experienced.

"I picked up the beacon."

"But—"

"And here's the audio track."

She gulped unspilled remnants of cold coffee, not tasting it, as she patched in the parallel signal.

"*Wa-waaah!*"

"What was that?" Jean-Paul's voice was quietly serious.

"Tsk, tsk." Dorothy shook her head. "The lonely life of the dedicated scientist."

"Dorothy—"

"Have you never heard a baby cry before?"

"Damn you!"

The voice sounded from far away, waking her.

"Just let me in to see her!"

Muted arguments, then a metallic rattle as the door slid open.

"Karyn."

"Hello, Sensei." She raised her head slightly, then let it fall back weakly onto the soft pillow: the nearest she could come to a bow. "Nice to see you."

But she saw nothing. The world was darkness.

"Thank God." His beard brushed against her cheek in a swift kiss, then he took one of her hands—still so weak—in his callused grip.

"I heard you cursing at the medical officer."

"They told me you'd made it OK, but I had to see . . ."

"I know."

It was total darkness, but the bed's softness pressed beneath her, and the covers felt solid and heavy, cocooning her. Not like a ship—

"Sensei. Dart . . . He didn't . . ."

I can't cry.

"Don't speak." Big hands squeezing hers gently. "I've been briefed."

They took my eyes and I can't cry.

"He saved us." A whisper.

Perhaps she drifted into sleep then. Sometimes it was hard to tell. But when she came back to full awareness, Sensei was still there, his warmth and strength a comfort.

"Sensei . . ."

"It's all right, Karyn."

"They won't let me see my baby."

Dart's baby.

She might have heard more arguments, but she was not sure. But Sensei, Mike, had come all this way to Metronome Station, and he was not going to let subordinate officers or trivial regulations get in his way. Blend and harmonize when possible, thrust when necessary.

Then the door was sliding open, and Sensei was helping to raise her into a sitting position.

"Hello." Faint Slavic accent as a woman's hands transferred the baby's tiny form. "I'm Dorothy."

Baby. A new reality.

Another individual, but part of her, part of Dart—

Suddenly frantic, she moved fluttering, scarcely touching fingertips across her baby's warm face, head, with its furlike patch of hair, and body, checking the limbs, counting the tiny fingers and toes.

"She's beautiful." Sensei.

"Definitely." The woman, Dorothy, agreed.

Relaxing, Karyn settled back into the cushioning pillow, her tiny, wriggling daughter held in her arms. She felt a smile tugging at her face.

She had never expected to smile again.

"Is she . . . really all right?" Turning slightly to face Dorothy, judging the position by her voice and the rustling of her clothes. "What scans have you done?"

"Ah, I don't know. I'm an astrophysicist, not a medic."

"Dorothy was the one," said Sensei, "who picked up your signal."

"Oh." Karyn shook her head, very slightly. "I don't know how to thank you."

"Least I could do." The words were light-hearted, but Karyn could hear the emotion catching in her throat.

"Tell me straight, Sensei." Laying her head to one side, facing him, knowing he would focus on the useless silver sockets where her eyes should be. "This is your granddaughter. Why wouldn't they let me see her?"

"The strain—" Dorothy began.

"I came to take her home." Sensei avoided the question. "I can retire, or work part time; I haven't decided the details. You don't have anything to worry about."

"*Nothing to worry—?*" She forced herself to calmness. Sensei was the last person she should be angry with.

"I mean, she won't be raised in an orphanage. Your daughter."

Dorothy said quickly, "Two whole tech crews came in on the same ship." Mu-space vessel: Karyn wondered who the Pilot was. "When you've recovered, they'll re-interface you right here."

If Sensei were to raise his granddaughter, would that mean giving up the priesthood, breaking his vows? It didn't matter, because Karyn had made her own decision, not realizing it until now.

"I'm not going back into mu-space." Quietly. "I'm going to be a mother, on Earth."

"But you'll be—"

"Blind, I know."

They took my eyes.

"But that's what I'm going to do."

Then there were arms around her, silently hugging her, and the warm tears which trickled down her cheek could have been Dorothy's or Sensei's, and she accepted them as though they were her own.

After a minute, when they had disengaged, she asked again: "So why didn't they let me see her?"

"There's nothing actually *wrong* . . ." Dorothy.

"What is it?"

Silence. Were the two of them communicating by subtle gesture?

"It's her eyes."

Dear God, no.

"But—"

"Visual reflex appears normal." Sensei's hand grasped her wrist. "She tracks moving objects."

"It's hard to—" Dorothy started, then shut up.

Not her eyes.

"They're black," said Sensei, very softly.

"I—Oh. But why should—?"

"He means totally black." Dorothy. "No surrounding whites at all. It's quite . . . eerie."

My daughter.

"But she's very beautiful."

<<MODULE ENDS>>

57

NULAPEIRON AD 3414

"It's about time."

The technician did not look up as Tom lowered the stallion on its black cord to the desktop and let go.

"What's he been doing with it?" the young man added, checking the depths of his display.

"Bedtime reading, I guess."

"My Lord!" He jerked upright, face paling as he looked up at Tom. "My apologies, sir. I—"

"It doesn't matter." Tom clapped his hand on the fellow's shoulder and looked around. The place was long and wide, low-ceilinged, and mostly in shadow: deserted workstations, holodisplays cycling through intricate routines no-one was observing. There were only two other people in a work chamber designed for fifty. "It doesn't look like any of us can sleep."

Not when dead children wait in my dreams.

"Ah, well, my Lord. That's because we're making progress." Swivelling on his seat, the technician waved subsidiary display volumes into being. "Look at this displacement algorithm . . ."

Tom let him talk for a few minutes, and followed as best he could. After asking a few questions—which the technician was kind enough to pretend were not totally naive—Tom congratulated him on his progress, and left.

There was no particular need, in his own demesne, to carry the crystal around inside his childhood talisman, but it seemed appropriate. One thing that everyone agreed on, though, was that it was never going to be repaired.

Instead, the hundreds of men and women working in Tom's palace were engaged on a clandestine reverse-engineering project, trying to decipher the comms relay's design from femtanalysis of its components and topology. Later the emphasis would swing the other way, as they started to manufacture their own crystals.

But that step was a year away, at least.

Will this never end?

"Sweet Fate!"

Jammed into the tiny space, arm wrapped around his knees, Tom felt sickened as the dark blue ceiling and floor outside the view slit suddenly spun around and they plunged down, then sideways.

"One minute." Elva's voice, muffled by her helmet.

"I hope so."

Crammed in behind the control seat, Tom swallowed bile as the black arachnabug spun, actually *leaped* across a sunken pit, and whipped into a narrow, twisting tunnel.

"We're here. Broke a world record or two, I'd say."

"And my bones."

Bright light burst into the small cabin as they came out into a wide hall and Elva threw out all tendrils to halt progress. They swung sickeningly for a few oscillations until the tendrils damped them out.

"Everybody out," Elva said, knowing that Tom would have to follow her.

"After you, please."

She popped the bug, swung her legs over the side, and lowered herself on a threadlike descent fibre to the ground.

Ignoring the muscle cramps, Tom grabbed another fibre and followed.

Some twenty executive officers, with various aides, were in the hall. Zhao-ji was there, raising a hand in greeting, and Viscount Vilkarzyeh was already hurrying over, bootsteps clacking across translucent violet flagstones.

"Tom. Good to see you."

"Hi, Alexei." They clasped wrists. "Mind telling me what the fuss is all about?"

Looking around, Tom counted three Planning Council representatives: Dr Sukhram, a big woman called Galvina Chalviro, and the blocky man whom he still knew only by his codename, Sentinel.

"There's no rush," Vilkarzyeh was saying, "now that you're here."

"Nice to know."

In one corner, a small buffet had been set up. Tom was relieved to see Elva refuse wine and opt for gripplejuice; if the journey back was even half as fast as the outward trip, she would need her wits about her.

"Really, Tom, they've just brought forward a meeting which would have been held anyway. In three tendays' time."

"I see."

"With the beta-net blown we've got to—"

"With the *what*?"

Tom swung round quickly and Vilkarzyeh flinched. Then he stepped back and coughed, covering his embarrassment, and said quickly: "Not my decision, Tom."

Fist clenched, Tom scanned the room—

Limp body. Elva laying the dead child down.

—as scarlet pinpoints blossomed everywhere—

Small hand disappearing beneath the turbulent flood.

—even on Elva, and Tom squeezed his eyes shut until yellow fluorescence appeared and the tacware overlay went away.

Then he stalked across the room, leaving Vilkarzyeh behind, to the buffet beside Elva.

"Tom? What's the—?"

Picking up a shot of dodecapear vodka, he tossed the hot spirit down his throat in one go. He coughed, blinking away nascent tears.

"Destiny!" said Elva. "That's the first time I've seen you drink alcohol."

It burned nicely inside him.

"Today I need it."

"Why?" Keeping her voice low, trying to calm him.

"Lord A'Dekal's counter-terrorist Chaos-blighted think-tank." Tom had been to three major sessions now, worked there for days at a time, even brought back some of their material to his own demesne. "I showed them, these bastards"—gesturing at Sentinel and Dr Sukhram, who were staring in his direction—"all of Corduven's infiltration plans. You know they were ready to crack open half our courier lines in this sector?"

Frowning, Elva nodded.

"So our clean-up teams could have taken out every one of Corduven's intelligence people. *Every single one of them.*" He was raising his voice again, so he made an effort to bring the volume down. "I handed it to them on a plate, that's all."

"But that's great news, isn't it?"

"It should be." Tom bit back a curse. "Except Vilkarzyeh says our network's completely blown, regardless."

Elva's face grew pale, and Tom wondered how many people she knew among the courier lines.

"Maybe some of them—" he began, then stopped.

At the room's centre, one of the aides had gestured lozenge-shaped lev-stools into formation, and Sentinel was calling the meeting to order.

They wanted to discuss the long-range future first.

It was very impressive: outline constitutions, local cultural variables factored in, a global cellular-automata network; it was the LudusVitae organization writ large, reworked into a framework for all governments in the planet.

"And you'll be playing a key role, Tom." Sentinel, trying to forestall his questions. "As one of our first ambassadors to the existing power structure"—with a nod, too, in Vilkarzyeh's direction—"you could eventually expect a sector chairmanship, in my opinion."

Nods of agreement among the executive officers.

I didn't start this to become a—

But then, why did he start this?

It's not just a technical project.

Wishing he could be back with his technicians.

"Why," he asked, forcing rationality into his tone, "does a cellular structure need leadership at this level?"

"People will still," said Vilkarzyeh smoothly, "need guidance from the top."

"Of course." Tom stood up.

"I think," Sentinel began, "we should postpone—"

"My point precisely." Tom enunciated his words carefully. "I'd like to see the new local-sector courier-network chart."

"That's on the agenda." Dr Sukhram gestured at a vertical stack of tricons.

"What I would like to see"—voice veering out of control—"is the new network, *compared to the old one*. So we can see the names, pardon me, the *codenames* of the dead."

A surprised murmur rippled through the seated ranks.

"Tom, I think you should sit down."

Who had spoken? Tom glanced around, then back at Sentinel.

"I've been to counter-terrorist meetings for five tendays"—*betraying Corduven, my friend*—"walking a tightrope you wouldn't believe, doing my best to appear a productive member of their team without giving anything away . . ."

"Please sit down, sir." One of the junior aides.

"You let them die."

His voice echoed back from the too elegant hall.

"We had to." Dr Sukhram, rubbing the yellow tattoo across his face. "There was no choice."

"The Planning Council—" Sentinel began, but Dr Sukhram continued talking: "It's a paradox, Tom."

For a moment, there was nothing Tom could say.

Then, "*What?* What kind of superstitious—?"

"Just as surely as predestination," said Dr Sukhram, "traps both the Oracles and us. If we'd acted on the information you gave us, then *they would have known you were the source.* You, or someone else in a very small group. It wouldn't have taken them long to work it out."

Icy chills swept across Tom.

My fault.

Like the dead child. Like Mother, sliding back into eternal death.

My fault again.

All the nerve-straining effort to appear calm before his former noble friends, to smile as he plotted their destruction at the hands of his people, while his people were busy betraying their own—

Had it gone wrong after he killed the Oracle, when he joined LudusVitae? Or much earlier?

"Tom." Elva was touching his sleeve. "Let's get out of here."

"Good idea. Oh, by the way, Dr Sukhram—"

"Yes?" Trying to remain civil.

"Watch your back. Vilkarzyeh wanted to use me as a scapegoat: presenting terms while the combat's in full flow, when surrender will be the last thing on their minds." He looked at Vilkarzyeh, whose face was blotched with white and red. "Without me, he'll need someone else to betray."

Sentinel was on his feet, calling to Tom even as the others were pushing their seats away—bobbing slightly in the combined lev-field—making room for him to leave. "Where are you going?"

"Does it matter?"

He tossed his cape back over his shoulder and headed for the arachnabug, still parked in one corner, hanging from ceiling and wall.

"*Everybody back.*" Elva's voice.

He stopped and turned, and saw that she was between him and the assembled meeting, covering them with her graser pistol.

Of course. They expected betrayal.

"Get the Chaos out of here, Tom." Briefly, over her shoulder, then jerking her attention back to the others. "No twitching, anybody. Let's not have any mistakes."

He reached up, and a black fibre whisked him upwards.

"You've chosen the wrong side!" the other senior officer, Galvina, called out to him.

I don't think so.

With a thump, he slid into the control seat. The all-black cockpit closed around him, seat spreading liquidly around his torso and chin to hold him in, as the control organ grew like a webbed gauntlet around his hand, joined to the front panel by a narrow umbilical.

Dead girl . . .

There might have been shouting from the hall but it was too late now, as Tom made a fist and the arachnabug whipped forwards, then sprang up, speeding along a near-vertical shaft, and made the dizzying turn into a main thoroughfare.

Just go!

Pushing his fist forwards, forcing the arachnabug to maximum speed as the tendrils became a blur.

58

NULAPEIRON AD 3414–3416

"You're going to be all right."

Concerned faces, somewhat blurred.

"Give him room."

He stood up and everything tilted—broad square tunnel, busy with foot traffic and lev-cars—and he would have pitched forwards but strong hands caught him.

"Thanks," he managed to say.

"I think you're lucky." It was a broad-faced woman who spoke, and he followed her gaze: the black arachnabug was flat against the junction wall, half of its tendrils hanging in limp coils.

Destiny. How fast was I going?

Fast enough to miss the turn, even with all the safety routines.

Passers-by must have pulled him clear but he could remember nothing—*What's the matter? Not heard of retrograde amnesia?*—or even estimate how long ago the crash had happened.

"Don't worry, son." An older man. "Medics'll be here soon."

It wasn't medics Tom was concerned about. "Thanks, but I have . . . have to get moving."

"I don't think—"

But he had already shaken them off, mumbling something about his boss—drawing sympathetic looks among the shaking heads—and stumbled away into the crowd.

He was jostled—"Sorry"—but the thoroughfare's teeming streams of people could only help him. This was the Secundum Stratum of a wealthy demesne, and under other circumstances he would have been impressed, and stayed to look around.

Uniforms.

Two pairs, working their way through the pedestrians, headed for the wrecked arachnabug. Tom had to get clear before they came back looking for him.

"Hey—"

"Excuse me."

A migraine beat heavily over his left eye but he could see it now: almost hidden between fern-surrounded pillars and spraying fountains, the shining silver disc.

It spun as soon as it sensed his weight, and took him down to the next stratum.

There, he made his way through more utilitarian corridors to the next hatch—plain ceramic-and-steel here—and descended once more. Hurrying, he found the next, and made his way down again. Fifth stratum.

Head pounding mercilessly, he stumbled along a dark, raw tunnel, making horizontal distance, trying to get ahead of the pursuers, real and imaginary, who even now were hunting him down.

It was the beginning of Tom's descent.

"Ganja, my friend?"

Tom shook his head.

"Suit yourself."

The tavern was shadowed, warm with bodies but not in social atmosphere: it held a certain grimness Tom could not define.

Dead girl—

"Golden Angel," he told the barmaid, and drank half of it down straight away.

He had walked all through the night and most of the morning, tried to sleep in a deserted service tunnel, but moved on again when the migraine returned. Now it was late evening, and he would have to do something to force himself to sleep.

Small white hand, limp. Dead-doll eyes.

Drank some more. Ordered a second glass.

Hot and hard, it hit the spot.

Many hours later, he went back out into the cooler tunnel air, and the sudden change in conditions made him vomit.

Damn . . .

Wiping his mouth with the back of his hand, he continued to walk.

When he reached the demesne's border, he saw the patrols and smiled to himself, feeling cunning. Backtracking his route, he found the thing—*see, I remembered*—gestured, and half stumbled down the spiral staircase to the stratum below.

Chuckling, thinking himself very wise, he watched the slats rise back into the ceiling.

There were guards here, too, but he took a narrow side tunnel, confident he would bypass them soon.

Awoke, with stiff joints and cold muscles.

He was huddled in an alcove, cape pulled around him—*not writing poetry, oh no*—and early-morning activity was beginning: cleaners, kitchen staff fetching fresh food for the restaurants and freemerchants' kitchens, market traders—*I remember, Father*—going to open up their stalls.

Everything had the bright, dislocated quality of his childhood memories.

The strangest thing was, he thought, that there were few servitors. The term itself was not used this far down, though some men and women were indentured in conditions that might as well have been servitude.

More egalitarian than up above, all the same.

Breakfast was a bowl of cheap broth, which he ate at a public bench. His cred-slivers would need to be conserved; here, his thumb ring was more a liability than a source of credit.

Are your people looking for me, Corduven?

Fragments of Sun Tzu—on the importance of intelligence agents —flashed across Tom's semi-logotropic awareness, and were gone.

LudusVitae, too, of course. Looking for him. Bound to be.

It was night-time. In the darkness, Tom had thought he would be able to sleep. But fear prickled across his skin when he saw groups of men with silvery steel and amber woven into their skin—and, occasionally, young titanium-clawed women with longblades at each hip and coldness in their eyes—haunting the corridors. He realized that here it was safer to sleep when it was bright.

Perhaps he should make his way to Lady V'Delikona's demesne, where public halls and tunnels were kept brightly lit constantly, and there was no consensual night.

But that would take many tendays on foot. When he tried to plot a mental map across the demesnes, the migraine would return, pounding above his left eye.

Another day.

Two or three nights had passed since the arachnabug crash. Already, he was losing count.

None of you bastards have caught me yet.

A passing youth looked at him, startled, and Tom wondered if he had spoken aloud.

"Ah, so what?" He laughed as the youth picked up the pace, and ducked into the first cross-corridor.

He sniffed once inside his tunic, and decided he really must buy some clean-gel.

My talisman! It was gone.

But then he remembered where it was. Lying on some technician's desk, in his palace. In his own bloody palace.

Bastards.

There were twelve of them, following him through the tunnels as the glowglimmers began to fade, so Tom did the only thing he could think of.

He stopped at the first hatch, prayed as its rusty flanges creaked into position that it would not seize up, then fell down the steps, hurrying, catching his fingers on the bent rail and feeling the warm spurt of blood.

Cackling laughter sounded from above, until the revolving steps snicked back into place in the ceiling, cutting off all sound.

Tom waited for the longest time, but no-one followed.

Spitting into a dirty puddle, he picked himself up and stumbled on.

Another tavern, at midday. Tom forced himself to order bread and cheese. Then he swilled it down with gripple-cider, feeling better than he had for days.

"Son? Are you OK?"

An old straggle-haired woman was peering at him, and Tom shooed her away. "'Course I am, you old hag."

Later, when the tavern was closing, strong hands carried him, not ungently, outside. He slept on a bench, sliding in and out of grey, wraithlike dreams.

When the migraine was at its worst, his nonexistent left arm no longer burned.

Hey. Can't be all bad.

"Better come back to my place first."

"Huh? Oh, yeah."

He had promised to buy her food, that was right.

In her tiny curtained-off alcove, she lay back on her cot without preamble, hitching up her skirt, and their coupling was swift, animal-like but intense. Then he rolled off her, and she took him to a ganja club where the food was hot and filling.

There were friends of hers, a confused jumble of faces, and he drank something whose name he did not know, but it lit up every vein and artery, every capillary in his body, with a dragon's fire.

When he woke the next morning, his ribs were bruised, and his thumb ring and high-denomination cred-slivers were gone.

"Try some of this."

There were four—no, five—of them, sitting around the makeshift fire, drinking from the stained jar. All of them wore capes or tunics like Tom's: stained and tattered. Probably smelled like his.

So he had nothing they could want, his friends, and he was safe for the moment.

"Drink."

Then he saw the hidden glint of a knife blade, the only clean thing here, among the folds of a dirty robe, so he muttered, "Takin' a piss," and lurched out of the fire's illumination, down a deserted, twisting tunnel, then walked on alone.

The courtyard looked nice—shining copper glimmerglow baskets; scrubbed flagstones; whitewashed walls and ceiling—and one of the men saw Tom watching, and asked what he wanted.

"How about a job?"

Careful examination, then: "Sure thing. I'll show you."

He lasted five days, going for long periods when he could stop his attention drifting and focus on his work. But finally the man who had given him the job pointed out his shortcomings—the poor quality of what he had achieved compared to the others: "Worth their weight in rubies, these cleaners"—and paid him off.

"Sorry," he called out, as Tom stumbled from the courtyard for the last time.

In the tavern he saw them watching—noticing his bundle of steel cred-slivers—so he pretended to go outside to look for someone, then half walked, half jogged to the nearest floor hatch and descended once more.

Hiss of a paintstick. She was decorating his face so that it would look like hers: blue stripes, silver pentangles.

Another animal coupling. Or had that been the other girl? And back to the tavern.

Later, he lay on the floor, half sleeping, while she shared her bed with one of the neighbours who stopped, suddenly, as she asked him outright for money.

"Understanding boyfriend you got," said the man, tugging on his trews.

Not me. Tom turned his face to the wall.

He left when she went to the public washroom at the corridor's end.

"Look, officer." Talking to an astymonia patrol, but it should be safe. No-one would be looking for Lord Corcorigan down here. "I just want a place to work, somewhere to clean up—"

"And get a new paint-job, sir?"

The other trooper laughed—*I forgot about the face-paint*—as they booked him for vagrancy.

He spent overnight in a cell, ate three meals the next day, and finally was taken out to see a magistrate in the late evening. His head felt fuzzy, but he was thinking more clearly than he had for a while, and as he stood before the bench he felt almost grateful.

The options were a three-tenday work detail or exile downstratum.

No choice at all.

$$\diamondsuit\diamondsuit\diamondsuit$$

It all flowed together.

Cold and heat, light and dark. Brief fumblings with yellow-toothed women. Jars of fiery liquid passed round grudgingly.

Always sleeping in the hours of brightness: the nights were dangerous. Without the drink, he would never have slept; but sometimes the migraines took the place of sleep, and kept him going.

Sometimes, when he awoke, there would be low-denomination cred-slivers lying beside him, dropped by charitable passers-by.

There was a period of lucidity. A scribe, astonished that Tom could even read, gave him brief employment as a clerk. But the other assistants, sensing Tom's abilities, did their best to damage his reputation. When a small sum was missing at the end of the second tenday, it was obvious that the last person to join would be blamed.

When he demanded his wages, the security guards came, and his tacware manifested itself as a sickening series of blurred red flashes while they beat him. The sound of his ribs breaking was a distant crunch.

This time, his descent was not even conscious. He awoke beneath a ceiling hatch, paralysed with pain, and assumed they had thrown him down.

Had anyone asked him to recount how he survived, he could not have answered. He lost count of the number of times he came to in strange places, body aching with new injuries or with recurring damage which never quite healed.

And the pain over his left eye sometimes blinded him.

Dead girl . . .

Once, he tried to calculate how long he had been wandering, and realized that whole chunks must be missing from his memory: his matted beard reached to his chest, entangled with his long, unwashed hair.

None of it mattered.

An old woman took him to her alcove, shared her booze—synthetic leth'aqua—and then her bed, but he could not satisfy her there so she kicked him out, cursing, and he walked out into a main tunnel, lay down in the middle of it, and fell asleep.

Broken ground, smoke-blackened ceiling. Shambles of human figures, huddled here and there: as derelict as he was.

Jerking awake.

A strange woman was sleeping—grey/black-toothed mouth open, snoring—with her head in his lap. Off to one side a wizened man—*but how old? older than me?*—dropped his trews and defecated on the smashed flagstones.

Disgusted, he pushed the protesting woman off him and stumbled towards the nearest hatch. No-one followed him.

They never did.

Screeches of torn metal, but finally it opened.

Another trip down.

He was tracing patterns with his fingertip on green-yellow rock, sitting cross-legged. Someone tossed him a cred-sliver and he stared at it, wondering what it was for.

Not bad.

This one opened smoothly. Descending, it was hard to keep his balance, but he liked the smooth feel of the rail beneath his grime-encrusted hand.

When it closed above him, it snicked softly into place.

Cleaner than he had expected, this tunnel. He found a dark alcove and slept.

Smooth black floor, polished to a shine. He passed a booth selling trinkets he could not focus on.

Something odd . . .

Pale and dark blues mixed in the next section, where the corridor curved and widened, and the smell of baking pies made his mouth ache, and he ran his hand—long, blackened nails, thick coating of grime—across his weakly protruding stomach. Where his sleeve was torn, he could see that his upper arm was white, emaciated.

Wavering . . .

Green/gold; orange/black.

Hard to focus on the tricon—*why do they make them so small?*—but eventually he deduced its meaning: Snake . . . no, Tiger-Year, Shyed'mday, fortieth of Jyu. Tiger 280. That meant . . .

Walk.

Halting steps, shuffling.

Leaving the café behind, then a jeweller's, he continued because he could think of nothing else to do.

Trying to work out what the date meant.

Corridor opening out, becoming a green-paved boulevard beneath titanic natural caverns. The path curved, but he continued in a straight line, descending—painfully slowly—the arced shallow steps.

With quivering hand, he pulled open his tunic: saw the blackened patches of grime, the sickly white skin, the big purple-red carbuncles growing across his torso. His whiskers covered his mouth, and smelled of old food, booze and vomit.

Lapping, very gently . . .

There were children laughing at the sea's edge.

Tiger-Year.

He had been wandering for over six hundred days.

Cathedral-high caverns, with their vast natural pillars, receding for ever across the calm, flat-surfaced sea. Glowfungus sparked pyrites highlights from the rock, the gentle waves; the air smelled fresh and clean.

Slowly, Tom turned his head, looking along the shore-hugging boulevard, then back the way he came. He knew what the strange thing was, but it took a while for the concept to coalesce in his mind, to achieve reality.

No floor hatches.

He had been wandering for two Standard Years, and he was at the edge of an underground sea which washed amid an endless forest of pillars, and he could descend no farther, for he had achieved the lowest stratum.

A child's giggle carried through the still air.

Slowly—incredibly slowly—he lowered himself to the smooth floor and sat there, watching the placid waves, the cool, clean waters, for an endless time.

Then, softly, he began to weep.

59

NULAPEIRON AD 3416

Children singing.

There was a clean white pavilion, standing out among the cool waves, joined by a slender footbridge to the shore. The pure, crystalline voices came from there.

Tom pulled himself upright on the smooth stone. Had he actually slept without dreaming?

"Hello." Child's voice.

"Er . . ." Tom's throat could only produce a croak.

The little girl looked at him wide-eyed. "Hello hello hello," she said, then popped her thumb in her mouth.

Don't be frightened—

But she backed off as he reached out his grime-blackened hand. Then she turned and scampered away, pigtails bouncing as she went.

Warm pies.

It was the liquid, mouth-tingling aroma that drew him back to the row of shops along the dark blue, polished corridor. The café was close to the curve where the corridor opened out, and had a nice view of the sea and the boulevard which ran along its shore.

What am I going to do?

Swaying, he stood there, looking at the shelves of pies and cakes in the clear display cases.

A big, chunky woman with cropped white hair and broad forearms carried a tray out from the rear of the café. She set the pie-laden tray down on a marble-topped table, then stopped, hands on hips, and stared at Tom.

"We're not open yet."

"I'm—" Croak. *Have to do better than that.* "Looking for . . . a job."

Gaze swept across his blackened, tattered clothes. Small nose wrinkled. Could she smell him from that far away?

"I can program"—forcing himself not to stoop, to stand upright—"a procblock."

Upturned grin. "Not many of those around here."

She turned away, then began loading display-case shelves from her tray.

Tom could only stand watching, swaying but unable to stop, not knowing what else to do.

Over her brawny shoulder: "Not many charity cases here, either."

"I really"—closing his eyes, as his balance began to go—"need a job."

Then her big hands were on his shoulders, grabbing him.

No . . .

"Sit down."

Forcing him onto a bench-seat.

"I . . ."

Pushing a pie into his hand: warm and golden, pastry flaking beneath his touch. "Consider this an advance against salary."

Flavour bursting in his mouth.

Closed eyes, savouring the moment.

"That's enough," she said, when he had eaten a third of it.

He set the remaining pie down on the table, and thought he was going to cry. Instead, he painfully, arm trembling, pushed himself up to a standing position and began to shuffle out of the café.

"No, no." Wrapping the pie in a cloth, she put it in his hand. "I meant, don't eat it too quickly."

It was true, he shouldn't: already his stomach was grumbling, with twinges of pain, unused to good food.

A grey-haired man in a long, elegant surcoat paused at the café's entrance, then continued walking.

"That's all right," muttered the woman. "Don't like having you in here, anyway."

Oh, Fate.

"I'm not a thief."

"What?" She looked at the tattered flap of his abbreviated left sleeve. "Oh. Good. All right, come on. Bring the pie with you."

She led him through the rear of the café, past the entrance to the small, clean kitchen, to a workroom. A short passage, curtained off at both ends, led to the washing facilities.

"I'm Vosie," she said.

"Tom."

"Well, Tom. Take as long as you like."

He lost count of the number of times he scrubbed, from face down to dirty feet, as pale-blue jets of recycling cleanser washed over him.

At some point Vosie called out to him above the shower's roar; when he looked out, his stinking clothes had gone, and there were a straight razor and a white towel lying on a stool.

Hair and beard were one long, tangled mess, now sopping wet. He massaged cleanser into the knotted mass, but those knots seemed solid.

There was clean-gel, but Tom was filthy: the long-unused cycle-shower, once used to hose down work drones, was what he needed and deserved.

Washed and rinsed again, while the grime was sluiced away into the drains. Carbuncles and cuts were sore when he scrubbed, but he cleaned them out regardless.

Then, feeling wobbly on his pitifully thin, white legs, he reached past the curtain and found the razor; before—*two years ago*—he had used only depil-gel.

Harder work than he thought.

The old-fashioned vibroblade was sharp, and he hacked off great chunks of beard, trimming it first, then scraping it away in patches. Bathing in cleanser. But the hair atop his head was equally problematic, so he continued the shaving process, starting at the temples and cutting back. A huge wet mass of hair grew in one corner of the cubicle.

When he looked around the curtain again, there were a disposable bag and nail clippers and, farther along the wall, clean trews and tunic hanging from a hook. Sandals on the floor.

He waved the shower jets off and wrestled with the hair, getting it into the bag. His nails were still grimy; he worked on his toes sitting down on the cubicle's wet floor. He thought he was going to have to ask for help to do his fingernails—more used to autocutter or shedding-fluid—but he finally worked out how he could jam the manual clippers in his left armpit and operate them with his stump.

His flesh tingled painfully as he showered for the final time, using the razor again to scrape away at the last stubble patches until his scalp and chin were smooth-skinned and clean.

Finally, he slapped clean-gel on his chest; it spread across his skin, cleansing, disinfecting his sores. After a short while, it sloughed off, flowing back into its container, leaving a faint woody scent.

Then Tom dressed in the clean, simple clothes and headed for the kitchen.

A beefy young man was slicing vat-grown vegetables with a lattice blade. Silently, he indicated the dirty dishes stacked by the tiny clean-beam; Tom nodded and started work.

Vosie had a small office. After thumbprint-locking the cabinets, she said Tom could sleep there until he found some place better.

His bedroll was made up of discarded towels: tattered but clean.

The first tenday passed like a warm dream. He worked every day in the kitchen, alongside the burly young man whose name, it turned out, was Gérard. He was Vosie's nephew, and amiable enough once he had accepted Tom's presence.

If Tom still dreamed of the other Gérard, he no longer remembered it on waking.

On the fourth day Vosie let him serve in the shop, when it was quiet. He fetched a cheese-and-herb omelette for the grey-haired man who had refused to come in on that first morning, confronting the filthy, stinking apparition which had been Tom.

No hint of recognition in the man's eyes.

Tom kept his face shaved clean, as clean stubble developed on his scalp. Every evening, work over, he took a long, slow walk along the edge of the placid sea. The boulevard was kept constantly spotless by civic cleaning-crews. Everyone he passed nodded a greeting or said hello.

Morning and evening he ate well in the kitchen. On the ninth day, Vosie handed over his wages, including a one-off "welcoming bonus" which he tried to give back; Vosie made him keep it.

"Tomorrow," she said, "is your day off."

A community noticeboard listed available dwellings. In a small, white-painted corridor, a lean-faced man accepted Tom's advance payment and showed him the dwelling-alcove. The washroom was communal, shared among a dozen small chambers, but everything was clean and well-kept.

His own room. Bed, table, stool. Shelf: nothing yet to put on it.

Late evening. He took a tunnel at right angles to the boulevard, exploring. Holoflames danced along the walls. Laughter drifted out of membrane-fronted chambers: taverns.

He stopped in the doorway of the nearest. The ganja scents were subdued. Behind the bar, crystal flasks of all colours beckoned.

Tom felt the dragon stirring inside, but forced it back into its shadowed cave. He turned around and walked back home.

◆ ◆ ◆

"Can I keep these?"

Gérard shrugged. "If you like."

The old trews had been discarded, lying among the cupboard's cleaning-rags; wearable, though not really presentable.

"Thanks. Can I help you with that?"

That night, Tom washed the trews in the communal facilities near his chamber.

He woke up very early next morning, as always. Putting on the old trews and nothing else, he padded on bare feet out of his dwelling—careful not to waken the still-sleeping families—and headed for the shore.

Even the mildest stretching was painful. How could his muscles be so weak and yet so tight? He paid special attention to his calves and Achilles tendons.

Slowly—very slowly—he began to jog.

That first morning, he managed only a few minutes along the sea's edge before he had to stop and walk, chest wheezing, back to his chamber.

But he tried again the next day, and the next, bare feet slapping against the gold-flecked stone as he jogged—later, ran—a little farther each time out.

On the fourth tenday, having saved sufficient, he purchased a pair of good trews. Two tendays later, a cheap pair of training-slippers.

They helped him to run faster.

He could not afford to buy an infotablet, but old Narvan who ran the antique shop had a battered Laksheesh holoterminal; he rented it to Tom for only a minim per week. And lent him some of the classics, though they were all in Laksheesh.

With a reference from Vosie, Tom was allowed to join the lending-library; for a small hall in a tiny community, its array of crystals was impressive.

Tenth tenday: an entire hectoday had passed.

By the time Tom had completed his fifteenth tenday in Vosie's employment, he was running five kilometres, fast, every morning. He would stretch; do his chin-ups from the solid clothes rail in his chamber; do press-ups with hand on the floor, feet on the bed; work his abdominal crunches and leg-raises. Shower, dress. Go early to work—it was usually Tom who opened up, nowadays—and clean the café thoroughly before making breakfast for himself and Gérard.

Vosie would eat at home: not, she assured Tom, because of his cooking.

"You're not the same man," she said one morning, "who came in here half a year ago."

Tom stopped, mop in hand. "You took a chance, Vosie."

"Well." She looked into one of the broad mirrors which ran along the café wall, and patted her short white hair into place. "Guess I did good, didn't I?"

"I don't know how I . . ." Tom stopped, voice thickening.

"You want a way to repay me, honey?"

What could he say? Tom nodded.

"Some day, for somebody else—help them out when they're in need. OK?"

"I will, Vosie." He leaned forwards and kissed her on the cheek.

"Good boy. Now go and help Gérard with the flans, why don't you. Make sure he doesn't burn them."

60

NULAPEIRON AD 3417

Restday. Leaning back on the steps, eyes closed, listening to the ripples. Children playing.

Rippling outwards:
Bursting onwards,
Entropy and Destiny.

Moving waveform
Traces outlines
Diabolic and divine;

Only children
Brave and foolish
Cast their laughter against time . . .

It had been such a long time since he had composed a poem.

"Mister, mister."

"Hello." He looked at them: girl and boy, maybe seven SY old. Stuffed white unicorn in the girl's small grasp.

"What happened to your arm, mister?"

Glanced at his left shoulder. "Lost it. Pretty careless of me, don't you think?"

The little girl giggled; the boy grinned.

"I lost Fredo"—the unicorn—"but Mummy found him for me."

"Oh, right." Tom kept his face straight. "See if she can find my arm, will you?"

"OK."

More giggles. Behind them, two slender adults appeared—with the similar gaits of long-married couples, hair tied back with identical bandannas—followed by more children, perhaps twenty of them.

"Have you been bothering the gentleman, Linya?"

Solemn shake of the head.

"They've been fine, ma'am," said Tom, and nodded a greeting to the man.

"That's good. Come along, children."

"You bastard!"

Tom flinched and turned, but there was laughter as the two youths tussled on the ground, close to the waves. Three others watched, then one of them tried to deliver a playful jumping-kick—as Tom winced: terrible technique, a threat only to the kicker's own ligaments—and all five of them mock-fought while Tom shook his head, smiling.

One of them had had some lessons, and afterwards they all tried to perform a traditional form—awkwardly, without balance—until they got bored and wandered off.

That evening, on the way home, Tom bought a second-hand cylindrical canvas bag—military-issue duffel, supposedly—from Narvan's store.

It took a few days to find sufficient rags to stuff it tightly. On the eighth day, after his morning run, he carried the bag to the shore and hung it, by one end, from the underside of the elevated footbridge which ran out to the Pavilion School.

Alone on the smooth stone, underneath the bridge, he worked the bag: circling around, keeping his footwork mobile as he dug in with the punches, whipped the curved elbow-strikes, threw kick after spinning kick into the thing—counting in his head: two-hundred-second rounds with forty-second rest intervals—over and over until he could barely stand.

"*Izvinitye . . .*" Gaunt woman standing in the doorway.

"We're not—" Tom paused, mop in hand.

Two thin children were behind her.

Blinking, he gestured them inside, made them sit. Digging a cred-sliver from his waistband, he inserted it in the socket behind the counter; then he fetched rolls and fruit from the kitchen and put them down before the starving trio.

"Waifs and strays?" Vosie, her big form almost filling the doorway.

Tom shrugged.

"Good man," said Vosie. "But I'm afraid they're not the last we'll see."

News of distant events was slow to arrive, but Tom had heard the rumours. Far upstratum, fighting and chaos. Vosie might be right: if trouble was on all sides, where could refugees go but downwards?

Was it the Prime Strike? Or had plans changed since Tom's time?

Behind Vosie, two others: Tom recognized the bandannas.

"We heard"—the woman spoke hurriedly—"that they were here, and only spoke Laksheesh. Are they all—?"

"*Sprazitne mir Laksheesh*," said Tom, and smiled at the startled family at the table. "But we haven't needed it so far."

A grin widened across Vosie's broad face. "Tom? Do you know Rislana and Trilvun, the school principals?"

"Only by sight."

They shook hands all round, then reassured the nervous woman with her children, and sat down to draw up plans for their welfare.

"*Hee-ya!*"

Tom spoke without thinking: "Keep your back straight. Twist your hips."

The youths—there were seven of them this time—stared at Tom. One of them, who had been carrying a small pebble in his hand, turned and threw it out across the waves; it vanished with a small splash.

"So what do you know about it, mate?"

"This."

Tom was standing side-on to the youth. Murderously fast, his leg whipped out: hooked *over* the boy's head, flicked back—instep against temple—hooked heel against the other temple—then lightly tapped the blade-edge of his foot against kneecap, hip and—as the boy involuntarily stepped back—stopped his foot just millimetres from the boy's throat.

Stunned silence.

Then, "Bleedin' Dissolution!"

The youths looked at Tom as he lowered his leg.

"Er, mister, could you teach us how to do that?"

"See you tomorrow night, Tom!" "Yeah, we'll be here." "Tomorrow!" "Thanks, Tom!"

Tom called after them: "Don't be late."

And turned away, grinning, to find the school principals, Rislana and Trilvun, looking at him.

"So," said Trilvun. "Fighter and linguist."

"Teacher, too," his wife said.

"I—" Tom shrugged. "I guess so." Looking back at the seven youths in the distance. "Guess I've got a commitment now."

"And they'll bring more of their friends tomorrow." Trilvun looked to Rislana for confirmation and she nodded.

"How many languages do you speak, Tom?"

A pause, then, "Seven fluently. Some smatterings."

Indrawn breath, but the couple did not look greatly surprised. "Anything else?"

"Logosophy . . ." Tom looked out across the sea, at the reflected ripples on the cavern ceiling. "All disciplines."

"Er . . ." Exchanged glances. Rislana said: "Only Lords study every branch of logosophy."

"Nevertheless."

Tom let the silence stand.

He watched as the couple communicated in the near-telepathy of long-term partners. Then they looked at him.

"Did you know," asked Rislana, "that Niltiva"—she meant the refugee woman—"used to be a cook?"

"Ah, no."

"Thing is," said Trilvun, "she needs a job, and Vosie's place would be ideal . . ."

". . . and it's really time," Rislana finished for him, "that you moved on, Tom."

"I don't . . ."

The ground seemed to shift beneath Tom's feet.

"So you're starting with us tomorrow." Rislana.

"In at the deep end." Trilvun, grinning. "You'll be teaching the seven-year-olds. Poor you."

"I . . ."

"The phrase you're looking for," said Rislana, "is thank you."

Tom swallowed. "Thank you."

61

NULAPEIRON AD 3417-3418

And he loved it.

Teaching. Academic classes during the day—the youngest children at first, then the older ones, with a chance to extend the curricula—and the physical arts in the evenings. At first only the boys learned to fight, then some girls—fascinated by Tom's regained lean good looks, giggling when they had to practise with the boys.

After a while, though, some of the girls took to the art for its own sake; soon groin-protectors as well as gum-shields were mandatory for the males.

Four times, Tom refused principalship of the Pavilion School when Rislana and Trilvun tried to step down in his favour.

But he kept reworking the curriculum: another three years, and he would have all the foundations in place. The eleven-year-olds who started on his accelerated programme at that time would eventually, aged eighteen, leave with an education equal to any Lord or Lady of the Primum Stratum.

A decade until the first of those students graduated. Tom looked forward to the day.

Only one year after Tom's arrival, though, his morning class was interrupted by a breathless student skidding to a halt in the room's archway.

"Sir, sir—"

"What is it, Filgrave?"

"It's . . ." Catching his breath. "Soldiers, sir. Down at the waterfront."

"Show me."

Outside Vosie's, the four soldiers were mirror-visored and heavily armed, guarding the doorway. They made no attempt to stop Tom as he strode inside.

"Are you OK, Vosie?"

"I'm all right." She nodded, clutching her white apron.

At one of the tables, near the back, an officer was sitting. There was a glass of warm daistral in front of him, and his helmet was beside him on the bench-seat.

"I'm a local schoolmaster," Tom said to him. "May I ask what's going on?"

"A magister, eh?" Raised eyebrows, then a gestured invitation. "Please sit down."

Tom slid in, facing the officer across the table.

"I'm Colonel Rashidorn," the man added. "And I have to say, I've heard good things about you. The Pavilion School, that is."

Tom grew cold. "What about the school?"

"That its reputation has grown somewhat . . . unusual. Excellent, of course." The colonel sipped from his daistral. "So much so that bright children are now being sent *down* to attend it, from two strata above."

"We try our best." Tom kept his voice neutral, watching the man's face, but his mind was racing: plotting ways out of the trap.

My fault, yet again . . .

The colonel moved and Tom's nerves screamed. Sweat broke out but he was only taking something from his pocket, that was all.

"And your best is impressive." If Rashidorn had noticed Tom's reaction, he gave no sign.

But Tom noted: there had been no blossoming of red dots across his vision. He had suspected it from his training sessions, but this was proof. His tacware was gone, disintegrated in the abuse of his two lost years.

"As is the breadth of subjects," added Colonel Rashidorn. "Including disciplines one would hardly expect to find this far down."

Clenched fist.

"This is for you. A token."

Tom made no move, so Colonel Rashidorn opened his hand and laid the thing on the table between them.

"Do you know where the Community Hall is, Mr Corcorigan?"

Lord Corcorigan, to you.

But, "Of course," was all Tom said. "I live here, after all."

"The general will see you there tomorrow morning, at oh-eight-hundred."

Which general? Tom could have asked, but said nothing as Colonel Rashidorn stood.

Then the colonel left, passing through the doorway, and his soldiers fell in step behind him. Their diminishing bootsteps echoed back from the boulevard outside.

"Tom?" Vosie, fearfully.

But the thing on the tabletop was a small stallion attached to a black cord, and there was only one person both subtle and knowledgeable enough to have sent that as a token.

You found me.

62
TERRA AD 2142
<<Karyn's Tale>>
[14]
Epilogue

They attacked from all directions.

The backdrop: icy Alps, grey and blue, capped with breathtaking whiteness. Clean, crisp air. A panoramic window displayed the view.

But in the blue-matted dojo, bodies were flying.

From every conceivable angle, they made their unrehearsed attacks: fit-looking white-jacketed men and women charging with strikes and kicks and attempted grabs, but they crashed into each other, were dropped in their steps or flung suddenly through the air.

At the centre of the maelstrom, the slender woman moved.

Her attackers tried again, but once more the bodies became entangled as she danced among them, long, grey hair flying, and the sunlight glinted from the silver sockets where her eyes should have been.

And then it was over.

"*Mokosu*," she ordered, as they knelt in straight ranks, and the class slipped into meditation.

As the trainees limped to the showers, their faces were drawn and bloodless. No-one spoke. There were twenty-one of them in total; after showering, they put on white UNSA jumpsuits and, bone-tired, made their way outside to the waiting silver bus.

"What a hard-ass!" said a young woman.

"Kicked the shit out of me." A big, wide-shouldered man with buzz-cut hair. "Jesus Christ! And she's so small."

Footsteps crunched on the gravel.

"Be thankful"—it was a black-jumpsuited nun who spoke, and the trainees stiffened—"that you have her as your teacher."

Behind her, a small boy waited silently. The UNSA trainees looked uncomfortable.

"Sorry, Sister," said the big man.

"Probably no-one's told you, but Karyn's classes have the highest pass rates of all Pilot Candidates."

The trainees exchanged glances; this was news to them.

"Can we watch Ro play now?" The little boy's upturned face was eager. "Please, Sister?"

"In a moment. The thing is"—a half-smile—"getting your asses kicked by a little blind grey-haired woman is the good Lord's way of encouraging some humility. God bless you." Then she took the little boy's hand and led him inside the building.

"See?" breathed one of the men. "Hard-asses. Every last one of them."

In single file, they trooped aboard the UNSA bus and headed back towards the Flight School.

Wooden dagger, gleaming.

The girl attacked.

Effortlessly, the grey-haired woman moved, blended, pinned the girl's arm to the ground. Then they regained their start positions, kneeling, facing each other.

The girl—young woman, now—was nineteen years old. Both women wore white jackets and black split-skirt *hakama*.

Over and over they worked the formal routines, from kneeling and standing, empty-handed and with weapons, while the nun and the little boy watched from a balcony. Then the two watchers departed.

"Your *shiho nage*'s improving," said the grey-haired woman.

Rare praise, indeed, from a sensei.

"Thanks, Mother." The black-haired girl smiled. "But it'll never be as good as yours."

Karyn gave a short bow of acknowledgement. Her daughter could be right: at ninth dan, Karyn McNamara was the highest-graded aiki-doka outside the Kyoto *honbu*.

"See you later, Dorothy," she called, as her daughter bowed out and left the *dojo*.

After meditation, Karyn left by the side door leading out into the cloisters. She had never seen the garden beyond, but knew it intimately by touch and smell; she smiled, breathing in the cold alpine air, enjoying the warm feel of sunlight upon her face.

There was a beeping, and the black-haired girl gestured: a holocube opened at her bedroom's geometric centre.

"Hello, Ro." Chojun Akazawa's head and shoulders filled the display volume. "How are things?"

"Hi, Uncle Cho." Sitting down on the bed, Ro folded her legs into lotus. "Let's see. Mother still calls me Dorothy. The place is still staffed with bloody nuns—*I admire their discipline, Dorothy, not always their beliefs*—and I'm still waiting for my exam results."

Chojun laughed.

"And apart from that," he said, "everything's fine?"

"I guess." Ro grinned.

"I'm lecturing students in the flesh." Chojun grimaced. "Would you believe that?"

"You love it, Uncle Cho. What else are you working on?"

"This."

The image of his head shrank and moved off to one side as a Four-Speak text lattice took over the volume.

"*Self Awareness in an N-Dimensional Continuum.*" Ro magnified the image. "What's this?"

The movement of her eyes was impossible to see.

"You're publishing this?" she added.

"What, and lose my tenure?" A wry smile. "I'm posting it anonymously, on a non-reviewed board."

"It'll be a hit anyway."

"Yeah, sure."

Chojun Akazawa had gained his Ph.D. at UTech the year Karyn had returned there to teach, when Ro was three years old. By the time Karyn and Ro had moved to Switzerland, four years later, Chojun had jumped on the connectivity-theory bandwagon, and his academic career was assured.

Ro downloaded the text and magnified Chojun's image.

"Will you let me know," he asked, "when you hear about your exams?"

"Of course, Uncle Cho."

"I'll be off then. Give my love to Karyn."

"Ciao." She blew him a kiss.

The display shut down.

Absorption.

Quickly, the last motes dwindle into nothingness. The ship is gone, evaporated, melded into the fabric of mu-space, as scarlet lightning flickers.

The pattern evolves, adapting to the new structures; changes recur infinitely through all the levels, instantiated in infinitesimal time.

None-life . . .

Strategies. Goals. Self-modification.

. . . becomes life.

In realspace, life is a paradox: DNA manufactures proteins, building bodies . . . but also replicates, builds copies of itself; a factory which is simul-

taneously its own blueprint, its own maker of factories. It is an impossible loop—which comes first, blueprint or factory?—a contradiction resolved only because an outside factor, RNA, triggers the process.

But in mu-space, self-referential conditions are not unsatisfiable.

Patterns, spreading . . .

The ultimate closed-feedback loop is conscious thought: neural processes which can perceive themselves; the essence of self-reflexiveness.

Consciousness.

And in mu-space . . .

It spreads, everywhere.

. . . self-reflexiveness is always resolved.

Chojun's article concluded with some observations:

1) That the incidence of lost mu-space ships dropped almost to zero immediately after Pilot Dart Mulligan's demise, and has remained low for almost two decades.

2) That the surviving Pilot, Karyn McNamara, reported in her debriefing a *sudden feeling of euphoria, of love*, immediately before her re-insertion to realspace.

3) That adaptive self-modification has been observed in many other . . .

A knock sounded on the door.

"Come in," said Ro. "Oh, it's you, Sister Francis Xavier."

It was the nun who had been watching earlier.

"Since you're home from college, Ro," she said, "would you like to come to evening prayers? It would be—"

"You don't give up, do you, Sister?"

"From you, that has to be a compliment." The nun glanced at the holotext, still glowing in mid-air. She stiffened. *"Self-Awareness in . . .* Does that mean what I think it does?"

"You were on your way, I believe"—Ro spoke carefully—"to pray to an anthropomorphic omnipresent consciousness, of whose existence you can have no direct proof. Am I right?"

From the cloisters outside, a ringing bell sounded.

"I'm late. I'll"—with a last glance at the holo—"talk to you later."

Sister Francis Xavier swept out.

Ro's silence lasted only a few seconds.

"Maybe your God is imaginary . . ."

Eyes of pure black, devoid of surrounding white. Orbs of jet.

Her voice rang out in the empty room.

". . . and maybe not . . ."

Suddenly, golden fire coruscated across those eyes, and the whole room lit up.

". . . but mine is real, for sure."

Then, slowly, the golden fire faded, was gone.

In its aftermath, Ro's obsidian eyes glittered, cold as stone, totally unreadable, as hard and implacable as death.

<<STORY ENDS>>

63

NULAPEIRON AD 3418

Mine is real, for sure . . .

Tom stared up at the shadowed ceiling, leaning back in his chair, but his thoughts were whirling.

Do you realize what you've given me?

Eerie silence. It was the main teaching-hall, all square lines and elegant, understated, carved decoration, now delineated in shadows: a hundred shades of grey.

A strange feeling of euphoric warmth, of loving benediction—Karyn's words, describing her exit from mu-space as her lover's ship dissolved into sparkling fragments . . . Tom did not need to replay that earlier fragment of Karyn's Tale: the words were fresh in his mind.

The implications . . . but he was here to say a farewell, of sorts. A full analysis would have to wait.

He was alone at night in the Pavilion School, wondering if he would ever see the place again.

Beneath his tunic, the talisman hung. He had resealed it after playing the final module, using the school's highest-resolution infotablet. The question was, had anyone ever guessed its contents? The crystal's nul-gel coating had been intact; impossible to tell.

Surely it was the stallion itself that was the gift, its secret core unknown.

Subtle, indeed.

Giving him time to think. Letting the night bring doubts among the shadows. It was not fair warning, not an opportunity to escape: there would be soldiers at every exit from the area. Many were patrolling the pedestrian corridors; Tom had seen them earlier.

My fault that they're here.

He got up from the chair and walked around the hall—noting the flat-sheet drawings of the eight-year-olds, the older kids' abstract holos which sprang into life as he passed—then out into the gallery, overlooking the placid, black-looking sea. It seemed that he could hear echoed childish laughter, scampering feet; but the only sound was of waves lapping endlessly against the pavilion.

Letting the doubts prey on him.

An old desire sparked inside: to go for a late-night run, escaping his demons. But there were soldiers around, neighbours who might be awoken.

That was the old way.

Near the water's edge, he sat down on the smooth stone and folded his legs into lotus posture. Closed his eyes, let the waves' plashing sound wash over him.

Then, one after another in his mind, he named the Pavilion Schools' students, starting at the youngest: pictured them, their budding personalities, their bursting potential.

When he had mentally bidden the last child farewell, he blanked out his thoughts, let the sea become his mind, a peaceful flow, and slid into perfect trance

There was a flickering quality to the eyes. It had always been there, just a hint, when they were younger. Now it was part of the man.

"Hello, Corduven," said Tom.

For a moment, just that flickering stare; then he gestured for Tom to sit.

The Community Hall was three-sided, opening onto the sea, but there was no escape that way. An encircling gallery, high up, was filled with troops: thirty, no, forty of them. Two flat boats floated on the waves outside.

Tom sat down before the green crystal desk, and waited for Corduven to speak. He noted that the soldiers at ground level stood far back, allowing privacy. That was security, not good manners.

How are you doing, old friend? But openness was not called for, here.

Tom's objective had been clear in his mind when his eyes snapped open this morning: it was to get these people out of here, so they would leave Tom's community alone.

"I wish I could say"—Corduven looked away, out across the waves—"that it's good to see you again, Tom."

He was even paler than before, stamped with the stress of two years' warfare.

Tom quoted: "'What enables the wise sovereign and the good general to strike and conquer, and achieve things beyond the reach of ordinary men, is foreknowledge.'"

Corduven did not smile.

"At the academy," he said, "we spent our first two tendays entirely immersed *without sleep* in logotropic simulation of *The Art of War.* Watching and feeling action scenarios while the principles wired themselves into our brains." He stood up, a narrow figure taut with nervous energy. "So don't quote Sun Tzu to me, my friend."

Tom's had been a twin-barbed comment: hinting of Oracles, but what Sun Tzu had referred to was the use of intelligence agents; in his view, espionage lay at the heart of war.

"But you found me," said Tom, "because of rumours about a good school. Who spotted the significance of that datum among all your infoflow?" He paused. "I was complimenting you, I guess."

A momentary flash: "*Maybe your God is imaginary, and maybe not . . .*" *Golden fire coruscating across Ro's eyes.* "*. . . but mine is not.*" Had Corduven accessed the crystal, understood its content?

Tom forced his attention back to the moment.

"A compliment?" Corduven stopped by his chair, put his hand on its back, then let go and resumed pacing. "If you say so . . . But this is a good location for a garrison; my aim is to have troops on the Ultimum Stratum of every demesne, and I might as well begin here."

Stare, flickering.

He knows.

Maybe not about the crystal, but . . .

Tom's mouth grew very dry. What would Corduven do to the community which had harboured his brother's murderer? The youthful Corduven would not have harmed them; but this driven man was different. And revenge was not pure logic, crystalline rationality.

I can be sure of that, can't I?

"I'm aware of the circumstances," Corduven added, finally standing still, "under which you deserted your own people. It's the one reason you're still alive right now."

But they could have come for Tom last night, dragged him out and arrested him or killed them. Instead, they had let him worry: softening him up.

They've got other ways of softening people up.

"In fact"—sliding a small silver infotablet across the desk, Corduven leaned over, looking down at Tom—"your actions probably screwed up Flashpoint. They can't have any love for you, either. Your own kind."

Tom exhaled slowly, keeping control. "What's Flashpoint?"

"Ah." Corduven pulled his chair back, and dropped heavily into it. "You'd have known it as Prime Strike, is that right? You were going to change the world; that would have been due to happen two years ago, almost exactly."

Tom sat very still.

"Well, it's changed all right." Corduven. "We've been fighting for two years, and I for one am getting tired of the bloodshed."

A kind of itch, a tingling. It had been a long time since Tom's non-existent left arm had actually burned.

"Take a look." Corduven nodded at the infotablet. "See what you've done. The sequence is for convenience only: they're all from around the same time, two years ago."

"What's in here?"

"Standard surveillance logs—most of which we recovered later, not acted on at the time—plus undercover people on the scene. Some reconstructions."

"From what? Interrogations?"

No answer.

FLASHPOINT ONE

Streamers. Floating platforms, bedecked with ribbons, fanciful sculptures: giant mushrooms, fantastical beasts. Dancing. All around is darkness, save for the candles; the corridor is alive with music and dancing crowds.

Darkday Carnival.

"In beneficence"—a reporter, speaking to the hovering cam-globe—"Lord Xaldrugen's steward distributes alms to his poorest subjects."

In a side corridor, among seated beggars with tattered robes, a paunchy alpha servitor roots in his embroidered pouch and scatters cred-spindles.

An old man, bent with age and poverty, patch over one eye and fingers missing from one hand, sits down at the back. The others, grudgingly, make way for him.

There is consternation among the beggars when the reporter tells them to hand the alms back—"So I can film again, for close-ups, you moronic fools!"—but eventually they get everything recorded. The reporter hurries off, following the carnival floats, and the beggars begin to disperse.

The surveillance system's viewpoint does not change.

One beggar's body ends at the waist, fastened somehow to a smoothplate, and he uses his arms to push himself along the ground. The alpha servitor watches him go, shaking his head as the other beggars limp away.

"Pitiful." Scorn in his tone. Then, "What are you still doing here?"

The last beggar: old man, hooked claws for a hand, eye-patch.

"It's time to go," says the old man.

Then his hand flashes out, very fast, to the steward's throat. Behind them both, the solid-seeming stone wall dissolves—chameleon membrane—and two hooded figures step out and grab the unconscious steward before he can fall.

Quickly, the old man and his accomplices drag the portly steward back through the membrane, and are gone.

The membrane hardens into opacity, and the wall looks like solid stone once more.

Tom looked up, carefully keeping his face blank. Corduven, too, revealed nothing with his eyes.

No matter. The thing was, not to betray any sign of recognition.

But the last time Tom had seen the one-eyed man was in a history lesson at the Ragged School, and he—the Captain—had given Tom a verbal roasting for not knowing the year in which Bilkranitsa Syektor had been founded.

"Don't stop there," said Corduven.

FLASHPOINT TWO

The young woman, bent over the console, hums softly to herself. From outside the studio, glowglobes cast gentle peach-orange hues: early morning, dark-period just ending.

Holovolumes flicker into being.

PRIMARY: "Outlying Argenia provinces report severe fluorofungal blight. Damages are estimated to total . . ."

SECONDARY: Lightball players, fluorescent costumes, the

piercing whine of the semi-sentient ball. "Just minutes into the final third . . ."

TERTIARY: Triconic lattices of economic-forecast data grow steadily more entangled.

QUATERNARY: "In the Zhinghuan Protectorate today, ambassadors gathered to pay homage to Lord Cheng Yat-Sen, and survey the site of . . ."

A scraping sound, and she gestures the displays to silence.

"Who's there?"

Three hooded figures walk into the room. Rainbows shimmer across the transmission ends of their graser weapons.

"I'm not stupid," the woman says hastily. "Whatever you want, I'll co-op—"

But she leaps then, grabbing a power-staff from the wall and spinning, with a yell. Two of the hooded figures are slow to react but the other sidesteps, uses a horizontal hammer-fist above the power-staff's trajectory and strikes the graser butt-first against the woman's forehead, and she drops like a stone.

"Damn it," says one of the others, voice muffled by her hood. "We need an editor with brains, not a concussed zombie. Did you have to hit her so hard?"

"Sorry."

The sea was gentle, its reflected waves a slow ripple of light across the cavern ceiling, the gold-flecked pillars.

But here in the Community Hall, the pressure was oppressive.

FLASHPOINT THREE

The woman trips.

"Seeya-seeya-seeya!" In the middle of the chamber, heavy

with ganja fumes from badly sealed masks, the dancers are clapping and chanting in time to broquadeco music.

Around the tavern's edges, the light is dim, and the woman may not have seen the man's outstretched legs before catching her ankle on his boot and dropping her glass.

"Sorry! Er . . ." The balding man helps her up. "My name's Jyaneto. I'll buy you another."

Anger in her fine green eyes, slowly dissipating.

"OK then," she says.

When he comes back with a tray of Salamander Fires from the bar, she giggles and introduces herself. "I'm Karlia."

Younger than Jyaneto. Very beautiful.

Entranced, they sit together in the booth, shouting above the music, but Jyaneto obviously does not care about the volume. It is the company that is important.

The suspicion comes only after the second drink, but by then he's already slumping sideways, and his attempts to move are useless.

"Don't hurt him," says the girl, as two burly men lift Jyaneto from the bench. "He's quite sweet, really."

Tom flicked to the next.

FLASHPOINT FOUR

Immensely huge, naked woman, shaven head, unconscious, being lifted by ten struggling hooded men—"Fate, she's even heavier than she looks!"—pulling her from her vat and into the mobile tank.

She slides beneath the surface of the glowing sapphire liquid.

$$\diamond \diamond \diamond$$

Flick.

FLASHPOINT FIVE

"For One-Eye!" yell the boys, rushing into the corridor, brandishing short staves and jagged broken flasks.

The militia captain orders his troops to fall back.

"But—" One of the men lowers his graser rifle.

"We're not here," says the captain, "to open fire on children."

Again.

FLASHPOINT SIX

"Call yourselves freedom fighters?" Behind the woman, hooded figures are setting the hydroponic nets alight. "Bastards!"

She spits.

They club her unconscious before they leave.

Again.

FLASHPOINT SEVEN

Silver-skinned trio, floating on their lev-discs.

The serried rows of tables are set out with best linen and cutlery: the officers are in full dress uniform; the dishes brought not by servitors but by enlisted men.

"Wonderful." Amid the chatter, Brigadier Count Devarel drinks his private toast to the singers.

"Sir." Younger officer, with the shoulder-patches of an arach-nargos company commander. "Shall we allow them to proceed?"

A nod. The younger officer gestures.

At the banquet hall's far end, they begin to sing: triple-braided melodies, inhumanly sweet, which reduce the men to silence. Perhaps some tears; but it has been a long evening, and much drink has been taken.

No instruments, save their voices.

But the song is beautiful, heart-stopping, as the surgically altered gender-neutral singers—long bodies, short limbs, necks held by silver braces—weave their magic.

As the song builds to climax, they float out among the tables . . .

"Beautiful."

. . . and the Brigadier's head rolls as the speeding disc separates it from his body. The singer spins in mid-air, his/her/its lev-disc stained with bright arterial blood, still singing as the hooded figures burst in and graser fire splits the air.

When the slaughter is over, one of the killers pulls off his hood: his grim, scarred face is splashed with a purple birthmark. He stands astride Brigadier Count Devarel's corpse, opens his own trews, and begins to urinate.

"That was the academy," said Corduven.

"After your time there?"

"Oh, yes." Unreadable expression. "I was busy by then."

FLASHPOINT EIGHT

The white-haired Lady stumbles back into the room—Lady Darinia—and the officer leads her to an ornate chair: a lev-throne, grounded now, its lev-field cut.

"Don't go back out there, Lieutenant Milran."

The mustachioed young officer smiles. "Don't worry, ma'am. That rabble have a surprise coming to them."

Spin, refocus. Viewpoint shift.

They are marching down Furqualry Boulevard—ancient tapestries on fire, statues smashed—with crude holo-banners and no energy weapons, just bits of furniture, anything that comes to hand.

At the riot's head, a broad-shouldered man: red hair, green jerkin. A glimpse of slender black sticks in a diagonal pocket across his back.

Then the reinforcements attack, driving in from the side tunnels using wide-angle fire. The rabble's centre is unarmed, many just children, and the red-haired man leads the attempt to get them out through one corridor. Whirling and spinning his black, deadly sticks, he disarms and drops a dozen men before an amber beam cuts through one foot, dropping him, and then he is submerged beneath a running mass of screaming people, hundreds trampling over the man who gave them an exit from the trap.

Tears.

For all his self-control, there were tears tracking down Tom's cheeks, and he did not attempt to wipe them away.

Dervlin, my friend.

But Corduven said: "She's still alive, thanks to Lieutenant Milran."

Tom remained silent.

Powering the infotablet off, he pushed it back across the table. There was plenty more on there, but nothing he was going to look at. Not voluntarily.

"One more." Corduven looked at him. "Just look at the next module, then we'll talk."

Tom shook his head. "I don't think so."

"Very well." After a moment, "I'll just describe it for you. One of the demesnes your people brought down. Dead bodies, dozens of them, hanging from the statues. A pogrom, and the nobility are being slaughtered."

Closing his eyes, opening them again, Tom said: "We're not going to agree on politics, are we?"

"Understatement." A short, bitter laugh. "Are you going to tell me why you left LudusVitae—oh, yes, by now I even know what they're called—or do you want me to guess?"

"You said it yourself." Tom watched Corduven's expression. "Too much bloodshed."

Corduven pushed his chair back, as though to get up again, then stopped. "Fine. Perhaps there's something we agree on, then."

"Perhaps."

This man is not my friend.

There was a temptation to think otherwise, but Tom had better bloody well resist it.

I killed his brother.

"Well then." Corduven pulled forwards, leaned his elbows on the green crystal desk. "Let me fill you in on world politics over the last four years."

"Keep it simple," said Tom. "We're pretty isolated here."

And two of those years are a blur.

"Simple. A question, first. Was Flashpoint, Prime Strike, supposed to be a simultaneous attack on every single Oracle in the world?"

Tom hesitated, but the action had already happened. Four SY ago. "Every one of them. Four thousand nine hundred and twenty-three individuals."

"Individuals, yes." A flicker of the eyelids. "Thank you. In the event, the attacks affected three thousand Oracles, many of whom were killed outright."

Tom looked away.

"I'm willing to believe"—Corduven—"that the original plans had more finesse. But it was more than enough to cause Chaos. We continued to receive truecasts, you see, but *no-one knew which ones to believe.* Nearly every sector was destabilized."

"So it worked."

Corduven's knuckles were white, gripping his chair-arms. He saw Tom watching, and released them. "There's hardly a sector without trouble by now. Some have occasional violence, some are in the midst of open warfare."

"And who controls them?" Tom asked. "The demesnes where there aren't pitched battles, I mean."

Corduven shrugged. "Original Lords, new warlords, interim governments. No-one at all. Take your pick. When I said I want troops in every demesne, I meant this sector: there's no such thing as a global political system, not any more."

Good.

"You're in my power, Tom. Any victory you think you've achieved should be outweighed by that."

"If you say so."

They stopped for breakfast.

Tom was appalled. Observing the niceties: it was a sign of Corduven's massive self-control, as well as confidence.

But it gave Tom a chance to remind himself of his own objective. He would do whatever it took to get Corduven's soldiers away from here. This was Tom's *home*.

"I still care for Sylvana." Corduven put down his daistral cup. "As a sister, if you like."

The remark was unexpected, and Tom very carefully put down his own cup. It would make a useful weapon, but that was unnecessary: he could use his hand before anyone had time to react.

"I don't know what to say to that."

"Ah, Tom." A twisted smile. "You obviously hid a lot of things when you were in service, but some emotions were plain upon your face. Every time she was in the same room as you."

Tom was too old to blush. He inclined his head, acknowledging the truth.

"They're going to execute her, Tom."

What? He felt the blood drain from his face.

"That is why"—Corduven laid his slender hands flat upon the table—"you're going to help me."

64

NULAPEIRON AD 3418

Creamy spume beneath the blue skimmer's bow. At the bow, the team leader's stance was wide as he steered avoidance around pillars while the sea flew past in a blur.

Four soldiers, plus Tom. Looking astern, he could see the other skimmer as it wove its path amid stone and sea: Corduven at its centre, plus another crew of four.

I can't stand this.

Worse: he might not be able to go through with it. Not capable.

It wasn't muscle that propelled me up the terraformer.

If his hate was no longer strong enough, would he be able to help Sylvana?

The motion became choppy, the waves white-capped, and the wind began to sting Tom's face as he huddled cross-legged on the deck with his black cape pulled tightly around him. The soldiers, in heavy jumpsuits, seemed unaffected.

It was not visible yet.

Cold, though: the temperature was definitely dropping by degrees as their trajectory across the waves became bumpier, even wild, and then they were truly in the maelstrom as waves smashed against pillars, flinging foam droplets upwards, halfway to the cavern's dark ceiling.

The skimmer dropped.

It fell metres into the trough and he reacted at panic speed, grabbing a smooth bolt—*not enough*—as momentum tried to carry him off the deck—*got it*—and into the roiling waters.

Whirlpool.

The vortex was beneath the ceiling's darkest shadows, not by coincidence; as they span through the turbulence he was splashed in turn by water hot enough to scald, cold enough to chill, while the winds below the shaft's black entrance rotated madly.

Two taps on his shoulder.

Twenty seconds.

Can't do it.

Dipped again, forty-five-degree tilt the other way, and this time he slid two metres along the deck before one of the soldiers caught him.

One tap.

Ten seconds—

Have to.

Churning seas.

For Sylvana.

Sharp crack and the red line unravelling upwards.

Three.

All of them crouching in a low squat.

Two.

A white eruption spun them but linear momentum took them onwards beneath the—

One.

—dark opening above.

Jump.

Boiling waves, thunderous current rushing past as the little girl's chubby hand reached above the surface, trying to grasp, then pulled downwards out of sight—

"Snap out of it."

Tom shook his head to clear it. "I'm OK."

"We have to—"

"Get *going*, will you?"

The soldier, grim-mouthed, climbed up the swaying red rope

while Tom clung on, conscious of the turbulent sea below but trying not to look down.

Not used to rope-climbing, he used his crossed feet and worked hard, careful to slide his hand upwards without fully loosening his grip. He was last man on the line. As the four soldiers, one by one, reached the vertical shaft above, the rope's oscillations grew wilder.

Second red line, snaking upwards.

No attention to spare for the other team. The other rope clung in position but that was all he could tell; his focus zeroed in on the rhythm of feet-hand, feet-hand.

Made it.

Rock-face.

Strange rhythm.

The other four—elite soldiers, all—were used to rope and piton, to harness and karabiner; above all, they knew how to climb as a team. Tom's presence, for all his driving force, was a discord, a tear in the fabric of their co-ordinated unity.

Directly opposite them, on the hundred-metre-wide shaft, Corduven's team made slightly better progress.

Foothold. Reach and pull.

Out of practice.

It took twenty minutes to reach the first membrane.

They would not let him see what they used.

The membrane was a shimmering, gossamer sheet which stretched horizontally across the shaft. It could deliver toxic fatal stings while shrieking alarms to local astymonia patrols; there would be more, a membrane before every stratum.

No smart-tech was allowed for any part of the climb, and this was the reason. Higher up, the more sophisticated sensor webs would occur, but the membranes were sufficient deterrent.

Whatever the tool they used—obviously undetectable by the membrane itself—the soldiers cut away huge swathes of the stuff, throwing them with gloved hands into the shaft's centre, where they fluttered downwards.

As they climbed up through the gap, Tom saw that the rest of the membrane was already degrading: from glistening gossamer to darkened, fibrous gel. It set a time limit, though perhaps not a critical one—sooner or later, someone was going to lean over a balcony in one of the horizontal view-slits and notice the damage.

Corduven's group were already on this stratum's window, sitting on the ledge with their feet dangling over the shaft. Tom's team drew level, then had to traverse nearly half the shaft's diameter to reach them.

"Have some daistral." Corduven offered a self-warming flask as Tom sat beside him.

"Thanks." A welcome sip. Hot and tart, stimulating. "Quite like old times."

Corduven took the flask back.

"I wouldn't go that far."

Next stage.

The rate of ascent, while they were actually climbing, increased; though fatigue was setting in, Tom was learning the rhythm. The other four took turns to act as lead climber; he was always last, in belay.

But the nature of the membranes changed, became more problematical. The last one they cut through, the fourteenth, took an hour of painstaking work to penetrate, and the shaft was deep in shadow by the time they had finished.

"We stay here tonight, if we can." Corduven's team went through the view-window first, slipping over the balustrade and sliding into crouched positions, weapons drawn.

"Clear."

Tom's team followed.

Purple shadows. The constant splash of water, spurting in tiny arcs between the copper cups; intertwined rivulets winding around the sculpture's flow-channels.

"How did you know I could climb?"

A spark of fluorescence.

"I know more than you think."

Spark.

The aquaria contained strange species: fish with long tendrils, gorgeous colours and the ability to glow, just for a second, in the darkness.

"The thing is—" Corduven stopped, reconsidering his words. "You've heard of impoverished nobility?"

Tom tried to read his expression, but it was too dark, here in the Aqua Hall. "I ran my own demesne, remember? I understand balances of payment."

"Then you'll know . . ." Rustling. Corduven was checking, Tom thought, whether his men were in earshot: they weren't. "Gérard and I both had the potential, you know. They do the tests before you learn to walk."

Potential.

"Sweet . . . Destiny."

"Not so sweet. They took Gérard away before I was born, of course. I came along sixteen years later: an accident, or an attempt to replace Gérard; I never found out for sure."

The words were worse, spoken in darkness.

Tom could not speak.

"But my family—my parents—were very well off by then. The payments are quite lavish, you know; not enough to keep a demesne running, but sufficient seed money to kick-start a small demesne's economy. My father"—Corduven's voice thickened—"was very able, you see. It was Grandfather who'd allowed our realm to decline."

"Did you see—I mean, did Gérard live with you or—?"

"Oh, there were visits." Unreadable emotion. "The Collegium Perpetuum Delphinorum allows family sessions; but they can't *predict* whether the subject's consciousness will be in normal timeflow on any given occasion."

"Fate."

"Exactly."

Later, Tom said: "It can't excuse . . . You know how Oracles treat their servitors. What they do for stimulation."

"Yes. But Gérard was better than the others." Pause. "He never lost his humanity."

Briefing session.

For the others, sitting cross-legged in a circle—save for the two lookouts—it was a recap. Tom was seeing the holo for the first time.

"The reason we travelled so far by sea-skimmer," Corduven said to Tom, "was to come up here directly, into Darinia Demesne."

"Understood."

The schematic hung in the air, glowing brightly in contrast: shadows still filled the Aqua Hall, though soon the ceiling's fluorofungus would awaken into its light-phase, and the glowclusters' reactants would phase-shift into illumination.

Tom had fallen asleep to the sound of running water, and awoken the same way. In other circumstances, it would have felt refreshing.

"The political significance"—Corduven pointed into the schematic—"is that Aleph Hall, here, has been fitted with newscast systems, camglobes and relays. If events of the last two years have achieved anything"—glancing at Tom—"it's the opening-up of comms. At any rate, this is the first trial that is being widely broadcast; eventually, within most of Nulapeiron."

"I don't understand." Tom.

"Plenty of nobles have been summarily executed." Corduven's taut face looked grim. "But this is a big show trial with all the trimmings."

Tom did not want to know the geopolitical background. "Where do we go once we reach the Primum Stratum?"

"Here. Or here." Arcs briefly flared as Corduven pointed. "Seven possible staging-points. We'll be relying on your knowledge, Tom, to proceed from there."

"OK. You don't know where they're actually being held?"

"No. Nor, in fact, how many nobles are on trial. But Sylvana and my Lady Darinia for sure. Possibly Lord Velond."

One of the soldiers asked about infiltration and egress, and Corduven highlighted the vectors one by one. Then the two team leaders repeated the briefing, in clipped abbreviation, confirming their understanding.

Corduven nodded.

"Breakfast now"—they'd had sweetened daistral, that was all—"and use the washrooms. Departing in fifteen minutes. Go."

Climbing.

Frog-position, reach, and boost.

The other four had adapted to him, too. Though they were four-limbed, their understanding of his needs had grown almost instinctively; he could now follow most of their holds, though not their moves.

"Having fun?" one of them asked.

"Oh, yeah."

Another said: "Girls? Can we keep the noise down?"

"Fate, we must be mad."

Foot, foot, and reach—

Climb.

Their overall ascent rate was slower, though they were climbing more quickly, as they spent increasing amounts of time working on the horizontal membranes. This had been included in Corduven's estimates; the plan was to reach the Quarternium Stratum tonight, and breach the last three membranes in the morning.

Climb . . .

They were six strata from their destination, in late afternoon, when amber beams split the air. The face of the man above blackened—*roast-meat aroma*—and he died instantly.

"On belay!" Tom yelled, but there was more to worry about than one falling climber.

Return fire spat from below: Corduven's team.

Part of Tom's awareness noted that the ambushers had fired too soon, not noticing the second team; but his immediate problem was hanging on—*my hold is unbreakable*—as the shock of the fallen soldier's weight jerked him, trying to pull him off—*unbreakable*—and one of the men above him screamed but did not fall.

Tom's forearm was burning with lactic acid build-up but he could not move. He hung there with the corpse weighing him down until somebody shifted overhead—*crackle of a lattice blade*—and Tom almost rebounded from reaction as the weight came off.

The red line snaked through his 'biner, was gone.

Beams flicking this way and that. A whimper sounded; Tom realized it was him, and forced himself to silence.

"Tom! Go!"

It was Corduven's voice but Tom shook his head—*what do you expect of me?*—as a wide, white beam tore upwards, missing him by centimetres.

Ozone stink in his nostrils, making him cough.

"*For Sylvana*—" Corduven's voice, cut off as the beams crackled again and a high-pitched scream laced the air.

The membrane above was blackened, shredded apart. Farther up, much farther, the next one, too, looked scorched—*Destiny, it's all the way up*—and he knew what he had to do.

Stump and two wide-braced feet: hold, using counter-pressure. He used his hand to free the harness, then tossed it clear into the void.

Climb.

Graser beams hit close by and molten rock spat white but Tom was already moving. He glanced back down, but the others were exchanging fire.

He was on his own.

Climb.

65

NULAPEIRON AD 3418

Although redolent of ancient sweat and fear-pheromones, the mat was soft and very comfortable as Tom lay on his side and closed his eyes.

Strange laughter.

It had bubbled up inside him, inappropriately: the silent laughter as he struggled through the last membrane, climbed the last stretch in the dark—*watch it*—hand slipping, correcting—*almost*—and he hauled himself over the balustrade.

The odd humour was twofold: he had almost fallen right at the last moment; and now he was in a long, shadowed gallery which was very familiar: *his* gallery.

So he picked himself up and began to run, just a slow jog. Despite the exhaustion, he moved very quietly.

No-one stepped from the shadows to shoot him down.

At the gallery's end, he took the old servitors' tunnels and made his way to the salle d'armes. An odd sense of homecoming as he slipped inside.

Adrenaline and sweat.

Microdrones cleaned the place every day, but the traces of decades' effort remained. How many times had he crashed into this mat, beneath Maestro da Silva's watchful gaze?

Lying down, he sighed. Slid into dreamless sleep.

Tickle.

"Wake up."

Not soft: sharp and stinging as it bit into the skin.

"You'd better have a good—"

Jerked awake, Tom could not react. Lean face above him, silver-grey goatee beard; hand holding the long blade perfectly steady.

Sword at his throat.

Then the eyes widened and the pressure came away. The warm trickle at Tom's throat might have been sweat or blood, but he dared not look down.

He can kill me faster than I can blink.

Lowering the blade.

"You'd better come with me."

"My Lord." Major-Steward Malkoril's full formal bow brought a flush to his face.

From his seat, Chef Keldur struggled up, looking stricken. He had forgotten Tom's status; he had remembered Tom only as a subordinate fellow servitor.

"I don't think"—Tom motioned them to sit—"I'm Lord of anything, any more."

Maestro da Silva spoke softly: "I think perhaps you've become Lord of yourself, which is more than most people achieve."

It was Tom's turn to bow: student to master.

"I thought you were dead, my Lord."

Astounded, Tom saw the dampness in Malkoril's eyes.

"I've missed you, my friends," he said, and realized he meant it.

The chamber was cramped: Malkoril's old office, piled high with battered boxes full of Fate-knew-what among the blue-glass pillars, and filled with crystal-cases and broken pieces of drones. A fine patina of white-grey dust overlay everything. The three were sitting on antique chairs in need of repair. Tom slid onto the desk and sat cross-legged.

"There are two more to come," said the maestro, "but we might as well start."

Tom let out a long, shaky breath. This was going to be hard.

"I gather the term LudusVitae is now well known?" he began.

A dignified nod from Maestro da Silva; Malkoril's fleshy face hardened while Chef Keldur looked ready to spit.

"Well—"

"We should all have joined them, before it was too late!" Square-faced, shaven-headed Zhongguo Ren, just head and shoulders inserted through the door membrane. Then, as he stepped inside: "Tom? Is that you?"

"Chaos, Tat! How are you?"

"I've heard a lot about you." As the other men exchanged puzzled glances, Tat added: "Don't you know who this is? Lord One-Arm himself. Legend of the movement."

Malkoril's face was blotched with conflicting emotions.

"I think I should explain"—Maestro da Silva's elegant voice was soft, measured—"that we are of all political persuasions in this room."

Like LudusVitae.

An image of his first meeting with Sentinel and the others sprang up in his mind, but Tom banished it.

"Our common interest," the maestro continued, "is concern about the fate of our imprisoned former masters."

"*Former* masters?" Chef Keldur's towering rages used to terrify kitchen servitors. "Allegiance is for life, as you damned well ought to—"

"Ahem." Tom coughed deliberately, and Keldur lapsed into silence.

"Go on, my Lord," said Maestro da Silva.

"I think it would be best if you called me Tom. For the sake of security"—as Malkoril started to object—"if for no other reason. Agreed?"

Reluctant nods.

"So then. Tat's correct: I was a ranking executive officer of LudusVitae, an umbrella organization of many factions. And, yes, I was one of the coup's planners."

"But—" Tat stopped.

"What is it?"

"Everyone knows—thinks—you were killed. You're a *martyr*."

A bitter laugh rising, but Tom suppressed it. "I've been away—let's say, in self-imposed exile—for the last two years. No"—*forgetting the lost time*—"make that four years."

"So you don't know about Jak?" Tat, quietly.

Chill on his skin.

"What about him?" Tom asked.

"When you disappeared . . . Your demesne, your palace, were investigated. One of your alpha-class people co-operated fully—"

Felgrinar. I should never have kept him on.

"—and Jak was blamed for misappropriation of funds, other things."

"Did they—?"

"He's imprisoned somewhere. Not executed: he convinced them that he wasn't a member of LudusVitae, luckily."

Good for you, Jak. That must have taken some persuasive talking.

More guilt.

"What else do you know, Tat?"

"Not much. They found the cleared-out remnants of some secret project that—"

Corduven's people. Tom started to reach for his talisman, stopped.

How had Corduven recognized it? Tom had worn a wide-necked shirt, instead of high-collared tunic, maybe once or twice in all their acquaintance. Scarily observant.

Don't underestimate him.

"—call it sorcery, but I don't—Damn, it's hard to believe you're here! Not some mythical hero."

Tom shook his head. "Do you know what happened to my security chief, Captain Elva Strelsthorm?"

"No, sorry. Your demesne was merged back into Lord Shinkenar's, I think. Though that's irrelevant now. He fled in the revolt, sought asylum from Duke Boltrivar."

The maestro cleared his throat. "You've come a long way, Tom. Can you tell us—?"

Soft chime.

A tall, elegant figure, wearing a gold/yellow cape. Her skin was very black, her features striking.

"You were my finest student, once."

"Mistress eh'Nalephi!"

She divested herself of the cape.

"So what went wrong, my Lord?"

No-one.

Moving quietly, head down. Plain black cloak.

Tom took a spiralling white tunnel to the smoke-sculpture garden, walked past gentle mag-chimes, and came to the library. Among the crystal-racks, a few browsers. One looked up, and Tom left quickly.

Next.

The third possibility was farther: near the outer courts, a small bonded godown for precious metals only. But the racks were empty, heavy cobwebs—trapped blindmoths unmoving, dead—hung in the corners, and the dust on the floor was undisturbed.

No go.

He worked his way through the entire sequence—*they have to be there* running through his mind—and stopped in the seventh, the last one, a children's ballet studio. No-one.

I can't do this without support.

But neither could he do it with his old servitor friends: they had the knowledge, but not the training.

Losing track of time in the empty studio, haunted by the dark spectre in the mirror: himself, hand resting loosely on the barre. *Did you learn to dance, Mother, in a place like this?* Then he heard the sound of approaching children.

He slipped outside.

Only one course of action suggested itself, so he began the entire exercise again, beginning with the first rendezvous-point and following the sequence, and on the fourth try he found them.

"Catch."

The crystal sparkled orange as Corduven caught it. "What's this?"

"Everything you need," said Tom. "Detailed schematics—more detailed than your own—with prisoner locations mapped. Estimated guard strengths."

Corduven was sitting at a white wrought-iron table beneath tall, dark-leaved bushes with bright flowers and cloying scents. Carp swam in a pool.

It had taken this long—too long—for Corduven's team to reach one of the prearranged rendezvous-points. But when Tom had asked how they had escaped the fighting, Corduven had ignored the question.

"All right," Corduven said now, leaning back in his chair. "How did you—?"

A low whistle, and he froze.

People coming, he mouthed.

But a second whistle came, the all-clear, and he continued: "Is it reliable?"

"I'd say so, yes." Tom turned a chair backwards, sat down.

"How . . . ?"

"Let's just say, the new masters need to keep the old place running. And keep the prisoners fed."

Corduven took out a small silver infotablet.

"Nice cells." The schematic blossomed. "The old guest suites. I remember them."

With teams of revolutionary guards in front of every membrane, on watch at every intersection.

"Me too. The thing is"—Tom gestured: the display rotated and magnified—"the interim council have anticipated, in my opinion, every possible action."

Corduven had the rank to mobilize a thousand soldiers for all-out assault—Tom understood that—but their movements would be detected days in advance and the prisoners would disappear. Stealth was the only option, but still uncertain.

"Fate damn it!" Corduven's eyelids flickered. He was showing the stress.

"How are your men?" Meaning: *how many casualties?*

This time Corduven answered. "We lost two. The other six are fine. The enemy was suppressed."

Tom looked away. Then, "Why are you here, Corduven? What's the real reason?"

Corduven answered too quickly: "Is life that simple?"

"Not in my experience. But your marriage with Sylvana was annulled."

You knew my feelings: that's why I'm here. But what about you?

"Do you think she's beautiful, Tom?"

It caught him unawares. "Oh, yes."

"I like beautiful women, too, Tom—"

"Naturally."

"—because I can identify with them, in a sense."

Tom stared at him. "I don't follow."

"Not because I desire a relationship with them."

It took a few moments to sink in.

"Bloody Chaos, Cord!"

I didn't realize.

"Yes, my friend." Corduven's voice was distant. "That's exactly what it is."

And it was grounds for disinheritance—at best—among the nobility; within the military, Tom had no idea of the consequences.

He knows the risks in telling me this.

Tom looked at his old friend for a long moment, then held out his hand. "Thank you."

Gravely, they clasped wrists.

Corduven called the others round for briefing, leaving one lookout.

"Tom, explain your thinking. I'll want pros and cons, gentlemen, so pay attention."

Two of the soldiers nodded as Tom started: "We can turn their own thinking against them. This is a show trial, so they want an audience in the Aleph Hall. It looks better for the cameras."

He pulled up a subsidiary holovolume. "They don't want any nasty surprises, of course, so the guest list has been planned. But that gives us something to work with: ID crystals, seating arrangements—I've hacked into those before—and the like."

"Weapon scans," interrupted one of the men. "You're not going to be able to suborn their sensor webs."

Tom noted the *suborn* and the patrician accent. These men held high rank.

"Granted. That's why we'll be going in unarmed."

Derisive looks, replaced almost immediately by thoughtful expressions.

You picked your men well, Corduven.

Elite-trained, certainly. But there was something else: Corduven's soul-baring had avoided Tom's pertinent question about why he was really here. This operation had the feel of a last-ditch attempt, as if his forces needed to pull off a spectacular *and very public* coup.

Suicide mission? With high-ranking patriotic officers?

". . . you think, Tom?"

"I'm sorry?"

"I said—"

"Never mind." Tom reached inside his tunic, pulled out the talisman and drew it over his head. "Watch carefully, gentlemen." Gestured, separated the halves, split the nul-gel with his fingernail. "See this?"

Corduven stiffened: a man used to giving nothing away, but surprised for once.

He didn't know what was inside.

"This," said Tom, "is a mu-space comms relay. Pilot tech."

"Chaos!" Troopers glanced at each other.

I've been getting blasé, Tom realized, *about the whole concept.* Once more, he was bringing ancient, whispered legends to life before people's eyes.

But if you knew what I now suspect, you'd kill me out of hand.

"Pilots, did you say?" A lean-faced soldier stared intently at the display.

"They do exist—"

Tom forced himself to silence.

"Go on." Corduven.

"This particular crystal is not, unfortunately, in complete working order." Tom indicated a tricon in Corduven's holodisplay; he gestured for drill-in to more detail. "We can deduce where the higher-ranking LudusVitae officers are staying. One of them should have a functional crystal."

Two troopers whispered; Tom caught the word *Pilot* mentioned twice.

Corduven said: "How do you know? About these crystals, I mean."

"You told me. Three thousand Oracles were affected in Flashpoint. That would have taken three thousand comms relays—probably—and I'm willing to bet the senior officers still have them."

Corduven and one of the men exchanged looks.

Tom understood: this was something their renowned intelligence services had not picked up, but should have. Which meant Tom could be lying.

He addressed Corduven directly: "You're going to have to trust me, and let me make my own preparations."

And if you knew whose help I intended to enlist—
A pause, then: "Agreed."

A hesitant ripple seemed to pass along the corridor wall, then it froze.

"Yes," murmured Tom. "It's me."

He touched the wall with a gentle palm, then hurried onwards. He needed complete isolation—*the timing's all wrong*—and the outer courts would be safer.

Timing. He should have had a crystal *first*, before he started: but it was not going to happen. Instead, he was going to have to construct the whole thing in his mind, an algorithmic network comprising thousands of processes in Avernon-metavector contexts.

And Corduven's men would have to get hold of a crystal.

Lev-bikes, hurtling through the air—

But the high-arched halls of Veneluza Galleria were empty, disused. Wild fluorofungus formed random clumps on the groined ceiling, the fluted columns. The thirteen-year-old monument—to the riders and spectators who had perished in the explosion—had been toppled over, and acid-etched tricon projections proclaimed freedom's cause across smoke-blackened walls.

66

NULAPEIRON AD 3418

Aleph Hall, reconfigured.

From inside: a vast, dark, hollow sphere, hundreds of metres across. Its shadows were relieved by floating holo-panels and ribbons of glowing blues—royal and eggshell, azure and sapphire, picked out here and there with exotic violet and startling turquoise.

Scalp tingling.

Hard to make out the walls, but they were faceted, with dark panels. The shadows held twisted sculptures: steel and dull gold, tortured figures struggling in the darkness.

Sombre crowds were filing in.

Tom started to reach up to run a hand across his scalp—*stop that*—but prevented himself in time. It would not be appropriate, that was all.

Least of his worries. He did not have that *bloody* crystal.

Other light sources: blood-red vertical bars of baleful light, slowly moving in unpredictable orbits around the hall.

"Excuse me, Your Reverence."

"Please, daughter." Tom moved aside to let her past.

Crowds, mostly silent: speaking, when they had to, in subdued whispers. There was just a faint susurration of rustling fabric—long, hooded robes predominating, their colours dark and plain—and the soft arrhythmic slapping of hundreds of padded sandals against the seven spiralling glassine ramps.

Relying on Corduven to come through with the goods.

The revolutionary guards wore crossed sashes—one crimson, one emerald—and, more importantly, bore black-and-silver graser rifles at port-arms. They were everywhere: in curved rows along the sloping ramps, around the crystal floor's perimeter, and stationed in a grid-pattern among the spectators themselves.

Elva, can I trust you?

If Corduven knew how Tom had obtained the IDs, he would have aborted the operation immediately. But in any case Tom had not seen any sign of—There! Small in the distance, a figure in the descending file. Grey, hooded cape, but it did not disguise Corduven's gait: highly strung and radiating tension.

Scalp tingling, ignore.

Seven ramps, seven men.

It had been a coincidence, and Tom wondered now whether that had influenced their judgement. Corduven and the six soldiers had split up, each coming down a separate ramp spiral. Perhaps they should have stuck together.

Itching—*Keep still!*

Too far for Corduven to signal success or failure.

A whisper: "May I have your blessing, Reverence?"

Urge to laugh.

"Of course, my son."

Do not laugh, do not even think of scratching your bloody head, or Sylvana will die, *is that plain enough for you?*

The thought came like an icy shock, and then Tom was forming the one-hand mudra and dredging his memory for the Old Eldraic words—"*Benehte, syen mir, pre' omnis greche*"—of formal benediction.

It was an image of torture.

The crystal floor was flat, maybe a hundred metres in diameter. High above, at the equatorial level, seven equidistant entrances formed a horizontal circle.

Torture, yes. It suggested torture, and by conscious design. Formed of dark iron and metre-long carbon rods, thousands of them:

a satanic cruciform nest of tortured metal floating at the hall's exact centre, a hundred metres above Tom's head.

Shaven head, tingling.

In the cruciform, restraining-straps hung limply.

Here and there, as Tom adjusted his flowing purple robes, people stopped and paused, craning their heads back to look up at the thing. Disappointed that it was unoccupied?

Some bowed or raised fist to forehead in respect as they passed Tom, and he blessed them with the mudra.

He could have had two acolytes with him, swinging thuribles and filling the place with perfumed violet incense smoke, but Corduven's men would *not* look like apprentice priests, even shaven-headed and purple-robed.

Ripples passed across the crystalline floor.

Melting, beginning to move. Tom and everyone else shifted as clear seats morphed into being. Then, by unspoken consent, the two thousand spectators sat down.

A murmur passed through them.

But the revolutionary guards did not look up: they were watching the crowd, scanning carefully, and Tom did not like that. Too well trained. There was the glitter of eyes upon him—*mistake: look up like everybody else*—and Tom forced himself to break eye contact and lean back.

Glowing, white.

At the ceiling's apex, a circular membrane glowed. It changed, bulging downwards in seven places, budding, then the buds burst. White light slid across silver as they dropped into view.

For a moment the tribunal bobbed in place, then the seven lev-spheres slowly descended. Open-topped, ringed with gold: one judge inside each.

Destiny!

He must have been mistaken.

Then seven great cubic holovolumes sprang up around the hall, close-ups of the judges, and Tom realized he was right.

Elva.

No surprise that she was here, a senior LudusVitae officer and locally born . . . except that she had said *nothing* of this last night.

Malkoril had furnished the information, and Tom had sneaked along to her temporary quarters to talk. To persuade her to furnish the eight IDs, which she had.

Closing his eyes to slits, as though in prayer.

There was no hint that he was the focus of special attention. The guards—at least a hundred and fifty of them—were watching everybody.

So he opened his eyes normally and checked the holos. Three judges were strangers to him, but four were not. Their heads and shoulders were so huge in the displays that it felt as though he could just reach out and touch them: a gentle fingertip along a cheek, or curved fingers raking eyes, take your pick.

His feelings were that mixed.

Sentinel: blocky and white-haired, formidable-looking.

Elva: face impassive, eyes giving nothing away.

Viscount Vilkarzyeh: in a simple uniform without decorations, one of the proletariat, trying his quondam peers.

A familiar pale, freckled face . . . Reddish-auburn hair, beautiful eyes, the nonfunctional one like a huge turquoise/aquamarine amber-flecked jewel at this magnification. Here to try her former mistress.

Arlanna.

He tried to catch Corduven's eye, but the vectors were all wrong, his view obscured by other spectators.

No crystal.

If Corduven's men had been successful, he would have got it to Tom by now.

"Are you sure you'll get one?" Tom had asked.

"My people," Corduven had replied, *"are proficient in neurointerroga-tion."*

A paradox-trap, then.

Corduven could not make his move without Tom; Tom needed a crystal.

Lady Darinia's expression is calm, authoritative: in close-up, her eyes are unnaturally steady.

"The Lady Sylvana will decide the boy's punishment."

Wide, blue eyes.

Blood pressure, EEG, normal. Verdict: not unduly stressed.

Clear, young voice. "An arm, perhaps?"

"Very well." Lady Darinia. "Before you deliver him, remove an arm."

Impersonal grey gaze.

"Either arm will do."

Why the Chaos had the prosecution begun with this illustration?

Because of the thing Tat had said: One-Arm had been a martyr to the cause, and the crowd would know that.

A subsidiary volume showed **bubbling fat, the rising smoke of burnt blood, as the blade cuts and the youthful Tom Corcorigan screams.**

THE FIRST ACCUSED. . .

Tricons flow, showing Arlanna's spoken words in light.

. . . SYLVANA LIRGOLAN, FORMERLY LADY SYLVANA . . .

High up, at the hall's apex, circles of light ripple outwards from the membrane's centre.

. . . CRIMES BEING: TREASON AGAINST THE PEOPLE . . .

The dark iron/graphite cruciform rises slowly to the light.

. . . AGAINST HUMANITY . . .

And descends.

Her face was captured in holovolumes, and Tom wondered if they had made a mistake: bound in the cruciform, fine blonde hair in disarray, she was nevertheless heart-stoppingly beautiful.

Sylvana. He had been right to come here.

Defence advocate.

"This trial is unfair, in that the outcome is predetermined. As we stand on the verge of a new age, on the world built by the courage"—raising her voice above the crowd's murmur—*"yes, and the mistakes of those who ruled before . . . But we should not repeat those mistakes, fellow citizens. The prosecution will argue that she is not without guilt; but I will submit that the defendant had little choice in her actions . . ."*

Prosecution.

". . . defence's claims force us to do this, though it seems unfair . . ."

Sylvana screams.

Tom's hand was clenched against his thigh, fingers digging in like claws. Around him, spectators drew in shaky breaths; even after the years of violence, such primitive means remained shocking.

As the cruciform's mag-field slowly draws them inwards, ten thousand iron rods and carbon fibres . . .

Biting his lip hard, tasting warm salty blood.

. . . penetrate Sylvana, writhing within the cruciform's core . . .

A muffled sob. Near Tom, a woman buries her face in her hood.

. . . and her blood trickles in rivulets, drips from the cruciform's myriad rods as she dies.

". . . truecast, utilizing an Oracle under our control, shows that the defendant's guilt is not only without question, but that the very sentence to be carried out by this court is predetermined . . ."

"Reverence?" A concerned whisper.

"Peace." Tom gave the mudra. "I'm praying, that's all."

Not entirely a lie.

". . . *since we already know the defendant will be executed, it becomes a matter of following procedure . . .*"

Bastards.

But the other Sylvana, the real one, was staring at the truecast holo. No panic; but no expectation of reprieve.

The prosecution lawyer smiled.

". . . *consider that, before we see the first log . . .*"—defence—". . . *by the prosecution's own argument, Destiny forced her to make the decision you are about to see . . .*"

". . . *just as we . . .*"—prosecution—". . . *will be forced by Fate to find her guilty and carry out the tribunal's sentence, as we have* already *seen . . .*"

"You'll know," Tom had said to Corduven.

"Not good enough!" Corduven had been livid: it was his men's lives at risk.

But Tom had shaken his head.

"It may not manifest itself the same way as before. Just get me a damned crystal . . ."

Sylvana.

Dark cruciform, hanging.

I can't do it without the crystal. He had no processing power . . .

And no choice.

Tom made his move.

67

NULAPEIRON AD 3418

Blue flame.

Shouldn't be happening.

A distinct barrier, invisible.

Not yet . . .

Pushing through.

Burning, against his chest.

I don't have a crystal.

The people sitting closest to him drew near as though to help, then shrank away, horror written across their faces as blue flames licked along his purple robes.

And he did have a crystal.

But it doesn't work. Does it?

Reaching inside, forming the control gesture with his hand hidden, and pulling out the crystal. It felt warm even through the nul-gel, before he slit the stuff with his thumbnail and pulled the crystal out.

Stallion in two halves: one on its neck cord, the other loose inside his shirt, beneath the priestly robes.

Fire in his hand.

This is it.

He put the crystal back inside the talisman, sealed it in—

"Run, Tom!"

—but without the nul-gel coating, and it burned.

No barrier now so he leaped forwards, freeing the quick-release seals, purple robes falling away—*run*—and as he moved, white beams cracked through the air—*run faster*—and someone screamed.

✧✧✧

High above, the judges' lev-spheres were changing shape: splitting into facets, light spilling out. Launching weapons: smart miasmas, seekautomata, neurospindles—but a silvery collimated beam of sparkling motes slid out of nowhere and struck. Femtoweapons annihilated each other in a flash.

Running.

Dozens of beams spat back and forth while the spectators huddled. Some panicked and headed for the spiral ramps, but the first few were cut down and all notions of exodus were stopped dead.

No weapons, Tom had said, and the others had agreed for one simple reason: they could take the weapons they needed from the revolutionary guards, when the time was right.

Time: now.

Run faster.

He had missed a trick.

"Lay down your weapons!"

Sizzle, crack. A scream.

Both sides were aiming for pinpoint accuracy, not trying to kill innocent civilians—if that's who the spectators were—but there were hundreds against seven men, and by now it should be all—

Foot of the ramp.

Running up the incline, thighs feeling the pump of uphill sprinting.

A glimpse: in the crowd, a young man—Zhongguo Ren—sprang from his seat and took down the nearest guard, disarming her. That was the trick Tom had missed: Corduven had not come here without allies, not at all.

Should have known.

Bitter admiration for Corduven's tactical sense, but no time to dwell on it.

Guards.

There were three guards on the ramp but they hesitated, seeing a one-armed weaponless man fleeing from the fighting, then realized their mistake.

The first pulled a graser pistol from his hip but Tom grabbed the hand, spinning, and the guard rolled into empty air and dropped.

Broken body on the ground, one arm flung out.

Knocking the barrel aside, a low, scything kick that took out both legs, and the second guard went down. The last had time to bring his weapon to bear—*too late*—but a needle-thin beam from below pierced his torso and he fell.

Clatter of graser rifle, but Tom was already swarming up twisted sculptures on black-shadowed walls, leaving the glassine ramp below.

Silence.

No time to look down: the ceiling sloped at forty-five degrees here among the tangled, angular shadows—*foot, foot, reach*—and was getting harder as he rose.

What was happening below?

But there were two reasons for not looking down: time was dwindling, and his face might be noticeable among the shadows.

It should have been easy going—raised, decorated metal plates hooked tangentially to soft, black inner walls, tortured metal sculptures everywhere—but there was the need for haste, and the nature of the tangled shapes. Already he was cut in a dozen places, blood trickling along his forearm.

Not serious, but his hand was slippery and one missed hold would mean Sylvana's death *so move it*, and he was climbing horizontally now, *do not look down*, hundreds of metres above the crystalline floor, all those people, *don't even think of it*, and he climbed to the metallic rim and stopped.

White membrane, glowing.

Damn it!
Stuck.

Wait for the moment of complete frustration, the Old Terran philosopher Pirsig had said, *and savour it, for it precedes enlightenment.*

Tom was waiting, but he didn't have much time.

A hundred metres below, the tangled cruciform hung—movement of blond hair: Sylvana still OK for now—but it was not *directly* below and that was the problem.

What's keeping you, Corduven?
Stand-off.

Tom hooked his feet, wide apart, into good holds and let go with his hand. He dangled from the waist, upside down, shaking his arm to relieve the tension.

Blood pooled into his head as he stared at the distant floor. No movement. Stand-off, or they were all dead.

No-one had made it to the lev-field controls.

The plan had been to raise the cruciform, not lower it, on the assumption that it would take longer for the guards to notice. And it would provide some protection while he worked to get Sylvana loose.

White membrane: eight, maybe ten metres in diameter.

He could not reach the ceiling's exact apex because of the membrane, so Tom's trajectory would have to carry him four or five metres horizontally during the hundred-metre vertical drop.

Planning. He thought he could judge the thrusting effort he would need, pushing off with his feet, but it was *pointless* because he could not hope to survive the impact: impaling himself on the cruciform would do Sylvana no good at all; just a bloody mess.

Intellectual exercise, pure theory.

Keep working on the known possibilities to distract the conscious mind, while the subconscious does the real work and lets the *unknown* possibilities rise to the surface.

Black movement stirring, and then he got it.

Do you feel pain?

It flowed like black liquid. As he thrust his hand inside, it webbed his forearm, holding strong.

Do you feel pain, my old friend?

"I'm ready."

Lowering now.

Blue fire.

Tom screamed silently as he burned, but then he was through another barrier and he was descending still, forearm gripped by flowing blackness.

Descent slowing.

The stallion was burning against his chest but cold sweat prickled his back.

What have I awoken?

Because he had been wrong. There was processing power available, sufficient to interface *of its own accord* with his comms-enabled crystal.

The Palace: a hundred cubic kilometres. Within its volume, untold lengths of femtotissue stretched: corridors and tunnels were its arteries; great halls and caverns, the chambers of its heart.

But not aware. Never aware.

Bypassing connection-inhibition protocols, in a structure one hundred billion times the size of a human brain, whose logic-gates were one-million-cubed times smaller than neurons . . .

"Thank you," he whispered.

He was addressing a structure with potentially *twenty-nine orders of magnitude* greater power than a human brain.

It released its grip.

✧✧✧

Straddle-stance.

Balanced on the cross-member, slipping the mag-clip. Wrist-restraint released, involuntary tension flipped Sylvana's hand forwards and her wrist struck Tom in the groin.

Sorry, Tom. Silently.

Fluorescent patches in his vision as the sickening sensation swept through him. Funny, under other circumstances. Tom's kind of joke.

No hysteria. She tried to free the other restraints but her hand was shaking too much. No sound, despite the pain of returning circulation.

Tom slipped the other wrist free, then throat and waist.

Looked up. The black tendril had snaked back up into the ceiling and was gone.

Has anyone ever asked if you feel pain? The metallic plates and twisted sculptures were embedded in the malleable stuff of the inner Palace itself. No-one wondered whether the Palace hurt, but pain is an emergent property of basic neural structures: Tom could write out the metavectors to prove it.

"Now what?" Sylvana, quietly.

Silver motion at the edge of his vision.

One of the judges' lev-spheres ascended to see what was going on—*their weapons are disabled*—then Tom saw the graser pistol swinging up, transmission-end glistening.

For a moment he saw knuckles whitening on the firing-stud—*white explosion tearing apart the world*—but there was a moment of shocked mutual recognition and Arlanna froze.

A sapphire inferno.

He did not know how to achieve the interface, but it had to happen. The Palace was enabling the comms, but there was more than that: it was destined.

Pushing through the barrier.

It was going to happen because these were its effects, pushed backwards in time. *So take action, now.*

A prayer, a *kata* without movement: a warrior's dance.

Barrier.

If there had been time, he could have investigated the Palace's capability. Perhaps he did not need to do this . . . Too late.

Will-power.

It had been years since his last femtocytic infusion but the knowledge was there, and the self-discipline. Forcing it, he fanned the flames of the tiniest spark, achieving logotropic trance.

Pushing through.

To *infinite* levels of processing.

Hard to think, but he remembered: Karyn's emotion, Ro's conviction. His own moment of insight. Desperately, he clasped the memory in his mind.

The crystal was in his hand, like fire, though he did not remember taking it out—*stallion*—and the pain's intensity grew—*my eyes!*—as it stroboscopically pulsed into his optic nerves—*fist and stallion*—and he dug deep, to his spirit's core, crying out with pain beyond belief, and then he was through.

##WE CAN'T INTERFACE—##

Going mad.

##—LIKE THIS FOR LONG.##

But if this were madness, he had to go with it.

"Can you . . ." Madness. Try anyway. "Take the model from my mind? Can you . . . ?"

##I'M READING IT.##

Impossible. Hallucination.

"Show them . . . future."

##WHICH FUTURE?##

He would have laughed if he had the strength but his eyes were close to burning out with the pulsing optic blast and it had to happen quickly.

"All of them," he said.

##CONNECT ME.##

Not entirely clear what was meant, but there had to be a decision so Tom took it.

Blue fire.

Through the sapphire haze he could see Arlanna and Sylvana, frozen, locked by conflicting emotions—

##QUICKLY.##

Crack! Graser fire, renewed fighting below.

Black streaks, tearing across the walls—*arachnabugs*—streaming in through the doorways, fanning out in all directions.

##BEFORE YOUR EYES BURN.##

—but he could not wait so he ran along the cross-beam—

"Tom! *No!*"

##HURRY.##

Jump.

—towards Arlanna as the graser pistol swung back up and he launched himself into space.

Reverence? The concerned person had touched his sleeve.

Peace, Tom, disguised as a priest, had replied. *I'm praying, that's all.*

Floating.

Physical awareness was distant: hard floor beneath him, tilting—

##GET UP.##

—lev-sphere floor, made it—

##GET UP NOW.##

—but he had *not* put the crystal in the socket—

##FADING . . . ##

"I'm *doing* it."

—as he forced himself back up into reality, staggered across the open-top lev-sphere, muttered apologies to Arlanna as he searched the golden console for what he needed, *got it*, and slammed the crystal in.

Graser fire, arachnabugs, people screaming as the fighting intensified.

"STOP NOW!"

Tom's voice was magnified a thousand times as he interfaced with the Palace and used the internal walls as a speaker membrane. For a moment everybody froze, two thousand people; even the arachnabugs stopped, clinging to metal-faceted walls, as Tom called on the power of Ro's god to cast huge holovisions before them.

One: Bodies hanging in blood-dripping rows from sculpted walls, while the triumphant army with their crimson/emerald colours march through burning tunnels, and a subsidiary volume shows the heaped tiny corpses.

Two: The LudusVitae dead, Vilkarzyeh's face recognizable among them. Outside, reinstated Lords direct the cleansing of the walls, and banquet halls are restored to former glory, while in the lower demesnes they use smoothcarts to take dead children to the acid vortices.

Three: Lords and LudusVitae facing each other across the elliptical quartz table. Triconic lattices show the details—and the numbers of casualties are huge, but those numbers have stopped growing.

✧✧✧

The holovolumes were immense, clustered into three main groups, and if this didn't convince them, nothing would.

"MAKE YOUR CHOICE: THERE ARE THREE OPTIONS."

The only place from which someone could take control of the holosystem was from a lev-sphere, and Tom could see the other judges working it out. Vilkarzyeh and Sentinel were the first to react.

"THEY ARE ALL TRUECASTS."

Arlanna lurched past Tom to the golden panel, hit a stud, and the whole lev-sphere spun aside as Vilkarzyeh's sphere shot past, his face white with rage.

"CHOOSE ONE."

Tom closed the voice interface but left the giant holodisplays running. It was their choice. For those who cared to look, tertiary displays provided stress-analyses demonstrating that Tom at least believed his own words.

Graser beam and now it was up to Fate—*save Sylvana*—and he shouted: "Arlanna, you've got to help me!" She spun the lev-sphere again.

Silver swarm.

"That way," he said.

She arced their trajectory, down, then up, and smashed into Vilkarzyeh's sphere. The impact threw them both across the console.

From each of seven doorways they came, flying into the hall and quickly dispersing: lev-bikes. Riders with crimson/emerald sashes fired grasers at the darting arachnabugs.

Vilkarzyeh was slumped in his lev-sphere, stunned or dead. Among the other five spheres, Elva was in control, her weapon trained directly on Sentinel but ready to blast anyone who moved.

I could always rely on you.

"Move closer to that thing." Tom pointed to the cruciform sculpture. "Please, Arlanna."

A tortured sound arose in Arlanna's throat, but she made the gesture and their lev-sphere moved.

She wanted Sylvana to die, Tom realized, *because of me.*

There was more than one interpretation of that, but one thing Tom was sure of: Arlanna had been surprised to see him because she thought he was dead. Believed her own organization's disinformation.

Sylvana climbed aboard. The tension between her and Arlanna was almost physical.

Hurtling lev-bikes and arachnabugs were everywhere.

"Arlanna!" Tom had to yell above the crack of weapons. "Who can order the guards to stand down?"

"Any of us."

"Who will they *listen* to?"

Too late.

Lev-field.

The Chaos of lev-bikes and arachnabugs faded into background as he saw the cruciform *quiver.*

"You think . . . I'm a . . . fool?" Vilkarzyeh, unsteady, pointed at the first group of holos.

A Lord, screaming under interrogation, while Vilkarzyeh impassively watches . . .

It was the future compatible with his own truecast; therefore he assumed it was the only possible future. And it showed him alive.

"Don't be a fool, Alexei!"

Build-up.

It was designed for execution, but not this way.

"Get down." Tom grabbed Sylvana, forced her down. "And you." Arlanna.

Rods, separating.

The cruciform shape was there, but it was a configuration: each rod trembled with potential, detached from those around it.

Pulse.

The cruciform exploded.

Ten thousand rods slammed through the air, ripped through bodies and arachnabug hulls alike.

Vilkarzyeh . . .

Tom glimpsed the rod which sliced through Vilkarzyeh's carotid artery, scarlet blood spurting. Then he threw himself across Sylvana and Arlanna—*my leg!*—as rods arrowed into the lev-sphere and smashed against the deck.

They were listing at an angle and it saved them from the worst of the cascade; bouncing rods whipped past but nothing serious, save the shaft impaling Tom's left leg.

A Zhongguo Ren. His face looked bloodless.

"Where's Zhao-ji?" Tom asked, or thought he did.

The cockpit was open; the youth was still looking down.

Whisper: "You know Siu Lung?"

Sliding in and out of consciousness. Strange fire in his thigh.

"Tom . . ." Arlanna.

Tearing sound. "Use this as a tourniquet." Sylvana.

The arachnabug was still there, suspended above them.

"*Zài nǎr?*" said Tom, but knew he needed more, a code-intro, and it came from intuition: "Paradox," and then the blackness fell.

68

NULAPEIRON AD 3418

Carnage.

Tom was leaning against a misshapen crystal blob, part of the damaged floor, and his bandaged leg was numb.

Whimpers. Here, a wounded woman, taken from the wreckage of her lev-bike; there, a man screaming as rescuers lifted him. Lev-gurneys, med-drones. Survivors sat amid the debris, looking stunned.

"Tom." Zhao-ji, left hand clasped over right fist, bowed.

A nod was all Tom could manage.

"Congratulations." Corduven's uniform was smeared with blood, not his own. "You worked things out rather quickly."

He meant, Tom had deduced the new alliance between Corduven's soldiers and the Strontium Dragons on remarkably little evidence. But Tom had always known that LudusVitae was a shaky alliance . . . and that Corduven was a master strategist.

"What's happening outside?" The fighting had spread far beyond the confines of Aleph Hall. Fate knew what state the rest of Darinia Demesne was in.

Crunch of bootsteps. Elva, walking across bright ceramic shards.

"There's still fighting," she said. "But it's dying down. News of the cease-fire is spreading."

"Let's hope it spreads quickly." Arlanna.

"Provided your people don't—" Sylvana stopped.

Tom raised his hand, ignoring torn muscles.

"If you two"—looking between Sylvana and Arlanna—"can't make peace, what hope is there for anyone?"

The two women stared in silence.

Crystal.

Elva held it out. "We recovered it from the lev-sphere."

Corduven and Sylvana watched intently as Tom took it. Fully trained, Lord and Lady, they appreciated the strangeness—

Glimmer of light.

"Is its strobe-output functional?" asked Corduven.

"No idea." Tom smiled grimly. "I didn't even know it could do that."

I thought it was nonfunctional.

Fading.

"Doesn't look like it." Corduven's eyelids flickered. "*Multiple* true-casts, Tom? And all of them genuine?"

The blue fire; the barrier. After killing the Oracle—*Corduven's brother*—that strange hallucination of committing suicide, hurling himself from the terraformer.

Parallel universes, or their ghosts.

"All true," said Tom.

Were they different beads of the Cosmic Necklace, sometimes impinging, as though Fate had carelessly tossed the Necklace down into a tangled heap? Or was the explanation more complex?

"I know enough," Tom added, "to have deduced my ignorance. Time's more subtle than we think."

Spark.

"Tom . . ."

Spark of light.

"Careful, now."

But he had already seen it.

"The medics said you need to take care of your eyes. The strobe nearly burned out—"

##DISCONNECTING NOW.##

Tom winced at the input's strength, but did not look away.

"Thank you."

##PILOTS DIED FOR THIS. IT WAS IMPORTANT.##

Firing the words directly into his brain.

"Yes," said Tom. "Are you who I think . . . ?"

##I AM A SYSTEM-REFLECTION OF WHAT LIES BEYOND.##

Head pounding. *Do* not *look away.*

"But you're not just an AI inside the comms system."

##LESS THAN THE WHOLE, BUT GREATER THAN THE SEED.##

"I know, but—"

No time left.

##DISCONNECT.##

"*Dart!*"

Crystal growing opaque.

"Thank you," he whispered.

Sylvana touched Tom's arm. "You'd better come with me."

Arlanna was frowning.

Tom shook his head.

"It's Maestro da Silva," Sylvana said.

Three rods impaled him.

"*Tom* . . ." Maestro da Silva's eyes fluttered.

"He saved me," Malkoril muttered. "Pushed me aside so fast—"

Tom cursed himself for not realizing that the maestro, with Malkoril and Keldur, had been here, amid the crowd.

". . . *best . . . bargain . . .*"

"Don't speak, Maestro. You'll be all—"

". . . *thousand merits . . . well . . . spent . . .*"

Tom's throat tightened.

No.

Breathing changed, rasping—

Not again.

—and he shouted for a medic but no-one came—

Damn it, not again.

—holding onto the maestro—quickening breaths, shallow and painful—hugging him tight as the throat-rattle came and life departed.

"It was you," he whispered to the maestro's corpse. "You gave me my start."

He held on until the body-bearers came.

Despite unsteady feet—his wounded leg felt increasingly numb, and odd pulsations drifted across his vision—Tom bowed to each in turn: Zhao-ji, Corduven, Arlanna, the beautiful Sylvana. Friends, but with their own agendas.

"Good Destiny," he said.

Sudden weakness, but she caught him: the one who was always faithful.

"What do you want to do, Tom?"

Whimpers of the wounded, cries of the bereaved.

Lords and revolutionaries, standing together.

"Take me home," he whispered.

He stumbled once, but Elva's strong arm held him, and they left the Palace together.

THE END

ACKNOWLEDGMENTS

Undying love and gratitude to Yvonne, who inspires, critiques and puts up with it all . . .

A thousand thanks to: Lisanne Norman, for the crucial psychotherapy; Bridget McKenna, Howard V. Hendrix and the assembled NadaHax, for kind criticism of a partial early draft; Simon Taylor (editor) and John Parker (agent), for unerringly pinpointing my weaknesses, (productively) stressing me out, and making me get rid of that epilogue (great move, guys!); to Jim Burns, for the cool artwork; and to everyone who enjoyed *To Hold Infinity* and was kind enough to say so. (Even if that makes me a filthypro—thanks, Roger Robinson!)

Also—if I dare place these names together in one sentence—thanks to Rog Peyton, Dick Jude, Ariel, Ken Slater, and the van der Voorts, for kind comments and for actually selling the book.

Some portions of this book appeared first (in different form: *c'est-à-dire*, before the rewrite) in *Interzone* magazine, under the title of *Parallax Transform*.

The "one-chopstick" problem is a thinly disguised version of that described in *Science*, 2 March 1984, p.917, and reprinted in *The New Physics*, ed. Paul Davies, pub. Cambridge University Press.

The form of logic proof-tree I've used (OK: abused) is that developed by Jim Woodcock and Jim Davies at Oxford University, and utilized in their book *Using Z*, pub. Prentice Hall. (I know you're going to make me suffer for this.)

Other sources—*pace* Einstein's famous advice—were various excellent works by: John Gribbin; William Poundstone; Huw Price; W.V. Quine; Jack Cohen and Ian Stewart . . . not to mention Ian Stewart and Jack Cohen.

In the absence of logotropes, this book came to fruition under the influence of massive doses of Green & Black's organic dark chocolate (thanks, Lucie!), Diet Coke, and the music of both Hans Zimmer and Eric Serra.

To the original Paradox, beloved Pip, *Osu, neko-sama!*

JOHN MEANEY has a degree in physics and computer science, and is a black belt in Shotokan karate. He has been hooked on science fiction since the age of eight, and his short fiction has appeared in *Interzone* and in a number of anthologies. His début novel, *To Hold Infinity*, was published to great acclaim in 1998, shortlisted for the BSFA Award and subsequently selected as one of the *Daily Telegraph*'s "Books of the Year." *Paradox* is John Meaney's second novel.